P9-CNI-019

**Praise for #1 *New York Times* bestselling author
Debbie Macomber**

"As always, Macomber draws rich, engaging
characters."

—*Publishers Weekly*

"Debbie Macomber is the queen of laughter and
love."

—*New York Times* bestselling author
Elizabeth Lowell

"I've never met a Macomber book I didn't love!"
—#1 *New York Times* bestselling author
Linda Lael Miller

**Praise for *USA TODAY* bestselling author
Patricia Davids**

"Faith becomes a strong suit in Patricia Davids'
heartwarming story and rewards readers with a
touching conclusion."

—*RT Book Reviews* on *Love Thine Enemy*

"*A Matter of the Heart* is a touching and wonderful
story that's not to be missed."

—*RT Book Reviews*

Debbie Macomber is a #1 *New York Times* bestselling author and a leading voice in women's fiction worldwide. Her work has appeared on every major bestseller list, with more than 170 million copies in print, and she is a multiple award winner. Hallmark Channel based a television series on Debbie's popular Cedar Cove books. For more information, visit her website, www.debbiemacomber.com.

After thirty-five years as a nurse, **Patricia Davids** hung up her stethoscope to become a full-time writer. She enjoys spending her free time visiting her grandchildren, doing some long-overdue yard work and traveling to research her story locations. She resides in Wichita, Kansas. Patricia always enjoys hearing from her readers. You can visit her online at patriciadavids.com.

#1 *New York Times* Bestselling Author

DEBBIE MACOMBER

DENIM AND DIAMONDS

**HARLEQUIN
BESTSELLING
AUTHOR
COLLECTION**

If you purchased this book without a cover you should be aware
that this book is stolen property. It was reported as "unsold and
destroyed" to the publisher, and neither the author nor the
publisher has received any payment for this "stripped book."

HARLEQUIN®
BESTSELLING
AUTHOR
COLLECTION

Recycling programs
for this product may
not exist in your area.

ISBN-13: 978-1-335-97995-7

Denim and Diamonds

First published in 1989. This edition published in 2020.

Copyright © 1989 by Debbie Macomber

A Military Match
First published in 2008. This edition published in 2020.
Copyright © 2008 by Patricia Macdonald

All rights reserved. No part of this book may be used or reproduced in
any manner whatsoever without written permission except in the case of
brief quotations embodied in critical articles and reviews.

This is a work of fiction. Names, characters, places and incidents
are either the product of the author's imagination or are used fictitiously.
Any resemblance to actual persons, living or dead, businesses,
companies, events or locales is entirely coincidental.

This edition published by arrangement with Harlequin Books S.A.

For questions and comments about the quality of this book,
please contact us at CustomerService@Harlequin.com.

Harlequin Enterprises ULC
22 Adelaide St. West, 40th Floor
Toronto, Ontario M5H 4E3, Canada
www.Harlequin.com

Printed in U.S.A.

CONTENTS

Also available from Debbie Macomber

MIRA

Cedar Cove

16 Lighthouse Road
204 Rosewood Lane
311 Pelican Court
44 Cranberry Point
50 Harbor Street
6 Rainier Drive
74 Seaside Avenue
8 Sandpiper Way
92 Pacific Boulevard
1022 Evergreen Place
Christmas in Cedar Cove
1105 Yakima Street
1225 Christmas Tree Lane

Heart of Texas

Texas Skies
Texas Nights
Texas Home
Promise, Texas
Return to Promise

Visit her Author Profile page on Harlequin.com,
or debbiemacomber.com, for more titles!

DENIM AND DIAMONDS

Debbie Macomber

To Karen Macomber, sister, dear friend and downtown-Seattle explorer.

Prologue

Dusk had settled; it was the end of another cold, harsh winter day in Red Springs, Wyoming. Chase Brown felt the chill of the north wind all the way through his bones as he rode Firepower, his chestnut gelding. He'd spent the better part of the afternoon searching for three heifers who'd gotten separated from the main part of his herd. He'd found the trio a little while earlier and bullied them back to where they belonged.

That tactic might work with cattle, but from experience, Chase knew it wouldn't work with Letty. She should be here, in Wyoming. With him. Four years had passed since she'd taken off for Hollywood on some fool dream of becoming a singing star. Four years! As far as Chase was concerned, that was three years too long.

Chase had loved Letty from the time she was a teenager. And she'd loved him. He'd spent all those lazy afternoons with her on the hillside, chewing on a blade of grass, talking, soaking up the warmth of the sun, and he knew she felt something deep and abiding for him. Letty had been innocent and Chase had sworn she would stay that way until they were married. Although, it'd been hard not to make love to her the way he'd wanted. But Chase was a patient man, and he was convinced a lifetime with Letty was worth the wait.

When she'd graduated from high school, Chase had come to her with a diamond ring. He'd wanted her to share his vision of Spring Valley, have children with him to fill the emptiness that had been such a large part of his life since his father's death. Letty had looked up at him, tears glistening in her deep blue eyes, and whispered that she loved him more than she'd thought she'd ever love anyone. She'd begged him to come to California with her. But Chase couldn't leave his ranch and Red Springs any more than Letty could stay. So she'd gone after her dreams.

Letting her go had been the most difficult thing he'd ever had to do. Everyone in the county knew Letty Ellison was a gifted singer. Chase couldn't deny she had talent, lots of it. She'd often talked of becoming a professional singer, but Chase hadn't believed she'd choose that path over the one he was offering. She'd kissed him before she left, with all the innocence of her youth, and pleaded with him one more time to come with her. She'd had some ridiculous idea that he could become her manager. The only thing Chase had ever wanted to manage was Spring Valley, his ranch. With ambition clouding her eyes, she'd turned away from him and headed for the city lights.

That scene had played in Chase's mind a thousand

times in the past few years. When he slipped the diamond back inside his pocket four years earlier, he'd known it would be impossible to forget her. Someday she'd return, and when she did, he'd be waiting. She hadn't asked him to, but there was only one woman for him, and that was Letty Ellison.

Chase wouldn't have been able to tolerate her leaving if he hadn't believed she *would* return. The way he figured it, she'd be back within a year. All he had to do was show a little patience. If she hadn't found those glittering diamonds she was searching for within that time, then surely she'd come home.

But four long years had passed and Letty still hadn't returned.

The wind picked up as Chase approached the barnyard. He paused on the hill and noticed Letty's brother's beloved Ford truck parked outside the barn. A rush of adrenaline shot through Chase, accelerating his heartbeat. Involuntarily his hands tightened on Firepower's reins. Lonny had news, news that couldn't be relayed over the phone. Chase galloped into the yard.

"Evening, Chase," Lonny muttered as he climbed out of the truck.

"Lonny." He touched the brim of his hat with gloved fingers. "What brings you out?"

"It's about Letty."

The chill that had nipped at Chase earlier couldn't compare to the biting cold that sliced through him now. He eased himself out of the saddle, anxiety making the inside of his mouth feel dry.

"I thought you should know," Lonny continued, his expression uneasy. He kicked at a clod of dirt with the toe of his boot. "She called a couple of hours ago."

Lonny wouldn't look him in the eye, and that bothered Chase. Letty's brother had always shot from the hip.

"The best way to say this is straight out," Lonny said, his jaw clenched. "Letty's pregnant and the man isn't going to marry her. Apparently he's already married, and he never bothered to let her know."

If someone had slammed a fist into Chase's gut it wouldn't have produced the reaction Lonny's words did. He reeled back two steps before he caught himself. The pain was unlike anything he'd ever experienced.

"What's she going to do?" he managed to ask.

Lonny shrugged. "From what she said, she plans on keeping the baby."

"Is she coming home?"

"No."

Chase's eyes narrowed.

"I tried to talk some sense into her, believe me, but it didn't do a bit of good. She seems more determined than ever to stay in California." Lonny opened the door to his truck, looking guilty and angry at once. "Mom and Dad raised her better than this. I thank God they're both gone. I swear it would've killed Mom."

"I appreciate you telling me," Chase said after a lengthy pause. It took him that long to reclaim a grip on his chaotic emotions.

"I figured you had a right to know."

Chase nodded. He stood where he was, his boots planted in the frozen dirt until Lonny drove off into the fading sunlight. Firepower craned his neck toward the barn, toward warmth and a well-deserved dinner of oats and alfalfa. The gelding's action caught Chase's attention. He turned, reached for the saddle horn and in one smooth movement remounted the bay.

Firepower knew Chase well, and sensing his mood, the gelding galloped at a dead run. Still Chase pushed him on, farther and farther for what seemed like hours, until both man and horse were panting and exhausted. When the animal stopped, Chase wasn't surprised the unplanned route had led him to the hillside where he'd spent so many pleasant afternoons with Letty. Every inch of his land was familiar to him, but none more than those few acres.

His chest heaving with exertion, Chase climbed off Firepower and stood on the crest of the hill as the wind gusted against him. His lungs hurt and he dragged in several deep breaths, struggling to gain control of himself. Pain choked off his breath, dominated his thoughts. Nothing eased the terrible ache inside him.

He groaned and threw back his head with an anguish so intense it could no longer be held inside. His piercing shout filled the night as he buckled, fell to his knees and covered his face with both hands.

Then Chase Brown did something he hadn't done in fifteen years.

He wept.

Chapter 1

Five years later

Letty Ellison was home. She hadn't been back to Red Springs in more than nine years, and she was astonished by how little the town had changed. She'd been determined to come home a star; it hadn't happened. Swallowing her pride and returning to the town, the ranch, without having achieved her big dream was one thing. But to show up on her brother's doorstep, throw her arms around him and casually announce she could be dying was another.

As a matter of fact, Letty had gotten pretty philosophical about death. The hole in her heart had been small enough to go undetected most of her life, but it was there, and unless she had the necessary surgery, it would soon be lights out, belly up, buy the farm, kick the bucket or whatever else people said when they were about to die.

The physicians had made her lack of options abundantly clear when she was pregnant with Cricket, her daughter. If her heart defect hadn't been discovered then and had remained undetected, her doctor had assured her she'd be dead before she reached thirty.

And so Letty had come home. Home to Wyoming. Home to the Bar E Ranch. Home to face whatever lay before her. Life or death.

In her dreams, Letty had often imagined her triumphant return. She saw herself riding through town sitting in the back of a red convertible, dressed in a strapless gown, holding bouquets of red roses. The high school band would lead the procession. Naturally the good people of Red Springs would be lining Main Street, hoping to get a look at her. Being the amiable soul she was, Letty would give out autographs and speak kindly to people she hardly remembered.

Her actual return had been quite different from what she'd envisioned. Lonny had met her at the Rock Springs Airport when she'd arrived with Cricket the evening before. It really had been wonderful to see her older brother. Unexpected tears had filled her eyes as they hugged. Lonny might be a onetime rodeo champ and now a hard-bitten rancher, but he was the only living relative she and Cricket had. And if anything were to happen to her, she hoped her brother would love and care for Cricket with the same dedication Letty herself had. So far, she hadn't told him about her condition, and she didn't know when she would. When the time felt right, she supposed.

Sunlight filtered in through the curtain, and draw-

ing in a deep breath, Letty sat up in bed and examined
her old bedroom. So little had changed in the past nine
years. The lace doily decorating the old bureau was the
same one that had been there when she was growing up.
The photograph of her and her pony hung on the wall.
How Letty had loved old Nellie. Even her bed was covered with the same quilted spread that had been there
when she was eighteen, the one her mother had made.

Nothing had changed and yet everything was different. Because *she* was different.

The innocent girl who'd once slept in this room was
gone forever. Instead Letty was now a woman who'd
become disenchanted with dreams and disillusioned by
life. She could never go back to the guileless teen she'd
been, but she wouldn't give up the woman she'd become, either.

With that thought in mind, she folded back the covers
and climbed out of bed. Her first night home, and she'd
slept soundly. *She* might not be the same, but the sense
of welcome she felt in this old house was.

Checking in the smallest bedroom across the hall,
Letty found her daughter still asleep, her faded yellow
"blankey" clutched protectively against her chest. Letty
and Cricket had arrived exhausted. With little more than
a hug from Lonny, she and her daughter had fallen into
bed. Letty had promised Lonny they'd talk later.

Dressing quickly, she walked down the stairs and was
surprised to discover her brother sitting at the kitchen
table, waiting for her.

"I was beginning to wonder if you'd ever wake up," he
said, grinning. The years had been good to Lonny. He'd
always been handsome—as dozens of young women had
noticed while he was on the rodeo circuit. He'd quit eight

years ago, when his father got sick, and had dedicated himself to the Bar E ever since. Still, Letty couldn't understand why he'd stayed single all this time. Then again, she could. Lonny, like Chase Brown, their neighbor, lived for his land and his precious herd of cattle. That was what their whole lives revolved around. Lonny wasn't married because he hadn't met a woman he considered an asset to the Bar E.

"How come you aren't out rounding up cattle or repairing fences or whatever it is you do in the mornings?" she teased, smiling at him.

"I wanted to welcome you home properly."

After pouring herself a cup of coffee, Letty walked to the table, leaned over and kissed his sun-bronzed cheek. "It's great to be back."

Letty meant that. Her pride had kept her away all these years. How silly that seemed now, how pointless and stubborn not to admit her name wasn't going to light up any marquee, when she'd lived and breathed that knowledge each and every day in California. Letty had talent; she'd known that when she left the Bar E nine years ago. It was the blind ambition and ruthless drive she'd lacked. Oh, there'd been brief periods of promise and limited success. She'd sung radio commercials and done some backup work for a couple of rising stars, but she'd long ago given up the hope of ever making it big herself. At one time, becoming a singer had meant the world to her. Now it meant practically nothing.

Lonny reached for her fingers. "It's good to have you home, sis. You've been away too long."

She sat across from him, holding her coffee mug with both hands, and gazed down at the old Formica table-top. In nine years, Lonny hadn't replaced a single piece of furniture.

It wasn't easy to admit, but Letty needed to say it. "I should've come back before now." She thought it was best to let him know this before she told him about her heart.

"Yeah," Lonny said evenly. "I wanted you back when Mom died."

"It was too soon then. I'd been in California less than two years."

It hurt Letty to think about losing her mother. Maren Ellison's death had been sudden. Although Maren had begged her not to leave Red Springs, she was a large part of the reason Letty had gone. Her mother had had talent, too. She'd been an artist whose skill had lain dormant while she wasted away on a ranch, unappreciated and unfulfilled. All her life, Letty had heard her mother talk about painting in oils someday. But that day had never come. Then, when everyone had least expected it, Maren had died—less than a year after her husband. In each case, Letty had flown in for the funerals, then returned to California the next morning.

"What are your plans now?" Lonny asked, watching her closely.

Letty's immediate future involved dealing with social workers, filling out volumes of forms and having a dozen doctors examine her to tell her what she already knew. Heart surgery didn't come cheap. "The first thing I thought I'd do was clean the house," she said, deliberately misunderstanding him.

A guilty look appeared on her brother's face and Letty chuckled softly.

"I suppose the place is a real mess." Lonny glanced

furtively around. "I've let things go around here for the past few years. When you phoned and said you were coming, I picked up what I could. You've probably guessed I'm not much of a housekeeper."

"I don't expect you to be when you're dealing with several hundred head of cattle."

Lonny seemed surprised by her understanding. He stood and grabbed his hat, adjusting it on his head. "How long do you plan to stay?"

Letty shrugged. "I'm not sure yet. Is my being here a problem?"

"Not in the least," Lonny rushed to assure her. "Stay as long as you like. I welcome the company— and decent meals for a change. If you want, I can see about finding you a job in town."

"I don't think there's much call for a failed singer in Red Springs, is there?"

"I thought you said you'd worked as a secretary."

"I did, part-time, and as a temp." In order to have flexible hours, she'd done what she'd had to in order to survive, but in following her dream she'd missed out on health insurance benefits.

"There ought to be something for you, then. I'll ask around."

"Don't," Letty said urgently. "Not yet, anyway." After the surgery would be soon enough to locate employment. For the time being, she had to concentrate on making arrangements with the appropriate authorities. She should probably tell Lonny about her heart condition, she decided reluctantly, but it was too much to hit him with right away. There'd be plenty of time later, after the arrangements had been made. No point in upsetting him now. Besides, she wanted him to become acquainted with Cricket before he found out she'd be listing him as her daughter's guardian.

"Relax for a while," Lonny said. "Take a vacation. There's no need for you to work if you don't want to."

"Thanks, I appreciate that."

"What are brothers for?" he joked, and drained his coffee. "I should get busy," he said, rinsing his cup and setting it on the kitchen counter. "I should've gotten started hours ago, but I wanted to talk to you first."

"What time will you be back?"

Lonny's eyes widened, as though he didn't understand. "Five or so, I guess. Why?"

"I just wanted to know when to plan dinner."

"Six should be fine."

Letty stood, her arms wrapped protectively around her waist. One question had been burning in her mind from the minute she'd pulled into the yard. One she needed to ask, but whose answer she feared. She tentatively broached the subject. "Will you be seeing Chase?"

"I do most days."

"Does he know I'm back?"

Lonny's fingers gripped the back door handle. "He knows," he said without looking at her.

Letty nodded and she curled her hands into fists. "Is he...married?"

Lonny shook his head. "Nope, and I don't imagine he ever will be, either." He hesitated before adding, "Chase is a lot different now from the guy you used to know. I hope you're not expecting anything from him, because you're headed for a big disappointment if you are. You'll know what I mean once you see him."

A short silence followed while Letty considered her brother's words. "You needn't worry that I've come home expecting things to be the way they were between Chase and me. If he's different…that's fine. We've all changed."

Lonny nodded and was gone.

The house was quiet after her brother left. His warning about Chase seemed to taunt her. The Chase Brown she knew was gentle, kind, good. When Letty was seventeen he'd been the only one who really understood her dreams. Although it had broken his heart, he'd loved her enough to encourage her to seek her destiny. Chase had loved her more than anyone before or since.

And she'd thrown his love away.

"Mommy, you were gone when I woke up." Looking forlorn, five-year-old Cricket stood in the doorway of the kitchen, her yellow blanket clutched in her hand and dragging on the faded red linoleum floor.

"I was just downstairs," Letty said, holding out her arms to the youngster, who ran eagerly to her mother, climbing onto Letty's lap.

"I'm hungry."

"I'll bet you are." Letty brushed the dark hair away from her daughter's face and kissed her forehead. "I was talking to Uncle Lonny this morning."

Cricket stared up at her with deep blue eyes that were a reflection of her own. She'd inherited little in the way of looks from her father. The dark hair and blue eyes were Ellison family traits. On rare occasions, Letty would see traces of Jason in their child, but not often. She tried not to think about him or their disastrous affair. He was out of her life and she wanted no part of him—except for Christina Maren, her Cricket.

"You know what I thought we'd do today?" Letty said. "After breakfast?"

"After breakfast." She smiled. "I thought we'd clean house and bake a pie for Uncle Lonny."

"Apple pie," Cricket announced with a firm nod.

"I'm sure apple pie's his favorite."

"Mine, too."

Together they cooked oatmeal. Cricket insisted on helping by setting the table and getting the milk from the refrigerator.

As soon as they'd finished, Letty mopped the floor and washed the cupboards. Lonny's declaration about not being much of a housekeeper had been an understatement. He'd done the bare minimum for years, and the house was badly in need of a thorough cleaning. Usually, physical activity quickly wore Letty out and she became breathless and light-headed. But this morning she was filled with an enthusiasm that provided her with energy.

By noon, however, she was exhausted. At nap time, Letty lay down with Cricket, and didn't wake until early afternoon, when the sound of male voices drifted up the stairs. She realized almost immediately that Chase Brown was with her brother.

Running a brush through her short curly hair, Letty composed herself for the coming confrontation with Chase and walked calmly down the stairs.

He and her brother were sitting at the table, drinking coffee.

Lonny glanced up when she entered the room, but Chase looked away from her. Her brother had made a point of telling her that Chase was different, and she could see the truth of his words. Chase's dark hair had become streaked with gray in her absence. Deep crevices marked his forehead and grooved the sides of his mouth. In nine years he'd aged twenty, Letty thought with a stab of regret. Part of her longed to wrap her arms around him the way she had so many years before. She yearned to bury her head in his shoulder and weep for the pain she'd caused him.

But she knew she couldn't.

"Hello, Chase," she said softly, walking over to the stove and reaching for the coffeepot.

"Letty." He lowered his head in greeting, but kept his eyes averted.

"It's good to see you again."

He didn't answer that; instead he returned his attention to her brother. "I was thinking about separating part of the herd, driving them a mile or so south. Of course, that'd mean hauling the feed a lot farther, but I believe the benefits will outweigh that inconvenience."

"I think you're going to a lot of effort for nothing," Lonny said, frowning.

Letty pulled out a chair and sat across from Chase. He could only ignore her for so long. Still his gaze skirted hers, and he did his utmost to avoid looking at her.

"Who are you?"

Letty turned to the doorway, where Cricket was standing, blanket held tightly in her hand.

"Cricket, this is Uncle Lonny's neighbor, Mr. Brown."

"I'm Cricket," she said, grinning cheerfully.

"Hello." Chase spoke in a gruff unfriendly tone, obviously doing his best to disregard the little girl in the same manner he chose to overlook her mother.

A small cry of protest rose in Letty's throat. Chase could be as angry with her as he wanted. The way she figured it, that was his right, but he shouldn't take out his bitterness on an innocent child.

"Your hair's a funny color," Cricket commented, fascinated. "I think it's pretty like that." Her yellow blanket in tow, she marched up to Chase and raised her hand to touch the salt-and-pepper strands that were more pronounced at his temple.

Chase frowned and moved back so there wasn't any chance of her succeeding.

"My mommy and I are going to bake a pie for Uncle Lonny. Do you want some?"

Letty held her breath, waiting for Chase to reply. Something about him appeared to intrigue Cricket. The child couldn't stop staring at him. Her actions seemed to unnerve Chase, who made it obvious that he'd like nothing better than to forget her existence.

"I don't think Mr. Brown is interested in apple pie, sweetheart," Letty said, trying to fill the uncomfortable silence.

"Then we'll make something he does like," Cricket insisted. She reached for Chase's hand and tugged, demanding his attention. "Do you like chocolate chip cookies? I do. And Mommy makes really yummy ones."

For a moment Chase stared at Cricket, and the pain that flashed in his dark eyes went straight through Letty's heart. A split second later he glanced away as though he couldn't bear to continue looking at the child.

"Do you?" Cricket persisted.

Chase nodded, although it was clearly an effort to do so.

"Come on, Mommy," Cricket cried. "I want to make them *now*."

"What about my apple pie?" Lonny said, his eyes twinkling.

Cricket ignored the question, intent on the cookie-making task. She dragged her blanket after her as she started opening and closing the bottom cupboards, searching for bowls and pans. She dutifully brought out two of each and rummaged through the drawers until she located a wooden spoon. Then, as though suddenly finding the blanket cumbersome, the child lifted it from the floor and placed it in Chase's lap.

Letty could hardly believe her eyes. She'd brought Cricket home from the hospital in that yellow blanket and the little girl had slept with it every night of her life since. Rarely would she entrust it to anyone, let alone a stranger.

Chase looked down on the much-loved blanket as if the youngster had deposited a dirty diaper in his lap.

"I'll take it," Letty said, holding out her hands.

Chase gave it to her, and when he did, his cold gaze locked with hers. Letty felt the chill in his eyes all the way through her bones. His bitterness toward her was evident with every breath he drew.

"It would've been better if you'd never come back," he said so softly she had to strain to hear.

She opened her mouth to argue. Even Lonny didn't know the real reason she'd returned to Wyoming. No one did, except her doctor in California. She hadn't meant to come back and disrupt Chase's life—or anyone else's, for that matter. Chase didn't need to spell out that he didn't want anything to do with her. He'd made that clear the minute she'd walked into the kitchen.

"Mommy, hurry," Cricket said. "We have to bake cookies."

"Just a minute, sweetheart." Letty was uncertain how to handle this new problem. She doubted Lonny had chocolate chips in the house, and a trip into town was more than she wanted to tackle that afternoon.

"Cricket..."

Lonny and Chase both stood. "I'm driving on over to Chase's for the rest of the afternoon," Lonny told her. He obviously wasn't accustomed to letting anyone know his whereabouts and did so now only as an afterthought.

"Can I go, too?" Cricket piped up, so eager her blue eyes sparkled with the idea.

Letty wanted her daughter to be comfortable with Lonny, and she would've liked to encourage the two of them to become friends, but the frown that darkened Chase's brow told her now wasn't the time.

"Not today," Letty murmured, looking away from the two men.

Cricket pouted for a few minutes, but didn't argue. It wouldn't have mattered if she had, because Lonny and Chase left without another word.

Dinner was ready and waiting when Lonny returned to the house that evening. Cricket ran to greet him, her pigtails bouncing. "Mommy and me cooked dinner for you!"

Lonny smiled down on her and absently patted her head, then went to the bathroom to wash his hands. Letty watched him and felt a tugging sense of discontent. After years of living alone, Lonny tended not to be as communicative as Letty wanted him to be. This was understandable, but it made her realize how lonely he must be out here on the ranch night after night without anyone to share his life. Ranchers had to be more stubborn than any other breed of male, Letty thought.

To complicate matters, there was the issue of Cricket staying with Lonny while Letty had the surgery. The little girl had never been away from her overnight.

Letty's prognosis for a complete recovery was good, but there was always the possibility that she wouldn't be coming home from the hospital. Any number of risks had to be considered with this type of operation, and if anything were to happen, Lonny would have to raise Cricket on his own. Letty didn't doubt he'd do so with the greatest of care, but he simply wasn't accustomed to dealing with children.

By the time her brother had finished washing up, dinner was on the table. He gazed down at the ample amount of food and grinned appreciatively. "I can't tell you how long it's been since I've had a home-cooked meal like this. I've missed it."

"What have you been eating?"

He shrugged. "I come up with something or other, but nothing as appetizing as this." He sat down and filled his plate, hardly waiting for Cricket and Letty to join him.

He was buttering his biscuit when he paused and looked at Letty. Slowly he put down the biscuit and placed his knife next to his plate. "Are you okay?" he asked.

"Sure," she answered, smiling weakly. Actually, she wasn't—the day had been exhausting. She'd tried to do too much and she was paying the price, feeling shaky and weak. "What makes you ask?"

"You're pale."

That could be attributed to seeing Chase again, but Letty didn't say so. Their brief meeting had left her feeling melancholy all afternoon. She'd been so young and so foolish, seeking bright lights, utterly convinced that she'd never be satisfied with the lot of a rancher's wife. She'd wanted diamonds, not denim.

"No, I'm fine," she lied as Lonny picked up the biscuit again.

"Mommy couldn't find any chocolate chips," Cricket said, frowning, "so we just baked the apple pie."

Lonny nodded, far more interested in his gravy and biscuits than in conversing with a child.

"I took Cricket out to the barn and showed her the horses," Letty said.

Lonny nodded, then helped himself to seconds on the biscuits. He spread a thick layer of butter on each half.

"I thought maybe later you could let Cricket give them their oats," Letty prompted.

"The barn isn't any place for a little girl," Lonny murmured, dismissing the suggestion with a quick shake of his head.

Cricket looked disappointed and Letty mentally chastised herself for mentioning the idea in front of her daughter. She should've known better.

"Maybe Uncle Lonny will let me ride his horsey?" Cricket asked, her eyes wide and hopeful. "Mommy had a horsey when *she* was a little girl—I saw the picture in her room. I want one, too."

"You have to grow up first," Lonny said brusquely, ending the conversation.

It was on the tip of Letty's tongue to ask Lonny if he'd let Cricket sit in a saddle, but he showed no inclination to form a relationship with her daughter.

Letty was somewhat encouraged when Cricket went in to watch television with Lonny while she finished the dishes. But no more than ten minutes had passed before she heard Cricket burst into tears. A moment later, she came running into the kitchen. She buried her face in

Letty's stomach and wrapped both arms around her, sobbing so hard her shoulders shook.

Lonny followed Cricket into the room, his face a study in guilt and frustration.

"What happened?" Letty asked, stroking her daughter's head.

Lonny threw his hands in the air. "I don't know! I turned on the TV and I was watching the news, when Cricket said she wanted to see cartoons."

"There aren't any on right now," Letty explained.

Cricket sobbed louder, then lifted her head. Tears ran unrestrained down her cheeks. "He said *no,* real mean."

"She started talking to me in the middle of a story about the rodeo championships in Vegas, for Pete's sake." Lonny stabbed his fingers through his hair.

"Cricket, Uncle Lonny didn't mean to upset you," Letty told her. "He was watching his program and you interrupted him, that's all."

"But he said it *mean.*"

"I hardly raised my voice," Lonny came back, obviously perplexed. "Are kids always this sensitive?"

"Not really," Letty assured him. Cricket was normally an easygoing child. Fits of crying were rare and usually the result of being overtired. "It was probably a combination of the flight and a busy day."

Lonny nodded and returned to the living room without speaking to Cricket directly. Letty watched him go with a growing sense of concern. Lonny hadn't been around children in years and didn't have the slightest notion how to deal with a five-year-old. Cricket had felt more of a rapport with Chase than she did her own uncle, and Chase had done everything he could to ignore her.

Letty spent the next few minutes comforting her

daughter. After giving Cricket a bath, Letty read her a story and tucked her in for the night. With her hand on the light switch, she acted out a game they'd played since Cricket was two.

"Blow out the light," she whispered.

The child blew with all her might. At that precise moment, Letty flipped the switch.

"Good night, Mommy."

"Night, sweetheart."

Lonny was waiting for her in the living room, still frowning over the incident between him and his niece. "I don't know, Letty," he said, apparently still unsettled. "I don't seem to be worth much in the uncle department."

"Don't worry about it," she said, trying to smile, but her thoughts were troubled. She couldn't schedule the surgery if she wasn't sure Cricket would be comfortable with Lonny.

"I'll try not to upset her again," Lonny said, looking doubtful, "but I don't think I relate well to kids. I've been a bachelor for too long."

Bachelor...

That was it. The solution to her worries. All evening she'd been thinking how lonely her brother was and how he needed someone to share his life. The timing was perfect.

Her gaze flew to her brother and she nearly sighed aloud with relief. What Lonny needed was a wife.

And Letty was determined to find him one.

Fast.

Chapter 2

It wasn't exactly the welcome parade Letty had dreamed about, with the bright red convertible and the high school marching band, but Red Springs's reception was characteristically warm.

"Letty, it's terrific to see you again!"

"Why, Letty Ellison, I thought you were your dear mother. I never realized how much you resemble Maren. I still miss her, you know."

"Glad you're back, Letty. Hope you plan to stay a while."

Letty smiled and shook hands and received so many hugs she was late for the opening hymn at the Methodist church the next Sunday morning.

With Cricket by her side, she slipped silently into a pew and reached for a hymnal. The hymn was a familiar one from her childhood and Letty knew the lyrics well. But even before she opened her mouth to join the others, tears welled up in her eyes. The organ music swirled around her, filling what seemed to be an unending void in her life. It felt so good to be back. So right to be standing in church with her childhood friends and the people she loved.

Attending services here was part of the magnetic pull that had brought her back to Wyoming. This comforting and spiritual experience reminded her that problems were like mountains. There wasn't one she couldn't handle with God's help. Either she'd climb it, pass around it or carve a tunnel through it.

The music continued and Letty reached for a tissue, dabbing at the tears. Her throat had closed up, and that made singing impossible, so she stood with her eyes shut, soaking up the words of the age-old hymn.

Led by instinct, she'd come back to Red Springs, back to the Bar E and the small Methodist church in the heart of town. She was wrapping everything that was important and familiar around her like a homemade quilt on a cold December night.

The organ music faded and Pastor Downey stepped forward to offer a short prayer. As Letty bowed her head, she could feel someone's bold stare. Her unease grew until she felt herself shudder. It was a sensation her mother had often referred to as someone walking over her grave. An involuntary smile tugged at Letty's mouth. That analogy certainly hit close to home. Much too close.

When the prayer was finished, it was all Letty could do not to turn around and find out who was glaring at her. Although she could guess...

"Mommy," Cricket whispered, loudly enough for half

the congregation to hear. "The man who likes chocolate chip cookies is here. He's two rows behind us."

Chase. Letty released an inward sigh. Just as she'd suspected, he was the one challenging her appearance in church, as if her presence would corrupt the good people of this gathering. Letty mused that he'd probably like it if she wore a scarlet A so everyone would know she was a sinner.

Lonny had warned her that Chase was different. And he was. The Chase Brown Letty remembered wasn't judgmental or unkind. He used to be fond of children. Letty recalled that, years ago, when they walked through town, kids would automatically come running to Chase. He usually had coins for the gum-ball machine tucked away in his pocket, which he'd dole out judiciously. Something about him seemed to attract children, and the fact that Cricket had taken to him instantly was proof of his appeal.

An icy hand closed around Letty's heart at the memory. Chase was the type of man who should've married and fathered a houseful of kids. Over the years, she'd hoped he'd done exactly that.

But he hadn't. Instead Chase had turned bitter and hard. Letty was well aware that she'd hurt him terribly. How she regretted that. Chase had loved her, but all he felt for her now was disdain. In years past, he hadn't been able to disguise his love; now, sadly, he had difficulty hiding his dislike.

Letty had seen the wounded look in his eyes when she'd walked into the kitchen the day before. She'd known then that she'd been the one to put it there. If she hadn't been so familiar with him, he might've been able to fool her.

If only she could alter the past....

"Mommy, what's his name again?" Cricket demanded.

"Mr. Brown."

"Can I wave to him?"

"Not now."

"I want to talk to him."

Exasperated, Letty placed her hand on her daughter's shoulder and leaned down to whisper, "Why?"

"Because I bet he has a horse. Uncle Lonny won't let me ride his. Maybe Mr. Brown will."

"Oh, Cricket, I don't think so...."

"Why not?" the little girl pressed.

"We'll talk about this later."

"But I can ask, can't I? Please?"

The elderly couple in front of them turned around to see what all the commotion was about.

"Mommy?" Cricket persisted, clearly running out of patience.

"Yes, fine," Letty agreed hurriedly, against her better judgment.

From that moment on, Cricket started to fidget. Letty had to speak to her twice during the fifteen-minute sermon; during the closing hymn, Cricket turned around to wave at Chase. She could barely wait for the end of the service so she could rush over and ask about his horse.

Letty could feel the dread mounting inside her. Chase didn't want anything to do with Cricket, and Letty hated the thought of him hurting the little girl's feelings. When the final prayer was offered, Letty added a small request of her own.

"Can we leave now?" Cricket said, reaching for her

mother's hand and tugging at it as the concluding burst of organ music filled the church.

Letty nodded. Cricket dropped her hand and was off. Letty groaned inwardly and dashed after her.

Standing on the church steps, Letty saw that Chase was walking toward the parking lot when Cricket caught up with him. She must have called his name, because Chase turned around abruptly. Even from that distance, Letty could see his dark frown. Quickening her step, she made her way toward them.

"Good morning, Chase," she greeted him, forcing a smile as she stood beside Cricket.

"Letty." His hat was in his hand and he rotated the brim, as though eager to make his escape, which Letty felt sure he was.

"I asked him already," Cricket blurted out, glancing up at her mother.

From the look Chase was giving Letty, he seemed to believe she'd put Cricket up to this. As if she spent precious time thinking up ways to irritate him!

"Mr. Brown's much too busy, sweetheart," Letty said, struggling to keep her voice even and controlled. "Perhaps you can ride his horse another time."

Cricket nodded and grinned. "That's what he said, too."

Surprised, Letty gazed up at Chase. She was grateful he hadn't been harsh with her daughter. From somewhere deep inside, she dredged up a smile to thank him, but he didn't answer it with one of his own. A fresh sadness settled over Letty. The past would always stand between them and there was nothing Letty could do to change that. She wasn't even sure she should try.

"If you'll excuse me," she said, reaching for Cricket's hand, "there are some people I want to talk to."

"More people?" Cricket whined. "I didn't know there were so many people in the whole world."

"It was nice to see you again, Chase," Letty said, turning away. Not until several minutes later did she realize he hadn't echoed her greeting.

Chase couldn't get away from the church fast enough. He didn't know why he'd decided to attend services this particular morning. It wasn't as if he made a regular practice of it, although he'd been raised in the church. He supposed that something perverse inside him was interested in knowing if Letty had the guts to show up.

The woman had nerve. Another word that occurred to him was *courage;* it wouldn't be easy to face all those people with an illegitimate daughter holding her hand. That kind of thing might be acceptable in big cities, but people here tended to be more conservative. Outwardly folks would smile, but the gossip would begin soon enough. He suspected that once it did, Letty would pack up her bags and leave again.

He wished she would. One look at her the day she'd arrived and he knew he'd been lying to himself all these years. She was paler than he remembered, but her face was still a perfect oval, her skin creamy and smooth. Her blue eyes were huge and her mouth a lush curve. There was no way he could continue lying to himself. He was still in love with her—and always would be.

He climbed inside his pickup and started the engine viciously. He gripped the steering wheel hard. Who was he trying to kid? He'd spent years waiting for Letty to come back. Telling himself he hated her was nothing more than a futile effort to bolster his pride. He wished there could be someone else for him, but there wasn't; there never would be. Letty was the only woman he'd ever loved, heart and soul. If she couldn't be the one to fill his arms during the night, then they'd remain empty. But there was no reason for Letty ever to know that. The fact was, he'd prefer it if she didn't find out. Chase Brown might be fool enough to fall in love with the wrong woman, but he knew better than to hand her the weapon that would shred what remained of his pride.

"You must be Lonny's sister," a feminine voice drawled from behind Letty.

Letty finished greeting one of her mother's friends before turning. When she did, she met a statuesque blonde, who looked about thirty. "Yes, I'm Lonny's sister," she said, smiling.

"I'm so happy to meet you. I'm Mary Brandon," the woman continued. "I hope you'll forgive me for being so direct, but I heard someone say your name and thought I'd introduce myself."

"I'm pleased to meet you, Mary." They exchanged quick handshakes as Letty sized up the other woman. Single—and eager. "How do you know Lonny?"

"I work at the hardware store and your brother comes in every now and then. He might have mentioned me?" she asked hopefully. When Letty shook her head, Mary shrugged and gave a nervous laugh. "He stops in and gets whatever he needs and then he's on his way." She paused. "He must be lonely living out on that ranch all by himself. Especially after all those years in the rodeo."

Letty could feel the excitement bubbling up inside her. Mary Brandon definitely looked like wife material to her, and it was obvious the woman was more than casually interested in Lonny. As far as Letty was concerned, there wasn't any better place to find a prospective mate for her brother than in church.

The night before, she'd lain in bed wondering where she'd ever meet someone suitable for Lonny. If he hadn't found anyone in the past few years, there was nothing to guarantee that she could come up with the perfect mate in just a few months. The truth was, she didn't know whether he'd had any serious—or even not-so-serious—relationships during her years away. His rodeo success had certainly been an enticement to plenty of girls, but since he'd retired from the circuit and since their parents had died, her brother had become so single-minded, so dedicated to the ranch, that he'd developed tunnel vision. The Bar E now demanded all his energy and all his time, and consequently his personal life had suffered.

"Your brother seems very nice," Mary was saying.

And eligible, Letty added silently. "He's wonderful, but he works so hard it's difficult for anyone to get to know him."

Mary sent her a look that said she understood that all too well. "He's not seeing anyone regularly, is he?"

"No." But Letty wished he was.

Mary's eyes virtually snapped with excitement. "He hides away on the Bar E and hardly ever socializes. I firmly believe he needs a little fun in his life."

Letty's own eyes were gleaming. "I think you may be right. Listen, Mary, perhaps we should talk…"

* * *

Chase was working in the barn when he heard Lonny's truck. He wiped the perspiration off his brow with his forearm.

Lonny walked in and Chase immediately recognized that he was upset. Chase shoved the pitchfork into the hay and leaned against it. "Problems?"

Lonny didn't answer him right away. He couldn't seem to stay in one place. "It's that fool sister of mine."

Chase's hand closed around the pitchfork. Letty had been on his mind all morning and she was the last person he wanted to discuss. Lonny appeared to be waiting for a response, so Chase gave him one. "I knew she'd be nothing but trouble from the moment you told me she was coming home."

Lonny removed his hat and slapped it against his thigh. "She went to church this morning." He turned to glance in Chase's direction. "Said she saw you there. Actually, it was her kid, Cricket, who mentioned your name. She calls you 'the guy who likes chocolate chip cookies.'" He grinned slightly at that.

"I was there," Chase said tersely.

"At any rate, Letty talked to Mary Brandon afterward."

A smile sprang to Chase's lips. Mary had set her sights on Lonny three months ago, and she wasn't about to let up until she got her man.

"Wipe that smug look off your face, Brown. You're supposed to be my friend."

"I am." He lifted a forkful of hay and tossed it behind him. Lonny had been complaining about the Brandon woman for weeks. Mary had done everything but stand on her head to garner his attention. And a wedding ring.

Lonny stalked aggressively to the other end of the barn, then returned. "Letty's overstepped the bounds this time," he muttered.

"Oh? What did she do?"

"She invited Mary to dinner tomorrow night."

Despite himself, Chase burst out laughing. He turned around to discover his friend glaring at him and stopped abruptly. "You're kidding, I hope?"

"Would I be this upset if I was? She invited that… woman right into my house without even asking me how I felt about it. I told her I had other plans for dinner tomorrow, but she claims she needs me there to cut the meat. Nine years in California and she didn't learn how to cut meat?"

"Well, it seems to me you're stuck having dinner with Mary Brandon." Chase realized he shouldn't find the situation so funny. But he did. Chase wasn't keen on Mary himself. There was something faintly irritating about the woman, something that rubbed him the wrong way. Lonny had the same reaction, although they'd never discussed what it was that annoyed them so much. Chase supposed it was the fact that Mary came on so strong. She was a little too desperate to snare herself a husband.

Brooding, Lonny paced the length of the barn. "I told Letty I was only staying for dinner if you were there, too."

Chase stabbed the pitchfork into the ground. "You did *what?*"

"If I'm going to suffer through an entire dinner with that…that woman, I need another guy to run interference. You can't expect me to sit across the dinner table from those two."

"Three," Chase corrected absently. Lonny hadn't included Cricket.

"Oh, yeah, that's right. Three against one. It's more than any man can handle on his own." He shook his head. "I love my sister, don't get me wrong. I'm glad she decided to come home. She should've done it years ago...but I'm telling you, I like my life exactly as it is. Every time I turn around, Cricket's underfoot asking me questions. I can't even check out the news without her wanting to watch cartoons."

"Maybe you should ask Letty to leave." A part of Chase—a part he wasn't proud of—prayed that Lonny would. He hadn't had a decent night's sleep since he'd found out she was returning to Red Springs. He worked until he was ready to drop, and still his mind refused to give him the rest he craved. Instead he'd been tormented by resurrected memories he thought he'd buried years before. Like his friend, Chase had created a comfortable niche for himself and he didn't like his peace of mind invaded by Letty Ellison.

"I can't ask her to leave," Lonny said in a burst of impatience. "She's my *sister!*"

Chase shrugged. "Then tell her to uninvite Mary."

"I tried that. Before I knew it, she was reminding me how much Mom enjoyed company. Then she said that since she was moving back to the community, it was only right for her to get to know the new folks in town. At the time it made perfect sense, and a few minutes later, I'd agreed to be there for that stupid dinner. But there's only one way I'll go through with this and that's if you come, too."

"Cancel the dinner, then."

"Chase! How often do I ask you for a favor?"

Chase glared at him.

"All right, *that* kind of favor!"

"I'm sorry, Lonny, but I won't have anything to do with Mary Brandon."

Lonny was quiet for so long that Chase finally turned to meet his narrowed gaze. "Is it Mary or Letty who bothers you?" his friend asked.

Chase tightened his fingers around the pitchfork. "Doesn't matter, because I won't be there."

Letty took an afternoon nap with Cricket, hoping her explanation wouldn't raise Lonny's suspicions. She'd told him she was suffering from the lingering effects of jet lag.

First thing Monday morning, she planned to contact the state social services office. She couldn't put it off any longer. Each day she seemed to grow weaker and tired more easily. The thought of dealing with the state agency filled her with apprehension; accepting charity went against everything in her, but the cost of the surgery was prohibitive. Letty, who'd once been so proud, was forced to accept the generosity of the taxpayers of Wyoming.

Cricket stirred beside her in the bed as Letty drifted into an uneasy sleep. When she awoke, she noticed Cricket's yellow blanket draped haphazardly over her shoulders. Her daughter was gone.

Yawning, she went downstairs to discover Cricket sitting in front of the television. "Uncle Lonny says he doesn't want dinner tonight."

"That's tomorrow night," Lonny shouted from the kitchen. "Chase and I won't be there."

Letty's shoulders sagged with defeat. She didn't understand how one man could be so stubborn. "Why not?"

"Chase flat out refuses to come and I have no intention of sticking around just to cut up a piece of meat for you."

Letty poured herself a cup of coffee. The fact that Chase wouldn't be there shouldn't come as any big shock, but it did, accompanied by a curious pain.

Scowling, she sat down at the square table, bracing her elbows on it. Until that moment, she hadn't realized how much she wanted to settle the past with Chase. She needed to do it before the surgery.

"I said Chase wasn't coming," Lonny told her a second time.

"I heard you—it's all right," she replied, doing her best to reassure her brother with an easy smile that belied the emotion churning inside her. It'd been a mistake to invite Mary Brandon to dinner without consulting Lonny first. In her enthusiasm, Letty had seen the other woman as a gift that had practically fallen into her lap. How was she to know her brother disliked Mary so passionately?

Lonny tensed. "What do you mean, 'all right'? I don't like the look you've got in your eye."

Letty dropped her gaze. "I mean it's perfectly fine if you prefer not to be here tomorrow night for dinner. I thought it might be a way of getting to know some new people in town, but I should've cleared it with you first."

"Yes, you should have."

"Mary seems nice enough," Letty commented, trying once more.

"So did the snake in the Garden of Eden."

Letty chuckled. "Honestly, Lonny, anyone would think you're afraid of the woman."

"This one's got moves that would be the envy of a world heavyweight champion."

"Obviously she hasn't used them, because she's single."

"Oh, no, she's too smart for that," Lonny countered, gesturing with his hands. "She's been saving them up, just for me."

"Oh, Lonny, you're beginning to sound paranoid, but don't worry, I understand. What kind of sister would I be if I insisted you eat Mama's prime rib dinner with the likes of Mary Brandon?"

Lonny's head shot up. "You're cooking Mom's recipe for prime rib?"

She hated to be so manipulative, but if Lonny were to give Mary half a chance, he might change his mind. "You don't mind if I use some of the meat in the freezer, do you?"

"No," he said, and swallowed. "I suppose there'll be plenty of leftovers?"

Letty shrugged. "I can't say, since I'm thawing out a small roast. I hope you understand."

"Sure," Lonny muttered, frowning.

Apparently he understood all too well, because an hour later, her brother announced he probably would be around for dinner the following night, after all.

Monday morning Letty rose early. The coffee had perked and bacon was sizzling in the skillet when Lonny wandered into the kitchen.

"Morning," he said.

"Morning," she returned cheerfully.

Lonny poured himself a cup of coffee and headed for the door, pausing just before he opened it. "I'll be back in a few minutes."

At the sound of a pickup pulling into the yard, Letty glanced out the kitchen window. Her heart sped up at the sight of Chase climbing out of the cab. It was as if those nine years had been wiped away and he'd come for her the way he used to when she was a teenager. He wore jeans and a shirt with a well-worn leather vest. His dark hair curled crisply at his sun-bronzed nape and he needed a haircut. In him, Letty recognized strength and masculinity.

He entered the kitchen without knocking and stopped short when he saw her. "Letty," he said, sounding shocked.

"Good morning, Chase," she greeted him simply. Unwilling to see the bitterness in his gaze, she didn't look up from the stove. "Lonny's stepped outside for a moment. Pour yourself a cup of coffee."

"No, thanks." Already he'd turned back to the door.

"Chase." Her heart was pounding so hard it felt as though it might leap into her throat. The sooner she cleared the air between them, the better. "Do you have a minute?"

"Not really."

Ignoring his words, she removed the pan from the burner. "At some point in everyone's life—"

"I said I didn't have time, Letty."

"But—"

"If you're figuring to give me some line about how life's done you wrong and how sorry you are about the past, save your breath, because I don't need to hear it."

"Maybe you don't," she said gently, "but I need to say it."

"Then do it in front of a mirror."

"Chase, you're my brother's best friend. It isn't as if we can ignore each other. It's too uncomfortable to pretend nothing's wrong."

"As far as I'm concerned nothing *is* wrong."

"But—"

"Save your breath, Letty," he said again.

Chapter 3

"Mr. Chase," Cricket called excitedly from the foot of the stairs. "You're here!"

Letty turned back to the stove, fighting down anger and indignation. Chase wouldn't so much as listen to her. Fine. If he wanted to pretend there was nothing wrong, then she would give an award-winning performance herself. He wasn't the only one who could be this childish.

The back door opened and Lonny blithely stepped into the kitchen. "You're early, aren't you?" he asked Chase as he refilled his coffee cup.

"No," Chase snapped impatiently. The look he shot Letty said he wouldn't have come in the house at all if he'd known she was up.

Lonny paid no attention to the censure in his neighbor's voice. He pulled out a chair and sat down. "I'm not ready to leave yet. Letty's cooking breakfast."

"Mr. Chase, Mr. Chase, did you bring your horsey?"

"It's Mr. *Brown*," Letty corrected as she brought two plates to the table. Lonny immediately dug into his bacon-and-egg breakfast, but Chase ignored the meal—as though eating anything Letty had made might poison him.

"Answer her," Lonny muttered between bites. "Otherwise she'll drive you nuts."

"I drove my truck over," Chase told Cricket.

"Do you ever bring your horsey to Uncle Lonny's?"

"Sometimes."

"Are you a cowboy?"

"I suppose."

"Wyoming's the Cowboy State," Letty told her daughter.

"Does that mean everyone who lives here has to be a cowboy?"

"Not exactly."

"But close," Lonny said with a grin.

Cricket climbed onto the chair next to Chase's and dragged her yellow blanket with her. She set her elbows on the table and cupped her face in her hands. "Aren't you going to eat?" she asked, studying him intently.

"I had breakfast," he said, pushing the plate toward her.

Cricket didn't need to be asked twice. Kneeling on the chair, she reached across Chase and grabbed his fork. She smiled up at him, her eyes sparkling.

Letty joined the others at the table. Lately her appetite hadn't been good, but she forced herself to eat a piece of toast.

The atmosphere was strained. Letty tried to avoid looking in Chase's direction, but it was impossible to ignore the man. He turned toward her unexpectedly, catching her look and holding it. His eyes were dark and intense. Caught off guard, Letty blushed.

Chase's gaze darted from her eyes to her mouth and stayed there. She longed to turn primly away from him with a shrug of indifference, but she couldn't. Years ago, Letty had loved staring into Chase's eyes. He had the most soulful eyes of any man she'd ever known. She was trapped in the memory of how it used to be with them. At one time, she'd been able to read loving messages in his eyes. But they were cold now, filled with angry sparks that flared briefly before he glanced away.

What little appetite Letty had was gone, and she put her toast back on the plate and shoved it aside. "Would it be all right if I took the truck this morning?" she asked her brother, surprised by the quaver in her voice. She wished she could ignore Chase altogether, but that was impossible. He refused to deal with the past and she couldn't make him talk to her. As far as Letty could tell, he preferred to simply overlook her presence. Only he seemed to find that as difficult as she found ignoring him. That went a long way toward raising her spirits.

"Where are you going?"

"I thought I'd do a little shopping for dinner tonight." It was true, but only half the reason she needed his truck. She had to drive to Rock Springs, which was fifty miles west of Red Springs, so she could talk to the social services people there about her eligibility for Medicaid.

"That's right—Mary Brandon's coming to dinner, isn't she?" Lonny asked, evidently disturbed by the thought.

It was a mistake to have mentioned the evening meal,

because her brother frowned the instant he said Mary's name. "I suppose I won't be needing the truck," he said, scowling.

"I appreciate it. Thanks," Letty said brightly.

Her brother shrugged.

"Are you coming to dinner with Mommy's friend?" Cricket asked Chase.

"No," he said brusquely.

"How come?"

"Because he's smart, that's why," Lonny answered, then stood abruptly. He reached for his hat, settled it on his head and didn't look back.

Within seconds, both men were gone.

"You'll need to complete these forms," the woman behind the desk told Letty, handing her several sheets.

The intake clerk looked frazzled and overburdened. It was well past noon, and Letty guessed the woman hadn't had a coffee break all morning and was probably late for her lunch. The clerk briefly read over the letter from the physician Letty had been seeing in California, and made a copy of it to attach to Letty's file.

"Once you're done with those forms, please bring them back to me," she said.

"Of course," Letty told her.

Bored, Cricket had slipped her arms around her mother's waist and was pressing her head against Letty's stomach.

"If you have any questions, feel free to ask," the worker said.

"None right now. Thank you for all your help." Letty stood, Cricket still holding on.

For the first time since Letty had entered the government office, the young woman smiled.

Letty took the sheets and sat at a table in a large lobby. One by one, she answered the myriad questions. Before she'd be eligible for Wyoming's medical assistance program, she'd have to be accepted into the Supplemental Security Income program offered through the federal government. It was a humiliating fact of life, but proud, independent Letty Ellison was about to go on welfare.

Tears blurred her eyes as she filled in the first sheet. She stopped long enough to wipe them away before they spilled onto the papers. She had no idea what she'd tell Lonny once the government checks started arriving. Especially since he seemed so confident he could find her some kind of employment in town.

"When can we leave?" Cricket said, close to her mother's ear.

"Soon." Letty was writing as fast as she could, eager to escape, too.

"I don't like it here," Cricket whispered.

"I don't, either," Letty whispered back. But she was grateful the service existed; otherwise she didn't know what she would've done.

Cricket fell asleep in the truck during the hour's drive home. Letty was thankful for the silence because it gave her a chance to think through the immediate problems that faced her. She could no longer delay seeing a physician, and eventually she'd have to tell Lonny about her heart condition. She hadn't intended to keep it a secret, but there was no need to worry him until everything was settled with the Medicaid people. Once she'd completed all the paperwork, been examined by a variety of knowledgeable doctors so they could tell her what she already knew, then she'd be free to explain the situation to Lonny.

Until then, she would keep this problem to herself.

"Letty!" Lonny cried from the top of the stairs. "Do I have to dress for dinner?"

"Please," she answered sweetly, basting the rib roast before sliding it back in the oven for a few more minutes.

"A tie, too?" he asked without enthusiasm.

"A nice sweater would do."

"I don't own a 'nice' sweater," he shouted back.

A couple of muffled curses followed, but Letty chose to ignore them. At least she knew what to get her brother next Christmas.

Lonny had been in a bad temper from the minute he'd walked in the door an hour earlier, and Letty could see that this evening was headed for disaster.

"Mommy!" Cricket's pigtails were flying as she raced into the kitchen. "Your friend's here."

"Oh." Letty quickly removed the oven mitt and glanced at her watch. Mary was a good ten minutes early and Letty needed every second of that time. The table wasn't set, and the roast was still in the oven.

"Mary, it's good to see you." Letty greeted her with a smile as she rushed into the living room.

Mary walked into the Ellison home, her eyes curious as she examined the living room furniture. "It's good to be here. I brought some fresh-baked rolls for Lonny."

"How thoughtful." Letty moved into the center of the room. "I'm running a little behind, so if you'll excuse me for a minute?"

"Of course."

"Make yourself comfortable," Letty called over her

shoulder as she hurried back to the kitchen. She looked around, wondering which task to finish first. After she'd returned from Rock Springs that afternoon and done the shopping, she'd taken a nap with Cricket. Now she regretted having wasted that time. The whole meal felt so disorganized and with Lonny's attitude, well—

"This is a lovely watercolor in here," Mary called in to her. "Who painted it?"

"My mother. She was an artist," Letty answered, taking the salad out of the refrigerator. She grabbed silverware and napkins on her way into the dining room. "Cricket, would you set the table for me?"

"Okay," the youngster agreed willingly.

Mary stood in the room, hands behind her back as she studied the painting of a lush field of wildflowers. "Your mother certainly had an eye for color, didn't she?"

"Mom was very talented," Letty replied wistfully.

"Did she paint any of the others?" Mary asked, gesturing around the living room.

"No…actually, this is the only painting we have of hers."

"She gave the others away?"

"Not exactly," Letty admitted, feeling a flash of resentment. With all her mother's obligations on the ranch, plus helping Dad when she could during the last few years of his life, there hadn't been time for her to work on what she'd loved most, which was her art. Letty's mother had lived a hard life. The land had drained her energy. Letty had been a silent witness to what had happened to her mother and swore it wouldn't be repeated in her own life. Yet here she was, back in Wyoming. Back on the Bar E, and grateful she had a home.

"How come we're eating in the dining room?" Lonny

muttered irritably as he came downstairs. He buried his hands in his pockets and made an obvious effort to ignore Mary, who stood no more than five feet away.

"You know Mary, don't you?" Letty asked pointedly.

Lonny nodded in the other woman's direction, but managed to do so without actually looking at her.

"Hello, Lonny," Mary cooed. "It's a real pleasure to see you again. I brought you some rolls—hot from the oven."

"Mary brought over some homemade dinner rolls," Letty reiterated, resisting the urge to kick her brother in the shin.

"Looks like those rolls came from the Red Springs Bakery to me," he muttered, pulling out a chair and sitting down.

Letty half expected him to grab his knife and fork, pound the table with them and chant, *Dinner, dinner, dinner.* If he couldn't discourage Mary by being rude, he'd probably try the more advanced "caveman" approach.

"Well, yes, I did pick up the rolls there," Mary said, clearly flustered. "I didn't have time after work to bake."

"Naturally, you wouldn't have," Letty responded mildly, shooting her brother a heated glare.

Cricket scooted past the two women and handed her uncle a plate. "Anything else, Mommy?"

Letty quickly checked the table to see what was needed. "Glasses," she mumbled, rushing back into the kitchen. While she was there, she took the peas off the burner. The vegetable had been an expensive addition to the meal, but Letty had bought them at the market in town, remembering how much Lonny loved fresh peas.

He deserved some reward for being such a good sport—
or so she'd thought earlier.

Cricket finished setting the table and Letty brought
out the rest of their dinner. She smiled as she joined the
others. Her brother had made a tactical error when he'd
chosen to sit down first. Mary had immediately taken the
chair closest to him. She gazed at him with wide adoring
eyes while Lonny did his best to ignore her.

As Letty had predicted earlier, the meal was a disaster, and the tension in the air was thick. Letty made several attempts at conversation, which Mary leaped upon,
but the minute either of them tried to include Lonny,
the subject died. It was all Letty could do to keep from
kicking her brother under the table. Mary didn't linger
after the meal.

"Don't ever do that to me again," Lonny grumbled
as soon as Letty was back from escorting Mary to the
front door.

She sank down in the chair beside him and closed her
eyes, exhausted. She didn't have the energy to argue with
her brother. If he was looking for an apology, she'd give
him one. "I'm sorry, Lonny. I was only trying to help."

"Help what? Ruin my life?"

"No!" Letty said, her eyes flying open. "You need
someone."

"Who says?"

"I do."

"Did you ever stop to think that's a bit presumptuous
on your part? You're gone nine years and then you waltz
home, look around and decide what you can change."

"Lonny, I said I was sorry."

He was silent for a lengthy moment, then he sighed.
"I didn't mean to shout."

"I know you didn't." Letty was so tired she didn't know how she was going to manage the dishes. One meal, and she'd used every pan in the house. Cricket was clearing the table for her and she was so grateful she kissed her daughter's forehead.

Lonny dawdled over his coffee, eyes downcast. "What makes you think I need someone?" he asked quietly.

"It seems so lonely out here. I assumed—incorrectly, it appears—that you'd be happier if there was someone to share your life with. You're a handsome man, Lonny, and there are plenty of women who'd like to be your wife."

One corner of his mouth edged up at that. "I intend to marry someday. I just haven't gotten around to it, that's all."

"Well, for heaven's sake, what are you waiting for?" Letty teased. "You're thirty-four and you're not getting any younger."

"I'm not exactly ready for social security."

Letty smiled. "Mary's nice—"

"Aw, come off it, Letty. I don't like that woman. How many times do I have to tell you that?"

"—but I understand why she isn't your type," Letty finished, undaunted.

"You do?"

She nodded. "Mary needs a man who'd be willing to spend a lot of time and money keeping her entertained. She wouldn't make a good rancher's wife."

"I knew that the minute I met her," Lonny grumbled. "I just didn't know how to put it in words." He mulled over his thoughts, then added, "Look at the way she let you and Cricket do all the work getting dinner on the table. She didn't help once. That wouldn't sit well with most folks."

"She was company." Letty felt an obligation to defend Mary. After all, she hadn't *asked* the other woman to help with the meal, although she would've appreciated it. Besides, Lonny didn't have a lot of room to talk; he'd waited to be served just like Mary had.

"Company, my foot," Lonny countered. "Could you see Mom or any other woman you know sitting around making idle chatter while everyone else is working around her?"

Letty had to ackowledge that was true.

"Did you notice how she wanted everyone to think she'd made those rolls herself?"

Letty had noticed, but she didn't consider that such a terrible thing.

Lonny reached into the middle of the table for a carrot stick, chewing on it with a frown. "A wife," he murmured. "I agree that a woman would take more interest in the house than I have in the past few years." He crunched down on the carrot again. "I have to admit it's been rather nice having my meals cooked and my laundry folded. Those are a couple of jobs I can live without."

Letty practically swallowed her tongue to keep from commenting.

"I think you might be right, Letty. A wife would come in handy."

"You could always hire a housekeeper," Letty said sarcastically, irritated by his attitude and unable to refrain from saying something after all.

"What are you so irked about? You're the one who suggested I get married in the first place."

"From the way you're talking, you seem to think of a wife as a hired hand who'll clean house and cook your meals. You don't want a *wife*. You're looking for a servant. A woman has to get more out of a relationship than that."

Lonny snorted. "I thought you females need to be needed. For crying out loud, what else is there to a marriage but cooking and cleaning and regular sex?"

Letty glared at her brother, stood and picked up their coffee cups. "Lonny, I was wrong. Do some woman the ultimate favor and stay single."

With that she walked out of the dining room.

"So how did dinner go?" Chase asked his friend the following morning.

Lonny's response was little more than a grunt.

"That bad?"

"Worse."

Although his friend wouldn't appreciate it, Chase had gotten a good laugh over this dinner date of Lonny's with the gal from the hardware store. "Is Letty going to set you up with that Brandon woman again?"

"Not while I'm breathing, she won't."

Chase chuckled and loosened the reins on Firepower. Mary Brandon was about as subtle as a jackhammer. She'd done everything but throw herself at Lonny's feet, and she probably would've done that if she'd thought it would do any good. Chase wanted to blame Letty for getting Lonny into this mess, but the Brandon woman was wily and had likely manipulated the invitation out of Letty. Unfortunately Lonny was the one who'd suffered the consequences.

Chase smiled, content. Riding the range in May, looking for newborn calves, was one of his favorite chores as a rancher. All creation seemed to be bursting out, fresh and alive. The trees were budding and the wind was warm and carried the sweet scent of wildflowers with it. He liked the ranch best after it rained; everything felt so pure then and the land seemed to glisten.

"That sister of yours is determined to find you a wife, isn't she?" Chase teased, still smiling. "She hasn't been back two weeks and she's matchmaking to beat the band. Before you know it, she'll have you married off. I only hope you get some say in whatever woman Letty chooses."

"Letty doesn't mean any harm."

"Neither did Lizzy Borden."

When Lonny didn't respond with the appropriate chuckle, Chase glanced in his friend's direction. "You look worried. What's wrong?"

"It's Letty."

"What about her?"

"Does she seem any different to you?"

Chase shrugged, hating the sudden concern that surged through him. The only thing he wanted to feel for Letty was apathy, or at best the faint stirring of re-membrance one had about a casual acquaintance. As it was, his heart, his head—every part of him—went into overdrive whenever Lonny brought his sister into the conversation.

"How do you mean—different?" Chase asked.

"I don't know for sure." He hesitated and pushed his hat farther back on his head. "It's crazy, but she takes naps every afternoon. And I mean *every* afternoon. At first she said it was jet lag."

"So she sleeps a lot. Big deal," Chase responded, struggling to sound disinterested.

"Hey, Chase, you know my sister as well as I do. Can

you picture Letty, who was always a ball of energy, taking naps in the middle of the day?"

Chase couldn't, but he didn't say so.

"Another thing," Lonny said as he loosely held his gelding's reins, "Letty's always been a neat freak. Remember how she used to drive me crazy with the way everything had to be just so?"

Chase nodded.

"She left the dinner dishes in the sink all night. I found her putting them in the dishwasher this morning, claiming she'd been too tired to bother after Mary left. Mary was gone by seven-thirty!"

"So she's a little tired," Chase muttered. "Let her sleep if it makes her happy."

"It's more than that," Lonny continued. "She doesn't sing anymore—not a note. For nine years she fought tooth and nail to make it in the entertainment business, and now it's as if…as if she never had a voice. She hasn't even touched the piano since she's been home—at least not when I was there to hear her." Lonny frowned. "It's like the song's gone out of her life."

Chase didn't want to talk about Letty and he didn't want to think about her. In an effort to change the subject he said, "Old man Wilber was by the other day."

Lonny shook his head. "I suppose he was after those same acres again."

"Every year he asks me if I'd be willing to sell that strip of land." Some people knew it was spring when the flowers started to bloom. Chase could tell when Henry Wilber approached him about a narrow strip of land that bordered their property line. It wasn't the land that interested Wilber as much as the water. Nothing on this earth would convince Chase to sell that land. Spring Valley Ranch had been in his family for nearly eighty years and each generation had held on to those acres through good times and bad. Ranching wasn't exactly making Chase a millionaire, but he would die before he sold off a single inch of his inheritance.

"You'd be a fool to let it go," Lonny said.

No one needed to tell Chase that. "I wonder when he'll give up asking."

"Knowing old man Wilber," Lonny said with a chuckle, "I'd say never."

"Are you going to plant any avocados?" Cricket asked as Letty spaded the rich soil that had once been her mother's garden. Lonny had protested, but he'd tilled a large section close to the house for her and Cricket to plant. Now Letty was eager to get her hands in the earth.

"Avocados won't grow in Wyoming, Cricket. The climate isn't mild enough."

"What about oranges?"

"Not those, either."

"What *does* grow in Wyoming?" she asked indignantly. "Cowboys?"

Letty smiled as she used the sturdy fork to turn the soil.

"Mommy, look! Chase is here…on his horsey." Cricket took off, running as fast as her stubby legs would carry her. Her reaction was the same whenever Chase appeared.

Letty stuck the spading fork in the soft ground and reluctantly followed her daughter. By the time she got to the yard, Chase had climbed down from the saddle and dropped the reins. Cricket stood awestruck on the steps leading to the back porch, her mouth agape, her eyes wide.

"Hello, Chase," Letty said softly.

He looked at her and frowned. "Didn't that old straw hat used to belong to your mother?"

Letty nodded. "She wore it when she worked in the garden. I found it the other day." Chase made no further comment, although Letty was sure he'd wanted to say something more.

Eagerly Cricket bounded down the steps to stand beside her mother. Her small hand crept into Letty's, holding on tightly. "I didn't know horsies were so big and *pretty*," she breathed.

"Firepower's special," Letty explained. Chase had raised the bay from a yearling, and had worked with him for long, patient hours.

"You said you wanted to see Firepower," Chase said, a bit gruffly. "I haven't got all day, so if you want a ride it's got to be now."

"I can ride him? Oh, Mommy, can I really?"

Letty's blood roared in her ears. She opened her mouth to tell Chase she wasn't about to set her daughter on a horse of that size.

Before she could voice her objection, however, Chase quieted her fears. "She'll be riding with me." With that he swung himself onto the horse and reached down to hoist Cricket into the saddle with him.

As if she'd been born to ride, Cricket sat in front of Chase on the huge animal without revealing the least bit of fear. "Look at me!" she shouted, grinning widely. "I'm riding a horsey! I'm riding a horsey!"

Even Chase was smiling at such unabashed enthusiasm. "I'll take her around the yard a couple of times," he told Letty before kicking gently at Firepower's sides. The bay obediently trotted around in a circle.

"Can we go over there?" Cricket pointed to some undistinguishable location in the distance.

"Cricket," Letty said, clamping the straw hat onto her head and squinting up. "Chase is a busy man. He hasn't got time to run you all over the countryside."

"Hold on," Chase responded, taking the reins in both hands and heading in the direction Cricket had indicated.

"Chase," Letty cried, running after him. "She's just a little girl. Please be careful."

He didn't answer her, and not knowing what to expect, Letty trailed them to the end of the long drive. When she reached it, she was breathless and light-headed. It took her several minutes to walk back to the house. She was certain anyone watching her would assume she was drunk. Entering the kitchen, Letty grabbed her prescription bottle—hidden from Lonny in a cupboard—and swallowed a couple of capsules without water.

Not wanting to raise unnecessary alarm, she went back to the garden, but had to sit on an old stump until her breathing returned to normal. Apparently her heart had gotten worse since she'd come home. Much worse.

"Mommy, look, no hands," Cricket called out, her arms raised high in the air as Firepower trotted back into the yard.

Smiling, Letty stood and reached for the spading fork.

"Don't try to pretend you were working," Chase muttered, frowning at her. "We saw you sitting in the sun.

What's the matter, Letty? Did the easy life in California make you lazy?"

Once more Chase was baiting her. And once more Letty let the comment slide. "It must have," she said and looked away.

Chapter 4

Chase awoke just before dawn. He lay on his back, listening to the birds chirping outside his half-opened window. Normally their singing would have cheered him, but not this morning. He'd slept poorly, his mind preoccupied with Letty. Everything Lonny had said the week before about her not being herself had bounced around in his brain for most of the night.

Something *was* different about Letty, but not in the way Chase would have assumed. He'd expected the years in California to transform her in a more obvious way, making her worldly and cynical. To his surprise, he'd discovered that in several instances she seemed very much like the naive young woman who'd left nine years earlier to follow a dream. But the changes were there, lots of them, complex and subtle, when he'd expected them to be simple and glaring. Perhaps what troubled Chase was his deep inner feeling that something was genuinely wrong with her. But try as he might, he couldn't pinpoint what it was. That disturbed him the most.

Sitting on the edge of the bed, Chase rubbed his hands over his face and glanced outside. The cloudless dawn sky was a luminous shade of gray. The air smelled crisp and clean as Wyoming offered another perfect spring morning.

Chase dressed in his jeans and a Western shirt. Downstairs, he didn't bother to fix himself a cup of coffee; instead he walked outside, climbed into his pickup and headed over to the Bar E.

Only it wasn't Lonny who drew him there.

The lights were on in the kitchen when Chase pulled into the yard. He didn't knock, but stepped directly into the large family kitchen. Letty was at the stove, the way he knew she would be. She turned when he walked in the door.

"Morning, Chase," she said with a smile.

"Morning." Without another word, he walked over to the cupboard and got himself a mug. Standing next to her, he poured his own coffee.

"Lonny's taking care of the horses," she told him, as if she needed to explain where her brother was.

Briefly Chase wondered how she would've responded if he'd said it wasn't Lonny he'd come to see.

"Cricket talked nonstop for hours about riding Firepower. It was the thrill of her life. Thank you for being so kind to her, Chase."

Chase held back a short derisive laugh. He hadn't planned to let Cricket anywhere near his gelding. His intention all along had been to avoid Letty's daughter entirely. To Chase's way of thinking, the less he had to do with the child the better.

Ignoring Cricket was the only thing he could do, because every time he looked at that sweet little girl, he felt nothing but pain. Not a faint flicker of discomfort, but a deep wrenching pain like nothing he'd ever experienced. Cricket represented everything about Letty that he wanted to forget. He couldn't even glance at the child without remembering that Letty had given herself to another man, and the sense of betrayal cut him to the bone.

Naturally Cricket was innocent of the circumstances surrounding her birth, and Chase would never do anything to deliberately hurt the little girl, but he couldn't help feeling what he did. Yet he'd given her a ride on Firepower the day before, and despite everything, he'd enjoyed himself.

If the truth be known, the ride had come about accidentally. Chase had been on the ridge above the Bar E fence line when he saw two faint dots silhouetted against the landscape, far in the distance. Almost immediately he'd realized it was Letty and her daughter, working outside. From that moment on, Chase hadn't been able to stay away. He'd hurried down the hill, but once he was in the yard, he had to come up with some logical reason for showing up in the middle of the day. Giving Cricket a chance to see Firepower had seemed solid enough at the time.

"Would you like a waffle?" Letty asked, breaking into his musings.

"No, thanks."

Letty nodded and turned around. "I don't know why

Cricket's taken to you the way she has. She gets excited every time someone mentions your name. I'm afraid you've made a friend for life, whether you like it or not."

Chase made a noncommital noise.

"I can't thank you enough for bringing Firepower over," Letty continued. "It meant a lot to me."

"I didn't do it for you," he said bluntly, watching her, almost wanting her to come back at him with some snappy retort. The calm way in which Letty swallowed his barbs troubled him more than anything else.

As he'd suspected, Letty didn't respond. Instead she brought butter and syrup to the table, avoiding his gaze.

The Letty Ellison he remembered had been feisty and fearless. She wouldn't have tolerated impatience or tactlessness from anyone, least of all him.

"This coffee tastes like it came out of a sewer," he said rudely, setting his cup down hard on the table.

The coffee was fine, but he wanted to test Letty's reactions. In years past, she would've flared right back at him, giving as good as she got. Nine years ago, Letty would've told him what he could do with that cup of coffee if he didn't like the taste of it.

She looked up, her face expressionless. "I'll make another pot."

Chase was stunned. "Forget it," he said quickly, not knowing what else to say. She glanced at him, her eyes large and shadowed in her pale face.

"But you just said there's something wrong with the coffee."

Chase was speechless. He watched her, his thoughts confused.

What had happened to his dauntless Letty?

* * *

Letty was working in the garden, carefully planting rows of corn, when her brother's pickup truck came barreling down the drive. When he slammed on the brakes, jumped out of the cab and slammed the door, Letty got up and left the seed bag behind. Her brother was obviously angry about something.

"Lonny?" she asked quietly. "What's wrong?"

"Of all the stupid, idiotic, crazy women in the world, why did I have to run into *this* one?"

"What woman?" Letty asked.

Lonny thrust his index finger under Letty's nose. "She—she's going to pay for this," he stammered in his fury. "There's no way I'm letting her get away with what she did."

"Lonny, settle down and tell me what happened."

"There!" he shouted, his voice so filled with indignation it shook.

He was pointing at the front of the pickup. Letty studied it, but didn't see anything amiss. "What?"

"Here," he said, directing her attention to a nearly indistinguishable dent in the bumper of his ten-year-old vehicle.

The entire truck was full of nicks and dents. When a rancher drove a vehicle for as many years as Lonny had, it collected its share of battle scars. It needed a new left fender, and a new paint job all the way around wouldn't have hurt, either. As far as Letty could tell, Lonny's truck was on its last legs, as it were—or, more appropriately, tires.

"Oh, you mean *that* tiny dent," she said, satisfied she'd found the one he was referring to.

"Tiny dent!" he shouted. "That...woman nearly cost me a year off my life."

"Tell me what happened," Letty demanded a second time. She couldn't remember ever seeing her brother this agitated.

"She ran a stop sign. Claimed she didn't see it. What kind of idiot misses a stop sign, for Pete's sake?"

"Did she slam into you?"

"Not exactly. I managed to avoid a collision, but in the process I hit the pole."

"What pole?"

"The one holding up the stop sign, of course."

"Oh." Letty didn't mean to appear dense, but Lonny was so angry, he wasn't explaining himself clearly.

He groaned in frustration. "Then, ever so sweetly, she climbs out of her car, tells me how sorry she is and asks if there's any damage."

Letty rolled her eyes. She didn't know what her brother expected, but as far as Letty could see, Lonny was being completely unreasonable.

"Right away I could see what she'd done, and I pointed it out to her. But that's not the worst of it," he insisted. "She took one look at my truck and said there were so many dents in it, she couldn't possibly know which one our *minor* accident had caused."

In Letty's opinion the other driver was absolutely right, but saying as much could prove dangerous. "Then what?" she asked cautiously.

"We exchanged a few words," he admitted, kicking the dirt and avoiding Letty's gaze. "She said my truck was a pile of junk." Lonny walked all the way around it before he continued, his eyes flashing. "There's no way I'm going to let some *teacher* insult me like that."

"I'm sure her insurance will take care of it," Letty said calmly.

"Damn straight it will." He slapped his hat back on his head. "You know what else she did? She tried to buy me off!" he declared righteously. "Right there in the middle of the street, in broad daylight, in front of God and man. Now I ask you, do I look like the kind of guy who can be bribed?"

At Letty's questioning look, her irate brother continued. "She offered me fifty bucks."

"I take it you refused."

"You bet I refused," he shouted. "There's two or three hundred dollars' damage here. Probably a lot more."

Letty bent to examine the bumper again. It looked like a fifty-dollar dent to her, but she wasn't about to say so. It did seem, however, that Lonny was protesting much too long and loud over a silly dent. Whoever this woman was, she'd certainly gained his attention. A teacher, he'd said.

"I've got her license number right here." Lonny yanked a small piece of paper from his shirt pocket and carefully unfolded it. "Joy Fuller's lucky I'm not going to report her to the police."

"Joy Fuller," Letty cried, taking the paper away from him. "I know who she is."

That stopped Lonny short. "How?" he asked suspiciously.

"She plays the organ at church on Sundays, and as you obviously know, she teaches at the elementary school. Second grade, I think."

Lonny shot a look toward the cloudless sky. "Do the good people of Red Springs realize the kind of woman they're exposing their children to? Someone should tell the school board."

"You've been standing in the sun too long. Come inside and have some lunch," Letty offered.

"I'm too mad to think about eating. You go ahead without me." With that he strode toward the barn.

Letty went into the house, and after pouring herself a glass of iced tea, she reached for the church directory and dialed Joy Fuller's number.

Joy answered brusquely on the first ring. "Yes," she snapped.

"Joy, it's Letty Ellison."

"Letty, I'm sorry, but your brother is the rudest… most arrogant, unreasonable man I've ever encountered."

"I can't tell you how sorry I am about this," Letty said, but she had the feeling Joy hadn't even heard her.

"I made a simple mistake and he wouldn't be satisfied with anything less than blood."

"Can you tell me what happened?" She was hoping Joy would be a little more composed than Lonny, but she was beginning to have her doubts.

"I'm sure my version is nothing like your brother's," Joy said, her voice raised. "It's simple, really. I ran the stop sign between Oak and Spruce. Frankly, I don't go that way often and I simply forgot it was there."

Letty knew the intersection. A huge weeping willow partially obscured the sign. There'd been a piece in the weekly paper about how the tree should be trimmed before a collision occurred.

"I was more than willing to admit the entire incident was my fault," Joy went on. "But I couldn't even tell which dent I'd caused, and when I said as much, your brother started acting like a crazy man."

"I don't know what's wrong with Lonny," Letty confessed. "I've never seen him like this."

"Well, I'd say it has something to do with the fact that I turned him down the last time he asked me out."

"*What?* This is the first I've heard of it. You and my brother had a…relationship?"

Joy gave an unladylike snort. "I wouldn't dignify it with that name. He and I… He— Oh, Letty, never mind. It's all history. Back to this so-called accident…" She drew in an audible breath. "I told him I'd contact my insurance company, but to hear him tell it, he figures it'll take at least two thousand dollars to repair all the damage I caused."

That was ridiculous. "I'm sure he didn't mean it—"

"Oh, he meant it, all right," Joy interrupted. "Personally, I'd rather have the insurance people deal with him, anyway. I never want to see your arrogant, ill-tempered, bronc-busting brother again."

Letty didn't blame her, but she had the feeling that in Joy Fuller, her brother had met his match.

At four o'clock, Lonny came into the house, and his mood had apparently improved, because he sent Letty a shy smile and said, "Don't worry about making me dinner tonight. I'm going into town."

"Oh?" Letty said, looking up from folding laundry.

"Chase and I are going out to eat."

She smiled. "Have a good time. You deserve a break."

"I just hope that Fuller woman isn't on the streets."

Letty raised her eyebrows. "Really?"

"Yeah, really," he snapped. "She's a menace."

"Honestly, Lonny, are you still mad about that…silly incident?"

"I sure am. It isn't safe for man or beast with someone like her behind the wheel."

"I do believe you protest too much. Could it be that you're attracted to Joy? *Still* attracted?"

Eyes narrowed, he stalked off, then turned back around and muttered, "I was *never* attracted to her. We might've seen each other a few times but it didn't work out. How could it? She's humorless, full of herself and... and she's a city slicker. From the West Coast, the big metropolis of Seattle, no less."

"I've heard it's a nice place," Letty said mildly.

Lonny did not consider that worthy of comment, and Letty couldn't help smiling.

His bathwater was running when he returned several minutes later, his shirt unbuttoned. "What about you, Letty?"

"What do you mean?" she asked absently, lifting the laundry basket onto the table. The fresh, clean scent of sun-dried towels made the extra effort of hanging them on the line worth it.

"What are you doing tonight?"

"Nothing much." She planned to do what she did every Saturday night. Watch a little television, polish her nails and read.

Her brother pulled out a chair, turned it around and straddled it. "From the minute you got home, you've been talking about marrying me off. That's the reason you invited that Brandon woman over for dinner. You admitted it yourself."

"A mistake that won't be repeated," she assured him, fluffing a thick towel.

"But you said I need a woman."

"A wife, Lonny. There's a difference."

"I've been thinking about what you said, and you might be right. But what about you?"

Letty found the task of folding bath towels vitally important. "I don't understand."

"When are you going to get married?"

Never, her mind flashed spontaneously.

"Letty?"

She shrugged, preferring to avoid the issue and knowing it was impossible. "Someday…maybe."

"You're not getting any younger."

Letty supposed she had that coming. Lonny's words were an echo of her own earlier ones to him. Now she was paying the penalty for her miserable attempt at matchmaking. However, giving Lonny a few pat answers wasn't going to work, any more than it had worked with her. "Frankly, I'm not sure I'll ever marry," she murmured, keeping her gaze lowered.

"Did…Cricket's father hurt you that much?"

Purposely she glanced behind her and asked stiffly, "Isn't your bathwater going to run over?"

"I doubt it. Answer me, Letty."

"I have no intention of discussing what happened with Jason. It's in the past and best forgotten."

Lonny was silent for a moment. "You're so different now. I'm your brother—I care about you—and it bothers me to see you like this. No man is worth this kind of pain."

"Lonny, please." She held the towels against her stomach. "If I'm different it isn't because of what happened between me and Jason. It's…other things."

"What other things?" Lonny asked, his eyes filled with concern.

That was one question Letty couldn't answer. At least

not yet. So she sidestepped it. "Jason taught me an extremely valuable lesson. Oh, it was painful at the time, don't misunderstand me, but he gave me Cricket, and she's my joy. I can only be grateful to Jason for my daughter."

"But don't you hate him for the way he deceived you and then deserted you?"

"No," she admitted reluctantly, uncertain her brother would understand. "Not anymore. What possible good would that do?"

Apparently absorbed in thought, Lonny rubbed his hand along the back of his neck. Finally he said, "I don't know, I suppose I want him to suffer for what he put you through. Some guy I've never even seen got you pregnant and walked away from you when you needed him most. It disgusts me to see him get off scot-free after the way he treated you."

Unexpected tears pooled in Letty's eyes at the protectiveness she saw in her brother. She blinked them away, and when she could speak evenly again, she murmured, "If there's anything I learned in all those years away from home, it's that there's an order to life. Eventually everything rights itself. I don't need revenge, because sooner or later, as the old adage says, what goes around, comes around."

"How can you be so calm about it, though?"

"Take your bath, Lonny," she said with a quick laugh. She shoved a freshly folded towel at him. "You're driving me crazy. And you say *Cricket* asks a lot of questions."

Chase arrived a couple of hours later, stepping gingerly into the kitchen. He completely avoided looking at or speaking to Letty, who was busy preparing her and

Cricket's dinner. He walked past Letty, but was waylaid by Cricket, who was coloring in her book at the dining room table.

Chase seemed somewhat short with the child, Letty noted, but Cricket had a minimum of ten important questions Chase needed to answer regarding Firepower. The five-year-old didn't seem to mind that Chase was a little abrupt. Apparently her hero could do no wrong.

Soon enough Lonny appeared. He opened a can of beer, and Letty listened to her brother relate his hair-raising encounter with "the Fuller woman" at the stop sign in town as if he were lucky to have escaped with his life.

The two men were in the living room while Letty stayed in the kitchen. Chase obviously wanted to keep his distance, and that was just as well. He'd gone out of his way to irritate her lately and she'd tolerated about all she could. Doing battle with Chase now would only deplete her energy. She'd tried to square things with him once, and he'd made his feelings abundantly clear. For now, Letty could do nothing but accept the situation.

"Where do you think we should eat?" Lonny asked, coming into the kitchen to deposit his empty beer can.

"Billy's Steak House?" Chase called out from the living room. "I'm in the mood for a thick sirloin."

Letty remembered that Chase had always liked his meat rare.

"How about going to the tavern afterward?" Lonny suggested. "Let's see if there's any action to be had."

Letty didn't hear the response, but whatever it was caused the two men to laugh like a couple of rambunctious teenagers. Amused, Letty smiled faintly and placed the cookie sheet with frozen fish sticks in the oven.

It wasn't until later, while Letty was clearing away the dinner dishes, that the impact of their conversation really hit her. The "action" they were looking for at the Roundup Tavern involved women.... Although she wouldn't admit it to Lonny—and he'd never admit it himself—she suspected he might be hoping Joy Fuller would show up.

But Chase—what woman was *he* looking for? Would anyone do, so long as she wasn't Letty? Would their encounter go beyond a few dances and a few drinks?

Tight-lipped, Letty marched into the living room and threw herself down on the overstuffed chair. Cricket was playing with her dolls on the carpet and Letty pushed the buttons on the remote control with a vengeance. Unable to watch the sitcom she usually enjoyed, she turned off the set and placed a hand over her face. Closing her eyes was a mistake.

Instantly she imagined Chase in the arms of a beautiful woman, a sexy one, moving suggestively against him.

"Oh, no," Letty cried, bolting upright.

"Mommy?"

Letty's pulse started to roar in her ears, drowning out reason. She looked at Cricket, playing so contentedly, and announced curtly, "It's time for bed."

"Already?"

"Yes... Remember, we have church in the morning," she said.

"Will Chase be there?"

"I...I don't know." If he was, she'd...she'd ignore him the way he'd ignored her.

Several hours later, Cricket was in bed asleep and Letty lay in her own bed, staring sightlessly into the dark. Her fury, irrational though it might be, multiplied with every passing minute. When she could stand it no longer, Letty hurried down the stairs and sat in the living room without turning on any lights.

She wasn't there long before she heard a vehicle coming up the drive. The back door opened and the two men stumbled into the house.

"Sh-h-h," she heard Chase whisper loudly, "you'll wake Letty."

"God forbid." Lonny's slurred words were followed by a husky laugh.

"You needn't worry, I'm already awake," Letty said righteously as she stood in the doorway from the dining room into the kitchen. She flipped on the light and took one look at her brother, who was leaning heavily against Chase, one arm draped across his neighbor's neck, and snapped, "You're drunk."

Lonny stabbed a finger in her direction. "Nothing gets past you, does it?"

"I'll get him upstairs for you," Chase said, half dragging Lonny across the kitchen.

Lonny's mood was jovial and he attempted to sing some ditty, off-key, the words barely recognizable. Chase shushed him a second time, reminding him that Cricket was asleep even if Letty wasn't, but his warning went unheeded.

Letty led the way, trudging up the stairs, arms folded. She threw open Lonny's bedroom door and turned on the light.

Once inside, Lonny stumbled and fell across the bed, glaring up at the ceiling. Letty moved into the room and, with some effort, removed his boots.

Chase got a quilt from the closet and unfolded it

across his friend. "He'll probably sleep for the rest of the night."

"I'm sure he will," Letty said tightly. She left Lonny's bedroom and hurried down the stairs. She was pacing the kitchen when Chase joined her.

"What's the matter with you?" he asked, frowning.

"How dare you bring my brother home in that condition," she demanded, turning on him.

"You wanted me to leave him in town? Drunk?"

If he'd revealed the slightest amount of guilt or contrition, Letty might've been able to let him go without another word. But he stood in front of her, and all she could see was the imagined woman in that bar. The one he'd danced with…and kissed and—

Fury surged up inside her, blocking out sanity. All week he'd been baiting her, wanting to hurt her for the pain she'd caused him. Tonight he'd succeeded.

"I hate you," she sobbed, lunging at him.

He grabbed her wrists and held them at her sides. "Letty, what's gotten into you?"

She squirmed and twisted in his arms, frantically trying to free herself, but she was trapped.

"Letty?"

She looked up at him, her face streaked with tears she didn't care to explain, her shoulders heaving with emotion.

"You're angry because Lonny's drunk?" he whispered.

"No," she cried, struggling again. "You went to that bar. You think I don't know what you did but—"

"*What* are you talking about?"

"You went to the Roundup to…to pick up some woman!"

Chase frowned, then shook his head. "Letty, no!"

"Don't lie to me...don't!"

"Oh, Letty," he murmured. Then he leaned down to settle his mouth over hers.

The last thing Letty wanted at that moment was his touch or his kiss. She meant to brace her hands against his chest and use her strength to push him away. Instead her hands inched upward until she was clasping his shoulders. The anger that had consumed her seconds before was dissolving in a firestorm of desire, bringing to life a part of her that had lain dormant from the moment she'd left Chase Brown's arms nine years before.

Chapter 5

Chase kissed her again and again while his hands roved up and down the curve of her spine as though he couldn't get enough of her.

His touch began to soothe the pain and disappointment that had come into her life in their long years apart. She was completely vulnerable to him in that moment. She *wanted* him.

And Chase wanted her.

"Letty…"

Whatever he'd intended to say was lost when his mouth covered hers with a hungry groan. Letty's lips parted in eager response.

She'd been back in Red Springs for several weeks, but she wasn't truly home until Chase had taken her in his arms and kissed her. Now that she was with him, a peace settled over her. Whatever lay before her, life or death, she was ready, suffused with the serenity his embrace offered. Returning to this small town and the Bar E were only a tiny part of what made it so important to come home for her surgery. Her love for Chase had been the real draw; it was what had pulled her back, and for the first time she was willing to acknowledge it.

Letty burrowed her fingers into his hair, her eyes shut, her head thrown back. Neither she nor Chase spoke. They held on to each other as though they were afraid to let go.

A sigh eased from Letty as Chase lifted his head and tenderly kissed her lips. He brought her even closer and deepened his probing kiss until Letty was sure her knees were about to buckle. Then his mouth abandoned hers to explore the hollow of her throat.

Tears welled in her eyes, then ran unheeded down her cheeks. Chase pressed endless kisses over her face until she forgot everything but the love she'd stored in her heart for him.

When she was certain nothing could bring her any more pleasure than his kiss, he lowered his hand to her breast—

"Mommy!"

Cricket's voice, coming from the top of the stairs, penetrated the fog of Letty's desire. Chase apparently hadn't heard her, and Letty had to murmur a protest and gently push him aside.

"Yes, darling, what's wrong?" Her voice sounded weak even to her own ears as she responded to her daughter.

Chase stumbled back and raised a hand to his face, as if he'd been suddenly awakened from a dream. Letty longed to go to him, but she couldn't.

"Uncle Lonny keeps singing and he woke me up!" Cricket cried.

"I'll be right there." Letty prayed Chase understood that she couldn't ignore her daughter.

"Mommy!" Cricket called more loudly. "Please hurry. Uncle Lonny sings terrible!"

"Just a minute." She retied her robe, her hands shaking. "Chase—"

"This isn't the time to do any talking," he said gruffly.

"But there's so much we need to discuss." She whisked the curls away from her face. "Don't you think so?"

"Not now."

"But—"

"Go take care of Cricket," he said and turned away.

Letty's heart was heavy as she started for the stairs. A dim light illuminated the top where Cricket was standing, fingers plugging her ears.

In the background, Letty heard her brother's drunken rendition of "Puff the Magic Dragon." Another noise blended with the first, as Chase opened the kitchen door and walked out of the house.

The next morning, Letty moved around downstairs as quietly as possible in an effort not to wake her brother. From everything she'd seen of him the night before, Lonny was going to have one heck of a hangover.

The coffee was perking merrily in the kitchen as Letty brushed Cricket's long hair while the child stood patiently in the bathroom.

"Was Uncle Lonny sick last night?" Cricket asked.

"I don't think so." Letty couldn't remember hearing him get out of bed during the night.

"He sounded sick when he was singing."

"I suppose he did at that," Letty murmured. "Or sickly, anyway." She finished tying the bright red ribbons in Cricket's hair and returned to the kitchen for a cup of coffee. To her astonishment, Lonny was sitting at the table, neatly dressed in a suit and tie.

"Lonny!"

"Morning," he greeted her.

Although his eyes were somewhat bloodshot, Lonny didn't look bad. In fact, he acted as though he'd gone sedately to bed at nine or ten o'clock.

Letty eyed him warily, unsure what to make of him. Only a few hours earlier he'd been decidedly drunk—but maybe not as drunk as she'd assumed. And Chase hadn't seemed inebriated at all.

"How are you feeling?" she asked, studying him carefully.

"Wonderful."

Obviously his escapades of the night before hadn't done him any harm. Unexpectedly he stood, then reached for his Bible, wiping the dust off the leather binding.

"Well, are you two coming to church with me or not?" he asked.

Letty was so shocked it took her a moment to respond. "Yes…of course."

It wasn't until they'd pulled into the church parking lot that Letty understood her brother's newly formed desire for religion. He was attending the morning service not because of any real longing to worship. He'd come hoping to see Joy Fuller again. The thought surprised Letty as much as it pleased her. Red Springs's second-grade teacher had managed to reignite her brother's interest. That made Letty smile. From the little Letty knew of the church organist, Joy would never fit Lonny's definition of the dutiful wife.

The congregation had begun to file through the wide doors. "I want to sit near the front," Lonny told Letty, looking around.

"If you don't mind, I'd prefer to sit near the back," Letty said. "In case Cricket gets restless."

"She'll be good today, won't you, cupcake?"

The child nodded, clearly eager for her uncle's approval. Lonny took her small hand in his and, disregarding Letty's wishes, marched up the center aisle.

Groaning inwardly, Letty followed her brother. At least his choice of seats gave Letty the opportunity to scan the church for any sign of Chase. Her quick survey told her he'd decided against attending services this morning, which was a relief.

Letty had been dreading their next encounter, yet at the same time she was eager to talk to him again. She felt both frightened and excited by their rekindled desire for each other. But he'd left her so brusquely the night before that she wasn't sure what to expect. So much would depend on his reaction to her. Then she'd know what he was feeling—if he regretted kissing her or if he felt the same excitement she did.

Organ music resounded through the church, and once they were settled in their pew, Letty picked up a hymnal. Lonny sang in his loudest voice, staring intently at Joy as she played the organ. Letty resisted the urge to remind him that his behavior bordered on rude.

When Joy faltered over a couple of notes, Lonny smiled with smug satisfaction. Letty moaned inwardly. So *this* was her brother's game!

"Mommy," Cricket whispered, standing backward on the pew and looking at the crowd. "Chase is here."

Letty's grip on the hymnal tightened. "That's nice, sweetheart."

"Can I go sit with him?"

"Not now."

"Later?"

"No."

"How come?"

"Cricket," Letty pleaded. "Sit down and be quiet."

"But I like Chase and I want to sit with him."

"Maybe next week," she said in a low voice.

"Can I ask him after the pastor's done talking at everybody?"

Letty nodded, willing to agree to just about anything by then. The next time her brother insisted on sitting in the front pew, he would do so alone.

No worship service had ever seemed to take longer. Cricket fidgeted during the entire hour, eager to run and talk to Chase. Lonny wasn't much better. He continued to stare at Joy and did everything but make faces at her to distract the poor woman. Before the service was half over, Letty felt like giving him a good, hard shake. Even as a young girl, she'd never seen her older brother behave more childishly. The only reason he'd come to church was to make poor Joy as uncomfortable as he possibly could.

By the time Letty was outside the church, Cricket had already found Chase. From his stiff posture, Letty knew he'd planned on escaping without talking to her and the last thing he'd wanted was to be confronted by Cricket. Letty's heart swelled with fresh pain. So this was how he felt.

He regretted everything.

Letty hastened to her daughter's side and took her small hand. "Uncle Lonny's waiting for us at the truck," she said, her eyes skirting Chase.

"But I haven't asked Chase if I can sit with him next week."

"I'm sure he has other friends he'd prefer to sit with," Letty answered, hiding her impatience.

"I can answer for myself." Chase's voice was clipped and unfriendly. "As it happens, Cricket, I think your mother's right. It would be best if you sat with her in church."

"Can't you sit in the same row as us?"

"No."

"Why not?"

Chase didn't say anything for an awkward moment, but when he did, he looked past Letty. "Because I'd rather not."

"Okay," Cricket said, apparently accepting that without a problem.

"It's time to go," Letty said tersely. Only a few hours earlier, Chase had held her in his arms, kissed her and loved her with a gentleness that had fired her senses back to life. And in the light of a new day, he'd told her as plainly as if he'd shouted it from the church steps that it had all been a mistake, that nothing had changed and he didn't want anything to do with her.

After all the hurt she'd suffered in California, Letty thought she was immune to this kind of pain. In the span of a few minutes Chase had taught her otherwise.

Cricket raced ahead of Letty to Lonny's truck and climbed inside. For his part, her brother seemed to be taking his time about getting back to the ranch. He talked to a couple of men, then finally joined Cricket and Letty.

"We're ready anytime you are," Letty said from inside the truck.

"In a minute," he returned absently, glancing around before he got in.

Letty realized Lonny was waiting for Joy to make an appearance. The parking lot was nearly deserted now. There were only three other cars left, and Lonny had parked next to one of them, a PT Cruiser. Letty had no trouble figuring out that it belonged to Joy.

Lonny was sitting in the truck, with the window down, his elbow resting on the frame, apparently content to laze away in the sunshine while he waited.

"Lonny?" Letty pressed. "Can we please go?" After the way he'd behaved in church, Letty had every intention of having a serious discussion with her brother, but she preferred to do it when Cricket wasn't around to listen. She'd also prefer not to witness another embarrassing skirmish between him and Joy Fuller.

"It'll only be another minute."

He was right; the church door opened and Joy came out. She hesitated when she saw Lonny's pickup beside her car.

"What are you going to say to her?" Letty whispered angrily.

"Oh, nothing much," Lonny murmured back, clearly distracted. When Joy approached her car, Lonny got out of the pickup and leaned indolently against the side, bracing one foot on the fender.

"I wouldn't do that if I were you," Joy said scathingly.

She was nearly as tall as Lonny, her dark hair styled so it fell in waves around her face. Her cheeks were a rosy hue and Letty couldn't help wondering if confronting Lonny again was why they were so flushed.

"Do what?" Lonny demanded.

"Put your foot on that truck. You might damage your priceless antique."

"I'll have you know, this truck isn't even ten years old!"

Joy feigned shock, opening her eyes wide while she held her hand against her chest. "Is that so? I could've sworn you claimed otherwise only yesterday. But, then, it seems you have a problem keeping your facts straight."

"You were impossible to talk to yesterday, and I can see today isn't going to be any better."

"Impossible?" Joy echoed. "Me? *You* were the one jumping up and down and acting like an idiot."

"Me?" Lonny tilted back his head and forced a loud laugh. "That's a good one."

Joy ignored him and continued to her car.

Lonny dropped his foot and yanked open the truck door. "I thought we might be able to settle our differences, but you're being completely unreasonable."

"Perhaps I am, but at least I don't throw temper tantrums in the middle of the street."

"Yeah, but *I* know how to drive."

"Based on *what?* Taking that…that unsafe rattletrap on a public road should be an indictable offense!"

"Rattletrap? *Unsafe?*" Lonny slapped his hat against his thigh. "Just who do you think you are, talking to me like that?"

"If you don't like the way I talk, Mr. Rodeo Star, then stay away from me."

"It'll be my pleasure."

Suddenly, Lonny couldn't seem to get out of the parking lot fast enough. He gripped the steering wheel as if he was driving in the Indy 500.

"Lonny," Letty ordered, "slow down."

When he reached the end of the street, he drove off as if the very fires of hell were licking at his heels.

"Lonny!" Letty cried a second time. If he continued to drive in this manner, she'd walk home. "You're driving like a maniac. Stop the truck this minute!"

"Didn't I tell you that woman's a living, breathing menace?" he snapped, but he reduced his speed. To his credit, he looked surprised by how fast he'd been traveling. "I swear she drives me over the edge."

"Then do as she says and stay away from her," Letty advised, shaking her head in wonder. But she doubted he would.

He ignored her comment. "Did you see the way she laid into me?"

"Lonny, you provoked her."

"Then you didn't see things the way they happened," he muttered, shooting Letty a look of indignation. "I was only trying to be friendly."

Her brother was as unreasonable as he'd claimed Joy was. "I like Joy and I think you were rude to her this morning," Letty returned primly.

"When?"

"Oh, honestly! The only reason you came to church was to intimidate her into making a mistake while she was playing the organ. When you succeeded, I thought you were going to stand up and cheer."

Lonny cast her a frown that said Letty should consider counseling. "You're totally wrong, little sister."

Letty rolled her eyes. "Have you figured out *why* you feel so strongly?"

"Because she needs to be put in her place, that's why!"

"And you think you're the one to do it?"

"Damn right! I'm not about to let any woman get away with the things she said to me."

"Calling this truck an antique or—" she grinned "—a rattletrap...well, they don't exactly sound like fighting words to me."

Lonny turned into the long dusty drive leading to the house. "You women really stick together, don't you?" he asked bitterly. "No matter how stupid you act."

"Stupid?"

He pulled the truck into his usual spot. "Yeah. Like the fact that Joy Fuller doesn't know how to drive and then blames me. And what about you? You're the perfect example, taking off on some fool dream. Chase should never have let you go."

"It wasn't up to Chase to stop me or not. He couldn't have, anyway—no one could. I wasn't going to end up like Mom, stuck out here in no-man's-land, working so hard... Why, she was little more than a slave."

Lonny's eyes widened as he turned to her. "That's the way you see Mom?"

"You mean you don't?" How could her brother be so blind? Their mother had worked herself into an early grave, sacrificing her talent and her dreams for a few head of cattle and an unforgiving land.

"Of course I don't! Mom had a good life here. She loved the ranch and everything about it."

"You're so oblivious you can't see the truth, can you? Mom hated it here, only she wasn't honest enough to admit it, not even to herself."

"And you hate it, too?" he asked, his voice dangerously quiet.

"I did."

Lonny climbed out of the pickup and slammed the door. "No one asked you to come back, Letty. You could turn around and go straight back to California." With that he stormed into the house.

Fueled by her anger, Letty stayed in the truck, tears streaming down her face. She and Lonny had both been furious and the conversation had quickly gotten out of control. She should never have said the things she did. And Lonny shouldn't have, either. Now wasn't the time to deal with the past.

"Mommy?" Cricket leaned against her mother, obviously confused and a little frightened. "Why was Uncle Lonny shouting at you?"

"He was angry, honey."

"You were shouting at him, too."

"I know." She climbed out of the cab and helped Cricket clamber down. They walked into the house, and Lonny glared at her. She glared right back, surprised by how heated her response to him remained. In an effort to avoid continuing their argument, Letty went upstairs and changed her clothes. She settled Cricket with her activity book and crayons, then went outside and grabbed the hoe. Venting her frustration in the garden was bound to help. Once they'd both cooled down, they could discuss the matter rationally.

Lonny left soon afterward, barreling down the driveway as if he couldn't get away from her fast enough.

She was happy to see him go.

Chase felt as though his world had been knocked off its axis and he was struggling with some unknown force to right it again.

Letty was to blame for this. A part of him yearned to take Letty in his arms, love her, care for her and make up to her for the pain and disappointment she'd suffered. Yet something powerful within him wouldn't allow him to do it. He found himself saying and doing things he'd never intended.

Telling her he preferred not to sit beside her daughter in church was a prime example. The only reason he even attended was to be close to Letty. He rarely listened to the sermons. Instead, he sat and pretended Letty was the one sitting next to him. He thought about what it would be like to hear her lovely voice again as she sang. He imagined how it would feel to hold her hand while the pastor spoke.

Cricket had provided him with the perfect excuse to do those things. His pride wouldn't have suffered, and he'd be doing something to appease the kid. No one needed to know that being with Letty was what he'd wanted all along.

Yet he'd rejected the child's request flat out. And he'd been equally unwilling to talk to Letty last night. Chase didn't know how to explain his own actions. He was behaving like an idiot.

On second thought, his actions made perfect sense. He was protecting himself, and with good reason. He figured that if Letty really planned to make a life for herself in Red Springs, she'd be doing something about finding a decent job and settling down. She hadn't done that. Every piece of evidence pointed in the direction of her leaving again. She behaved as if this was an extended vacation and once she'd rested, she'd be on her way. Other than the garden she'd planted, he couldn't see any sign of permanence.

Chase couldn't allow his emotions to get involved with Letty a second time. He hadn't fully healed from the first. It wasn't that simple, however. He loved her, and frankly, he doubted he'd ever stop.

Rubbing his face, Chase drew in a deep, shuddering breath. He hadn't meant to touch her the night before, but her outrage, her eyes shooting sparks, had reminded him of the old Letty. The Letty who'd been naive, perhaps, but confident and self-assured, certain of her own opinions. He'd forgotten that he'd promised himself he'd never touch her again. One kiss and he'd been lost....

Even now, hours later, the memory of the way she'd melted in his embrace had the power to arouse him. He pushed it out of his mind. The best thing to do was forget it ever happened.

He went outside and got into the truck, deciding he'd go into town and do some shopping. Perhaps keeping busy would ease the ache in his heart.

Still confused, Chase wondered if he'd feel differently if Letty had made more of an effort to acknowledge their kisses. Cricket had come running up to him after the church service and Letty wouldn't even meet his eye. Obviously the memory of their encounter embarrassed her.

That pleased him.

And it infuriated him.

If Letty was disconcerted by their kissing, it said she didn't often let men touch her like that—which made him glad. The thought of another man making love to her was enough to produce a fireball of resentment in the pit of his stomach.

But her actions that morning also infuriated him, because she so obviously regretted what they'd done. While he'd spent the night dreaming of holding her and kissing her, she'd apparently been filled with remorse. Maybe she thought he wasn't good enough for her.

Telephone poles whizzed past him as he considered that bleak possibility.

A flash of red caught his attention. He looked again. It was Cricket, standing alone at the end of the Bar E driveway, crying. She was wearing the same dress she'd worn at church.

Chase stepped on his brakes and quickly backed up. When he reached the little girl, she looked up and immediately started running to him.

"Chase...oh, Mr. Chase!"

"Cricket," he said sternly, climbing out of the truck, angry with Letty for being so irresponsible. "What are you doing here? Where's your mother?"

Sobbing, the little girl ran and hugged his waist. "Uncle Lonny and Mommy shouted at each other. Then Uncle Lonny left and Mommy went outside. Now she's sleeping in the garden and I can't wake her up."

Chapter 6

Letty sat on the porch steps, rubbing her eyes. Her knees felt weak and her eyes stubbornly refused to focus. It had been through sheer force of will that she'd made it from the garden to the back steps. She trembled with fear and alarm. Although she'd called for Cricket, the little girl was nowhere in the house or garden. Letty had to find her daughter despite the waves of nausea and weakness.

The last thing Letty remembered clearly was standing in the garden, shoveling for all she was worth, weeding because she was furious with Lonny and equally upset with herself for being drawn into such a pointless argument.

"Cricket," Letty called out again, shocked by how unsteady her voice sounded. Her daughter had been standing beside her only a few minutes before. Now she was gone.

The roar of an approaching truck was nearly deafening. Letty didn't have the strength to get up, so she sat there and waited. Whoever it was would have to come to her.

"Letty?"

"Mommy! Mommy!"

Chase leaped out of the pickup and quickly covered the space that separated them. Cricket was directly behind him, her face wet and streaked with tears.

Confused, Letty glanced up at them. She had no idea how Cricket had come to be with Chase. Even more surprising was the way he looked, as though he was ill himself. His face was gray, set and determined, but she couldn't understand why.

"What happened?" Chase demanded.

For a long moment her mind refused to function. "I…I think I fainted."

"Fainted?"

"I must have." She wiped her forehead, forcing a smile. By sheer resolve, she started to stand, but before she was fully on her feet, Chase had scooped her up in his arms.

"Chase," she protested. "Put me down…I'm perfectly all right."

"Like hell you are."

He seemed furious, as if she'd purposely fainted in a ploy to gain his sympathy. That added to her frustration and she tried to get free. Her efforts, however, were futile; Chase merely tightened his grip.

Cricket ran ahead of him and opened the back door. "Is Mommy sick?"

"Yes," Chase answered, his mouth a white line of impatience. He didn't so much as look at Letty as he strode through the house.

"I'm fine, sweetheart," Letty countered, trying to reassure her daughter, who ran beside Chase, intently studying her mother. Cricket looked so worried and frightened, which only distressed Letty more.

Chase gently deposited Letty on the sofa, then knelt beside her, his gaze roaming her face, inspecting her for any injury. Reluctantly, as if he was still annoyed, he brought his hand to her forehead. "You're not feverish," he announced.

"Of course I'm not," she shot back, awkwardly rising to an upright position. If everyone would give her a few minutes alone and some breathing room, she'd feel better. "I'm fine. I was weeding the garden, and next thing I knew I was on the ground. Obviously I got too much sun."

Cricket knelt on the carpet. "I couldn't wake you up," she murmured, her blue eyes round, her face shiny with tears.

Letty reached out to hug her. "I'm sorry I scared you, honey."

"Did you hit your head?" Chase asked.

"I don't think so." Tentatively she touched the back of her skull. As far as she could tell, there wasn't even a lump to suggest she'd hit anything besides the soft dirt.

"Cricket, go get your mother a glass of water."

The child took off running as if Chase's request was a matter of life and death.

"How did Cricket ever find you?" Letty asked, frowning. Her daughter wouldn't have known the way to

Chase's ranch, and even if she had, it was several minutes away by car.

"I saw her on the road."

"The road," Letty repeated, horrified. "She got that far?"

"She was in a panic, and with Lonny gone, she didn't know what else to do."

Letty stared at Chase. "I'm grateful you stopped. Thank you."

Cricket charged into the living room with the glass of water, which was only partially full. Letty assumed the other half had spilled. She planted a soft kiss on her daughter's cheek as a thank-you.

"I think your mother could use a blanket, too," Chase murmured. His mouth was set and obstinate, but for what reason Letty could only speculate. It was unreasonable for him to be angry with her because she'd fainted!

Once more Cricket raced out of the room.

Chase continued to frown at Letty. He seemed to think that if he did that long enough, he'd discover why she'd taken ill. She boldly met his look and did her best to reassure him with a smile, but obviously failed.

Chase closed his eyes, and when he opened them again, the agony that briefly fluttered into his gaze was a shock. He turned away from her as if he couldn't bear to have her look at him.

"Letty, I didn't know what to think when I found Cricket," he said, and dragged a breath between clenched teeth. "For all I knew you could have been dead."

Motivated by something other than reason, Letty raised her hand to his face, running the tips of her fingers along his tense jaw. "Would you have cared?" she whispered.

"Yes," he cried. "I don't want to, but heaven help me, I do."

He reached for her, kissing her awkwardly, then hungrily, his mouth roving from one side of her face to the other, brushing against her eyes, her cheek, her ears and finally her throat.

They were interrupted by Cricket, who dashed into the room.

"I brought Mommy a blankey," Cricket said. She edged her way between Letty and Chase and draped her yellow knit blanket across Letty's lap.

"Thank you, sweetheart."

Chase rose and paced the floor in front of the sofa. "I'm calling Doc Hanley."

Letty was overcome with panic. She'd purposely avoided the physician, who'd been seeing her family for as long as she could remember. Although she trusted Doc Hanley implicitly, he wasn't a heart specialist, and if she was seen going in and out of his office on a regular basis there might be talk that would filter back to Lonny or Chase and cause them concern.

"Chase," she said, "calling Doc Hanley isn't necessary. I was in the sun too long—that's all. I should've known better."

"You're in the sun every day. Something's wrong. I want you to see a doctor."

"All right," she agreed, thinking fast. "I'll make an appointment, if you want, but I can't today—none of the offices are open."

"I'll drive you to the hospital," he insisted.

"The nearest hospital's an hour from here."

"I don't care."

"Chase, please, I'm a little unsettled, but basically

I'm fine. What I need more than anything is some rest. The last thing I want to do is sit in a hot, stuffy truck and ride all the way into Rock Springs so some doctor can tell me I got too much sun."

Chase paced back and forth, clearly undecided.

"I'll just go upstairs and lie down. It's about time for Cricket's nap, anyway," Letty said calmly, although her heart was racing. She really did feel terrible. Dizzy. Disoriented. Nauseous.

Chase wasn't pleased about Letty's proposal, but nodded. "I'll stay here in case you need me later."

"That really isn't necessary," she said again.

He turned and glared at her. "Don't argue with me. I'm not in the mood."

That was obvious. With some effort, although she struggled to conceal it, Letty stood and walked up the stairs. Chase followed her as though he suspected she might not make it. Letty was exhausted by the time she entered her bedroom.

"I'll take a nap and feel totally refreshed in a couple of hours. You wait and see."

"Right," Chase said tersely. As soon as she was lying down, he left.

Letty sat across the desk from Dr. Faraday the next afternoon. He'd wanted to talk to her after the examination.

"I haven't received your records from your physician in California yet, but I'm expecting them any day," he said.

Letty nodded, making an effort to disguise her uneasiness. As she'd promised Chase, she'd contacted the heart specialist in Rock Springs first thing Monday morning. She'd seen Dr. Faraday the week before and he'd asked that she come in right away. His brooding look troubled her.

"Generally speaking, how are you?"

"Fine." That was a slight exaggeration, but other than being excessively tired and the one fainting spell, she *had* felt healthy most of the time.

Dr. Faraday nodded and made a notation in her file. It was all Letty could do not to stand up and try to read what he'd written. He was a large man, his face dominated by a bushy mustache that reminded Letty of an umbrella. His eyes were piercing, and Letty doubted that much got past him.

"The results from the tests we did last week are in, and I've had a chance to review them. My opinion is that we shouldn't delay surgery much longer. I'll confer with my colleague, Dr. Frederickson, and make my report to the state. I'm going to ask that they put a rush on their approval."

Letty nodded and watched as he lifted his prescription pad from the corner of his desk. "I want you to start taking these pills right away."

"Okay," Letty agreed. "How long will I be in the hospital, Doctor?" Although she tried to appear calm, Letty was frightened. She'd never felt more alone. Her sense of humor, which had helped her earlier, seemed to have deserted her.

"You should plan on being in the hospital and then the convalescent center for up to two weeks," he replied absently, writing out a second prescription.

"Two weeks?" Letty cried. That was far longer than she'd expected.

His eyes met hers. "Is that a problem?"

"Not…exactly." It seemed foolish now, but Letty had automatically assumed that Lonny would be able to watch Cricket for her. He'd be happy to do that, she was confident, if her hospital stay was going to be only a few days. Even with the responsibilities of the ranch, he'd have found a way to look after the five-year-old, maybe hiring a part-time babysitter. True, it would have been an inconvenience for him, but Lonny was family. But two weeks was too long for Letty to even consider asking him.

Lonny and Cricket were just beginning to find their footing with each other. Cricket had accepted him, and Lonny seemed to think that as kids went, his niece was all right. Letty smiled to herself—she didn't want to do anything that would threaten their budding relationship.

A list of people who could possibly watch Cricket flashed through Letty's mind. There were several older women from church who'd been her mother's friends, women Letty would feel comfortable asking. Any one of them would take excellent care of her daughter. Whoever Letty found would have her hands full, though. Cricket had never spent much time away from Letty.

"I'd like you to make an appointment for Thursday," Dr. Faraday said, adding a couple of notes to her file. "See my receptionist before you leave and she'll give you a time."

Letty nodded, chewing on her lower lip. She wondered what she was going to say to Lonny about needing the truck again so soon.

Cricket was waiting for her in the hallway outside Dr. Faraday's office. She sat next to the receptionist and was busy coloring in her activity book. The child looked up and smiled when Letty came out. She placed her crayons neatly back in the box, closed her book and crawled down from the chair, hurrying to Letty's side.

Letty made her appointment for later in the week, then she and Cricket headed for the parking lot.

It was during the long drive home that Letty decided to broach the subject of their being separated.

"Cricket, Mommy may have to go away for a few days."

"Can I go with you?"

"Not this time. Uncle Lonny will be busy with the ranch, so you won't be able to stay with him, either."

Cricket shrugged.

Letty didn't think she'd mind not staying with Lonny. Her brother still hadn't come to appreciate the finer points of watching cartoons.

"Do you remember Mrs. Martin from church?" Letty asked. "She was my mommy's good friend." Dorothy Martin was a dear soul, although she'd aged considerably since her husband's death. Letty knew her mother's friend would agree to care for Cricket until Letty was able to do so herself.

"Does Mrs. Martin have gray hair and sing as bad as Uncle Lonny?"

"That's the one. I was thinking you could stay with her while I'm away."

"Don't want to." Cricket rejected Mrs. Martin without further comment.

"I see." Letty sighed. There were other choices, of course, but they were all women Cricket had met only briefly.

"What about—"

Cricket didn't allow her to finish.

"If you're going away and I can't go with you, then I

want to stay with Chase. I bet he'd let me ride Firepower again, and we could make chocolate chip cookies."

Letty should've guessed Chase would be her first choice.

"He'd read me stories like you do and let me blow out the lights at bedtime," Cricket continued. "We'd have lots of fun together. I like Chase better than anyone 'cept you." She paused, then added as extra incentive, "We could sit in church together and everything."

A tight knot formed in Letty's throat. In making her decision to return to Red Springs, she could never have predicted that Cricket would take such a strong and instant liking to Chase Brown.

"Mommy, could I?"

"I'm afraid Chase has to work on his ranch the same way Uncle Lonny does."

"Oh." Cricket sighed in disappointment.

"Think of all the people we've met since we came to live with Uncle Lonny," Letty suggested. "Who do you like best other than Chase?"

Cricket seemed to need time to mull over the question. She crossed her legs and tugged at one pigtail, winding the dark hair around her index finger as she considered this important decision.

"I like the lady who plays the organ second-best."

Joy Fuller was the perfect choice, although Letty was certain Lonny wouldn't take Cricket's preference sitting down. "I like Ms. Fuller, too," she told her daughter. "I'll talk to her. But my going away isn't for sure yet, honey, so there's no need to say anything to anyone. Okay?"

"Is it a surprise?"

"Yes." Letty's fingers tightened on the steering wheel. She hated to mislead Cricket, but she couldn't have her daughter announce to Chase or her brother that she was going away and leaving Cricket behind.

"Oh, goody. I won't tell anyone," she said, pretending to zip her mouth closed.

"It's so nice to see you, Letty," Joy said as she stood in the doorway of her small rental house. "You, too, Cricket." A smile lit up Joy's face. "Your phone call came as a pleasant surprise."

Cricket followed Letty inside.

"I made some iced tea. Would you like some?"

"Please." Letty sat in the compact living room; as always, Cricket was at her side.

"Cricket, I have some Play-Doh in the kitchen if you'd like to play with that. My second-graders still enjoy it. I've also got some juice just for you."

Cricket looked to her mother and Letty nodded. The child trotted into the kitchen after Joy. Letty could hear them chatting, and although it was difficult to stay where she was, she did so the two of them could become better acquainted.

Joy returned a few minutes later with frosty glasses of iced tea. She set one in front of Letty, then took the chair opposite her.

"Cricket certainly is a well-behaved child. You must be very proud of her."

"Thank you, I am." Letty's gaze fell to her fingers, which were tightly clenched on the glass of iced tea. "I take it you and Lonny have come to some sort of agreement?"

Joy sighed, her shoulders rising reflexively, then sagging with defeat. "To be honest, I think it's best if he and I don't have anything to do with each other. I don't know what it is about your brother that irritates me so much. I mean, last fall we seemed to get along okay. But—and I'm sorry to say this, Letty—he's just so *arrogant.* He acted like I was supposed to be really impressed that he was a rodeo champion back in the day. *And* he kept calling me a hopeless city slicker because I'm from Seattle." She shook her head. "Now we can't even talk civilly to each other."

Letty doubted Joy would believe her if she claimed Lonny was still attracted to her. The problem was that he was fighting it so hard.

"You may find this difficult to believe," she said, "but Lonny's normally a calm, in-control type of guy. I swear to you, Joy, I've never seen him behave the way he has lately."

"I've known him for almost a year, but I had no idea he was that kind of hothead."

"Trust me, he usually isn't."

"He phoned me last Sunday."

At Letty's obvious surprise, Joy continued, eyes just managing to avoid her guest. "He started in about his stupid truck again. Then he mentioned something about an argument with you and how that was my fault—and then apparently you fainted, but he didn't really explain. Anyway, I hung up on him." She glanced over at Letty. "What happened to you? He sounded upset."

"He was, but mostly he was angry with himself. We got into an argument—which was *not* your fault—and, well, we both said things we didn't mean and immediately regretted. I went outside to work in the garden and…I don't know," she murmured. "The sun must've bothered me, because the next thing I knew, I'd fainted."

"Oh, Letty! Are you all right?"

"I am, thanks." Letty realized she was beginning to get good at exaggerating the state of her health.

"Did you see a doctor?"

"Yes. Everything's under control, so don't worry."

Cricket wandered in from the kitchen with a miniature cookie sheet holding several flat Play-Doh circles. "Mommy, I'm baking chocolate chip cookies for Chase."

"Good, sweetheart. Will you bake me some, too?"

The child nodded, then smiled shyly up at Joy. "Did you ask her, Mommy?"

"Not yet."

Letty's gaze followed Cricket back into the kitchen. She could feel Joy's curiosity, and wished she'd been able to lead into the subject of Cricket's staying with her a little more naturally.

"There's a possibility I'll need to be away for a week or two in the near future," she said, holding the glass with both hands. "Unfortunately I won't be able to take Cricket with me, and I doubt Lonny could watch her for that length of time."

"I wouldn't trust your brother to care for Cricket's *dolls*," Joy said stiffly, then looked embarrassed.

"Don't worry, I don't think I'd feel any differently toward my brother if I were in your shoes," Letty said, understanding her friend's feelings.

"As you were saying?" Joy prompted, obviously disturbed that the subject of Lonny had crept into the conversation.

"Yes," Letty said, and straightened. This wasn't easy; it was a lot to ask of someone she'd only known for a little while. "As I explained, I may have to go away for a couple of weeks, and since I can't leave Cricket with my brother, I'm looking for someone she could stay with while I'm gone."

Joy didn't hesitate for a second. "I'd be more than happy to keep her for you. But there's one problem. I've still got three more weeks of school. I wouldn't be able to take her until the first week of June. Would you need to leave before then?"

"No…I'd make sure of that." For the first time, Letty felt the urge to tell someone about her condition. It would be so good to share this burden with someone she considered a friend, someone who'd calm and reassure her. Someone she trusted.

But Joy was a recent friend, and it seemed wrong to shift the burden onto her shoulders. And if Lonny somehow discovered Letty's secret, he'd be justifiably angry that she'd confided her troubles in someone she barely knew and not her own flesh and blood.

"Letty…"

She looked up then and realized her thoughts had consumed her to the point that she'd missed whatever Joy had been saying. "I'm sorry," she said, turning toward her.

"I was just suggesting that perhaps you could leave Cricket with me for an afternoon soon—give us the opportunity to get better acquainted. That way she won't feel so lost while you're away."

"That would be wonderful."

As if knowing the adults had been discussing her, Cricket came into the living room. "Your chocolate chip cookies are almost cooked, Mommy."

"Thank you, sweetheart. I'm in the mood for something chocolate."

"Me, too," Joy agreed, smiling.

"Mommy will share with you," Cricket stated confidently. "She *loves* chocolate."

All three laughed.

"Since Cricket's doing so well, why don't you leave her here for an hour or two?"

Letty stood. "Cricket?" She looked at her daughter, wanting to be sure the child felt comfortable enough to be here alone with Joy.

"I have to stay," Cricket said. "My cookies aren't finished cooking yet."

"I'd be delighted with the company," Joy said so sincerely Letty couldn't doubt her words. "I haven't got anything planned for the next hour or so, and since you're already here, it would save you a trip into town later on."

"All right," Letty said, not knowing exactly where she'd go to kill time. Of course, she could drive back to the Bar E, but there was nothing for her there. She reached for her purse. "I'll be back...soon."

"Take your time," Joy said, walking her to the door. Cricket came, too, and kissed Letty goodbye with such calm acceptance it tugged at her heart.

Once inside her brother's battered pickup, she drove aimlessly through town. That was when she decided to visit the town cemetery. No doubt her parents' graves had been neglected over the years. The thought saddened her and yet filled her with purpose.

She parked outside the gates and ambled over the green lawn until she arrived at their grave sites. To her surprise they were well maintained. Lonny had obviously been out here recently.

Standing silent, feeling oppressed by an overwhelming sense of loss, Letty bowed her head. Tears gathered in her eyes, but Letty wiped them aside; she hadn't come here to weep. Her visit had been an impromptu one, although the emotions were churning inside her.

"Hi, Daddy," she whispered. "Hi, Mom. I'm back… I tried California, but it didn't work out. I never knew there were so many talented singers in the world." She paused, as though they'd have some comment to make, but there was only silence. "Lonny welcomed me home. He didn't have to, but he did. I suppose you know about my heart…that's what finally convinced me I had to be here."

She waited, not expecting a voice of authority to rain down from the heavens, yet needing something…except she didn't know what.

"What's it like…on the other side?" Letty realized that even asking such a question as if they could answer was preposterous, but after her visit with Dr. Faraday, she'd entertained serious doubts that she'd ever recover. "Don't worry, I don't actually think you're going to tell me. Anyway, I always did like surprises."

Despite her melancholy, Letty smiled. She knelt beside the tombstones and reverently ran the tips of her fingers over the names and dates engraved in the marble. Blunt facts that said so little about their lives and those who'd loved them so deeply.

"I went to the doctor today," she whispered, her voice cracking. "I'm scared, Mom. Remember how you used to comfort me when I was a little girl? I wish I could crawl into your lap now and hear you tell me that everything's going to be all right." With the back of her hand she dashed away the tears that slid unrestrained down her cheeks.

"There's so much I want to live for now, so many things I want to experience." She remembered how she'd joked and kidded with the California doctors about her condition. But the surgery was imminent, and Letty wasn't laughing anymore.

"Mom. Dad." She straightened, coming to her feet. "I know you loved me—never once did I doubt that—and I loved you with all my heart…damaged though it is," she said with a hysterical laugh. "I wish you were with me now…I need you both so much."

Letty waited a couple of minutes, staring down at the graves of the two people who'd shaped and guided her life with such tender care. A tranquillity came to her then, a deep inner knowledge that if it had been humanly possible, her mother would have thrown both arms around her, hugged her close and given her the assurance she craved.

"I need someone," Letty admitted openly. Her burden was becoming almost more than she could bear. "Could you send me a friend?" she whispered. "Someone I can talk to who'll understand?" Names slipped in and out of her mind. The pastor was a good choice. Dorothy Martin was another.

"Letty?"

At the sound of her name, she turned and looked into Chase's eyes.

Chapter 7

"I saw Lonny's pickup on the road," Chase said, glancing over his shoulder. His hat was tipped back on his head as he studied her, his expression severe. "What are you doing here, Letty?"

She looked down at her parents' graves as a warm, gentle breeze blew over her. "I came to talk to Mom and Dad."

Her answer didn't seem to please him and he frowned. "Where's Cricket?"

"She's with Joy Fuller."

"Joy Fuller." He repeated the name slowly. "Lonny's Joy Fuller?"

"One and the same."

A sudden smile appeared on his face. "Lonny's certainly taken a dislike to that woman, although he was pretty keen on her for a while there."

"Lonny's making an utter fool of himself," Letty said.

"That's easy enough to do," Chase returned grimly. His face tightened. "Did you make an appointment with the doctor like you promised?"

Letty nodded. She'd hoped to avoid the subject, but she should've known Chase wouldn't allow that.

"And?" he barked impatiently. "Did you see him?"

"This afternoon." She would've thought that would satisfy him, but apparently it didn't. If anything, his frown grew darker.

"What did he say?"

"Not to vent my anger in the hot sun," she told him flippantly, then regretted responding to Chase's concern in such a glib manner. He was a friend, perhaps the best she'd ever had, and instead of answering him in an offhand way, Letty should be grateful for his thoughtfulness. Only minutes before she'd been praying for someone with whom she could share her burdens, and then Chase had appeared like someone out of a dream.

He could, in every sense, be the answer to her prayer.

"Chase," she said, moving between the headstones, unsure how to broach the difficult subject. "Have you thought very much about death?"

"No," he said curtly.

Strangely stung by his sharp reaction, she continued strolling, her hands behind her back. "I've thought about it a lot lately," she said, hoping he'd ask her why.

"That's sick, Letty."

"I don't think so," she said, carefully measuring each word. "Death, like birth, is a natural part of life. It's sunrise and sunset, just the way the song says."

"Is that the reason you're wandering among the tombstones like…like some vampire?"

It took her several minutes to swallow a furious response. Did she need to hit this man over the head before he realized what she was trying to tell him? "Oh, Chase, that's a mean thing to say."

"Do you often stroll through graveyards as if they're park grounds?" he asked, his voice clipped. "Or is this a recent pastime?"

"Recent," she said, smiling at him. She hoped he understood that no matter how much he goaded her, she wasn't going to react to his anger.

"Then may I suggest you snap out of whatever trance you're in and join the land of the living? There's a whole world out there just waiting to be explored."

"But the world isn't always a friendly place. Bad things happen every day. No one said life's fair. I wish it was, believe me, but it isn't."

"Stop talking like that. Wake up, Letty!" He stepped toward her as if he'd experienced a sudden urge to shake her, but if that was the case, he restrained himself.

"I'm awake," she returned calmly, yearning for him to understand that she loved life, but was powerless to control her own destiny. She felt a deep need to prepare him for her vulnerability to death. Now if only he'd listen.

"It's really very lovely here, don't you think?" she asked. "The air is crisp and clear, and there's the faint scent of sage mingled with the wildflowers. Can't you smell it?"

"No."

Letty ignored his lack of appreciation. "The sky is lovely today. So blue… When it's this bright I sometimes think it's actually going to touch the earth." She paused, waiting for Chase to make some kind of response, but he remained resolutely silent. "Those huge white clouds resemble Spanish galleons sailing across the seas, don't they?"

"I suppose."

Her linked hands behind her back, she wandered down a short hill. Chase continued to walk with her, but the silence between them was uneasy. Just when Letty felt the courage building inside her to mention the surgery, he spoke.

"You lied to me, Letty."

His words were stark. Surprised, she turned to him and met his gaze. It was oddly impassive, as if her supposed deceit didn't matter to him, as though he'd come to expect such things from her.

"When?" she demanded.

"Just now. I phoned Doc Hanley's office and they said you hadn't so much as called. You're a liar—on top of everything else."

Letty's breath caught painfully in her throat. The words to prove him wrong burned on her lips. "You don't have any right to check up on me." She took a deep breath. "Nevertheless, I didn't lie to you. I never have. But I'm not going to argue with you, if that's what you're looking for."

"Are you saying Doc Hanley's office lied?"

"I'm not going to discuss this. Believe what you want." She quickened her steps as she turned and headed toward the wrought-iron gates at the cemetery entrance. He followed her until they stood next to the trucks.

"Letty?"

She looked at him. Anger kindled in his eyes like tiny white flames, but Letty was too hurt to appease him with an explanation. She'd wanted to reveal a deep part of herself to this man because she trusted and loved him. She couldn't now. His accusation had ruined what she'd wanted to share.

He reached out and clasped her shoulders. "I need to know. Did you or did you not lie to me?"

The scorn was gone from his eyes, replaced with a pain that melted her own.

"No…I did see a doctor, I swear to you." She held her head at a proud angle, her gaze unwavering, but when she spoke, her voice cracked.

His eyes drifted closed as if he didn't know what to believe anymore. Whatever he was thinking, he didn't say. Instead he pulled her firmly into his embrace and settled his mouth on hers.

A tingling current traveled down her body at his touch. Letty whimpered—angry, hurt, excited, pleased. Still kissing her, Chase let his hands slide down to caress her back, tugging her against him. Her body was already aflame and trembling with need.

Chase held her tightly as he slipped one hand up to tangle in her short curls. His actions were slow, hesitant, as if he was desperately trying to stop himself from kissing her.

"Letty…" he moaned, his breath featherlight against her upturned face. "You make me want you.…"

She bowed her head. The desire she felt for him was equally ravenous.

Chase dragged in a heavy breath and expelled it loudly. "I don't want to feel the things I do."

"I know." It was heady knowledge, and Letty took delight in it. She moved against him, craving the feel of his arms around her.

Chase groaned. His mouth found hers once more and he kissed her tentatively, as if he didn't really want to be touching her again, but couldn't help himself. This increased Letty's reckless sensation of power.

He slid his hands up her arms and gripped her shoulders. Letty shyly moved her body against him; unfortunately the loving torment wasn't his alone, and she halted abruptly at the intense heat that surged through her.

A car drove past them, sounding its horn.

Letty had forgotten that they were standing on the edge of the road. Groaning with embarrassment, she buried her face against his heaving chest. Chase's heart felt like a hammer beating against her, matching her own excited pulse.

"Listen to me, Letty," he whispered.

He held her head between his hands and gently lifted her face upward, his breath warm and moist against her own.

"I want you more than I've ever wanted a woman in my life. You want me, too, don't you?"

For a moment she was tempted to deny everything, but she couldn't.

"Don't you?" he demanded. His hands, which were holding her face, were now possessive. His eyes, which had so recently been clouded with passion, were now sharp and insistent.

Letty opened her mouth to reply, but some part of her refused to acknowledge the truth. Her fear was that Chase would find a way to use it against her. He didn't trust her; he'd told her that himself. Desire couldn't be confused with love—at least not between them.

"Don't you?" he questioned a second time.

Knowing he wouldn't free her until she gave him an answer, Letty nodded once.

The instant she did, he released her. "That's all I wanted to know." With that he turned and walked away.

For the three days after her confrontation with Chase, Letty managed to avoid him. When she knew he'd be over at the house, she made a point of being elsewhere. Her thoughts were in chaos, her emotions so muddled and confused that she didn't know what to think or feel toward him anymore.

Apparently Chase was just as perplexed as she was, because he seemed to be avoiding her with the same fervor. Normally he stopped by the house several mornings a week. Not once since they'd met in the cemetery had he shown up for breakfast. Letty was grateful.

She cracked three eggs in a bowl and started whipping them. Lonny was due back in the house any minute and she wanted to have his meal ready when he arrived. Since her argument with her brother, he'd gone out of his way to let her know he appreciated her presence. He appeared to regret their angry exchange as much as Letty did.

The back door opened, and Lonny stepped inside and hung his hat on the peg next to the door. "Looks like we're in for some rain."

"My garden could use it," Letty said absently as she poured the eggs into the heated frying pan, stirring them while they cooked. "Do you want one piece of toast or two?"

"Two."

She put the bread in the toaster. Her back was to her brother when she spoke. "Do you have any plans for today?"

"Nothing out of the ordinary."

She nodded. "I thought you were supposed to see the insurance adjuster about having the fender on your truck repaired."

"It isn't worth the bother," Lonny said, walking to the stove to refill his coffee cup.

"But I thought—"

Lonny had made such a fuss over that minuscule dent in his truck that Letty had assumed he'd want to have it fixed, if for no other reason than to irritate Joy.

"I decided against it," he answered shortly.

"I see." Letty didn't, but that was neither here nor there. She'd given up trying to figure him out when it came to his relationship with Joy Fuller.

"I hate it when you say that," he muttered.

"Say what?" Letty asked, puzzled.

"'I see' in that prim voice, as if you know exactly what I'm thinking."

"Oh."

"There," he cried, slamming down his coffee cup. "You did it again."

"I'm sorry, Lonny. I didn't mean anything by it." She dished up his eggs, buttered the toast and brought his plate to the table.

He glanced at her apologetically when she set his breakfast in front of him, picked up his fork, then hesitated. "If I turn in a claim against Joy, her insurance rates will go up. Right?"

Letty would've thought that would be the least of her brother's concerns. "That's true. She'd probably be willing to pay you something instead. Come to think of it, didn't she offer you fifty dollars to forget the whole thing?"

Lonny's eyes flared briefly. "Yes, she did."

"I'm sure Joy would be happy to give you the money if you'd prefer to handle the situation that way. She wants to be as fair as she can. After all, she admitted from the first that the accident was her fault."

"What else could she do?"

Letty didn't respond.

"I don't dare contact her, though," Lonny said, his voice low.

As she sat down across from him, Letty saw that he hadn't taken a single bite of his eggs. "Why not?"

He sighed and looked away, clearly uncomfortable. "The last time I tried to call her she hung up."

"You shouldn't have blamed her for our argument. That was a ridiculous thing to do. Ridiculous and unfair."

A lengthy pause followed. "I know," Lonny admitted. "I was lashing out at her because I was furious with myself. I was feeling bad enough about saying the things I did to you. Then I found out you fainted soon afterward and I felt like a real jerk. The truth is, I had every intention of apologizing when I got back to the house. But you were upstairs sleeping and Chase was sitting here, madder than anything. He nearly flayed me alive. I guess I was looking for a scapegoat, and since Joy was indirectly involved, I called her."

"Joy wasn't involved at all! Directly *or* indirectly. You just wanted an excuse to call her."

He didn't acknowledge Letty's last comment, but said, "I wish I hadn't done it."

"Not only that," she went on as though he hadn't spoken, "Chase had no right to be angry with you."

"Well, he thought he did." Lonny paused. "Sometimes I wonder about you and Chase. You two have been avoiding each other all week. I mention your name and he gets defensive. I mention him to you and you change the subject. The fact is, I thought that once you got home and settled down, you and Chase might get married."

At those words, Letty did exactly what Lonny said she would. She changed the subject. "Since you won't be taking the truck in for body work, someone needs to tell Joy. Would you like me to talk to her for you?"

Lonny shrugged. "I suppose."

"What do you want me to say?"

Lonny shrugged again. "I don't know. I guess you can say I'm willing to drop the whole insurance thing. She doesn't need to worry about giving me that fifty dollars, either—I don't want her money."

Letty ran one finger along the rim of her coffee cup. "Anything else?"

Her brother hesitated. "I guess it wouldn't do any harm to tell her I said I might've overreacted just a bit the day of the accident, and being the sensitive kind of guy I am, I regret how I behaved.... This, of course, all depends on how receptive she is to my apology."

"Naturally," Letty said, feigning a sympathetic look. "But I'm sure Joy will accept your apology." Letty wasn't at all certain that was true, but she wanted to reassure her brother, who was making great leaps in improving his attitude toward her friend.

Digging his fork into his scrambled eggs, Lonny snorted softly. "Now *that's* something I doubt. Knowing that woman the way I do, I'll bet Joy Fuller demands an apology written in blood. But this is the best she's going to get. You tell her that for me, will you?"

"Be glad to," Letty said.

Lonny took a huge bite of his breakfast, as if he'd

suddenly realized how hungry he was. He picked up a piece of toast with one hand and waved it at Letty. "You might even tell her I think she does a good job at church with the organ. But play that part by ear, if you know what I mean. Don't make it sound like I'm buttering her up for anything."

"Right."

"Do you want the truck today?"

"Please." Letty had another doctor's appointment and was leading up to that request herself.

Lonny stood up and carried his plate to the sink. "I'll talk to you this afternoon, then." He put on his hat, adjusted it a couple of times, then turned to Letty and smiled. "You might follow your own advice, you know."

"What are you talking about?"

"You and Chase. I don't know what's going on, but I have a feeling that a word or two from you would patch everything up. Since I'm doing the honorable thing with Joy, I'd think you could do the same with Chase."

With that announcement he was gone.

Letty sat at the table, both hands around the warm coffee mug, while she mulled over Lonny's suggestion. She didn't know what to say to Chase, or how to talk to him anymore.

More than a week had passed since Chase had seen Letty. Each day his mood worsened. Each day he grew more irritable and short-tempered. Even Firepower, who had always sensed his mood and adjusted his own temperament, seemed to be losing patience with him. Chase didn't blame the gelding; he was getting to the point where he hated himself.

Something had to be done.

The day Chase had found Letty wandering through the cemetery, he'd been driving around looking for her. She'd promised him on Sunday that she'd see Doc Hanley. Somehow, he hadn't believed she'd do it. Chase had been furious when he discovered she hadn't seen the doctor. It'd taken him close to an hour to locate Letty. When he did, he'd had to exercise considerable restraint not to blast her for her lack of common sense. She'd fainted, for crying out loud! A healthy person didn't just up and faint. Something was wrong.

But before Chase could say a word, Letty had started in with that macabre conversation about death and dying. His temper hadn't improved with her choice of subject matter. The old Letty had been too full of life even to contemplate death. It was only afterward, when she was in his arms, that Chase discovered the vibrant woman he'd always known. Only when he was kissing her that she seemed to snap out of whatever trance she was in.

It was as though Letty was half-alive these days. She met his taunts with a smile, refused to argue with him even when he provoked her. Nothing had brought a response from her, with the exception of his kisses.

Chase couldn't take any more of this. He was going to talk to her and find out what had happened to change her from the lively, spirited woman he used to know. And he didn't plan to leave until he had an answer.

When he pulled into the yard, Cricket was the only one he saw. The child was sitting on the porch steps, looking bored and unhappy. She brightened as soon as he came into view.

"Chase!" she called and jumped to her feet.

She ran toward him with an eagerness that grabbed his heart. He didn't know why Cricket liked him so much. He'd done nothing to deserve her devotion. She was so pleased, so excited, whenever she saw him that her warm welcome couldn't help but make him feel… good.

"I'm glad you're here," she told him cheerfully.

"Hello, Cricket. It's nice to see you, too."

She slipped her small hand into his and smiled up at him. "It's been ages and *ages* since you came over to see us. I missed you a whole bunch."

"I know."

"Where've you been all this time? Mommy said I wasn't supposed to ask Uncle Lonny about you anymore, but I was afraid I wouldn't see you again. You weren't in church on Sunday."

"I've been…busy."

The child sighed. "That's what Mommy said." Then, as though suddenly remembering something important, Cricket tore into the house, returning a moment later with a picture that had been colored in with the utmost care. "This is from my book. I made it for you," she announced proudly. "It's a picture of a horsey."

"Thank you, sweetheart." He examined the picture, then carefully folded it and put it in his shirt pocket.

"I made it 'cause you're my friend and you let me ride Firepower."

He patted her head. "Where's your mother?"

"She had to go to Rock Springs."

"Who's watching you?"

Cricket pouted. "Uncle Lonny, but he's not very good at it. He fell asleep in front of the TV, and when I changed the channel, he got mad and told me to leave it 'cause he was watching it. But he had his eyes closed. How can you watch TV with your eyes closed?"

She didn't seem to expect an answer, but plopped herself down and braced her elbows on her knees, her small hands framing her face.

Chase sat down next to her. "Is that why you're sitting out here all by yourself?"

Cricket nodded. "Mommy says I'll have lots of friends to play with when I go to kindergarten, but that's not for months and months."

"I'm sure she's right."

"But you're my friend and so is Firepower. I like Firepower, even if he's a really big horse. Mommy said I could have a horsey someday. Like she did when she was little."

He smiled at the child, fighting down an emotion he couldn't identify, one that kept bobbing to the surface of his mind. He remembered Letty when she was only a few years older than Cricket. They had the same color hair, the same eyes and that same stubborn streak, which Chase swore was a mile wide.

"My pony's going to be the best pony *ever*," Cricket prattled on, clearly content to have him sitting beside her, satisfied that he was her friend.

It hit Chase then, with an impact so powerful he could hardly breathe. His heart seemed to constrict, burning within his chest. The vague emotion he'd been feeling was unmistakable now. Strong and unmistakable. He loved this little girl. He didn't *want* to love Cricket, didn't want to experience this tenderness, but the child was Letty's daughter. And he loved Letty. In the last few weeks he'd been forced to admit that nine long years hadn't altered his feelings toward her.

"Chase—" Lonny stepped outside and joined them on the back porch. "When did you get here?"

"A few minutes ago." He had trouble finding his voice. "I came over to talk to Letty, but she's not here."

"No, she left a couple of hours ago." He checked his watch, frowning as he did. "I don't know what time to expect her back."

"Did she say where she was going?"

Lonny glanced away, his look uncomfortable. "I have no idea what's going on with that woman. I wish I did."

"What do you mean?" Chase knew his friend well enough to realize Lonny was more than a little disturbed.

"She's been needing the truck all week. She's always got some errand or another. I don't need it that much myself, so I don't mind. But then yesterday I noticed she's been putting a lot of miles on it. I asked her why, but she got so defensive and closemouthed we nearly had another fight."

"So did you find out where she's going?"

"Rock Springs," Lonny said shortly. "At least, that's what she claims."

"Why? What's in Rock Springs?"

Lonny shrugged. "She never did say."

"Mommy goes to see a man," Cricket interjected brightly. "He looks like the one on TV with the mustache."

"The one on TV with the mustache," Lonny repeated, exchanging a blank stare with Chase. "Who knows what she means by that?"

"He's real nice, too," Cricket went on to explain patiently. "But he doesn't talk to me. He just talks to Mommy. Sometimes they go in a room together and I have to wait outside, but that's all right 'cause I work in my book."

Lonny's face tensed as he looked at Chase again. "I'm sure that isn't the way it sounds," he murmured.

"Why should I care what she does," Chase lied. "I don't feel a thing for her. I haven't in years."

"Right," Lonny returned sarcastically. "The problem is, you never could lie worth a damn."

Chapter 8

The arrival of Letty's first welfare check had a curious effect on her. She brought in the mail, sat down at the kitchen table and carefully examined the plain beige envelope. Tears filled her eyes, then crept silently down her face. Once she'd been so proud, so independent, and now she was little more than a charity case, living off the generosity of taxpayers.

Lonny came in the back door and wiped his feet on the braided rug. "Mail here?" he asked impatiently.

Her brother had been irritated with her for the past couple of weeks without ever letting her know exactly why. Letty realized his displeasure was connected to her trips into Rock Springs, and her secrecy about them, but he didn't mention them again. Although he hadn't said a word, she could feel his annoyance every time they were together. More than once over the past few days,

Letty had toyed with the idea of telling Lonny about her heart condition, but whenever she thought of approaching him, he'd look at her with narrow, disapproving eyes.

Without waiting for her to respond, Lonny walked over to the table and sorted through the bills, flyers and junk mail.

Letty stood and turned away from him. She wiped her cheeks, praying that if he did notice her tears he wouldn't comment.

"Mommy!" Cricket crashed through the back door, her voice high with excitement. "Chase is here on Firepower and he's got another horsey with him. Come and look." She was out the door again in an instant.

Letty smiled, tucked the government check in her pocket and followed her daughter outside. Sure enough, Chase was riding down the hillside on his gelding, holding the reins of a second horse, a small brown-and-white pinto trotting obediently behind the bay.

"Chase! Chase!" Cricket stood on the top step, jumping up and down and frantically waving both arms.

Chase slowed his pace once he reached the yard. Lonny joined his sister, trying to hide a smile. Bemused, Letty stared at him. The last time she could remember seeing him with a silly grin like that, she'd been ten years old and he was suffering through his first teenage crush.

Unable to wait a second longer, Cricket ran out to greet her friend. Smiling down at the child, Chase lowered his arms and hoisted her into the saddle beside him. Letty had lost count of the times Chase had "just happened" to stop by with Firepower in the past few weeks. Cricket got as excited as a game show winner whenever he was around. He'd taken her riding more than once. He was so patient with the five-year-old, so gentle. The only time Chase had truly laughed in Letty's presence was when he was with her daughter—and Cricket treasured every moment with her hero.

In contrast, Letty's relationship with Chase had deteriorated to the point that they'd become, at best, mere acquaintances. Chase went out of his way to avoid talking to her. It was as if their last meeting in the cemetery, several weeks before, had killed whatever love there'd ever been between them.

Letty watched from the porch as Chase slid out of the saddle and onto the ground, then lifted Cricket down. He wore the same kind of silly grin as Lonny, looking exceptionally pleased with himself.

"Well, what do you think?" Lonny asked, rocking back on his heels, hands in his pockets. He seemed almost as excited as Cricket.

"About what?" Letty felt as if everyone except her was in on some big secret.

Lonny glanced at her. "Chase bought the pony for Cricket."

"What?" Letty exploded.

"It's a surprise," Lonny whispered.

"You're telling me! Didn't it cross his mind—or yours—to discuss the matter with *me?* I'm her mother... I should have some say in this decision, don't you think?"

For the first time, Lonny revealed signs of uneasiness. "Actually, Chase did bring up the subject with me, and I'm the one who told him it was okay. After all, I'll be responsible for feeding it and paying the vet's bills, for that matter. I assumed you'd be as thrilled as Cricket."

"I am, but I wish one of you had thought to ask me first. It's...it's common courtesy."

"You're not going to make a federal case out of this,

are you?" Lonny asked, his gaze accusing. "Chase is just doing something nice for her."

"I know," she sighed. But that wasn't the issue.

Chase and Cricket were standing next to the pony when Letty approached them in the yard. Apparently Chase had just told her daughter the pony now belonged to her, because Cricket threw her arms around Chase's neck, shouting with glee. Laughing, Chase twirled her in a circle, holding her by the waist. Cricket's short legs flew out and she looked like a tiny top spinning around and around.

Letty felt like an outsider in this touching scene, although she made an effort to smile and act pleased. Perhaps Cricket sensed Letty's feelings, because as soon as she was back on the ground, she hurried to her mother's side and hugged her tightly.

"Mommy, did you see Jennybird? That's the name of my very own pony."

Chase walked over and placed his hands on the little girl's shoulders. "You don't object, do you?" he asked Letty.

How could she? "Of course not. It's very thoughtful of you, Chase." She gazed down at her daughter and restrained herself from telling him she wished he'd consulted her beforehand. "Did you thank him, sweetheart?"

"Oh, yes, a hundred million, zillion times."

Letty turned back to the porch, fearing that if she stood there any longer, watching the two of them, she'd start to weep. The emotions she felt disturbed her. Crazy as it seemed, the most prominent one bordered on jealousy. How she yearned for Chase to look at her with the same tenderness he did Cricket. Imagine being envious of her own daughter!

Chase didn't hide his affection for the child. In the span of a few weeks, the pair had become great friends, and Letty felt excluded, as if she were on the outside looking in. Suddenly she couldn't bear to stand there anymore and pretend everything was fine. As unobtrusively as possible, she walked back to the house. She'd almost reached the door when Chase stopped her.

"Letty?"

She turned to see him standing at the bottom of the steps, a frown furrowing his brow.

"You dropped this." He extended the plain envelope to her.

The instant she realized what it was, Letty was mortified. Chase stood below her, holding out her welfare check, his face distorted with shock and what she was sure must be scorn. When she took the check, his eyes seemed to spark with questions. Before he could ask a single one, she whirled around and raced into the house.

It shouldn't have surprised Letty that she couldn't sleep that night, although she seemed to be the only member of the family with that problem. After all the excitement with Jennybird, Cricket had fallen asleep almost immediately after dinner. Lonny had been snoring softly when Letty had dressed and tiptoed past his bedroom on her way downstairs.

Now she sat under the stars, her knees under her chin, on the hillside where she'd so often met Chase when they were young. Chase had listened to her talk about her dreams and all the wonderful things in store for her. He'd held her close and kissed her and believed in her and with her.

That secure feeling, that sense of being loved, had

driven Letty back to this spot now. There'd been no place else for her to go. She felt more alone than ever, more isolated—cut off from the people she loved, who loved her. She was facing the most difficult problem of her life and she was doing it utterly alone.

Letty knew she should be pleased with the unexpected change in Chase's attitude toward Cricket…and she was. It was more than she'd ever expected from him, more than she'd dared to hope. And yet, she longed with all her heart for Chase to love *her*.

But he didn't. That was a fact he'd made abundantly clear.

It was hard to be depressed out here, Letty mused as she studied the spectacular display in the heavens. The stars were like frosty jewels scattered across black velvet. The moon was full and brilliant, a madcap adventurer in a heaven filled with like-minded wanderers.

Despite her low spirits, Letty found she was smiling. So long ago, she'd sat under the same glittering moon, confident that nothing but good things would ever come into her life.

"What are you doing here?"

The crisp voice behind her startled Letty. "Hello, Chase," she said evenly, refusing to turn around. "Are you going to order me off your land?"

Chase had seen Letty approach the hillside from the house. He'd decided the best tactic was to ignore her. She'd leave soon enough. Only she hadn't. For more than an hour she'd sat under the stars, barely moving. Unable to resist anymore, he'd gone over to the hill, without knowing what he'd say or do.

"Do you want me to leave?" she asked. He hadn't answered her earlier question.

"No," he answered gruffly.

His reply seemed to please her and he felt her tension subside. She relaxed, clasped her bent knees and said, "I haven't seen a night this clear in...forever." Her voice was low and enticing. "The stars look like diamonds, don't they?"

They did, but Chase didn't respond. He shifted his weight restlessly as he stood behind her, gazing up at the heavens, too.

"I remember the last time I sat on this hill with you, but...but that seems a million years ago now."

"It was," he said brusquely.

"That was the night you asked me to marry you."

"We were both young and foolish," he said, striving for a flippant air. He would've liked Letty to believe the ridiculous part had been in *wanting* her for his wife, but the truth was, he'd hoped with everything in him that she'd consent. Despite all the heartbreak, he felt the same way this very moment.

To his surprise, Letty laughed softly. "Now we're both older and wiser, aren't we?"

"I can't speak for anyone but myself." Before he was even conscious of moving, Chase was on the ground, sitting next to her, his legs stretched out in front of him.

"I wish I knew then what I do now," she continued. "If, by some miracle, we were able to turn back the clock to that night, I'd like you to know I'd jump at your proposal."

A shocked silence followed her words. Chase wished he could believe her, but he couldn't.

"You were after diamonds, Letty, and all I had to offer you was denim."

"But the diamonds were here all along," she whispered, staring up at the stars.

Chase closed his eyes to the pain that squeezed his heart. He hadn't been good enough for her then, and he wasn't now. He didn't doubt for an instant that she was waiting to leave Red Springs. When the time came she'd run so fast his head would spin. In fact, he didn't know what was keeping her here now.

The crux of the problem was that he didn't trust Letty. He couldn't—not anymore, not since he'd learned she was seeing some man in Rock Springs. Unfortunately it wasn't easy to stop caring for her. But in all the years he'd cherished Letty, the only thing his love had gotten him had been pain and heartache.

When she'd first come back to Wyoming, he'd carefully allowed himself to hope. He'd dreamed that they'd find a way to turn back time, just as she'd said, and discover a life together. But in the past few weeks she'd proved to him over and over how impossible that was.

Chase's gut twisted with the knowledge. He'd done everything he could to blot her out of his life. In the beginning, when he'd recognized his feelings for Cricket, he'd thought he would fight for Letty's love, show her how things could change. But could they really? All he could offer her was a humble life on a cattle ranch—exactly what he'd offered her nine years ago. Evidently someone else had given her something better. She'd fallen for some bastard in California, someone unworthy of her love, and now, apparently she was doing it again, blatantly meeting another man. Good riddance, then. The guy with the mustache was welcome to her.

All Chase wanted was for her to get out of his life, because the pain of having her so close was more than he could stand.

"I think Cricket will remember today as long as she lives," Letty said, blithely unaware of his thoughts. "You've made her the happiest five-year-old in the world."

He didn't say anything; he didn't want to discuss Cricket. The little girl made him vulnerable to Letty. Once he'd lowered his guard, it was as if a dam of love had broken. He didn't know what he'd do when Letty moved away and took the little girl with her.

"She thinks you're the sun and the moon," Letty said in a way that suggested he need not have done a thing for Cricket to worship him.

"She's a sweet kid." That was the most he was willing to admit.

"Jason reminded me of you." She spoke so softly it was difficult to make out her words.

"I beg your pardon?"

"Jason was Cricket's father."

That man was the last person Chase wanted to hear about, but before he could tell Letty so, she continued in a voice filled with pain and remembered humiliation.

"He asked me out for weeks before I finally accepted. I'd written you and asked you to join me in California, and time and again you turned me down."

"You wanted me to be your manager! I'm a rancher. What did I know about the music business?"

"Nothing…I was asking the impossible," she said, her voice level, her words devoid of blame. "It was ridiculous—I realize that now. But I was so lonely for you, so lost."

"Apparently you found some comfort."

She let the gibe pass, although he saw her flinch and knew his words had hit their mark. He said things like that to hurt her, but the curious thing was, *he* suffered, too. He hurt himself as much as he hurt Letty, maybe more.

"He took me to the best restaurants in town, told me everything I wanted to hear. I was so desperate to believe him that a few inconsistencies didn't trouble me. He pretended to be my friend, and I needed one so badly. He seemed to share my dream the way you always had. I couldn't come back to Wyoming a nobody. You understand that, don't you?"

Chase didn't give her an answer and she went on without waiting for one.

"I was still chasing my dreams, but I was so lonely they were losing their appeal.

"I never planned to go so far with Jason, but it happened, and for days afterward I was in shock. I was—"

"Letty, stop, I don't want to hear this." Her relationship with Cricket's father was a part of her life he wanted to remove completely from his mind.

Letty ignored him, her voice shaky but determined. "Soon afterward I found out I was pregnant. I wanted to crawl into a hole and die, but that wasn't the worst part. When I told Jason, he misunderstood… He seemed to think I wanted him to marry me. But I didn't. I told him because, well, because he was Cricket's father. That's when I learned he was married. *Married.* All that time and he'd had a wife."

"Stop, Letty. I'm the last person you should be telling this to. In fact, I don't want to hear any of it," Chase shouted. He clenched his fists in impotent rage, hating the man who'd used and deceived Letty like this.

"It hurts to talk about it, but I feel I have to. I want you to know that—"

"Whatever you have to say doesn't matter anymore."

"But, Chase, it does, because as difficult as you may find this to believe, I've always loved you...as much then as I do now."

"Why didn't you come home when you found out you were pregnant?"

"How could I have? Pregnant and a failure, too. Everyone expected me to make a name for Red Springs. I was so ashamed, so unhappy, and there was nowhere to go."

She turned away and Chase saw her wipe the tears from her eyes. He ached to hold and comfort her, his heart heavy with her grief, but he refused to make himself vulnerable to her again. She spoke of loving him, but she didn't mean it. She couldn't, not when there was someone else in her life.

"What changed your mind?" he asked. "What made you decide to come back now?"

Several minutes passed, far longer than necessary to answer a simple question. Obviously something had happened that had brought her running back to the Bar E when she'd managed to stay away all those years. Something traumatic.

"I suppose it was a matter of accepting defeat," she finally said. "In the years after Cricket's birth, the determination to succeed as a singer left me. I dabbled in the industry, but mainly I did temp work. As the years passed, I couldn't feel ashamed of Cricket. She's the joy of my life."

"But it took you nine years, Letty. *Nine* years."

She looked up at him, her eyes filled with pain, clearly revealed in the moonlight that seemed as bright as day.

The anger was still with him. The senselessness of it all—a dream that had ruined their lives. And for what? "I loved you once," he said starkly, "but I don't now, and I doubt I ever will again. You taught me that the only thing love brings is heartache."

She lowered her head and he saw new tears.

"I could hate you for the things you've done," he said in a low, angry voice.

"I think you do," she whispered.

Chase hadn't known what to expect, but it wasn't this calm, almost humble acceptance of his resentment.

Maybe the proud, confident Letty was gone forever, but he couldn't believe that was true. Every once in a while, he saw flashes of the old Letty. Just enough to give him hope.

"I *don't* hate you, Letty," he murmured in a tormented whisper. "I wish I could, but I can't…I can't."

Chase intended to kiss her once, then release her and send her back to the house. It was late, and they both had to get up early. But their kiss sparked, then caught fire, leaping to sudden brilliance. She sighed, and the sound was so soft, so exciting, that Chase knew he was lost even before he pressed her against the cool, fragrant grass.

Lying down beside her, Chase felt helpless, caught in a maze of love and desire. He tried to slow his breathing, gain control of his senses, but it was impossible, especially when Letty raised her hand and stroked his shoulders through the fabric of his shirt, then glided her fingers around to his back.

Chase felt engulfed by his love for her, lost, drowning, and it didn't matter, nothing did, except the warm feeling of her beside him, longing for him as desperately as he longed for her.

Again and again he kissed her, and when he paused to collect his senses, she eased her hand around his neck and gently brought his mouth back to hers.

Their need for each other was urgent. Fierce. Chase couldn't get enough of her. He kissed her eyes, her cheeks, her forehead and tenderly nuzzled her throat.

Eventually he released her and she sagged breathlessly against him. No other woman affected him the way Letty did. Why her? Of all the women in the world, why did he have to love *her?* For years she'd rewarded his loyalty with nothing but pain.

But it wasn't distress he was feeling now. The pleasure she brought him was so intense he wanted to cry out with it. He kissed her and her soft, gasping breaths mingled with his own. Chase was shaking and he couldn't seem to stop—shaking with anticipation and desire, shaking with the resolve not to make love to her, not to claim her completely, because once he did, he'd never be able to let her go. He wanted her, but he needed her to love him as much as he loved her. A love that came from their hearts and minds—not just the passionate dictates of their bodies.

His jaw tight with restraint, he closed his hands around hers and gently lifted her away from him.

"Chase?" she whispered, perplexed.

If she was confused, it was nothing compared to the emotions churning inside him. He'd always loved her, still did, yet he was turning her away again, and it was agonizing. She wanted him, and she'd let him know that. But he wouldn't make love to her. Not now.

"Letty...no."

She bowed her head. "You...don't want to make love to me?" she whispered tremulously. "Just one time..."

"No," he told her bluntly. "It wouldn't be enough."

He stroked her hair and kissed her gently. Then he realized the true significance of what she'd said. She only wanted him to love her *one time*. "You're going away, aren't you, Letty?" He felt her tense in his arms before her startled gaze found his.

"Who told you?"

Without responding, he pushed her away from him and stood.

"Chase?"

"No one told me," he said, the love and tenderness he felt evaporating in the heat of her betrayal. "I guessed."

Chapter 9

"What happened with you and Letty last night?" Lonny asked Chase early the next morning. They'd planned on repairing the fence that separated their property lines.

"What's between Letty and me is none of your business."

Lonny paused to consider this while rubbing the side of his jaw. "Normally I'd agree with you, but my sister looked really bad this morning. To be honest, I haven't been particularly pleased with her myself lately."

Lonny followed him to the pile of split cedar fence posts. "When Cricket mentioned Letty meeting some man in Red Springs," he continued, "I was madder 'n anything. But after all the fuss I made about her interfering in my life, I didn't think I had the right to ask her a whole lot of questions."

"Then why start with me now?" After that, Chase ignored his friend and loaded the posts into the back of his pickup. His mood hadn't improved since he'd left Letty only a few hours ago.

"I'm sticking my nose where it doesn't belong because you're the best friend I've got."

"Then let's keep it that way." Chase wiped the perspiration from his brow, then went back to heaving posts, still trying to pretend Lonny hadn't introduced the subject of his sister.

"You're as bad as she is," Lonny shouted.

"Maybe I am."

Lonny jerked on his gloves and walked toward the pile of wood. He pulled one long piece free, balanced it on his shoulder and headed toward the truck.

"I don't think she slept all night," Lonny muttered.

It was difficult for Chase to feel any sympathy when he hadn't, either.

"I got downstairs this morning and she was sitting in the kitchen, staring into space. I swear there were enough damp tissues on that table to insulate the attic."

"What makes you think I had anything to do with Letty crying?"

"Because she more or less told me so—well, less rather than more," Lonny muttered, shaking his head. "She wouldn't say a word at first, mind you—she's as tight-lipped as you are, but harder to reason with, Letty being a woman and all."

"Listen, if your sister wants to shed a few tears, that's her concern. Not mine. Not yours. Understand?"

Lonny tipped back the rim of his hat. "Can't say I do. Look, Chase, I know you're furious at me for butt-ing in, and I don't blame you. But the least you can do is hear me out."

"I'm a busy man, Lonny, and I'd appreciate it if you kept your thoughts to yourself."

Lonny disregarded his suggestion. "Like I said, I don't know what happened between you, but—"

"How many times do I have to tell you? It's none of your business."

"It is if it's hurting my sister," Lonny said darkly. "And she's hurting plenty."

"That's her problem." Chase had to take care of himself, protect his own heart; he couldn't worry about hers, or so he told himself.

"Why don't you talk to her?" Lonny was saying.

"What do you expect me to say? Are you going to tell me that, too? I respect you, Lonny, but I'm telling you right now to butt out. What's between Letty and me doesn't have anything to do with you." It would be a shame to ruin a lifetime friendship because of Letty, but Chase wasn't about to let Lonny Ellison direct his actions toward her.

They worked together for the next few hours without exchanging another word. Neither seemed willing to break the icy silence. They were repairing the fence, replacing the rotting posts with new ones. Normally, a day like that was an opportunity to joke and have a little fun. Today, it seemed, they could barely tolerate each other.

"I'm worried about her," Lonny said when they broke for lunch. He stared at his roast beef sandwich, then took a huge bite, quickly followed by another.

Chase sighed loudly. "Are you back to talking about Letty again?" Although she hadn't left his mind for an instant, he didn't want to discuss her.

"I can't help it!" Lonny shouted as he leaped to his feet and threw the remains of his lunch on the ground with such force that bits of apple flew in several directions. "Be mad at me if you want, Chase. Knock me down if it'll make you feel better. But I can't let you do this to Letty. She's been hurt enough."

"That isn't my fault!"

"I've never seen her like this—as if all the life's gone out of her. She sits and stares into space with a look that's so pathetic it rips your heart out. Cricket started talking to her this morning and she hardly noticed. You know that's not like Letty."

"She's leaving," Chase shouted, slamming his own lunch against the tree. "Just like she did before—she's walking away. It nearly destroyed me the first time, and I'm not letting her do that to me again."

"Leaving?" Lonny cried. "What do you mean? Did she tell you that herself?"

"Not exactly. I guessed."

"Well, it's news to me. She enrolled Cricket in kindergarten the other day. That doesn't sound like she's planning to move."

"But…" Chase's thoughts were in chaos. He'd assumed that Letty would be leaving; she'd certainly given him that impression. In fact, she'd said so—hadn't she?

"Would it be so difficult to ask her directly?" Lonny said. "We've repaired all the fence we're going to manage today. Come to the house and ask her point-blank. Letty doesn't lie. If she's planning to leave Red Springs, she'll admit it."

Chase expelled his breath forcefully. He might as well ask her, since Lonny wasn't going to quit bugging him until he did. And yet…

"Will you do that, at least?" Lonny urged.

"I..." Indecision tore at Chase. He didn't want any contact with Letty; he was still reeling from their last encounter. But he'd never seen Lonny behave like this. He was obviously worried about Letty. It wasn't typical of Lonny to get involved in another man's business and that alone was a more convincing argument than anything he'd said.

"You're driving me back to the house, aren't you?" Lonny asked matter-of-factly.

"What about Destiny?"

"I'll pick him up later."

Lonny said this casually, as if he often left his horse at Spring Valley. As far as Chase could remember, he'd never done so in all the years they'd been friends and neighbors.

"All right, I'll ask her," Chase agreed, but reluctantly. He'd do it, if for nothing more than to appease Lonny, although Chase wanted this issue with Letty cleared up. From what he remembered, she'd made her intentions obvious. Yet why she'd enrolled Cricket in kindergarten—which was several months away—was beyond him. It didn't make sense.

Lonny muttered something under his breath as he climbed into the cab of the truck.

The first thing Chase noticed when he rolled into the yard at Lonny's place was that his friend's battered pickup was missing. He waited outside while Lonny hurried into the kitchen.

"She's not here," Lonny said when he returned, holding a note. "She's gone into town to see Joy Fuller."

Chase frowned. Now that he'd made the decision to

confront Letty, he was disappointed about the delay. "I'll ask her another time," he said.

"No." Lonny had apparently sensed Chase's frustration. "I mean...I don't think it would do any harm to drive to Joy's. I've been wanting to talk to her, anyway, and this business with Letty gives me an excuse."

"You told me it was completely over. What possible reason could you have to talk to her?"

Lonny was already in the truck. Chase couldn't help noticing the color that tinged his face. "I might've been a bit...hasty. She might not have a sense of humor, but if Letty thinks she's okay, maybe I should give her another chance."

"Well, she is cute. But does she want to give *you* another chance?"

Lonny swallowed and glanced out the window. He didn't answer Chase's question—but then, how could he? Whether or not Joy would be willing to get involved with him again was debatable. Chase suspected Lonny was a lot more interested in Joy than he'd let on; he also suspected Joy might not feel quite the same way.

"Take a right at the next corner," Lonny said as they entered town. "Her house is the first one on the left."

Chase parked under the row of elms. "I'll wait here," he said abruptly.

Lonny got out of the truck and hesitated before he shut the door. "That might not be such a good idea."

"Why not?"

"Well, I'm not sure if Joy's going to talk to me. And what about Letty? Don't you want to see her?"

Chase sighed. Now that he'd had time to think about it, running into town to find Letty wasn't that brilliant a plan.

"Come with me, okay?" Lonny said. "That way Joy might not throw me out the second she sees me."

Sighing loudly, Chase left the truck, none too pleased by any of this. He accompanied Lonny to Joy Fuller's door and watched in surprise as Lonny licked his fingertips and smoothed down the sides of his hair before ringing the bell. It was all Chase could do not to comment.

Cricket answered the door. "Hi, Uncle Lonny. Hi, Chase." She whirled around and shouted over her shoulder. "Joy, it's my uncle Lonny and Chase! You remember Chase, don't you? He's my very best friend in the whole world." Then she ran back into the house.

A minute or so passed before Joy came to the door, Cricket on her heels.

"Yes?" she said stiffly.

She wore a frilly apron tied around her waist, and traces of flour dusted her nose. She'd obviously been baking, and knowing Cricket, it was probably chocolate chip cookies.

Lonny jerked the hat from his head. "We were wondering…me and Chase, my neighbor here, if it would be convenient to take a moment of your time."

Chase had never heard his friend more tongue-tied. Lonny made it sound as though they were old-fashioned snake oil salesmen, come to pawn their wares.

"We can't seem to talk to each other without yelling, Mr. Ellison," Joy returned. Her hands were neatly clasped in front of her, and her gaze was focused somewhere in the distance.

"I'd like to talk to Letty," Chase said. The way things were going, it could be another half hour before anyone learned the reason for their visit. Not that he actually knew what his friend planned to say to Joy—or if Lonny had even figured it out himself.

"Mommy's gone," Cricket piped up.

"She left a few minutes ago," Joy explained.

"Did she say where she was going?"

"No…but I'm sure you can catch her if it's important."

"Go, man," Lonny said, poking his elbow into Chase's ribs. "I'll stay here—that is, if Miss Fuller has no objections."

"*Ms*. Fuller," Joy corrected, her eyes narrowing.

"*Ms*. Fuller," Lonny echoed.

"You can stay, but only if you promise you won't insult me in my own home. Because I'm telling you right now, Lonny Ellison, I won't put up with it."

"I'll do my best."

"That may not be good enough," she said ominously.

"Which way did Letty go?" Chase demanded, decidedly impatient with the pair.

"Toward downtown," Joy said, pointing west. "You shouldn't have any trouble finding her. She's driving that piece of junk Mr. Ellison seems so fond of."

For a moment Lonny looked as if he'd swallowed a grapefruit. His face flamed red, he swallowed hard and it was obvious he was doing everything in his power not to let loose with a blistering response. His efforts were promptly rewarded with a smile from Joy.

"Very good, Mr. Ellison. You've passed the test." She stepped aside to let him enter.

"I won't be long," Chase told them.

Lonny repeatedly twisted the brim of his hat. "Take your time," he muttered. "But go!"

Chase didn't need any more incentive and ran toward his pickup. As soon as the engine roared to life, he shifted gears and swerved out into the traffic, such as it was.

Red Springs's main street was lined with small businesses that had diagonal parking in front. Chase could determine at a single glance that Lonny's truck wasn't in sight. He drove the full length of the town and down a couple of side streets, but she wasn't there, either.

Mystified, he parked and stood outside his truck, looking down Main Street in both directions. Where could she possibly have gone?

Letty came out of Dr. Faraday's office and sat in Lonny's truck for several minutes before she started the engine. After waiting all these weeks, after stringing out the medical and financial details of her life as though they were laundry on a clothesline—after all this, she should feel some sort of release knowing that the surgery was finally scheduled.

But she didn't.

Instead she experienced an overwhelming sadness. Tears burned in her eyes, but she held her head high and drove toward the freeway that would take her back to Red Springs. Now that everything had been cleared with the doctor and the state, Letty felt free to explain what was wrong with her to her brother. She'd leave it to him to tell Chase—if he wanted.

Chase. Quickly she cast all thoughts of him aside, knowing they'd only bring her pain.

A few miles out of town, Letty saw another truck in her rearview mirror, several cars back. Her first reaction was that someone was driving a model similar to the one Chase had.

Not until the truck started weaving in and out of traf-

fic in an effort to catch up with her did Letty realize it
was Chase's.

Why was he following her? All she could think was
that something terrible must have happened... Cricket!
Oh, no, it had to be Cricket.

Letty pulled to the side of the road.

Chase was right behind her.

Shutting off the engine, she climbed out and saw him
leap from his vehicle and come running toward her.

"Letty. Letty." He wrapped his arms around her, holding her with a tenderness she thought he could no longer feel.

She loosened his grip enough to raise her head. "Is
anything wrong with Cricket?" she asked urgently.

He frowned. "No," he said before he kissed her with
a thoroughness that left her weak and clinging.

"Then what are you doing here?"

Chase closed his eyes briefly. "That's a long story.
Letty, we've got to talk."

She broke free from his embrace. "I don't think we
can anymore. Every time we get close to each other, we
end up arguing. I know I hurt you, Chase, but I don't
know how much longer I can stand being hurt back.
After last night, I decided it was best if we didn't see
each other again."

"You make us sound as bad as Lonny and Joy."

"Worse."

"It doesn't have to be that way."

"I don't think we're capable of anything else," she
whispered. "Not anymore."

His eyes blazed into hers. "Letty, I *know*."

Chase wasn't making any sense. If he knew they were
incapable of sustaining a relationship, then why had he

been driving like a madman to catch her? Frankly, she wasn't in the mood for this. All she wanted to do was get Cricket and go home.

Chase dropped his arms and paced in front of her. "The day you fainted in the garden, I should've figured it out. For weeks before, Lonny had been telling me how tired you were all the time, how fragile you'd become." He shook his head. "I thought it was because you were depressed and California had spoiled you."

"It did. I'm a soft person, unaccustomed to anything resembling hard work."

Chase ignored her sarcasm. "Then that day in the cemetery...you tried to tell me, didn't you?" But he didn't allow her to answer his question. "You started talking about life and death, and all I could do was get angry with you because I thought you'd lied. I wasn't even listening. If I had been, I would've heard what you were trying to tell me."

Tears blurred her vision as she stood silent and unmoving before him.

"It's the reason you dragged Mary Brandon over to the house for dinner that night, isn't it?" Again he didn't wait for her response. "You figured that if Lonny was married and anything happened to you, Cricket would have a secure home."

"Not exactly," she managed. In the beginning her thoughts had leaned in that direction. But she wasn't the manipulative type, and it had soon become obvious that Lonny wanted nothing to do with her schemes.

Chase placed his hands on her shoulders. "Letty, I saw Dr. Faraday." A hint of a smile brushed the corners of his mouth. "I wanted to go over to the man and hug him."

"Chase, you're still not making any sense."

"Cricket told me that when you came to Rock Springs, you visited a man with a mustache—a man who looked like someone on TV."

"When did she tell you that?"

"Weeks ago. But more damning was that she claimed you went into a room together, and she had to stay outside and wait for you."

"Oh, dear…"

"You can imagine what Lonny and I thought."

"And you believed it?" It seemed that neither Chase nor her brother knew her. Both seemed willing to condemn her on the flimsiest evidence. If she *were* meeting a man, the last person she'd take with her was Cricket. But apparently that thought hadn't so much as entered their minds.

"We didn't know what to believe," Chase answered.

"But you automatically assumed the worst?"

Chase looked properly chagrined. "I know it sounds bad, but there'd been another man in your life before. How was I to know the same thing wasn't happening again?"

"How were you to know?" Letty echoed, slumping against the side of the truck. "How were you to know?" she repeated in a hurt whisper. "What kind of person do you think I am?"

"Letty, I'm sorry."

She covered her eyes and shook her head.

"From the moment you returned, everything's felt wrong. For a while I thought my whole world had been knocked off its axis. Nothing I did seemed to balance it. Today I realized it wasn't my world that was off-kilter, but yours, and I couldn't help feeling the effects."

"You're talking in riddles," she said.

Once more he started pacing, running his fingers through his hair. "Tell me what's wrong. Please. I want to know—I need to know."

"It's my heart," she whispered.

He nodded slowly. "I figured that's what it had to be. Dr. Faraday's specialty was the first thing I noticed when I saw you walk into his office."

"You saw me walk into his office?"

His gaze skirted away from hers. "I followed you to Rock Springs." He continued before she could react. "I'm not proud of that, Letty. Lonny convinced me that you and I needed to talk. After last night, we were both hurting so badly…and I guess I wasn't the best company this morning. Lonny and I went back to the ranch and found your note. From there, we went to Joy's place and she said you'd just left and were heading into town. I drove there and couldn't find you anywhere. That was when I realized you'd probably driven to Rock Springs. If you were meeting a man, I wanted to find out who it was. I had no idea what I'd do—probably nothing—but I had to know."

"So…so you followed me."

He nodded. "And after you walked back to the truck, I went into the office—where I caught sight of the good doctor…and his mustache."

She sighed, shaking her head.

"Letty, you have every reason in the world to be angry. All I can do is apologize."

"No." She met his eyes. "I wanted to tell you. I've kept this secret to myself for so long and there was no one…no one I could tell and I needed—"

"Letty…please, what's wrong with your heart?"

"The doctors discovered a small hole when I was pregnant with Cricket."

"What are they going to do?"

"Surgery."

His face tightened. "When?"

"Dr. Faraday's already scheduled it. I couldn't afford it.... When you saw my first welfare check I wanted to die. I knew what you thought and there wasn't any way to tell you how much I hate being a recipient of... charity."

Chase shut his eyes. "Letty, I failed you—you needed me and I failed you."

"Chase, I'm not going to blame you for that. I've failed you, too."

"I've been so blind, so stupid."

"I've suffered my share of the same afflictions," she said wryly.

"This time I can change things," he said, taking her by the shoulders.

"How?"

"Letty." His fingers were gentle, his eyes tender. "We're getting married."

Chapter 10

"Married," Letty said, repeating the word for the twentieth time in the past hour. Chase sat her down, poured her a cup of coffee and brought it to the kitchen table. Only a few days earlier, he'd thought nothing of watching her do a multitude of chores. Now he was treating her as if she were an invalid. If Letty hadn't been so amused by his change in attitude, she would've found his behavior annoying.

"I'm not arguing with you, Letty Ellison. We're getting married."

"Honestly, Chase, you're being just a little dramatic, don't you think?" She loved him for it, but that didn't alter the facts.

"No!" His face was tormented with guilt. "Why didn't I listen to you? You tried to tell me, and I was so pigheaded, so blind." He knelt in front of her and took both her hands in his, eyes dark and filled with emotion. "You aren't in any condition to fight me on this, Letty, so just do as I ask and don't argue."

"I'm in excellent shape." Chase could be so stubborn, there were times she found it impossible to reason with him. Despite all that, she felt a deep, abiding love for this man. Yet there were a multitude of doubts they hadn't faced or answered.

Chase hadn't said he loved her or even that he cared. But then, Chase always had been a man of few words. When he'd proposed the first time, he'd told her, simply and profoundly, how much he loved her and wanted to build a life with her. That had been the sweetest, most romantic thing she'd ever heard. Letty had supposed that what he'd said that night was going to be all the poetry Chase would ever give her.

"You're scheduled for heart surgery!"

"I'm not on my deathbed yet!"

He went pale at her joke. "Letty, don't even say that."

"What? That I could die? It's been known to happen. But I hope it won't with me. I'm otherwise healthy, and besides, I'm too stubborn to die in a hospital. I'd prefer to do it in my own bed with my grandchildren gathered around me, fighting over who'll get my many jewels." She said this with a hint of dark drama, loving the way Chase's eyes flared with outrage.

In response, he shook his head. "It's not a joking matter."

"I'm going to get excellent care, so don't worry, okay?"

"I'll feel better once I talk to Dr. Faraday myself. But when I do, I'm telling you right now, Letty Ellison, it'll be as your husband."

Letty rolled her eyes. She couldn't believe they were having this discussion. Yet Chase seemed so adamant, so certain that marrying now was the right thing to do. Letty loved him more than ever, but she wasn't nearly as convinced of the need to link their lives through marriage while the surgery still loomed before her. Afterward would be soon enough.

Her reaction seemed to frustrate Chase. "All right, if my words can't persuade you, then perhaps this will." With that he wove his fingers into her hair and brought his lips to hers. The kiss was filled with such tenderness that Letty was left trembling in its aftermath.

Chase appeared equally shaken. His eyes held hers for the longest moment, then he kissed her again. And again—

"Well, isn't this peachy?"

Lonny's harsh tone broke them apart.

"Lonny." Chase's voice sounded odd. He cast a glance at the kitchen clock.

"'I won't be long,'" Lonny mimicked, clearly agitated. "It's been *four* hours, man! Four minutes with that...that woman is more than any guy could endure."

"Where's Cricket?" Letty asked, instantly alarmed.

"With *her*." He turned to Chase, frowning. "Did you know all women stick together, even the little ones? I told Cricket to come with me, and she ran behind Joy and hid. I couldn't believe my eyes—my own niece!"

Letty sprang to her feet. "I'm going to call Joy and find out where Cricket is."

"How'd you get back here?" Chase asked his friend.

"Walked."

Letty paused in the doorway, anxious to hear more of her brother's reply.

"But it's almost twenty miles into town," she said.

"You're telling me?" Lonny moaned and slumped into a chair. The first thing he did was remove his left boot, getting it off his swollen foot with some difficulty. He released a long sigh as it fell to the floor. Next he flexed his toes.

"What happened?"

"She kicked me out! What do you think happened? Do I look like I'd stroll home for the exercise?" His narrowed eyes accused both Letty and Chase. "I don't suppose you gave me another thought after you dropped me off, did you? Oh, no. You two were so interested in playing kissy face that you conveniently forgot about *me*."

"We're sorry, Lonny," Letty said contritely.

Lonny's gaze shifted from Letty to Chase and back again. "I guess there's no need to ask if you patched things up—that much is obvious." By this time, the second dust-caked boot had hit the floor. Lonny peeled off his socks. "Darn it, I've got blisters on my blisters, thanks to the two of you."

"We're getting married," Chase announced without preamble, his look challenging Letty to defy him.

Lonny's head shot up. "What?"

"Letty and I are getting married," Chase repeated. "And the sooner the better."

Lonny's eyes grew suspicious, and when he spoke his voice was almost a whisper. "You're pregnant again, aren't you?"

Letty burst out laughing. "I wish it was that simple."

"She's got a defective heart," Chase said, omitting the details and not giving Letty the opportunity to explain more fully. "She has to have an operation—major surgery from the sound of it."

"Your heart?" Shocked, Lonny stared at her. "Is that why you fainted that day?"

"Partially."

"Why didn't you tell me?"

"I couldn't. Not until I had everything sorted out with the government, and the surgery was scheduled. You would've worried yourself into a tizzy, and I didn't want to dump my problems on top of all your other responsibilities."

"But…" He frowned, apparently displeased with her response. "I could've helped…or at least been more sympathetic. When I think about the way you've cleaned up around here… You had no business working so hard, planting a garden and doing everything else you have. I wish you'd said something, Letty. I feel like a jerk."

"I didn't tell anyone, Lonny. Please understand."

He wiped the back of his hand over his mouth. "I hope you never keep anything like this from me again."

"Believe me, there were a thousand times I wanted to tell you and couldn't."

"I'm going to arrange for the wedding as soon as possible," Chase cut in. "You don't have any objections, do you, Lonny?" His voice was demanding and inflexible.

"Objections? Me? No…not in the least."

"Honestly, Chase," Letty said, patting her brother's shoulder. "This whole conversation is becoming monotonous, don't you think? I haven't agreed to this yet."

"Call Joy and find out where Cricket is," he told her.

Letty moved to the phone and quickly dialed Joy's number. Her friend answered on the second ring. "Joy, it's Letty. Cricket's with you, right?"

"Yes, of course. I wouldn't let that brother of yours take her, and frankly, she wouldn't have gone with him, anyway. I'm sorry, Letty. I really am. You're my friend and I adore Cricket, but your brother is one of the most—" She stopped abruptly. "I...I don't think it's necessary to say anything else. Lonny's your brother—you know him better than anyone."

In some ways Letty felt she didn't know Lonny at all. "Joy, whatever happened, I'm sorry."

"It's not your fault. By the way, did Chase ever catch up with you? I didn't think to mention until after he'd gone that you'd said something about a doctor's appointment."

"Yes, he found me. That's the reason it's taken me so long to get back to you. I'm home now, but Chase and I have been talking for the past hour or so. I didn't mean to leave Cricket with you all this time."

"Cricket's been great, so don't worry about that. We had a great time—at least, we did until your brother decided to visit." She paused and Letty heard regret in her voice when she spoke again. "I don't know what it is with the two of us. I seem to bring out the worst in Lonny—I know he does in me."

Letty wished she knew what it was, too. Discussing this situation over the phone made her a little uncomfortable. She needed to see Joy, read her expression and her body language. "I'll leave now to pick up Cricket."

"Don't bother," Joy said. "I was going out on an errand and I'll be happy to drop her off."

"You're sure that isn't a problem?"

"Positive." Joy hesitated again. "Lonny got home all right, didn't he? I mean it *is* a long walk. When I told him to leave, I didn't mean for him to hike the whole way back. I forgot he didn't have the truck. By the time

I realized it, he'd already started down the sidewalk and he ignored me when I called him."

"Yes, he's home, no worse for wear."

"I'll see you in a little while, then," Joy murmured. She sounded guilty, and Letty suspected she was bringing Cricket home hoping she'd get a chance to apologize. Unfortunately, in Lonny's mood, that would be nearly impossible.

Letty replaced the phone, but not before Lonny shouted from the kitchen, "What do you mean, 'no worse for wear'? I've got blisters that would've brought a lesser man to his knees."

"What did you want me to tell her? That you'd dragged yourself in here barely able to move?"

"Letty, I don't think you should raise your voice. It can't be good for your heart." Chase draped his arm around Letty's shoulders, led her back to the table and eased her onto a chair.

"I'm not an invalid!" she shouted, immediately sorry for her outburst. Chase flinched as if she'd attacked him, and in a way she had.

"Please, Letty, we have a lot to discuss. I want the details for this wedding ironed out before I leave." He knelt in front of her again, and she wondered if he expected her to keel over at any moment.

She sighed. Nothing she'd said seemed to have reached Chase.

"I'm taking a bath," Lonny announced. He stuffed his socks inside his boots and picked them up as he limped out of the kitchen.

"Chase, listen to me," Letty pleaded, her hands framing his worried face. "There's no reason for us to marry now. Once the surgery's over and I'm back on my feet, we can discuss it, if you still feel the same."

"Are you turning me down a second time, Letty?"

"Oh, Chase, you know that isn't it. I told you the other night how much I love you. If my feelings for you didn't change in all the years we were apart, they won't in the next few months."

"Letty, you're not thinking clearly."

"It's my heart that's defective, not my brain."

"I'll arrange for the license right away," he continued as if she hadn't spoken. "If you want a church wedding with all the trimmings, we'll arrange for that later."

"Why not bring Pastor Downey to the hospital, and he can administer the last rites while he's there," she returned flippantly.

"Don't say that!"

"If I agree to this, I'll be married in the church the first time."

"You're not thinking."

"Chase, you're the one who's diving into the deep end here—not me. Give me one solid reason why we should get married now."

"Concern for Cricket ought to be enough."

"What's my daughter got to do with this?"

"She loves me and I love her." His mouth turned up in a smile. "I never guessed I could love her as much as I do. In the beginning, every time I saw her it was like someone had stuck a knife in my heart. One day—" he lowered his gaze to the floor "—I realized that nothing I did was going to keep me from loving that little girl. She's so much a part of you, and I couldn't care about you the way I do and *not* love her."

Hearing him talk about his feelings for Cricket lifted

Letty's sagging spirits. It was the closest he'd come to admitting he loved her.

"More than that, Letty, if something did happen to you, I'd be a better parent than Lonny. Don't you agree?"

Chase was arguably more of a natural, and he had greater patience; to that extent she did agree. "But," she began, "I don't—"

"I know," he said, raising his hand. "You're thinking that you don't have to marry me to make me Cricket's legal guardian, and you're right. But I want you to consider Lonny's pride in all this. If you give me responsibility for Cricket, what's that going to say to your brother? He's your only living relative, and he'd be hurt if he felt you didn't trust him to properly raise your child."

"But nothing's going to happen!" Letty blurted out, knowing she couldn't be completely sure of that.

"But what if the worst *does* happen? If you leave things as they are now, Lonny might have to deal with a grief-stricken five-year-old child. He'd never be able to cope, Letty."

She knew he was right; Lonny would be overwhelmed.

"This situation is much too important to leave everything to fate," he said, closing his argument. "You've got Cricket's future to consider."

"This surgery is a fairly standard procedure." The doctor had told her so himself. Complicated, yes, but not uncommon.

"Yes, but as you said before, things can always go wrong. No matter how slight that chance is, we need to be prepared," Chase murmured.

Letty didn't know what to think. She'd asked Chase to come up with one good argument and he'd outdone himself. In fact, his preoccupation with morbid possibilities struck her as a bit much, considering that he wouldn't let her make even a slight joke about it. However, she understood what he was doing—and why. There were other areas Chase hadn't stopped to consider, though. If they were married, he'd become liable for the cost of her medical care.

"Chase, this surgery isn't cheap. Dr. Faraday said I could be in the hospital as long as two weeks. The hospital bill alone will run into five figures, and that doesn't include the doctor's fee, convalescent care or the pharmaceutical bills, which will add up to much, much more."

"As my wife, you'll be covered by my health insurance policy."

He said this with such confidence that Letty almost believed him. She desperately wanted to, but she was pretty sure that wouldn't be the case. "In all likelihood, your insurance company would deny the claim since my condition is preexisting."

"I can find that out easily enough. I'll phone my broker and have him check my policy right now." He left and returned five minutes later. "It's just as I thought. As my wife, you'd automatically be included for all benefits, no matter when we found out about your heart condition."

It sounded too good to be true. "Chase...I don't know."

"I'm through with listening to all the reasons we can't get married. The fact is, you've rejected one proposal from me, and we both suffered because of it. I won't let you do it a second time. Now will or won't you marry me?"

"You're *sure* about the insurance?"

"Positive." He crouched in front of her and took both her hands in his. "You're going to marry me, Letty. No more arguments, no more ifs, ands or buts." He grinned at her. "So we're getting married?"

Chase made the question more of a statement. "Yes," she murmured, loving him so much. "But you're taking such a risk…"

His eyes narrowed. "Why?"

"Well, because—" She stopped when Cricket came running through the door and held out her arms to her daughter, who flew into them.

"I'm home." Cricket hugged Letty, then rushed over to Chase and threw her arms around his neck with such enthusiasm it nearly knocked him to the floor.

Letty watched them and realized, above anything else, how right Chase was to be concerned about Cricket's welfare in the unlikely event that something went wrong. She drew in a shaky breath and held it until her lungs ached. She loved Chase, and although he hadn't spelled out his feelings for her, she knew he cared deeply for her and for Cricket.

Joy stood sheepishly near the kitchen door, scanning the area for any sign of Lonny. Letty didn't doubt that if her brother were to make an appearance, Joy would quickly turn a designer shade of red.

"Joy, come in," Letty said, welcoming her friend.

She did, edging a few more feet into the kitchen. "I just wanted to make sure Cricket was safely inside."

"Thanks so much for watching her for me this afternoon," Letty said, smiling broadly. "I appreciate it more than you know."

"It wasn't any problem."

A soft snicker was heard from the direction of the hallway. Lonny stood there, obviously having just gotten out of the shower. His dark hair glistened and his shirt was unbuttoned over his blue jeans. His feet were bare.

Joy stiffened. "The only difficulty was when unexpected company arrived and—"

"Uncle Lonny was yelling at Joy," Cricket whispered to her mother.

"Don't forget to mention the part where she was yelling at me," Lonny said.

"I'd better go." Joy stepped back and gripped the doorknob.

"I'm not stopping you," Lonny said sweetly, swaggering into the room.

"I'm on my way out, *Mr.* Ellison. The less I see of you, the better."

"My feelings exactly."

"Lonny. Joy." Letty gestured at each of them. They were both so stubborn. Every time they were within range of each other, sparks ignited—and, in Letty's opinion, they weren't *just* sparks of anger.

"I'm sorry, Letty, but I cannot tolerate your brother."

Lonny moved closer to Joy and Letty realized why his walk was so unusual. He was doing his utmost not to limp, what with all his blisters. Lonny stopped directly in front of Joy, his arms folded over his bare chest. "The same goes for you—only double."

"Goodbye, Letty, Chase. Goodbye, Cricket." Joy completely ignored Lonny and walked out of the house.

The instant she did, Lonny sat down and started to rub his feet. "Fool woman."

"I won't comment on who's acting like a fool here, brother dearest, but the odds are high that you're in the competition."

* * *

Chase sat in the hospital waiting room and picked up a *Time* magazine. He didn't even notice the date until he'd finished three news articles and realized everything he'd read about had happened months ago.

Like the stories in the out-of-date magazine, Chase's life had changed, but the transformation had taken place within a few days, not months.

A week after following Letty into Rock Springs and discovering her secret, he was both a husband and a father. He and Letty had a small wedding at which Pastor Downey had been kind enough to officiate. And now they were facing what could be the most difficult trial of their lives together—her heart surgery.

Setting the magazine aside, Chase wandered outside to the balcony, leaning over the railing as he surveyed the foliage below.

Worry entangled his thoughts and dominated his emotions. And yet a faint smile hovered on his lips. Even when they'd wheeled Letty into the operating room, she'd been joking with the doctors.

A vision of the nurses, clad in surgical green from head to foot, who'd wheeled Letty through the double doors and into the operating room, came back to haunt him. They'd taken Letty from his side, although he'd held her hand as long as possible. Only Chase had seen the momentary look of stark fear, of panic, in her eyes. But her gaze had found his and her expression became one of reassurance.

She was facing a traumatic experience and she'd wanted to encourage *him*.

Her sweet smile hadn't fooled him, though. Letty was

as frightened as he was, perhaps more; she just wouldn't let anyone know it.

She could die in there, and he was powerless to do anything to stop it. The thought of her death made him ache with an agony that was beyond description. Letty had been back in Wyoming for less than two months and already Chase couldn't imagine his life without her. The air on the balcony became stifling. Chase fled.

"Chase!" Lonny came running after him. "What's happened? Where's Letty?"

Chase's eyes were wild as he stared at his brother-in-law. "They took her away twenty minutes ago."

"Hey, are you all right?"

The question buzzed around him like a cloud of mosquitoes, and he shook his head.

"Chase." Lonny clasped his shoulders. "I think you should sit down."

"Cricket?"

"She's fine. Joy's watching her."

Chase nodded, sitting on the edge of the seat, his elbows on his knees, his hands covering his face. Letty had come into his life when he'd least expected her back. She'd offered him love when he'd never thought he'd discover it a second time. Long before, he'd given up the dream of her ever being his wife.

They'd been married less than a day. Only a few hours earlier, Letty had stood before Pastor Downey and vowed to love him—Chase Brown. Her *husband.* And here she was, her life on the line, and they had yet to have their wedding night.

Chase prayed fate wouldn't be so cruel as to rip her from his arms. He wanted the joy of loving her and being loved by her. The joy of fulfilling his dreams and building happiness with her and Cricket and whatever other children they had. A picture began to form in his mind. Two little boys around the ages of five and six. They stood side by side, the best of friends, each with deep blue eyes like Letty's. Their hair was the same shade as his own when he was about their age.

"She's going to make it," Lonny said. "Do you think my sister's going to give up on life without a fight? You know Letty better than that. Relax, would you? Everything's going to work out."

His friend's words dispelled the vision. Chase wished he shared Lonny's confidence regarding Letty's health. He felt so helpless—all he could do was pray.

Chase stood up abruptly. "I'm going to the chapel," he announced, appreciating it when Lonny chose to stay behind.

The chapel was empty, and Chase was grateful for the privacy. He sat in the back pew and stared straight ahead, not knowing what to say or do that would convince the Almighty to keep Letty safe.

He rotated the brim of his hat between his fingers while his mind fumbled for the words to plead for her life. He wanted so much more than that, more than Letty simply surviving the surgery, and then felt selfish for being so greedy. As the minutes ticked past, he sat and silently poured out his heart, talking as he would to a friend.

Chase had never been a man who could speak eloquently—to God or, for that matter, to Letty or anyone else. He knew she'd been looking for words of love the day he'd proposed to her. He regretted now that he hadn't said them. He'd felt them deep in his heart, but something had kept them buried inside. Fear, he suspected.

He'd spoken them once and they hadn't meant enough to keep her in Red Springs. He didn't know if they'd mean enough this time, either.

An eternity passed and he stayed where he was, afraid to face whatever would greet him upon his return. Several people came and went, but he barely noticed them.

The chapel door opened once more and Chase didn't have to turn around to know it was Lonny. Cold fear dampened his brow and he sat immobilized. The longest seconds of his life dragged past before Lonny joined him in the pew.

"The surgery went without a hitch—Letty's going to be just fine," he whispered. "You can see her, but only for a minute."

Chase closed his eyes as the tension drained out of him.

"Did you hear me?"

Chase nodded and turned to his lifelong friend. "Thank God."

The two men embraced and Chase was filled with overwhelming gratitude.

"Be warned, though," Lonny said on their way back to the surgical floor. "Letty's connected to a bunch of tubes and stuff, so don't let it throw you."

Chase nodded.

One of the nurses who'd wheeled his wife into surgery was waiting when Chase returned. She had him dress in sterile surgical garb and instructed him to follow her.

Chase accompanied her into the intensive care unit. Letty was lying on a gurney, perfectly still, and Chase stood by her side. Slowly he bent toward her and saw that her eyes were closed.

"Letty," he whispered. "It's Chase. You're going to be fine."

Chase thought he saw her mouth move in a smile, but he couldn't be sure.

"I love you," he murmured, his voice hoarse with emotion. "I didn't say it before, but I love you—I never stopped. I've lived my life loving you, and nothing will ever change that."

She was pale, so deathly pale, that he felt a sudden sharp fear before he realized the worst of the ordeal was over. The surgery had etched its passing on her lovely face, yet he saw something else, something he hadn't recognized in Letty before. There was a calm strength, a courage that lent him confidence. She was his wife and she'd stand by his side for the rest of their days.

Chase kissed her forehead tenderly before turning to leave.

"I'll see you in the morning," he told her. *And every morning after that,* he thought.

Chapter 11

"Here's some tea," Joy said, carrying a tray into the living room, where Letty was supposed to be resting.

"I'm perfectly capable of getting my own tea, for heaven's sake," Letty mumbled, but when Joy approached, she offered her friend a bright smile. It didn't do any good to complain—and she didn't want to seem ungrateful—although having everyone wait on her was frustrating.

She was reluctant to admit that the most difficult aspect of her recovery was this lengthy convalescence. She'd been released from the hospital two weeks earlier, still very weak; however, she was regaining her strength more and more every day. According to Dr. Faraday, this long period of debility was to be expected. He was pleased with her progress, but Letty found herself becoming increasingly impatient. She yearned to go back to the life she'd just begun with Chase. It was as if their marriage had been put on hold.

They slept in the same bed, lived in the same house, ate the same meals, but they might as well have been brother and sister. Chase seemed to have forgotten that she was his *wife*.

"You're certainly looking good," Joy said as she took the overstuffed chair across from Letty. She poured them each a cup of tea and handed the first one to Letty. Then she picked up her own and sat back.

"I'm feeling good." Her eyes ran lovingly over the room with its polished oak floors, thick braided rug and the old upright piano that had once been hers. The house at Spring Valley had been built years before the one on the Bar E, and Chase had done an excellent job on the upkeep. When she'd been released from the hospital, Chase had brought her to Spring Valley and dutifully carried her over the threshold. But that had been the only husbandly obligation he'd performed the entire time she'd been home.

During her hospital stay, Lonny and Chase had packed her things and Cricket's, and moved them to the house at Spring Valley. Perhaps that had been a mistake, because Letty's frustration mounted as she hungered to become Chase's wife in every way.

She took a sip of the lemon-scented tea, determined to exhibit more patience with herself and everyone else. "I can't thank you enough for all you've done."

Joy had made a point of coming over every afternoon and staying with Letty. Chase had hired an extra man to come over in the early mornings so he could be with her until it was nearly noon. By then she'd showered and dressed and been deposited on the living room couch, where Chase and Cricket made a game of serving her breakfast.

"I've hardly done anything," Joy said, discounting Letty's appreciation. "It's been great getting better acquainted. Cricket is a marvelous little girl, and now that I know you, I understand why. You're a good mother, Letty, but even more important, you're a wonderful person."

"Thank you." Letty smiled softly, touched by Joy's tribute. She'd worked hard to be the right kind of mother, but there were plenty of times when she had her doubts, as any single parent did. Only she wasn't single anymore....

"Speaking of Cricket, where is she?"

"Out visiting her pony," Letty said, and grinned. Cricket thought that marrying Chase had been a brilliant idea. According to her, there wasn't anyone in the whole world who'd make a better daddy. Chase had certainly lived up to her daughter's expectations. He was patient and gentle and kind to a fault. The problem, if it could be termed that, was the way Chase treated *her,* which was no different from the way he treated Cricket. But Letty yearned to be a wife. A real wife.

"What's that?" Joy asked, pointing at a huge box that sat on the floor next to the sofa.

"Lonny brought it over last night. It's some things that belonged to our mother. He thought I might want to sort through them. When Mom died, he packed up her belongings and stuck them in the back bedroom. They've been there ever since."

Joy's eyes fluttered downward at the mention of Lonny's name. Letty picked up on that immediately. "Are you two still not getting along?" she asked, taking a chance, since neither seemed willing to discuss the other.

"Not exactly. Didn't you ask me to write down the recipe for that meatless lasagna? Well, I brought it along and left it in the kitchen."

From little things Letty had heard Lonny, Chase and Joy drop, her brother had made some effort to fix his relationship with Joy while Letty was in the hospital. Evidently whatever he'd said or done had worked, because the minute she mentioned Joy's name to Lonny he got flustered.

For her part, Joy did everything but stand on her head to change the subject. Letty wished she knew what was going on, but after one miserable attempt to involve herself in her brother's love life, she knew better than to try again.

"Mommy," Cricket cried as she came running into the living room, pigtails skipping. "Jennybird ate an apple out of my hand! Chase showed me how to hold it so she wouldn't bite me." She looped her small arms around Letty's neck and squeezed tight. "When can you come and watch me feed Jennybird?"

"Soon." At least, Letty hoped it would be soon.

"Take your time," Joy said. "There's no reason to push yourself, Letty."

"You're beginning to sound like Chase," Letty said with a grin.

Joy shook her head. "I doubt that. I've never seen a man more worried about anyone. The first few days after the surgery, he slept at the hospital. Lonny finally dragged him home, fed him and insisted he get some rest."

Joy wasn't telling Letty anything she didn't already

know. Chase had been wonderful, more than wonderful, from the moment he'd learned about her heart condition. Now, if he'd only start treating her like a wife instead of a roommate....

"I want you to come and see my new bedroom," Cricket said, reaching for Joy's hand. "I've got a new bed with a canopy and a new bedspread and a new pillow and everything."

Joy turned to Letty. "Chase again?"

Letty nodded. "He really spoils her."

"He loves her."

"He loves me," Cricket echoed, pointing a finger at her chest. "But that's okay, because I like being spoiled."

Letty sighed. "I know you do, sweetheart, but enough is enough."

Chase had been blunt about the fact that Cricket was his main consideration when he asked Letty to marry him. His point had been a valid one, but Letty couldn't doubt for an instant that Chase loved them both. Although he hadn't said the words, they weren't necessary; he'd shown his feelings for her in a hundred different ways.

"I'd better go take a gander at Cricket's room, and then I should head back into town," Joy said as she stood. "There's a casserole in the refrigerator for dinner."

"Joy!" Letty protested. "You've done enough."

"Shush," Joy said, waving her index finger under Letty's nose. "It was a new recipe, and two were as easy to make as one."

"You're going to have to come up with a better excuse than that, Joy. You've been trying out new recipes all week." Although she chided her friend, Letty was grateful for all the help Joy had given her over the past month. Her visits in the afternoons had brought Chase peace of mind so he could work outside without constantly worrying about Letty. The casseroles and salads Joy contributed for dinner were a help, too.

Chase wouldn't allow Letty to do any of the household chores yet and insisted on preparing their meals himself. Never in a thousand years would Letty have dreamed that she'd miss doing laundry or dishes. But there was an unexpected joy in performing menial tasks for the people she loved. In the past few weeks, she'd learned some valuable lessons about life. She'd experienced the nearly overwhelming need to do something for someone else instead of being the recipient of everyone else's goodwill.

The house was peaceful and still as Joy followed Cricket up the stairs. When they returned a few minutes later, Cricket was yawning and dragging her blanket behind her.

"I want to sleep with you today, Mommy."

"All right, sweetheart."

Cricket climbed into the chair across from Letty, which Joy had recently vacated, and curled up, wrapping her blanket around her. Letty knew her daughter would be asleep within five minutes.

Watching the child, Letty was grateful that Cricket would be in the morning kindergarten class, since she still seemed to need an afternoon nap.

Joy worked in the kitchen for a few minutes, then paused in the doorway, smiled at Cricket and waved goodbye. Letty heard the back door close as her friend left the house.

In an hour or so Chase would come to check her. Letty cherished these serene moments alone and lay down on the couch to nap, too. A few minutes later she realized she wasn't tired, and feeling good about that, she sat up. The extra time was like an unexpected gift and her gaze fell on the carton her brother had brought. Carefully Letty pried open the lid.

Sorting through her mother's personal things was bound to be a painful task, Letty thought as she lovingly removed each neatly packed item from the cardboard container.

She pulled out a stack of old pattern books and set those aside. Her mother had loved to sew, often spending a winter evening flipping through these pages, planning new projects. Letty had learned her sewing skills from Maren, although it had been years since she'd sat down at a sewing machine.

Sudden tears welled up in Letty's eyes at the memories of her mother. Happy memories of a loving mother who'd worked much too hard and died far too young. A twinge of resentment struck her. Maren Ellison had given her life's blood to the Bar E ranch. It had been her husband's dream, not hers, and yet her mother had made the sacrifice.

Letty wiped away her tears and felt a surge of sorrow over her mother's death, coming so soon after her father's. Maren had deserved a life so much better than the one she'd lived.

Once Letty's eyes had cleared enough to continue her task, she lifted out several large strips of brightly colored material in odd shapes and sizes and set them on the sofa. Bits and pieces of projects that had been carefully planned by her mother and now waited endlessly for completion.

Then Letty withdrew what had apparently been her

mother's last project. With extreme caution, she unfolded the top of a vividly colored quilt, painstakingly stitched by hand.

Examining the patchwork piece produced a sense of awe in Letty. She was astonished by the time and effort invested in the work, and even more astonished that she recognized several swatches of the material her mother had used in the quilt. The huge red star at the very center had been created from a piece of leftover fabric from a dress her mother had made for Letty the summer she'd left home. A plaid piece in one corner was from an old Western shirt she'd worn for years. After recognizing one swatch of material after another, Letty realized that her mother must have been making the quilt as a Christmas or birthday gift for her.

Lovingly she ran the tips of her fingers over the cloth as her heart lurched with a sadness that came from deep within. Then it dawned on her that without too much difficulty she'd be able to finish the quilt herself. Everything she needed was right here. The task would be something to look forward to next winter, when the days were short and the nights were Arctic-cold.

After folding the quilt top and placing it back in the box, Letty discovered a sketchbook, tucked against the side of the carton. Her heart soared with excitement as she reverently picked it up. Her mother had loved to draw, and her talent was undeniable.

The first sketch was of a large willow against the backdrop of an evening sky. Letty recognized the tree immediately. Her mother had sketched it from their front porch years ago. The willow had been cut down when Letty was in her early teens, after lightning had struck it.

Letty had often found her mother sketching, but the

opportunity to complete any full-scale paintings had been rare. The book contained a handful of sketches, and once more Letty felt a wave of resentment. Maren Ellison had deserved the right to follow her own dreams. She was an artist, a woman who'd loved with a generosity that touched everyone she knew.

"Letty." Chase broke into her thoughts as he hurried into the house. He paused when he saw Cricket asleep in the chair. "I saw Joy leave," he said, his voice a whisper.

"Chase, there's no need to worry. I can stay by myself for an hour or two."

He nodded, then wiped his forearm over his brow and awkwardly leaned over to brush his lips over her cheek. "I figured I'd drop in and make sure everything's under control."

"It is." His chaste kiss only frustrated Letty. She wanted to shout at him that the time had come for him to act like a married man instead of a saint.

"What's all this?" Chase asked, glancing around her. Letty suspected he only slept three hours a night. He never went to bed at the same time she did, and he was always up before she even stirred. Occasionally, she heard him slip between the sheets, but he stayed so far over on his side of the bed that they didn't even touch.

"A quilt," Letty said, pointing at the cardboard box.

"Is that the box Lonny brought here?"

"Yes. Mom was apparently working on it when she died. She was making it for me." Letty had to swallow the lump in her throat before she could talk again. She turned and pointed to the other things she'd found. "There's some pieces of material in here and pattern books, as well."

"What's this?"

"A sketch pad. Mom was an artist," Letty said proudly.

His eyebrows drew together. "I didn't realize that," he said slowly. He flipped through the book of pencil sketches. "She was very talented."

Chase sounded a little surprised that he hadn't known about her mother's artistic abilities. "Mom was an incredible woman. I don't think anyone ever fully appreciated that—I know I didn't."

Chase stepped closer and massaged Letty's shoulders with tenderness and sympathy. "You still miss her, don't you?"

Letty nodded. Her throat felt thick, and she couldn't express everything she was feeling, all the emotion rising up inside her.

Chase knelt in front of her, his gaze level with hers. He slipped his callused hands around the nape of her neck as he brought her into his arms. Letty rested her head against his shoulder, reveling in his warm embrace. It had been so long since he'd held her and even longer since he'd kissed her...really kissed her.

Raising her head slightly, she ran the moist tip of her tongue along the side of his jaw. He filled her senses. Chase tensed, but still Letty continued her sensual movements, nibbling at his earlobe, taking it into her mouth...

"Letty," he groaned, "no."

"No what?" she asked coyly, already knowing his answer. Her mouth roved where it wanted, while she held his face in her hands, directing him as she wished. She savored the edge of his mouth, teasing him, tantalizing him, until he moaned anew.

"Letty." He brought his hands to her shoulders. Letty was certain he'd meant to push her away, but before he could, she raised her arms and slid them around his neck. Then she leaned against him. Chase held her there.

"Letty." Her name was a plea.

"Chase, kiss me, please," she whispered. "I've missed you so much."

Slowly, as if uncertain he was doing the right thing, Chase lowered his mouth to touch her parted lips with his. Letty didn't move, didn't breathe, for fear he'd stop. She would've screamed in frustration if he had. His brotherly pecks on the cheeks were worse than no kisses at all; they just made her crave everything she'd been missing. Apparently Chase had been feeling equally deprived, because he settled his mouth over hers with a passion and need that demanded her very breath.

"What's taken you so long?" she asked, her voice urgent.

He answered her with another fiery kiss that robbed her of what little strength she still had. Letty heard a faint moan from deep within his chest.

"Letty…this is ridiculous," he murmured, breaking away, his shoulders heaving.

"What is?" she demanded.

"My kissing you like this."

He thrust his fingers through his hair. His features were dark and angry.

"I'm your *wife,* Chase Brown. Can't a man kiss his wife?"

"Not like this…not when she's— You're recovering from heart surgery." He moved away from her and briefly closed his eyes, as though he needed an extra moment to compose himself. "Besides, Cricket's here."

"I'm your wife," Letty returned, not knowing what else to say.

"You think I need to be reminded of that?" he shot back. He got awkwardly to his feet and grabbed his hat and gloves. "I have to get to work," he said, slamming his hat on top of his head. "I'll be home in a couple of hours."

Letty couldn't have answered him had she tried. She felt like a fool now.

"Do you need anything before I go?" he asked without looking at her.

"No."

He took several steps away from her, stopped abruptly, then turned around. "It's going to be months before we can do—before we can be husband and wife in the full sense," he said grimly. "I think it would be best if we avoided situations like this in the future. Don't you agree?"

Letty shrugged. "I'm sorry," she whispered.

"So am I," he returned grimly and left the house.

"Mommy, I want to learn how to play another song," Cricket called from the living room. She was sitting at the upright piano, her feet crossed and swinging. Letty had taught her "Chopsticks" earlier in the day. She'd been impressed with how easily her daughter had picked it up. Cricket had played it at least twenty times and was eager to master more tunes.

"In a little while," Letty said. She sat at the kitchen table, peeling potatoes for dinner and feeling especially proud of herself for this minor accomplishment. Chase would be surprised and probably a little concerned when he realized what she'd done. But the surgery was several weeks behind her and it was time to take on some of the lighter responsibilities. Preparing dinner was hardly an onerous task; neither was playing the piano with her daughter.

Seeking her mother's full attention, Cricket headed into the kitchen and reached for a peeler and a potato. "I'll help you."

"All right, sweetheart."

The chore took only a few minutes, Letty peeling four spuds to Cricket's one. Next the child helped her collect the peelings and clean off the table before leading her back into the living room.

"Play something else, Mommy," the little girl insisted, sitting on the bench beside Letty.

Letty's fingers ran lazily up and down the keyboard in a quick exercise. She hadn't touched the piano until after her surgery. Letty supposed there was some psychological reason for this, but she didn't want to analyze it now. Until Cricket's birth, music had dominated her life. But after her daughter's arrival, her life had turned in a different direction. Music had become a way of entertaining herself and occasionally brought her some paying work, although—obviously—*that* was no longer the case.

"Play a song for me," Cricket commanded.

Letty did, smiling as the familiar keys responded to her touch. This piano represented so much love and so many good times. Her mother had recognized Letty's musical gift when she was a child, only a little older than Cricket. Letty had started taking piano lessons in first grade. When she'd learned as much as the local music instructors could teach her, Maren had driven her into

Rock Springs every week. A two-hour drive for a half-hour lesson.

"Now show me how to do it like you," Cricket said, completely serious. "I want to play just as good as you."

"Sweetheart, I took lessons for seven years."

"That's okay, 'cause I'm five."

Letty laughed. "Here, I'll play 'Mary Had a Little Lamb' and then you can move your fingers the way I do." Slowly she played the first lines, then dropped her hands on her lap while Cricket perfectly mimicked the simple notes.

"This is fun," Cricket said, beaming with pride.

Ten minutes later, she'd memorized the whole song. With two musical pieces in her repertoire, Cricket was convinced she was possibly the most gifted musical student in the history of Red Springs.

The minute Chase was in the door, Cricket flew to his side. "Chase! Chase, come listen."

"Sweetie, let him wash up first," Letty said with a smile.

"What is it?" Chase asked, his amused gaze shifting from Cricket to Letty, then back to Cricket again.

"It's a surprise," Cricket said, practically jumping up and down with enthusiasm.

"You'd better go listen," Letty told him. "She's been waiting for you to come inside."

Chase washed his hands at the kitchen sink, but hesitated when he saw the panful of peeled potatoes. "Who did this?"

"Mommy and me," Cricket told him impatiently.

"Letty?"

"And I lived to tell about it. I'm feeling stronger every

day," she pointed out, "and there's no reason I can't start taking up the slack around here a little more."

"But—"

"Don't argue with me, Chase," she said in what she hoped was a firm voice.

"It hasn't been a month yet," he countered, frowning.

"I feel fine!"

It looked as if he wanted to argue, but he apparently decided not to, probably because Cricket was tugging anxiously at his arm, wanting him to sit down in the living room so he could hear her recital.

Letty followed them and stood back as Cricket directed Chase to his favorite overstuffed chair.

"You stay here," she said.

Once Chase was seated, she walked proudly over to the piano and climbed onto the bench. Then she looked over her shoulder and ceremoniously raised her hands. Lowering them, she put every bit of emotion her five-year-old heart possessed into playing "Chopsticks."

When she'd finished, she slid off the seat, tucked her arm around her middle and bowed. "You're supposed to clap now," she told Chase.

He obliged enthusiastically, and Letty stifled a laugh at how seriously Cricket was taking this.

"For my next number, I'll play—" she stopped abruptly. "I want you to guess."

Letty sat on the armchair, resting her hand on his shoulder. "She's such a ham."

Chase grinned up at her, his eyes twinkling with shared amusement.

"I must have quiet," Cricket grumbled. "You aren't supposed to talk now...."

Once more Cricket gave an Oscar-quality performance.

"Bravo, bravo," Chase shouted when she'd slipped off the piano bench.

Cricket flew to Chase's side and climbed into his lap. "Mommy taught me."

"She seems to have a flair for music," Letty said.

"I'm not as good as Mommy, though." Cricket sighed dramatically. "She can play anything…and she sings pretty, too. She played for me today and we had so much fun."

Letty laughed. "I'm thinking of giving Cricket piano lessons myself," Letty said, sure that Chase would add his wholehearted approval.

To her surprise, Letty felt him tense beneath her fingers. It was as if all the joy had suddenly and mysteriously disappeared from the room.

"Chase, what's wrong?" Letty whispered.

"Nothing."

"Cricket, go get Chase a glass of iced tea," Letty said. "It's in the refrigerator."

"Okay," the child said, eager as always to do anything for Chase.

As soon as the little girl had left, Letty spoke. "Do you object to Cricket taking piano lessons?"

"Why should I?" he asked, without revealing any emotion. "As you say, she's obviously got talent."

"Yes, but—"

"We both know where she got it from, don't we," he said with a resigned sigh.

"I would think you'd be pleased." Chase had always loved it when she played and sang; now he could barely stand it if she so much as looked at the piano.

"I *am* pleased," he declared. With that, he walked into the kitchen, leaving Letty more perplexed than ever.

For several minutes, Letty sat there numbly while Chase talked to Cricket, praising her efforts.

Letty had thought Chase would be happy, but he clearly wasn't. She didn't understand it.

"Someday," she heard him tell Cricket, his voice full of regret, "you'll play as well as your mother."

Chapter 12

Astride Firepower at the top of a hill overlooking his herd, Chase stared vacantly into the distance. Letty was leaving; he'd known it from the moment he discovered she'd been playing the piano again. The niggling fear had been with him for days, gnawing at his heart.

Marrying her had been a gamble, a big one, but he'd accepted it, grateful for the opportunity to have her and Cricket in his life, even if it was destined to be for a short time. Somehow, he'd find the courage to smile and let her walk away. He'd managed it once and, if he had to, he could do it again.

"Chase."

At the sound of his name, carried softly on the wind, Chase twisted in the saddle, causing the leather to creak. He frowned as he recognized Letty, riding one of his mares, advancing slowly toward him. Her face was lit with a bright smile and she waved, happy and elated. Sadly he shared little of her exhilaration. All he could think about was his certainty that she'd soon be gone.

Letty rode with a natural grace, as if she'd been born to it. Her beauty almost broke his heart.

Chase swallowed, and a sense of dread swelled up inside him. Dread and confusion—the same confusion that being alone with Letty always brought. He wanted her, and yet he had to restrain himself for the sake of her health. He wanted to keep her with him, and yet he'd have to let her go if that was her choice.

Sweat broke out across his upper lip. He hadn't touched Letty from the moment he'd learned of her heart condition. Now she needed to recover from her surgery. It was debatable, however, whether he could continue to resist her much longer. Each day became more taxing than the one before. Just being close to her sapped his strength. Sleeping with her only inches away had become almost impossible and as a result he was constantly tired…as well as frustrated.

Chase drew himself up when she joined him. "What are you doing here?" he asked. He sounded harsher than he'd intended.

"You didn't come back to the house for lunch," she murmured.

"Did it occur to you that I might not be hungry?" He was exhausted and impatient and hated the way he was speaking to her, but he felt himself fighting powerful emotions whenever he was near her.

"I brought you some lunch," Letty said, not reacting to his rudeness. "I thought we…we might have a picnic."

"A picnic?" he echoed with a short sarcastic laugh.

Letty seemed determined to ignore his mood, and

smiled up at him, her eyes gleaming with mischief. "Yes," she said, "a picnic. You work too hard, Chase. It's about time you relaxed a little."

"Where's Cricket?" he asked, his tongue nearly sticking to the roof of his mouth. It was difficult enough keeping his eyes off Letty without having to laze around on some nice, soft grass and pretend he had an appetite. Oh, he was hungry, all right, but it was Letty he needed; only his wife would satisfy his cravings.

"Cricket went into town with Joy," she said, sliding down from the mare. "She's helping Joy get her new classroom ready, although it's questionable how much help she'll actually be. School's only a couple of weeks away, you know."

While she was speaking, Letty emptied the saddlebags. She didn't look back at him as she spread a blanket across the grass, obviously assuming he'd join her without further argument. Next she opened a large brown sack, then knelt and pulled out sandwiches and a thermos.

"Chase?" She looked up at him.

"I...I'm not hungry."

"You don't have to eat if you don't want, but at least take a break."

Reluctantly Chase climbed out of the saddle. It was either that or sit where he was and stare down her blouse.

Despite the fact that Letty had spent weeks inside the house recuperating, her skin was glowing and healthy, Chase noted. Always slender, she'd lost weight and had worked at putting it back on, but he'd never guess it, looking at her now. Her jeans fit snugly, and her lithe, elegant body seemed to call out to him....

"I made fresh lemonade. Would you like some?" She

interrupted his tortured thoughts, opening the thermos and filling a paper cup, ready to hand it to him.

"No...thanks." Chase felt both awkward and out of place. He moved closer to her, drawn by an invisible cord. He stared at her longingly, then dropped to his knees, simply because standing demanded so much energy.

"The lemonade's cold," she coaxed. As if to prove her point, she took a sip.

The tip of her tongue came out and she licked her lips. Watching that small action, innocent yet sensuous, was like being kicked in the stomach.

"I said I didn't want any," he said gruffly.

They were facing each other, and Letty's gaze found his. Her eyes were wide, hurt and confused. She looked so beautiful.

He realized he should explain that he knew she was planning to go back to California, but his tongue refused to cooperate. Letty continued to peer at him, frowning slightly, as though trying to identify the source of his anger.

At that instant, Chase knew he was going to kiss her and there wasn't a thing he could do to stop himself. The ache to touch her had consumed him for weeks. He reached out for her now, easing her into his embrace. She came willingly, offering no resistance.

"Letty..."

Intuitively she must have known his intent, because she closed her eyes and tilted back her head.

At first, as if testing the limits of his control, Chase merely touched his mouth to hers. The way her fingers curled into his chest told him she was as eager for his touch as he was for hers. He waited, savoring the taste and feel of her in his arms, and when he could deny himself no longer, he deepened the kiss.

With a soft sigh, Letty brought her arms around his neck. Chase's heart was pounding and he pulled back for a moment, breathing in her delectable scent—wildflowers and some clean-smelling floral soap.

He ran his fingers through her hair as he kissed her again. He stopped to breathe, then slowly lowered them both to the ground, lying side by side. Then, he sought her mouth once more. He felt consumed with such need, yet forced himself to go slowly, gently....

Since Letty had returned to Red Springs, Chase had kissed her a number of times. For the past few weeks he'd gone to sleep each night remembering how good she'd felt in his arms. He had treasured the memories, not knowing when he'd be able to hold her and kiss her again. *Soon,* he always promised himself; he'd make love to her soon. Every detail of every time he'd touched her was emblazoned on his mind, and he could think of little else.

Now that she was actually in his arms, he discovered that the anticipation hadn't prepared him for how perfect it would be. The reality outdistanced his memory—and his imagination.

His mouth came down hard on hers, releasing all the tension inside him. Letty's breathing was labored and harsh and her fingers curled more tightly into the fabric of his shirt, then began to relax as she gave herself completely over to his kiss.

Chase was drowning, sinking fast. At first he associated the rumbling in his ears with the thunder of his own heartbeat. It took him a moment to realize it was the sound of an approaching horse.

Chase rolled away from Letty with a groan.

She sat up and looked at him, dazed, hurt, confused.

"Someone's riding toward us," he said tersely.

"Oh."

That one word bespoke frustration and disappointment and a multitude of other emotions that reflected his own. He retrieved his gloves and stood, using his body to shield Letty from any curious onlooker.

Within seconds Lonny trotted into view.

"It's your brother," Chase warned, then added something low and guttural that wasn't meant for her ears. His friend had quite the sense of timing.

Chase saw Letty turn away and busy herself with laying out their lunch.

As Lonny rode up, pulling on his horse's reins, Chase glared at him.

More than a little chagrined, Lonny muttered, "Am I interrupting something?"

"Of course not," Letty said, sounding unlike herself. She kept her back to him, making a task of unfolding napkins and unwrapping sandwiches.

Chase contradicted her words with a scowl. The last person he wanted to see was Lonny. To his credit, his brother-in-law looked as if he wanted to find a hole to hide in, but that didn't help now.

"Actually, I was looking for Letty," Lonny explained, after clearing his throat. "I wanted to talk to her about... something. I stopped at the house, but there wasn't anyone around. Your new guy, Mel, was working in the barn and he told me she'd come out here. I guess, uh, I should've figured it out."

"It would've been appreciated," Chase muttered savagely.

"I brought lunch out to Chase," Letty said.

Chase marveled that she could recover so quickly.

"There's plenty if you'd care to join us," she said.

"You might as well," Chase said, confirming the invitation. The moment had been ruined and he doubted they'd be able to recapture it.

Lonny's gaze traveled from one to the other. "Another time," he said, turning his horse. "I'll talk to you later, sis."

Letty nodded, and Lonny rode off.

"You should go back to the house yourself," Chase said without meeting her eyes.

It wasn't until Letty had repacked the saddlebags and ridden after her brother that Chase could breathe normally again.

Lonny was waiting for Letty when she trotted into the yard on Chase's mare. His expression was sheepish, she saw as he helped her down from the saddle, although she was more than capable of doing it on her own.

"I'm sorry, Letty," he mumbled. Hot color circled his ears. "I should've thought before I went traipsing out there looking for you."

"It's all right," she said, offering him a gracious smile. There was no point in telling him he'd interrupted a scene she'd been plotting for days. Actually, her time with Chase told her several things, and all of them excited her. He was going crazy with desire for her. He wanted her as much as she wanted him.

"*You* may be willing to forgive me, but I don't think Chase is going to be nearly as generous."

"Don't worry about it," she returned absently. Her

brother had foiled Plan A, but Plan B would go into action that very evening.

"Come on in and I'll get you a glass of lemonade."

"I could use one," Lonny said, obediently following his sister into the kitchen.

Letty could see that something was troubling her brother, and whatever it was appeared to be serious. His eyes seemed clouded and stubbornly refused to meet hers.

"What did you want to talk to me about?"

He sat down at the scarred oak table. Removing his hat, he set it on the chair beside him. "Do you remember when you first came home you invited Mary Brandon over to the house?"

Letty wasn't likely to forget it; the evening had been a catastrophe.

"You seemed to think I needed a wife," Lonny continued.

"Yes…mainly because you'd become consumed by the ranch. Your rodeo days are over—"

"My glory days," he said with a self-conscious laugh.

"You quit because you had to come back to the Bar E when Dad got sick. Now you're so wrapped up in the ranch, all your energy's channeled in that one direction."

He nodded, agreeing with her, which surprised Letty.

"The way I see it, Lonny, you work too hard. You've given up—been forced to give up—too much. You've grown so…short-tempered. In my arrogant way I saw you as lonely and decided to do something about it." She was nervous about her next remark but made it anyway. "I was afraid this place was going to suck the life out of you, like I thought it had with Mom."

"Are you still on that kick?" he asked, suddenly angry. Then he sighed, a sound of resignation.

"We had a big fight over this once, and I swore I wouldn't mention it again, but honestly, Letty, you're seeing Mom as some kind of martyr. She loved the ranch…she loved Wyoming."

"I know," Letty answered quietly.

"Then why are you arguing with me about it?"

Letty ignored the question, deciding that discretion was well-advised at the moment. "It came to me after I sorted through the carton of her things that you brought over," she said, toying with her glass. "I studied the quilt Mom was making and realized that her talent *wasn't* wasted. She just transferred it to another form—quilting. At first I was surprised that she hadn't used the sewing machine to join the squares. Every stitch in that quilt top was made by hand, every single one of them."

"I think she felt there was more of herself in it that way," Lonny suggested.

Letty smiled in agreement. "I'm going to finish it this winter. I'll do the actual quilting—and I'll do it by hand, just like she did."

"It's going to be beautiful," Lonny said. "Really beautiful."

Letty nodded. "The blending of colors, the design—it all spells out how much love and skill Mom put into it. When I decided to leave Red Springs after high school, I went because I didn't want to end up like Mom, and now I realize I couldn't strive toward a finer goal."

Lonny frowned again. "I don't understand. You left for California because you didn't want to be a rancher's wife, and yet you married Chase…."

"I know. But I love Chase. I always have. It wasn't

being a rancher's wife that I objected to so much. Yes, the life is hard. But the rewards are plentiful. I knew that nine years ago, and I know it even more profoundly now. My biggest fear was that I'd end up dedicating my life to ranching like Mom did and never achieve my own dreams."

"But Mom was happy. I never once heard her complain. I guess that's why I took such offense when you made it sound as if she'd wasted her life. Nothing could be farther from the truth."

"I know that now," Letty murmured. "But I didn't understand it for a long time. What upset me most was that I felt she could never paint the way she wanted to. There was always something else that needed her attention, some other project that demanded her time. It wasn't until I saw the quilt that I understood.... She sketched for her own enjoyment, but the other things she made were for the people she loved. The quilt she was working on when she died was for me, and it's taught me perhaps the most valuable lesson of my life."

Lonny's face relaxed into a smile. "I'm glad, Letty. In the back of my mind I had the feeling that once you'd recuperated from the surgery, you'd get restless. But you won't, will you?"

"You've got to be kidding," she said with a laugh. "I'm a married woman, you know." She twisted the diamond wedding band around her finger. "My place is here, with Chase. I plan to spend the rest of my life with him."

"I'm glad to hear that," he said again, his relief evident.

"We got off the subject, didn't we?" she said apologetically. "You wanted to talk to me." He hadn't told her why, but she could guess....

"Yes.... Well, it has to do with..." He hesitated, as if saying Joy Fuller's name would somehow conjure her up.

"Joy?" Letty asked.

Lonny nodded.

"What about her?"

In response, Lonny jerked his fingers through his hair and glared at the ceiling. "I'm telling you, Letty, no one's more shocked by this than me. I've discovered that I like her. I...mean I *really* like her. The fact is, I can't stop thinking about Joy, but every time I try to talk to her, I say something stupid, and before I know it, we're arguing."

Letty bent her head to show she understood. She'd witnessed more than one of her brother's clashes with Joy.

"We don't just argue like normal civilized people," Lonny continued. "She can make me so angry I don't even know what I'm saying anymore."

Letty lowered her eyes, afraid her smile would annoy her brother, especially since he'd come to her for help. Except that, at the moment, she didn't feel qualified to offer him any advice.

"The worst part is," he went on, "I was in town this morning, and I heard that Joy's agreed to go out with Glen Brewster. The thought of her dating another man has me all twisted up inside."

"Glen Brewster?" That surprised Letty. "Isn't he the guy who manages the grocery store?"

"One and the same," Lonny confirmed, scowling. "Can you imagine her going out with someone like Glen? He's all wrong for her!"

"Have you asked Joy out yourself?"

The way the color streaked his face told Letty what she needed to know. "I don't think I should answer that." He lifted his eyes piteously. "I want to take her out, but everyone's working against me."

"Everyone?"

He cleared his throat. "No, not everyone. I guess I'm my own worst enemy—I know that sounds crazy. I mean, it's not like I haven't had girlfriends before. But she's different from the girls I met on the rodeo circuit." He stared down at the newly waxed kitchen floor. "All I want you to do is tell me what a woman wants from a man. A woman like Joy. If I know that, then maybe I can do something right—for once."

The door slammed in the distance. Lonny's gaze flew up to meet Letty's. "Joy?"

"Probably."

"Oh, great," he groaned.

"Don't panic."

"Me?" he asked with a short, sarcastic laugh. "Why should I do that? The woman's told me in no uncertain terms that she never wants to see me again. Her last words to me were—and I quote—'take a flying leap into the nearest cow pile.'"

"What did you say to her, for heaven's sake?"

He shrugged, looking uncomfortable. "I'd better not repeat it."

"Oh, Lonny! Don't you ever learn? She's not one of your buckle bunnies—but you already know that. Maybe if you'd quit insulting her, you'd be able to have a civil conversation."

"I've decided something," he said. "I don't know how

or when, but I'm going to marry her." The words had no sooner left his lips than the screen door opened.

Cricket came flying into the kitchen, bursting to tell her mother about all her adventures with Joy at the school. She started speaking so fast that the words ran together. "I-saw-my-classroom-and-I-got-to-meet-Mrs.-Webber…and I sat in a real desk and everything!"

Joy followed Cricket into the kitchen, but stopped abruptly when she saw Lonny. The expression on her face suggested that if he said one word to her—one word—she'd leave.

As if taking his cue, Lonny reached for his hat and stood. "I'd better get back to work. Good talking to you, Letty," he said stiffly. His gaze skipped from his sister to Joy, and he inclined his head politely. "Hello, *Ms.* Fuller."

"*Mr.* Ellison." Joy dipped her head, too, ever so slightly.

They gave each other a wide berth as Lonny stalked out of the kitchen. Before he opened the screen door, he sent a pleading glance at Letty, but she wasn't sure what he expected her to do.

Chase didn't come in for dinner, but that didn't surprise Letty. He'd avoided her so much lately that she rarely saw him in the evenings anymore. Even Cricket had commented on it. She obviously missed him, although he made an effort to work with her and Jennybird, the pony.

The house was dark, and Cricket had been asleep for hours, when Letty heard the back door open. Judging by the muffled sounds Chase was making, she knew he was in the kitchen, washing up. Next he would shower. Some nights he came directly to bed; others he'd sit in front of the TV, delaying the time before he joined her. In the mornings he'd be gone before she woke. Letty didn't know any man who worked as physically hard as Chase did on so little rest.

"You're later than usual tonight," she said, standing barefoot in the kitchen doorway.

He didn't turn around when he spoke. "There's lots to do this time of year."

"Yes, I know," she answered, willing to accept his lame excuse. "I didn't get much of a chance to talk to you this afternoon."

"What did Lonny want?"

So he was going to change the subject. Fine, she'd let him. "Joy problems," she told him.

Chase nodded, opened the refrigerator and took out a carton of milk. He poured himself a glass, then drank it down in one long swallow.

"Would you like me to run you a bath?"

"I'd rather take a shower." Reluctantly he turned to face her.

This was the moment Letty had been waiting for. She'd planned it all night. The kitchen remained dark; the only source of light was the moon, which cast flickering shadows over the wall. Letty was leaning against the doorjamb, her hands behind her back. Her nightgown had been selected with care, a frothy see-through piece of chiffon that covered her from head to foot, yet revealed everything.

Letty knew she'd achieved the desired effect when the glass Chase was holding slipped from his hand and dropped to the floor. By some miracle it didn't shatter. Chase bent over to retrieve it, and even standing several yards away, Letty could see that his fingers were trembling.

"I saw Dr. Faraday this morning," she told him, keeping her voice low and seductive. "He gave me a clean bill of health."

"Congratulations."

"I think this calls for a little celebration, don't you?"

"Celebration?"

"I'm your wife, Chase, but you seem to have conveniently forgotten that fact. There's no reason we should wait any longer."

"Wait?" He was beginning to sound like an echo.

Letty prayed for calm.

Before she could say anything else, he added abruptly, "I've been out on the range for the past twelve hours. I'm dirty and tired and badly in need of some hot water."

"I've been patient all this time. A few more minutes won't kill me." She'd never thought it would come to this, but she was going to have to seduce her own husband. So be it. She was hardly an expert in the techniques of seduction, but instinct was directing her behavior—instinct and love.

"Letty, I'm not in the mood. As I said, I'm tired and—"

"You were in the mood this afternoon," she whispered, deliberately moistening her lips with the tip of her tongue.

He ground out her name, his hands clenched at his sides. "Perhaps you should go back to bed."

"Back to bed?" She straightened, hands on her hips. "You were supposed to take one look at me and be overcome with passion!"

"I was?"

He was silently laughing at her, proving she'd done an excellent job of making a fool of herself. Tears sprang to her eyes. Before the surgery and directly afterward, Chase had been the model husband—loving, gentle, concerned. He couldn't seem to spend enough time with her. Lately just the opposite was true. The man who stood across from her now wasn't the same man she'd married, and she didn't understand what had changed him.

Chase stood where he was, feet planted apart, as if he expected her to defy him.

Without another word, Letty turned and left. Tears blurred her vision as she walked into their room and sank down on the edge of the bed. Covering her face with both hands, she sat there, her thoughts whirling, gathering momentum, until she lost track of time.

"Letty."

She vaulted to her feet and wiped her face. "Don't you *Letty* me, you…you arrogant cowboy." That was the worst thing she could come up with on short notice.

He was fresh from the shower, wearing nothing more than a towel around his waist.

"I had all these romantic plans for seducing you—and…and you made me feel I'm about as appealing as an old steer. So you want to live like brother and sister? Fine. Two can play this game, fellow." She pulled the chiffon nightie over her head and yanked open a drawer, grabbing an old flannel gown and donning that. When she'd finished, she whirled around to face him.

To her chagrin, Chase took one look at her and burst out laughing.

Chapter 13

"Don't you *dare* laugh at me," Letty cried, her voice trembling.

"I'm not," he told her. The humor had evaporated as if it had never been. What he'd told her earlier about being tired was true; he'd worked himself to the point of exhaustion. But he'd have to be a crazy man to reject the very thing he wanted most. Letty had come to him, demolished every excuse not to hold and kiss her, and like an idiot he'd told her to go back to bed. Who did he think he was? A man of steel? He wasn't kidding anyone, least of all himself.

Silently he walked around the end of the bed toward her.

For every step Chase advanced, Letty took one away from him, until the backs of her knees were pressed against the mattress and there was nowhere else to go.

Chase met her gaze, needing her love and her warmth so badly he was shaking with it.

Ever so gently he brought his hands up to frame her face. He stroked away the moisture on her cheeks, wanting to erase each tear and beg her forgiveness for having hurt her. Slowly, he slid his hands down the sides of her neck until they settled on her shoulders.

"Nothing in my life has been as good as these past months with you and Cricket," he told her, although the admission cost him dearly. He hadn't wanted to tie her to him with words and emotional bonds. If she stayed, he wanted it to be of her own free will, not because she felt trapped or obliged.

"I can't alter the past," he whispered. "I don't have any control of the future. But we have now…tonight."

"Then why did you…laugh at me?"

"Because I'm a fool. I need you, Letty, so much it frightens me." He heard the husky emotion in his voice, but didn't regret exposing his longing to her. "If I can only have you for a little while, I think we should take advantage of this time, don't you?"

He didn't give her an opportunity to respond, but urged her toward him and placed his mouth on hers, kissing her over and over until her sweet responsive body was molded against him. He'd dreamed of holding Letty like this, pliable and soft in his arms, but once again reality exceeded his imagination.

"I was beginning to believe you hated me," she whimpered against his mouth. Then, clinging to him, she resumed their kiss.

"Let's take this off," he said a moment later, tugging at the flannel gown. With a reluctance that excited him all the more, Letty stepped out of his arms just far enough to let him pull the gown over her head and discard it.

"Oh, Letty," he groaned, looking at her, heaving a sigh of appreciation. "You're so beautiful." He felt humble seeing her like this. Her beauty, so striking, was revealed only to him, and his knees went weak.

"The scar?" Her eyes were lowered.

The red line that ran the length of her sternum would fade in the years to come. But Chase viewed it as a badge of courage. He leaned forward and kissed it, gently, lovingly, breathing her name.

"Oh, Chase, I thought…maybe you found me ugly and that's why…you wouldn't touch me."

"No," he said. "Never."

"But you *didn't* touch me. For weeks and weeks you stayed on your side of the bed, until…until I thought I'd go crazy."

"I couldn't be near you and not want you," he admitted hoarsely. "I had to wait until Dr. Faraday said it was okay." If those weeks had been difficult for Letty, they'd been doubly so for him.

"Do you want to touch me now?"

He nodded. From the moment they'd discarded her gown, Chase hadn't been able to take his eyes off her.

"Yes. I want to hold you for the rest of my life."

"Please love me, Chase." Her low, seductive voice was all the encouragement he needed. He eased her onto the bed, securing her there with his body. He had to taste her, had to experience all the pleasure she'd so unselfishly offered him earlier.

Their lovemaking was everything he could've hoped for—everything he *had* hoped for. She welcomed him readily and he was awed by her generosity, lost in her love.

Afterward, Chase lay beside Letty and gathered her in his arms. As he felt the sweat that slid down her face, felt the heavy exhaustion that claimed his limbs, he wondered how he'd been able to resist her for so long.

Letty woke at dawn, still in Chase's arms. She felt utterly content—and excited. Plan B hadn't worked out exactly the way she'd thought it would, but it had certainly produced the desired effect. She felt like sitting up and throwing her arms in the air and shouting for sheer joy. She was a wife!

"Morning," Chase whispered.

He didn't look at her, as if he half expected her to be embarrassed by the intimacies they'd shared the night before. Letty's exhilarated thoughts came to an abrupt halt. Had she said or done something a married woman shouldn't?

She was about to voice her fears when her husband turned to her, bracing his arms on either side of her head. She met his eyes, unsure of what he was asking. Slowly he lowered his mouth to hers, kissing her with a hungry need that surprised as much as delighted her.

"How long do we have before Cricket wakes up?" he whispered.

"Long enough," she whispered back.

In the days that followed, Letty found that Chase was insatiable. Not that she minded. In fact, she was thrilled that his need to make love to her was so great. Chase touched and held her often and each caress made her long for sundown. The nights were theirs.

Cricket usually went to bed early, tired out from the long day's activities. As always, Chase was endlessly patient with her, reading her bedtime stories and making up a few of his own, which he dutifully repeated for Letty.

Cricket taught him the game of blowing out the light that Letty had played with her from the time she was a toddler. Whenever she watched Chase with her daughter, Letty was quietly grateful. He was so good with Cricket, and the little girl adored him.

Letty had never been happier. Chase had never told her he loved her in so many words, but she was reassured of his devotion in a hundred different ways. He'd never communicated his feelings freely, and the years hadn't changed that. But the looks he gave her, the reverent way he touched her, his exuberant lovemaking, told her everything she needed to know.

The first week of September Cricket started kindergarten. On the opening day of school, Letty drove her into town and lingered after class had begun, talking to the other mothers for a few minutes. Then, feeling a little melancholy, she returned to the ranch. A new world was opening up for Cricket, and Letty's role in her daughter's life would change.

Letty parked the truck in the yard and walked into the kitchen. Chase wasn't due back at the house until eleven-thirty for lunch; Cricket would be coming home on the school bus, but that wasn't until early afternoon, so Letty's morning was free. She did some housework, but without much enthusiasm. After throwing a load of clothes in the washer, she decided to vacuum.

Once in the living room, she found herself drawn to the old upright piano. She stood over the keys and with one finger plinked out a couple of the songs she'd taught Cricket.

Before she knew it, she was sitting on the bench, running her fingers up and down the yellowing keys, playing a few familiar chords. Soon she was singing, and it felt wonderful, truly wonderful, to release some of the emotion she was experiencing in song.

She wasn't sure how long she'd been sitting there when she looked up and saw Chase watching her. His eyes were sad.

"Your voice is still as beautiful as it always was," he murmured.

"Thank you," she said, feeling shy. It had been months since she'd sat at the piano like this and sung.

"It's been a long time since I've heard you," he told her, his voice flat.

She slipped off the piano bench and closed the keyboard. She considered telling him she didn't do this often; she knew that, for some reason, her playing made him uncomfortable. That saddened Letty—even more so because she didn't understand his feelings.

An awkward silence passed.

"Chase," she said, realizing why he must be in the house. "I'm sorry. I didn't realize it was time for lunch already."

"It isn't," he said.

"Is something wrong?" she asked, feeling unnerved and not knowing why.

"No." The look in his eyes was one of tenderness… and fear? Pain? Either way, it made no sense to her.

Without a word, she slipped into his arms, hugging him close. He was tense and held himself stiffly, but she couldn't fathom why.

Tilting her head, Letty studied him. He glided his thumb over her lips and she captured it between her teeth. "Kiss me," she said. That was one sure way of comforting him.

He did, kissing her ravenously. Urgently. As if this was the last opportunity they'd have. When he ended the kiss, Letty finally felt him relax, and sighed in relief.

"I need you, Letty," he murmured.

Chase's mouth was buried in the hollow of her throat. She burrowed her fingers in his hair, needing to continue touching him.

He kissed her one more time, then drew back. "I want to have you in my arms and in my bed as often as I can before you go," he whispered, refusing to meet her gaze.

"Before I go?" she repeated in confusion. "I'm not going anywhere—Cricket's taking the bus home."

Chase shook his head. "When I married you, I accepted that sooner or later you'd leave," he said, his voice filled with resignation.

Letty was so stunned, so shocked, that for a second she couldn't believe what she was hearing. "Let me see if I understand you," she said slowly. "I married you, but you seem to think I had no intention of staying in the relationship and that sooner or later I'd fly the coop? Am I understanding you correctly?" It was an effort to disguise her sarcasm.

"You were facing a life-or-death situation. I offered you an alternative because of Cricket."

Chase spoke as if that explained everything. "I love you, Chase Brown. I loved you when I left Wyoming. I loved you when I came back.... I love you even more now."

He didn't look at her. "I never said I felt the same way about you."

The world seemed to skid to a halt; everything went perfectly still except for her heart, which was ramming loudly against her chest.

"True," she began when she could find her voice. "You never *said* you did. But you *show* me every day how much you love me. I don't need the words, Chase. You can't hide what you feel for me."

He was making his way to the door when he turned back and snorted softly. "Don't confuse great sex with love, Letty."

She felt unbelievably hurt and fiercely angry.

"Do you *want* me to leave, Chase? Is that what you're saying?"

"I won't ask you to stay."

"In...in other words, I'm free to walk out of here anytime?"

He nodded. "You can go now, if that's what you want."

"Generous of you," she snapped.

He didn't respond.

"I get it," she cried sharply. "Everything's falling into place now. Every time I sit down at the piano, I can feel your displeasure. Why did you bring it here if it bothered you so much?"

"It wasn't my bright idea," he said curtly. "Joy thought it would help you recuperate. If I'd had my way, it would never have left Lonny's place."

"Take it back, then."

"I will once you're gone."

Letty pressed her hand against her forehead. "I can't believe we're having this conversation. I love you, Chase... I don't ever want to leave you."

"Whatever you decide is fine, Letty," he said, and again his voice was resigned. "That decision is yours." He walked out of the house, letting the back door slam behind him.

For several minutes, Letty did nothing but lean against the living room wall. Chase's feigned indifference infuriated her. Hadn't the past few weeks meant *anything* to him? Obviously that was what he wanted her to think. He was pretending to be so damn smug...so condescending, that it demanded all her restraint not to haul out her suitcases that instant and walk away from him just to prove him right.

His words made a lie of all the happiness she'd found in her marriage. Angry tears scalded her eyes. For some reason she didn't grasp, Chase wanted her to think he was using her, and he'd paid a steep price for the privilege—he'd married her.

Letty sank down onto the floor and covered her face with her hands, feeling wretched to the marrow of her bones.

Like some romantic fool, she'd held on to the belief that everything between her and Chase was perfect now and would remain that way forever after. It was a blow to discover otherwise.

When she'd first come back to Wyoming, Letty had been afraid her life was nearly over and the only things awaiting her were pain and regret. Instead Chase had given her a glimpse of happiness. With him, she'd experienced an immeasurable sense of satisfaction and joy, an inner peace. She'd seen Chase as her future, seen the two of them as lifelong companions, a man and a woman in love, together for life.

Nearly blinded by her tears, she got up and grabbed

her purse from the kitchen table. She had to get away to think, put order to her raging thoughts.

Chase was in the yard when she walked out the door. He paused, and out of the corner of her eye, Letty saw that he moved two steps toward her, then abruptly stopped. Apparently he'd changed his mind about whatever he was going to say or do. Which was just as well, since Letty wasn't in the mood to talk to him.

His gaze followed her as she walked toward the truck, as if he suspected she was leaving him right then and there.

Perhaps that was exactly what she should do.

Chapter 14

Letty had no idea where she was going. All she knew was that she had to get away. She considered driving to town and waiting for Cricket. But it was still a while before the kindergarten class was scheduled to be dismissed. In addition, Cricket was looking forward to riding the bus home; to her, that seemed the height of maturity. Letty didn't want to ruin that experience for her daughter.

As she drove aimlessly down the country road, Letty attempted to put the disturbing events of the morning in perspective. Leaving Chase, if only for a day or two, would be an overreaction, but she didn't know how else to deal with this situation. One moment she had everything a woman could want; the next it had all been taken away from her for reasons she couldn't understand or explain. The safe harbor she'd anchored in—her marriage to Chase—had been unexpectedly invaded by an enemy she couldn't even identify.

Without realizing where she'd driven, Letty noticed that the hillside where she'd so often sat with Chase was just over the next ridge. With an ironic smile, she stopped the truck. Maybe their hillside would give her the serenity and inner guidance she sought now.

With the autumn sun warm on her back, she strolled over to the crest of the hill and sat down on a soft patch of grass. She saw a few head of cattle resting under the shade of trees near the stream below, and watched them idly while her thoughts churned. How peaceful the animals seemed, how content. Actually, she was a little surprised to see them grazing there, since she'd heard Chase say that he was moving his herd in the opposite direction. But where he chose to let his cattle graze was the least of her worries.

A slow thirty minutes passed. What Letty found so disheartening about the confrontation with Chase was his conviction that she'd leave him and, worse, his acceptance of it. Why was he so certain she'd pack up and move away? Did he trust her so little?

To give up on their love, their marriage and all the happiness their lives together would bring was traumatic enough. For her and, she was convinced, for him. But the fact that he could do so with no more than a twinge of regret was almost more than Letty could bear. Chase's pride wouldn't let him tell her he loved her and that he wanted her to stay.

Yet he *did* love her and he loved Cricket. Despite his heartless words to the contrary, Letty could never doubt it.

Standing, Letty let her arms hang limply at her sides.

She didn't know what she should do. Perhaps getting away for a day or two wasn't such a bad plan.

The idea started to gather momentum. It was as she turned to leave that Letty noticed one steer that had separated itself from the others. She paused, then stared at the brand, surprised it wasn't Chase's. Before she left Spring Valley she'd let Chase know that old man Wilber's cattle were on his property.

Chase was nowhere to be seen when Letty got back to the house. That was fine, since she'd be in and out within a matter of minutes. She threw a few things in a suitcase for herself and dragged it into the hallway. Then she rushed upstairs to grab some clothes for Cricket. Letty wasn't sure what she'd tell her daughter about this unexpected vacation, but she'd think of something later.

Chase was standing in the kitchen when she reached the bottom of the stairs. His eyes were cold and cruel in a way she hadn't seen since she'd first returned home. He picked up her suitcase and set it by the back door, as if eager for her to leave.

"I see you decided to go now," he said, leaning indolently against the kitchen counter.

His arms were folded over his chest in a gesture of stubborn indifference. If he'd revealed the least bit of remorse or indecision, Letty might have considered reasoning with him, but it was painfully apparent that he didn't feel anything except the dire satisfaction of being proven right.

"I thought I'd spend a few days with Lonny."

"Lonny," Chase repeated with a short, sarcastic laugh. "I bet he'll love that."

"He won't mind." A half-truth, but worth it if Chase believed her.

"You're sure of that?"

It was obvious from Chase's lack of concern that he wasn't going to invite her to stay at the ranch so they could resolve their differences—which was what Letty had hoped he'd do.

"If Lonny *does* object, I'll simply find someplace in town."

"Do you have enough money?"

"Yes…" Letty said, striving to sound casual.

"I'll be happy to provide whatever you need."

Chase spoke with such a flippant air that it cut her to the quick. "I won't take any money from you."

Chase shrugged. "Fine."

Everything in Letty wanted to shout at him to give her some sign, anything, that would show her he wanted her to stay. It was the whole reason she was staging this. His nonchalant response was so painful, that not breaking down, not weeping, was all Letty could manage.

"Is this what you really want?" she asked in a small voice.

"Like I said before, if you're set on leaving, I'm not going to stop you."

Letty reached down for her suitcase, tightening her fingers around the handle. "I'll get Cricket at school. I'll think up some excuse to tell her." She made it all the way to the back door before Chase stopped her.

"Letty…"

She whirled around, her heart ringing with excitement until she saw the look in his eyes.

"Before you go, there's something I need to ask you," he said, his face drawn. "Is there any possibility you could be pregnant?"

His question seemed to echo against the walls.

"Letty?"

She met his gaze. Some of his arrogance was gone, replaced with a tenderness that had been far too rare these past few hours. "No," she whispered, her voice hardly audible.

Chase's eyes closed, but she didn't know if he felt regret or relief. The way things had been going, she didn't want to know.

"I...went to the hillside," she said in a low voice that wavered slightly despite her effort to control it. She squared her shoulders, then continued. "There were several head of cattle there. The brand is Wilber's."

Chase clenched his jaw so tightly that the sides of his face went pale under his tan. "So you know," he said, his voice husky and filled with dread. His gaze skirted hers, fists at his sides.

Letty was baffled. Chase's first response to the fact that she'd seen his neighbor's cattle on his property made no sense. She had no idea why he'd react like that.

Then it struck her. "You sold those acres to Mr. Wilber, didn't you? Why?" That land had been in Chase's family for over three generations. Letty couldn't figure out what would be important enough for him to relinquish those acres. Not once in all the weeks they'd been married or before had he given her any indication that he was financially strapped.

"I don't understand," she said—and suddenly she did. "There wasn't any insurance money for my surgery, was there, Chase?"

She'd been so unsuspecting, so confident when he'd told her everything had been taken care of. She should've known—in fact, did know—that an insurance company wouldn't cover a preexisting condition without a lengthy waiting period.

"Chase?" She held his eyes with her own. Incredulous, shocked, she set the suitcase down and took one small step toward her husband. "Why did you lie to me about the insurance?"

He tunneled his fingers through his hair.

"Why would you do something like that? It doesn't make any sense." Very little of this day had. "Didn't you realize the state had already agreed to cover all the expenses?"

"You hated being a charity case. I saw the look in your eyes when I found your welfare check. It was killing you to accept that money."

"Of course I hated it, but I managed to swallow my pride. It was necessary. But what you did wasn't. Why would you sell your land? I just can't believe it." Chase loved every square inch of Spring Valley. Parting with a single acre would be painful, let alone the prime land near the creek. It would be akin to his cutting off one of his fingers.

Chase turned away from her and walked over to the sink. His shoulders jerked in a hard shrug as he braced his hands on the edge. "All right, if you must know. I did it because I wanted you to marry me."

"But you said the marriage was for Cricket's sake… in case anything happened to me…. Then you could raise her."

"That was an excuse." The words seemed to be wrenched from him. After a long pause, he added, "I love you, Letty." It was all the explanation he gave her.

"I love you, too…I always have," she whispered, awed by what he'd done and, more importantly, the reason behind it. "I told you only three hours ago how I felt about you, but you practically threw it back in my face. If you love me so much," she murmured, "why couldn't you let me know it? Would that have been so wrong?"

"I didn't want you to feel trapped."

"Trapped?" How could Chase possibly view their marriage in such a light? He made it sound as if he'd taken her hostage!

"Sooner or later I realized you'd want to return to California. I knew that when I asked you to marry me. I accepted it."

"That's ridiculous!" Letty cried. "I don't ever want to go back. There's nothing for me there. Everything that's ever been good in my life is right here with you."

Chase turned to face her. "What about the fight you and Lonny had about your mother? You said—"

"I realized how wrong I was about Mom," she interrupted, gesturing with her hands. "My mother was a wonderful woman, but more significant than that, she was fulfilled as a person. I'm not going to say she had an easy life—we both know differently. But she loved the challenge here. She loved her art, too, and found ways to express her talent. I was just too blind to recognize it. I was so caught up in striving toward my dreams, I failed to see that my happiness was right here in Red Springs with you. The biggest mistake I ever made was leaving you. Do you honestly believe I'd do it again?"

A look of hope crept into Chase's eyes.

"Telling me I'm free to walk away from you is one thing," Letty said softly. "But you made it sound as if you wanted me gone—as if you couldn't wait to get me out of your life. You weren't even willing to give us a chance. That hurt more than anything."

"I was afraid to," he admitted, his voice low.

"Over and over again, you kept saying that you wouldn't stop me from leaving. It was almost as if you'd been waiting for it to happen because I'd been such a disappointment to you."

"Letty, no, I swear that isn't true."

"Then why are you standing way over there—and I'm way over here?"

"Oh, Letty." He covered the space between them in three giant strides, wrapping his arms around her. When he lifted his head, their eyes melted together. "I love you, Letty, more than I thought it was possible to care about anyone. I haven't told you that, and I was wrong. You deserve to hear the words."

"Chase, you didn't need to say them for me to know how you feel. That's what was so confusing. I couldn't doubt you loved me, yet you made my leaving sound like some long-anticipated event."

"I couldn't let you know how much I was hurting."

"But I was hurting, too."

"I know, my love, I know."

He rained hot, urgent kisses down upon her face. She directed his mouth to hers, and his kiss intensified. Letty threaded her fingers through his hair, glorying in the closeness they shared. She was humbled by the sacrifice he'd made for her. He could have given her no greater proof of his love.

"Chase." His name was a broken cry on her lips. "The land...you sold...I can't bear to think of you losing it."

He caressed her face. "It's not as bad as it sounds. I have the option of buying it back at a future date, and I will."

"But—"

He silenced her with his mouth, kissing away her objections and concerns. Then he tore his mouth from hers and brought it to the hollow of her throat, kissing her there. "I would gladly have sold all of Spring Valley if it had been necessary."

Letty felt tears gather in her eyes. Tears of gratitude and joy and need.

"You've given me so much," he whispered. "My life was so empty until you came back and brought Cricket with you. I love her, Letty, as if she were our own. I want to adopt her and give her my name."

Letty nodded through her tears, knowing that Cricket would want that, too.

Chase inhaled deeply, then exhaled a long, slow breath. "As much as I wanted you to stay, I couldn't let you know that. When I asked if you might be pregnant, it was a desperate attempt by a desperate man to find a way to keep you here, despite all my claims to the contrary. I think my heart dropped to my feet when you told me you weren't."

Letty wasn't sure she understood.

He stared down at her with a tender warmth. "I don't know if I can explain this, but when I mentioned the possibility of you being pregnant, I had a vision of two little boys."

Letty smiled. "Twins?"

"No," Chase said softly. "They were a year or so apart. I saw them clearly, standing beside each other, and somehow I knew that those two were going to be our sons. The day you had the surgery—I saw them then, too. I wanted those children so badly.... Today, when you were about to walk out the door, I didn't know if you'd ever come back. I knew if you left me, the emptiness would return, and I didn't think I could bear it. I tried to prepare myself for your going, but it didn't work."

"I couldn't have stayed away for long. My heart's here with you. You taught me to forgive myself for the past and cherish whatever the future holds."

His eyes drifted shut. "We have so much, Letty." He was about to say more when the kitchen door burst open and Cricket came rushing into the room.

Chase broke away from Letty just in time for the five-year-old to vault into his arms. "I have a new friend, and her name's Karen and she's got a pony, too. I like school a whole bunch, and Mrs. Webber let me hand out some papers and said I could be her helper every day."

Chase hugged the little girl. "I'm glad you like school so much, sweetheart." Then he put his hand on Letty's shoulder, pulling her to him.

Letty leaned into his strength and closed her eyes, savoring these few moments of contentment. She'd found her happiness in Chase. She'd come home, knowing she might die, and instead had discovered life in its most abundant form. Spring Valley was their future—here was where they'd thrive. Here was where their sons would be born.

Cricket came to her mother's side, and Letty drew her close. As she did, she looked out the kitchen window. The Wyoming sky had never seemed bluer. Or filled with greater promise.

* * * * *

Books by Patricia Davids

Love Inspired

North Country Amish

An Amish Wife for Christmas
Shelter from the Storm

The Amish Bachelors

An Amish Harvest
An Amish Noel
His Amish Teacher
Their Pretend Amish Courtship
Amish Christmas Twins
An Unexpected Amish Romance
His New Amish Family

Brides of Amish Country

Plain Admirer
Amish Christmas Joy
The Shepherd's Bride
The Amish Nanny
An Amish Family Christmas: A Plain Holiday
An Amish Christmas Journey
Amish Redemption

Visit the Author Profile page
at Harlequin.com for more titles.

A MILITARY MATCH

Patricia Davids

The horse is made ready for the day of battle,
but victory rests with the Lord.
—*Proverbs* 21:31

This book is dedicated to my brother,
Bob Stroda—a real cowboy and a funny,
funny guy. Thanks for putting up with
your bossy big sister and for making me laugh
more times than I can count.

Chapter 1

"Stay here…and honk if you see *anyone* going inside."

Jennifer Grant pushed open the door of her old dark blue pickup, but paused to glance at her passenger. "Got it?"

Fifteen-year-old Lizzie Grant, the second of Jennifer's three younger siblings, hooked a lock of curly brown hair behind one ear. She didn't bother looking up from her math book. "I've got it."

"I'm serious." Jennifer stressed each word.

Lizzie shut her book and pulled her pink T-shirt collar up to cover the lower half of her face, mocking her sister's intensity. She glanced in all directions. "Have no fear, Agent Double oh six, Double oh seven is on the job."

"Don't be a smart aleck."

Dropping the fabric, Lizzie opened her book again.

"Fine. Then stop acting like a wimp. If I see *Avery,* which is who you're really trying to avoid, I'll honk three times so you'll know your ex-boyfriend is coming."

"Very funny." Jennifer gave her sister a dour look, but knew in her heart that Lizzie was right. Private Avery Barnes was exactly who she wanted to avoid.

"Why do we have to do this now?" Lizzie demanded. "It's Saturday."

"Because Dr. Cutter needs the follow-up films on Dakota's leg done today." *And because Avery should be away from the stable for at least another hour.*

Sighing with teenage impatience, Lizzie focused on her homework once more. "Is it going to take long? I don't want to be late and neither should you."

"It'll take ten minutes, tops. I can get you to your chess meeting, drop the films off at the Large Animal Clinic and still get to my horse show on time."

Jennifer was used to making the most of the limited hours in her day. To save time, she was already dressed in her tan riding breeches and white shirt beneath her pale blue lab coat. Her black show jacket hung in a garment bag behind the driver's seat. Her knee-high riding boots, polished to a high shine, sat ready to be pulled on before she took the field.

After she stepped out of the truck, Jennifer pulled a large yellow case from the front seat and glanced around. The narrow strip of white gravel between the close, single-story stone buildings reflected the heat of the warm September morning. The parking area contained only a few cars, but one was the sleek lapis-blue Jaguar she knew belonged to Avery.

Glancing into the horse trailer hitched behind her truck, she saw McCloud, her gray ten-year-old gelding, standing quietly, his head up and eyes alert. It was a sign he was ready to get down to business. Both of them needed to be on their game today or she would have wasted an entry fee.

Money was tight in the Grant household, and the possibility that she could earn an extra five hundred dollars in prize money wasn't to be taken lightly. Her riding, plus her work for Dr. Cutter, were paying her way though vet school. This semester's fees were due in the next few weeks and she didn't yet have the full amount she needed.

She walked quickly to the wide doorway of the old limestone-and-timber stable, pausing to check down the dim, cobblestone paved corridor. It was empty. She glanced over her shoulder at a small building a dozen yards away. It housed the offices of the Commanding General's Mounted Color Guard at Fort Riley, Kansas.

No one stepped out to greet her. She relaxed and blew out the breath she had been holding. She had permission to be here, she just didn't want to encounter a certain soldier.

The men who made up Fort Riley's unique cavalry living history unit should be at their training corrals now. When the unit wasn't performing around the country they practiced daily to hone their exceptional equestrian skills and train their horses. She didn't expect anyone back for at least another hour.

Part of her was glad that the maddening Avery Barnes was nowhere in sight. Another part of her half-hoped she'd be able to show him exactly how little she cared if he was. Grasping her equipment case tightly, she walked down the corridor to the last stall on the left.

Inside the old building, the air was cool and laced

with the smell of horses, hay and oiled leather. All scents she loved. Opening the upper half of the Dutch door, she spoke softly to the brown horse dozing with his head lowered near the back wall. "Hey, Dakota. What're ya doing?"

When his head came up and she was sure he wasn't startled by her presence, she opened the lower half of the door, stepped inside and held out her hand. Dakota whinnied and came to collect the slice of apple resting in her palm.

She patted his neck as she checked behind her. There was still no one in sight.

"Okay, fella, let's make this quick. I want to get done before you-know-who shows up."

Dropping to her knees, she felt along Dakota's leg, checking for any tenderness or swelling. To her satisfaction she didn't find anything but a nicely healed scar on the big bay's pastern. She popped open the fasteners on the cumbersome yellow case and removed the new portable X-ray machine her boss and mentor, equine surgeon Dr. Brian Cutter, had entrusted her with.

It only took a few minutes to set up and position the machine, and get Dakota to stand with his foot on the X-ray cassette. Taking the series of shots Brian needed to monitor the healing progress of Dakota's fractured leg took only a couple minutes more. She propped one used cassette against the side of the stall behind her so she wouldn't accidentally take two exposures on it, and set up for one final shot.

"Well, well, look who's here. If it isn't my darling Jenny."

As always, the broad New England accent in his deep

voice did funny things to the pit of her stomach. Apparently just telling herself she was over him wasn't enough.

When Avery had asked her out the previous winter, Jenny had been flattered but cautious. His playboy reputation was no secret. She'd accepted because she'd sensed that beneath that smooth charm was a lonely man who needed her, and God, in his life.

Getting Avery to open up proved more difficult than she had imagined, but because she cared about him, she hadn't been willing to give up. Jennifer Grant never walked away from a challenge.

In the end, she'd turned to a mutual friend, Lindsey Cutter, for help. Avery and Lindsey had served together in the CGMCG. Lindsey told her that Avery had joined the army after a falling-out with his only remaining family member, his grandfather.

Sensing she had found the key to understanding him, Jennifer had tried repeatedly to talk to Avery about his family, but he shut her out. After wrestling with her conscience, she'd made the decision to contact his grandfather herself. Her good intentions blew up in her face. Avery had found out and had been furious.

Their breakup that day at her clinic was both public and humiliating. Then, as if to prove he'd never really cared about her, Avery spent the next several weeks dating a series of Jenny's classmates.

Which only confirmed that he didn't care about me.

Choosing to ignore her reaction to the sound of his voice, Jennifer snapped the last shot, braced herself, then rose to face him.

Lizzie was in so much trouble. A heads-up really would have been nice.

Leaning with his tan forearms resting on the half

door, he grinned at her with a cocky smile that had probably melted more female hearts than she could count. It had certainly softened hers the first time she saw it. Fortunately, she knew him better now. *Un*fortunately, the lesson had been an emotionally painful one to learn.

He wore the unit's standard issue red T-shirt. His matching red ball cap was pushed back on his head revealing his military cut dark brown hair above his deep-set hazel eyes.

Eyes that a woman could get lost in—if she didn't have the good sense to see Avery Barnes for what he was—a playboy who broke hearts without a second thought.

"I'm not *your* anything, Private Barnes, and you know that I don't like being called Jenny."

It had taken months, but she had patched her heart back together with will power and hard work. She wasn't about to let him think she still cared. She didn't. She was *so* over him.

"It's Corporal Barnes now. I've been promoted since we last met and now that you mention it, Jenny, I do recall that you don't like being called Jenny."

"I'm busy. Go away if you can't be nice." She imbued her voice with as much toughness as she could muster.

A second soldier came up to stand beside Avery. Jennifer recognized another member of the mounted color guard. Private Lee Gillis was dressed in the same red shirt with the unit's logo embroidered on it. His smile, unlike Avery's, showed genuine warmth.

"Hi, Jennifer," Lee said brightly. "What are you doing here? I thought you'd be riding in the Deerfield Open today."

Lee, like many soldiers assigned to the CGMGC, had

never been on a horse before his transfer into the special unit a year ago. Everyone who came into the unit trained in cavalry tactic from manuals the U.S. Army had used during the Civil War. Once exposed to the world of equestrian sports, Lee had quickly become a fan of all things horse related, particularly show jumping and dressage. Jennifer often saw him at the local events when she was competing.

"Yes, Jenny, what are you doing here?" Avery interjected with mock interest. "Besides looking for me."

"I have absolutely no interest in seeing you. Dr. Cutter sent me to take Dakota's follow up films this month and if you call me Jenny one more time, I'm going to make you regret it."

Avery shook his head as he gave her a reproachful look. "Shame on you—threatening a member of the U.S. military. I could get you in serious trouble for that."

Jennifer smiled at Lee. "You'll short sheet his bed or put a large snake in it for me, won't you?"

Lee's eyes brightened. "Gladly."

Folding her arms over her chest, she said, "You see, Avery, I can get to you whenever I want."

"Lee, do you know why she doesn't like to be called Jenny?"

Holding up both hands, Lee took a step back. "I think you two should leave me out of this."

"Because a jenny is a female donkey," Avery said with a smirk. "Can you see the resemblance? Cute, with big ears and a long nose that gets into everyone's business, and too stubborn for her own good—that's my Jenny in a nutshell."

"I didn't come here to be abused by you. I'm here to do a job and you're interfering. Do I need to tell Captain

Watson that you're ignoring your own work and keeping me from doing mine? I'm sure it won't be the first time he's heard that you're slacking."

"She's got you there, Avery." Grinning, Lee slapped his buddy on the back then walked away.

"You can tattle to the captain if it makes you feel better, Jenny, but the truth is I'm not doing a thing to prevent you from working. I'm just standing here watching."

Jennifer bit back a retort. The last thing she wanted was to get into a verbal battle with the man. Instead, she turned away and stuffed the X-ray machine into the carrying case before snapping it shut. "I'm finished anyway."

Picking up the case, she spun around and marched toward the stall door. Avery pulled it open, swept his arm out and bowed low in a courtly gesture as she passed. She wasn't sure, but she thought she heard him chuckling behind her.

The man was insufferable. Why she had ever considered him handsome and interesting was a complete mystery.

The bright sunshine made her squint after the dimness of the barn's interior. She shaded her eyes with one hand as she crossed to her truck and yanked open the door. After depositing the equipment inside, she slid behind the wheel.

"Thanks a lot, Lizzie. I thought I told you to honk if you saw anyone coming."

Tapping her lips with her pencil, Lizzie frowned at her book. "I didn't see anyone."

Jennifer took a few deep breaths before inserting her key in the ignition. "Dr. Cutter is just going to have to get one of his other students to come do these films."

"Didn't you volunteer to do them?" Lizzie scowled as she wrote in her notebook.

"I did, but good grades are only worth so much aggravation."

"Oh, *he* was there." Lizzie turned the page and copied a set of numbers on her paper.

"I could care less about Avery Barnes," Jennifer stated firmly, hoping to convince herself as much as her sister.

"You were drooling over him last winter when the army had Dakota at your clinic."

"I don't recall drooling over anyone."

"You went out with him last winter and every other word out of your mouth was Avery this and Avery that and Avery is so charming."

Jennifer still wasn't certain how she could have been so mistaken about him. Her first impression had been that Avery was devoted to his friends and to helping care for injured animals. Both were qualities she greatly admired. She had sensed something special in him. She had begun to see a future with him.

A future, as it turns out, based on foolish daydreams with no basis in reality.

"He's charming all right. He's also as shallow as a petri dish. We saw each other for a few months, but then I learned how superficial and self-centered he really is."

"Why? Because he stopped asking you out?"

Her sister's comment hit a little too close to home. "I'm not having this conversation with you."

Rolling her eyes, Lizzie said, "Whatever. If we don't get going, I'll be late for my chess club."

Jennifer started the engine and checked her rearview mirror as she pulled away from the stable, but she wasn't granted another glimpse of the unbearable Avery Barnes. Which was just as well, she decided as she headed toward the checkpoint at the east entrance of the post. If she never had to see him again, it would be too soon.

Chapter 2

As Avery listened the sound of Jennifer's truck driving away, he tried to ignore the ache in the back of his throat. He rubbed his hands on the sides of his jeans and hoped the fact that she still took his breath away had gone unnoticed. Acting like a jerk wasn't usually so hard.

He hadn't expected to see her again after the painful brush off he'd given her. Certainly not here in his company's stable. The harshness of his behavior after their breakup pricked what little conscience he had left, but he tried to ignore that, too.

He thought he'd put his feelings for her behind him. Now, standing here with the lingering scent of her perfume filling him with warmth, he knew he hadn't. It had been a long time since a woman had affected his equilibrium the way Jennifer Grant did.

It wasn't that she was such a knockout in the looks

department. She wasn't overly tall, but she had a trim figure and a self-assured way of tossing her blond hair back with a flip of her hand that made a man sit up and take notice. Her nose had a little bump in the middle that the women in his circles would have had smoothed out by a plastic surgeon before they finished high school.

Jennifer's appeal wasn't in her deep blue eyes or in her looks. It was how she looked at others. Her kindness and her compassion lit her from the inside like a candle in the darkness. She was unlike anyone he had ever met. The only trouble with Jennifer was that she never knew when to quit.

His first reaction when he saw her today in Dakota's stall had been a surge of happiness. He was thankful her back had been turned and he'd had time to school his features into a smirk he knew would annoy her.

What he should have done was keep walking and let her leave without speaking to her. Even now he wasn't sure why he'd felt compelled to engage her in conversation. He knew she wouldn't have anything nice to say to him. Perhaps he had been hoping for a tongue lashing from her. Maybe he even had it coming.

Dakota thrust his head out the stall door and whinnied after Jennifer. Avery reached up to scratch the horse behind his ear. "Sorry I ran her off, big boy. I know you like her."

Dakota had gone through a rough time after his fracture the previous autumn. For a while, it had looked like the horse wouldn't survive. Jennifer had been one of the people involved in his care, and his recovery was due in part to the hours she spent helping take care of him.

Avery remembered Dakota's stay at the Large Animal Clinic with more fondness than the circumstances warranted. It had been Jennifer's company, her upbeat attitude and her bossy but kind nature that had helped everyone from the mounted color guard cope during those difficult days.

It was only later that Avery had realized what a danger she posed to his peace of mind. She was far too likable—and good. Definitely not what he looked for in the women he dated.

He patted Dakota's neck. "If she wasn't so cute when she gets mad I might have been able to stop egging her on. Did you see the way that fire leaps in those deep blue eyes?" Giving himself a mental shake for discussing Jennifer with a horse, Avery walked on toward the equipment room.

Lee came out of the door with two long-handled pitchforks and handed one to Avery. It was their turn to muck out the stalls before the rest of the unit returned from exercising the horses.

"Why do you razz Jennifer like that?" Lee asked as he pushed a wheelbarrow toward the first empty stall.

Avery wasn't in the habit of sharing his feelings or explaining his actions. He shrugged. "She can take it."

"And dish it out, but you seem to take a special delight in ruffling her feathers. What did she ever do to you?"

"Nothing."

"I seem to remember that the two of you had a thing going for a while. What happened?"

"We went out a couple of times. It didn't work." Avery began pitching the straw from the first stall into the wheelbarrow.

Lee stopped and grinned at him. "She dumped you."

"Get real. Women don't dump me."

Only one had. After that, he never gave another

woman the chance. He was always the first to call it quits in a relationship.

"Jennifer didn't fall for your smooth-talking ways, did she? That must have bruised your ego."

"My ego is unscathed, thank you. It just so happens the woman can't leave well enough alone."

"What does that mean?"

"She wanted me to go to church with her."

Lee resumed his work. "I go to church. It wouldn't hurt you to give it a try."

"Believing that someone or something is in charge of my life doesn't do it for me. Anyway, she didn't stop there. After I turned her down and expressed my views on the subject, she made a point of telling all the women at the clinic to steer clear of me."

"So that's what the big ears and long nose comment was about?"

"She thinks she knows what's best for everyone." She thought she knew what was best for him.

"I heard she was the one who got Dr. Cutter and Lindsey Mandel to patch things up. Now look at them."

"Exactly. They're married. In a year they'll both be miserable and filing for divorce because they hate each other."

Lee paused and leaned on his pitchfork. "Not every marriage ends in misery."

"Enough do. If flying in a plane was as risky as marriage, nobody would be racking up frequent flyer miles."

One look at his parents' marriage and his own near miss proved his point.

"That's a grim view."

"I call it like I see it."

"I wonder if that's true." Lee propped his pitchfork

against the wall and lifted the handles of the wheelbarrow.

Avery looked at him sharply. "What does that mean?"

"It means you might not want to admit it, but you've still got a thing for Jennifer." Lee maneuvered the loaded cart out the doorway, leaving Avery to stare after him.

Jennifer pulled up in front of the youth center at the Community Christian Church and checked her watch. "See, I told you I'd get you here on time. Is your math done? You know I'm not going to let you shirk your school work just to have a wild time with your chess-loving friends."

Lizzie scribbled one more number on her sheet and snapped the textbook shut. "I'm done."

"Okay, but I still need to check it before I turn you loose."

Handing over her work, Lizzie said, "Like that's a surprise. You're way stricter than Mom is."

"That's because, unlike our mother, I believe your education is more important than a silly hobby."

As soon as the words were out of her mouth, Jennifer's conscience pricked her. She shouldn't be criticizing her mother's behavior, or calling her sister's hobby silly.

Still, Mary Grant's obsession with history and re-enacting the life of frontier widow Henrietta Dutton had been taking up more and more her time. Her involvement with the local historical society's plans for the town's upcoming Founder's Day Festival had turned into a time-consuming passion that left all of her kids feeling ignored.

There were times when Jennifer wondered if the line

between reality and re-enactment were blurring a bit too much even for their eccentric mother.

"Your horse shows are a hobby," Lizzie said defensively.

"Yes, they are, but I don't let them interfere with my education or my job."

Someone in the family had to keep a level head. Since her father's death eight years ago, that lot had fallen to Jennifer. It wasn't that she resented it, because she did love her family, but there were times when she felt stifled in responsibility.

She glanced at her sister's downcast face and realized that she had sounded much too stern. Reaching over, she playfully tweaked Lizzie's nose. "Only God and shoe shopping are more important. Right?"

Jennifer was rewarded with the smile she had been hoping for. Lizzie rolled her eyes and shook her head. "Whatever. Is my math right?"

Jennifer checked it. "As usual, it's perfect. Go on and have a good time."

Lizzie pushed open her door, hopped out and slung her tattered black backpack over one shoulder. "Bobby Pinkerton has been telling everyone he's going to beat me in fifteen moves. I can't wait to make him eat his words."

Jennifer grinned. "You go, girl. Trounce that boy."

"I will. I hope you and McCloud win today, too."

"If we do, I'll get pizza for supper. Mom is picking you up, right?"

"Yup. I told her four o'clock."

A teenage girl came racing across the parking lot and Jennifer recognized her as one of Lizzie's friends. Slamming the door shut, Lizzie hurried toward her friend and the two of them entered the building.

After dropping her sister off, Jennifer drove a few more miles to the Kansas State University campus. The Large Animal Clinic was part of the Veterinary Teaching Hospital and Jennifer's boss, Dr. Brian Cutter, was the chief equine surgeon at the facility.

She parked her truck and trailer at the side of the building. Getting out, she turned and grabbed the X-ray machine. The second she did, she realized her mistake.

"Oh, I can't believe it!" She stamped her foot in sheer frustration.

"What's wrong, Jennifer?"

She whirled around to see Brian coming out of the building. Dressed in his usual dark slacks and pristine white lab coat, he leaned heavily on his cane as he walked toward her. Under his arm, he held a small, tan pet carrier.

Jennifer's shoulders slumped as she admitted her mistake. "I took the films you wanted of Dakota's leg, but I left one of the cassettes in his stall. Can you send someone else to get it?"

"It's Saturday. No one is in today except Deborah and I, and of course, Isabella." He nodded toward the crate under his arm where his pet rabbit rested, her nose pressed against the cage door and quivering with excitement.

The brown French lop was a favorite with everyone who worked at the clinic. She had the run of Brian's office plus a small enclosed pen outside the building where she happily napped in the shade or nibbled grass. It was well known that she had her owner and half the staff wrapped around her dainty paw.

Jennifer sighed. "I'm going to go out on a limb here and guess that Isabella doesn't have a driver's license."

He grinned. "Not even a learner's permit."

"And if an emergency came in they would need you and you need Deborah to answer the phone and check people in, so that leaves me to make the trip back to the base. Are you sure you need the films today?"

"Very sure. My grant money depends on accurate and up-to-date information on the results of my gene therapy subjects. The bone growth study Dakota is part of is one of my most important projects. I wouldn't ask you to make another trip to the fort if I didn't need it today. Do you want me to call and see if they have someone who can bring it over?"

Jennifer checked her watch and blew her breath out through pursed lips. She didn't want to miss her competition, but she didn't want Avery doing her work for her. "No, I'll go back."

"Before you leave, I wanted to ask if you could rabbit-sit for a few days. Well, actually a week. Lindsey and I are going out of town and I know how much you like Isabella. We'd pay you the same as last time."

"I'd be happy to watch her." Every extra dime helped, but Jennifer would have done it for free.

"Great." He deposited Isabella in her run and took the X-ray case from Jennifer. "I'm sorry you have to make a second trip to the post. This won't make you miss your show, will it?"

"No, I can still get there." She smiled but it took more effort than usual.

Getting back into her truck, she made a tight turn and sped out of the parking lot back toward the fort. If she picked up the film and got back in thirty minutes, she could still make her events, but it wouldn't leave her much time to warm up McCloud. The show jumping would be first with the more intricate dressage class scheduled for the afternoon. If she missed the first event she could still enter the later one, but only the horse and rider with the best overall score in both classes would win the top prize money being offered.

It was money she sorely needed. Both her younger brothers had outgrown last year's school clothes and she had noticed Lizzie's backpack was falling apart. Every extra bit of cash came in handy to help her mother support a family of four children and two horses.

Ten minutes later, Jennifer stopped at the gates of the fort to hand over her identification. As she waited for permission to enter, she mentally braced herself to face Avery again. Having to admit he had rattled her enough to make her forget her job was a sobering thought.

After being waved through the checkpoint, she quickly drove to the stables and parked beside them. She got out of her truck just as a black limousine drove up and stopped in front of the CGMCG office building. A chauffeur in a dark blue uniform stepped out and moved to open the door for his passenger. A white-haired man in a beautifully tailored gray pinstriped suit emerged.

Distinguished was the first word that popped into Jennifer's mind when she saw him. Money was the second word.

She tilted her head as she studied him. There was something familiar about him, but he entered the office building before she could place where she might have seen him before.

It didn't matter. What mattered was getting her job done and getting to her contest on time. She got out of her vehicle and walked boldly into the stable all the while praying she wouldn't run into Avery again.

Reaching Dakota's stall without meeting anyone, she opened the door and stepped inside, speaking softly to the big bay who had his nose buried in his feed bucket. The X-ray film cassette was exactly where she had left it leaning against the wall. Snatching it up, she turned and started toward the door when she heard someone call Avery's name.

"Coming," he shouted back. He was just outside.

Without thinking, Jennifer dropped into a crouch behind the half door. He must have been in the tack room on the other side of the walkway. She heard the creak of the door and his boots on the stone floor, but they didn't pass by. They stopped right outside Dakota's stall.

Jennifer closed her eyes and let her chin drop onto her chest. Realizing just what a ridiculous position she had placed herself in, she tried to think of a way to exit with her dignity intact but couldn't come up with anything.

"What are you doing here?" Avery demanded with cool disdain.

Chapter 3

Jennifer looked up expecting to see Avery glaring at her over the stall door, but the space above her was empty. He wasn't talking to her.

"Can't I pay my only grandson a visit?"

It was Avery's grandfather. The man Jennifer had tried and failed to contact. His dragon of a secretary had refused to put Jennifer's call through the day she'd attempted to call.

"I don't have anything to say to you. Did *she* put you up to this?" Avery's cold tone made Jennifer cringe.

Great! He's going to blame me anyway.

"I don't know who you're talking about. No one put me up to this. Coming here was my own idea. Can't we at least try to let bygones be bygones?"

"Why should I?"

"I thought perhaps you would have seen the error of your ways by now."

"I knew you didn't come to apologize."

"I have nothing to apologize for. I was protecting you. You would see that if you opened your eyes."

Jennifer pressed a hand to her mouth. Her foolish pride had placed her in the awkward position of eavesdropping on a family quarrel. There was no other way out of the stall. She braced herself to stand up and let them know she was there when Avery's next words stopped her.

"I don't have to stay and listen to this."

Jennifer heard his footsteps moving away and she breathed a sigh of relief. She just might get out of this with her dignity intact.

"She didn't love you. All she cared about was your money," Avery's grandfather called out loudly.

"No, all *you* ever cared about was money," Avery shot back.

"It never bothered you to spend the money I earn," the older man answered sharply. "You never had to work for anything…and that was my fault as much as anyone's."

"What you really mean is that I'll never amount to anything. I've heard this speech before."

"I have been guilty of saying that in the past, that's true, but I simply wanted you to stop wasting your life."

"It's my life. Which is something you never understood."

Dakota had finished his meal and walked over to Jennifer. He nickered softly and nuzzled at her pocket. She pushed his head away. He gave a loud snort and she tensed. He snorted again and whinnied.

"Shh," she whispered with her fingertips pressed

to her lips, hoping to quiet him and praying the men wouldn't notice anything unusual.

"Thanks for the visit, Grandfather. I'm sure you can find your own way out." Avery's voice drifted to her from the front of the barn and she knew he had walked away.

"Wait!" the older man called out. "I didn't mean for this to become one of our shouting matches. Please come back."

There was no answer. Jennifer heard his heavy sigh, then his unsteady footsteps faded, too.

A wave of sympathy engulfed her. How terribly sad for both men. Avery had always avoided talking about his family except to tell her that his parents were dead. He had never mentioned his grandfather. Now she knew why.

Rising, she opened the stall door and stepped out. A few feet away, the elderly man from the limousine sat on a bale of straw. His eyes opened wide at the sight of her.

Heat rushed to her cheeks. "I'm so sorry," she stammered. "I didn't mean to, but I couldn't help...overhearing."

He closed his eyes and waved his hand. "It doesn't matter. I've lost him. He's all I have and he hates me."

The resignation and pain in his voice touched her deeply.

"You mustn't think that. There is always a chance for reconciliation."

He shook his head. "You don't know all that stands between us."

She took a step closer. "You're right. I don't, but I do know that faith is a powerful tool. Faith and hard work can overcome the most insurmountable problems."

"Wise advice from someone so young, but my grandson isn't the forgiving kind."

The old man tried to rise to his feet, but sat down abruptly with his hand pressed to his chest. Beads of sweat popped out on his forehead and his face grew bright red. She dropped to her knees in front of him. "Are you okay?"

Nodding, he fumbled at the breast pocket of his jacket. He pulled out a small, dark glass bottle but couldn't hold on to it. It tumbled from his trembling hand. Jennifer caught it before it hit the stone floor.

A quick glance at the prescription label confirmed her suspicions. It was heart medication.

She opened the cap and shook one tiny white tablet onto her palm. Pinching it between her thumb and forefinger, she held it out to him. "Put this under your tongue."

He nodded, took the pill from her and put it in his mouth. She closed her hand around his wrist to check his pulse. It was fast, but not irregular. "I'm going to call 9-1-1."

He managed a tight smile. "No. The medicine will help. I don't need an ambulance."

"Shall I get Avery?"

Shaking his head, he said, "I don't want him to see me like this."

"Sir, you aren't well. You grandson should know that."

"I'm fine now."

Although she was relieved to see his color returning to normal and his voice growing stronger, his statement didn't fool her. "Not to be disrespectful, sir, but you are not fine. Those pills are for angina. If you are having heart pain, you need to see a doctor, ASAP."

"I thought perhaps I was talking to one."

"Me? I'm a veterinary student. Give me a lame horse and I can help, but I don't treat people."

"That is a pity." He patted her hand. "You have an excellent bedside manner and you're much prettier than the crusty old fellow who treats me."

She relaxed a fraction and smiled at his teasing. "Flattery—while always deeply appreciated—will get you nowhere."

"I really am feeling better. As you must have heard, I'm Avery's grandfather. My name is Edmond Barnes. I don't believe I caught your name, young lady."

"Pleased to meet you, Mr. Barnes. I'm Jennifer Grant and I should still call an ambulance."

He rose to his feet. "I'll simply refuse treatment."

Rising, she planted her hands on her hips. "When I first saw you I thought I noticed something familiar. Now I see the resemblance. You and Avery share the same strong chin, the same eyes and the same hole in your head where your common sense belongs."

He chuckled. "You must have more than a passing acquaintance with my grandson."

Heat rose in her cheeks. "We've met," she admitted.

Edmond studied her intently. "What do you think of him?"

His question caught her off guard. Should she tell the truth, or amend it to make a sick old man feel better? She didn't want to do either. "Perhaps you should ask his commanding officer that question."

"I'm asking you."

"Avery and I don't exactly see eye to eye on things,"

she admitted slowly. "Sometimes, I think he is his own worst enemy."

"That's very astute." Edmond began walking toward the stable door. Jennifer took his elbow to steady him. When they reached his car, his driver got out and opened the door for him.

Edmond paused, but glanced back at her and said, "When I was a young man, I started a small real estate firm. Over my lifetime I turned it into a multi-million dollar corporation. I learned to read people well and quickly because I had to, but I've never been able to tell what Avery is thinking."

Jennifer hesitated, then found herself saying, "You shouldn't give up on him."

Where had that come from? She was the last person who should be sticking up for Avery.

"I'll admit things didn't go well today, but thanks to my crusty doctor and a triple bypass surgery, I've been given the chance to make things right. I'm not giving up on my grandson. I'll find a way to reach him."

She smiled. "Good."

"Thank you again for your kindness, Miss Grant."

After he drove away, Jennifer glanced at her watch. If she left right now she might just make the first round of jumping at the Deerfield Open. Even though she knew she should leave, she found herself staring toward the Commanding General's Mounted Color Guard office.

Edmond Barnes was a sick man who wanted to reconcile with his grandson. Could she help? Had God placed her here today for that reason? If it were only Avery's feelings to consider she might drive off without a backward glance. She bit her lip in indecision.

As if summoned by her thoughts of him, the office

door opened and Avery stepped out into the sunshine. "I saw your truck was here again. Where were you? Hiding in the hay loft?"

"I forgot an X-ray film in Dakota's stall. Avery, I honestly had nothing to do with his coming here."

"A likely story. Just admit you can't stay away from me, Jenny."

She struggled with her rising indignation. Why did he have to turn everything into a joke? "Trust you to kill any kindness I might be feeling."

"Kindness? Don't tell me that manipulative old man made you feel sorry for me? Does he want you to help us patch things up?"

"Would that be such a bad thing?"

A shadow flickered in his eyes and she understood what Edmond had meant about not being able to read him.

"Careful, Jenny. Your nose is cute but it doesn't belong in my business." The edge in his voice should have been enough to send her on her way, but for some reason it wasn't.

"Our families are an important part of who we are. You shouldn't dismiss him out of hand. Forgiveness heals the forgiver as well as the forgiven."

"Shame on you for eavesdropping."

Heat rushed to her cheeks. She folded her arms across her chest. "I wasn't eavesdropping. I accidentally overheard part of your conversation," she conceded.

Raising one eyebrow, he asked, "How is that not eavesdropping?"

She glanced down at the toe of her work boot. "Okay, I'm sorry I didn't let you know I was in Dakota's stall."

"Skip it, Jennifer. It doesn't matter." There was a touch of defeat in his tone.

She looked up and met his gaze. "I honestly didn't mean to listen in on a private family matter. I am sorry."

A smile twitched the corner of his mouth. "I can't believe I lived to see the day Miss Jenny Grant acknowledged a fault. I'm going to have to mark this on my calendar."

Raising her chin a notch higher, she countered, "Unlike some people I know, I can admit when I'm wrong."

"Unlike some people I know, I mind my own business."

She touched a finger to her lips as she pressed them together, then pointed at him. "You know what? You're right. It's none of my business if you shun your own family, but in the end, you are the one who is going to suffer."

The sound of horses approaching at a rapid trot heralded the return of the troop. Avery took a step closer to her. "Do you charge for your advice, Dr. Jenny? I hope not, because it isn't worth anything."

Jennifer drew a deep breath to keep from making another comment. No matter what she said, he would always find a way to have the last word at her expense.

She spun on her heels and marched to her truck. Trying to help Avery had been a total waste of time.

Avery started to go after Jennifer and apologize, but stopped himself. It was better to let her believe he was a complete jerk. That way she wouldn't be tempted to interfere again. She was better off staying out of his family feud. His grandfather might pass himself off as a caring old man, but Avery knew better.

Edmond wasn't above using anyone or anything to gain the upper hand. He had certainly proved that to Avery beyond a shadow of a doubt.

Yet the old man still possessed the ability to make Avery feel worthless and insignificant.

No one could live up to the expectations his grandfather had set. Avery had given up trying years ago. It wasn't until he saw his grandfather again today that Avery realized he still cared what Edmond thought of him.

As the column of riders approached the stable yard, a jeep stopped on the roadway in front of them and a young corporal got out. Captain Watson reined his horse to a halt beside him as the rest of the unit continued on. The corporal saluted, handed the captain a thick envelope, then jumped in the jeep and drove off.

The previously quiet stable became a hive of activity around Avery as the group dismounted and led their animals into their stalls. The men's jovial chatter, the eager nickering of hungry mounts and the clatter of iron shod hooves on the old cobblestone floors brought the stable to life as it had for more than a century.

Although Avery would never admit it out loud, he was proud of his part in keeping the cavalry's heritage alive. He loved the unit and all it stood for. The Army had been good to him.

Captain Watson rode up, dismounted and handed the reins to Avery. "Tell the men to gather in the ready room. We have new orders."

"Yes, sir." Avery saluted and led the captain's horse into the barn where he passed the word, then rubbed down and stabled the captain's mount.

Twenty minutes later, the sixteen soldiers of the Commanding General's Mounted Color Guard were seated in gray folding chairs in a small meeting room at one end of the barn. They rose to their feet when Captain Watson walked in.

"Take your seats, men. As most of you know, the American Cavalry Competition is being held at Fort Riley this year and we've just received permission to participate."

A cheer went up from the group. Grinning, the captain motioned for silence. "We also have three major performances scheduled during the next few weeks. That means a lot of travel for some of you, but I'm confident that this year we're going to bring the Sheridan's Cup back where it belongs. To the home of America's cavalry!"

Avery observed the buzz of excitement in the group with mild amusement. The chance for the CGMCG to showcase their skills and outshine the unit that had won last year's contest had them trash-talking like a pumped up high school football squad.

"Okay, men," the captain continued. "This isn't just about beating the socks off the Fort Humphrey boys. We'll be facing police mounted units, National Guard mounted units and quite a few re-enactor units in the Platoon Drill event.

"All of you are free to enter the individual riding classes. They include Mounted Saber, Mounted Pistol, Military Horsemanship and Military Field Jumping. A plaque will also be awarded for the outstanding horse at the competition."

"It should go to Dakota," Lee suggested.

Captain Watson smiled. "Dakota has certainly earned a special place in this unit, but I'm not sure he is up to performing at such a high level. Dr. Cutter will give us his opinion on that soon."

Avery had been riding Dakota in the various parades and performances where jumping and rapid stops weren't required, but he suspected the horse was strong enough to compete.

Shuffling through the papers in his hand, the captain found the one he was seeking. "Winners of the individual events will be invited to compete in a combination test of skills for the Sheridan Cup. Besides the silver trophy and a one thousand dollar cash prize, the winner will have his name added to the bronze plaque displayed in the U.S. Cavalry Memorial Research Library. I don't need to tell you that Command is hoping it will be a Fort Riley soldier this year."

Captain passed out the entry forms to the men crowding around him and then dismissed the group. Avery rose and left the building. He had just reached his car when he heard Captain Watson call his name. Turning, he saw his commander approaching holding out a sheet of paper. "Aren't you going to enter?"

"I wasn't planning on it."

The captain pressed his lips together and frowned. "The Sheridan Cup carries a lot of prestige for the brass here. You are better than anyone I've ever seen with a saber and just as good as most with a pistol. I think you could win."

Taken aback by the praise, Avery found himself at a loss for words. In the back of his mind he heard his grandfather's voice telling him he'd never amount to anything. Yet here was his captain, a man he admired, telling him he believed he could win the most coveted prize in the modern cavalry.

"I can't order you to enter the individual classes," the captain continued, "but I'm asking you to do it for the honor of this company."

What if he entered and failed to win?

His grandfather would expect him to fail.

According to him, I fail at everything except spending money. So why do I still care what he thinks? I'm not a failure.

He did care what his captain and the men in the unit thought of him. Could he face disappointing them? "I'll think about it, sir."

"Let me know by tomorrow. Dakota is assigned to you, but you can pick another horse for the competition if Dr. Cutter doesn't think Dakota should participate."

Lee, who had been waiting nearby, came over after the captain walked away. "Are you going to enter?"

"I said I'd think about it."

"You can enter, but don't plan on winning."

Avery cocked his head to the side. "And why is that?"

"I've seen a couple of the riders from the National Guard Volunteers in action. You'll be outclassed."

"You just heard the captain say that I'm the best he's ever seen with a saber."

"Oh, I agree, but that's only a quarter of the overall score. You might be as good with a pistol as those boys, but they'll ride you into the dirt in Military Horsemanship. That's like dressage and no offence, but you stink at that."

"Okay, my fancy riding could use some work. You seem to know so much about it, why don't you give me a few lessons?"

"Me? I'm worse than you are. You need someone who really knows how to work with you and your horse."

Avery glanced at the men leaving the building. "So which of the guys in the unit is better?"

Lee shoved his hands in his pockets. "I hate to say it, but most of us are pretty average."

Exasperated, Avery said, "All right, you go to horse shows all the time. Who's the best in this area? Who can I get a few pointers from?"

Lee burst out laughing.

Avery scowled at him. "What's so funny?"

Controlling his mirth with difficulty, Lee managed to say, "Jennifer Grant is the best dressage rider in the area, but from what I've seen, she isn't going to give *you* the time of day."

Chapter 4

It was almost dark by the time Jennifer turned into the gravel drive that led to her family's double-wide mobile home on their twenty acres outside Dutton. To her relief she saw her mother's green-and-white pickup and horse trailer sitting in front of their small barn. She had been half afraid that her mother wouldn't be home yet.

The front stoop light came on and Lizzie, followed by twelve-year-old Toby and eight-year-old Ryan, piled out of the door to race toward her. She stopped beside the chain link fence that surrounded their tiny overgrown yard and rolled down her window.

"I smell pizza," Toby shouted as he pulled open the gate.

Picking up the warm cardboard box from the seat beside her, Jennifer passed it out the window to her eager siblings.

Lizzie took the box, holding it over her head to keep Toby from grabbing it. "I told you she would win."

Toby snatched the box from his sister's hand. "I hope it's pepperoni."

Lizzie snatched it back. "I hope it's cheese."

"Be careful or it will be a dirt pizza," Jennifer warned, but the two of them were already on their way into the house.

Ryan, the youngest and quietest of the Grant kids, looked up at Jennifer. "Did you win?"

She gave him a tired smile. "I won the dressage class."

"But not the jumping class?"

"No."

"Why? Did McCloud miss some jumps?"

"I wish I could blame him, but the truth is, I didn't get there in time to enter."

"Oh." He shoved his hands in the pocket of his jeans and kicked at a bit of gravel with the toe of his shoe. "I guess that means you didn't win enough to get me a new bike."

"No. I'm sorry, sweetheart. I only won enough to cover the money I spent to enter, the pizza and feed for the horses." Jennifer stepped out and began walking to the back of the trailer.

Ryan followed her. "That's okay. I don't really need it. It's almost winter anyway."

She wanted to hug him, but she knew he wouldn't appreciate the gesture. He hadn't been able to go dirt bike riding with his friends since their mother had accidentally run over his bicycle. Jennifer knew he missed hanging out with his buddies, but there were so many other things the family needed first.

"You should go inside before your brother eats your slices of pizza."

"I'm not hungry. Can I help you put your stuff away?"

"Sure. You get the saddle and pad and I'll take Mc-Cloud. I almost forgot to mention that Dr. Cutter has asked me to keep Isabella for a few day."

His eyes lit up. "Really? That's great. She's a cool rabbit, but won't Mom be upset? She got kind of mad when Isabella was here last time."

He stood aside as Jennifer backed her horse out of the trailer. "Mom was just upset because Isabella liked to run in and out of her long skirts and chew on the lace. We'll keep Isabella in her cage when Mom is in one of her costumes."

"Maybe we should keep her in the barn."

Jennifer stopped and looked down at him. "Mom or the rabbit?"

Ryan's mouth fell open, then he started to laugh and Jennifer grinned, too.

Ten minutes later, they finished putting McCloud out into the pasture with Lollypop, their mother's black mare. The two horses greeted each other with soft whinnies. Soon they moved off and began grazing together as the last golden rays of sunlight faded from the western sky.

When Jennifer and Ryan entered the house, she sent him to wash up. Lizzie and Toby were sitting on the worn blue sofa in front of the TV. The pizza box, with two small slices remaining, sat open on the kitchen table.

Jennifer washed up at the kitchen sink, then put both slices in the microwave. When Ryan returned, she handed him the plate and a glass of milk. He took it and joined his brother and sister on the couch.

Jennifer settled for a glass of milk and the last apple in the vegetable drawer. After tossing the empty pizza box in the trash, she retrieved her textbooks from her room and returned to the table to study.

A few minutes later, Jennifer looked up as Mary Grant came out of her bedroom and entered the kitchen. Her mother was wearing one of her 1850s-style dresses, a deep blue and white plaid cotton dress with a full skirt over layers of white petticoats.

"Oh, good, you're home," Mary said, turning around. "Can you hook me?"

"Are you going out like that?"

"The historical society is meeting at the Dutton mansion in Old Towne tonight."

"So?" Old Towne was a collection of log cabins, restored businesses and homes from the early 1850s. The Dutton mansion was a simple two-story house with pretentious white columns supporting a small balcony across the front of the building. It was the town historical society's fondest hope that they could turn the area into a profitable tourist attraction.

"Really, Jennifer. You know as an employee of Old Towne I can't go onto the property unless I'm in period dress. I am, after all, Henrietta Dutton. I'm not about to greet visitors to my home in anything but my freshest gown."

Jennifer tugged on the tight bodice and began fastening the long row of hooks down the back of the garment. "It seems kind of silly to dress up when there won't be any tourists to see you."

"Perhaps, but this keeps me in the spirit of my role. I can practice greeting important people with the grace and charm of a southern belle."

Jennifer fastened the last hook. "Don't you think you're carrying this a little far?"

Her mother spun around and flipped open a fan suspended from her wrist by a silken cord. "Of course not, darling," she drawled as she fluttered the dark blue silk and ivory fan beside her face. "I'm simply enjoying my job. Wait until you see my performance on Founder's Day. This year, for the first time ever, we are staging a stunning re-enactment of Henrietta Dutton's charge up Dutton Heights. I get goose bumps just thinking about it."

Snapping shut her accessory, Mary lifted her skirts with both hands and headed for the door. "I won't be back until late, so don't wait up. Thank goodness I don't have to wear a hoop under this thing. I'd never be able to drive in it. But I do wish I had a carriage to ride in. It would so much more appropriate to arrive in a horse-drawn buggy than in my truck."

As her mother departed in a flurry of petticoats, Jennifer glanced to where her brothers and sister sat on the sofa. They were all watching her with various degrees of concern on their faces.

Lizzie said, "It's tough enough being the brainy girl in school. Having a mother who thinks she is Betsy Ross on top of that is the pits."

"Mom does get a bit carried away," Jennifer admitted.

Toby rose and brought his empty plate to the sink. "Carried away? Our mother is a nut case. She knows more about old Colonel Dutton and his weirdo wife than they did. Who cares what was happening in 1859, anyway?"

Their mother's passion for re-enacting the past sometimes seemed to border on an obsession, but Jennifer felt the need to defend her.

"If it wasn't for Mom's respect for the history of our town and her determination to save our heritage, Henrietta Dutton's deeds of valor would be forgotten."

"And the town council wouldn't have an excuse to hold a money-making festival every year and exploit mother's zeal, not to mention her time and energy," Lizzie added.

"When did you get to be such a cynic?" Jennifer asked.

"Between your job and school and riding, I'm the only one left to listen to her grand schemes to expand the widow Dutton's ride into a national event."

"I'm here," Toby said, elbowing his sister when he sat down beside her.

Lizzie elbowed him back. "Oh, like you listen to her. All she talks about is making the exact same ride to show the world how brave Henrietta Dutton was. Mom doesn't even ask about school or how my chess match went."

"How did your match go?" Jennifer asked, feeling guilty for not asking sooner.

"I won—as usual. Most boys only think they're smarter."

Her comment started another round of elbowing with Toby. Ryan moved to the floor to get away from his jousting siblings.

"Cut it out," Jennifer said sternly. "I'm sure things will get back to normal after the Founder's Day Festival. Making the past come alive is Mother's dream. We need to support her."

Jennifer opened her textbook and prayed that she was right, but she couldn't quite silence the nagging doubts at the back of her mind. The kids needed a mother who was involved in their lives, not one so involved with the past that she couldn't see the present. How did one tell their own parent that they were falling down on their job?

The Founder's Day Festival was only three weeks away. Jennifer would hold her peace until then, but after her mother made her big ride, they were going to have a mother-daughter heart to heart.

On Monday afternoon, when Jennifer was done with her classes for the day, she made her way through the veterinary hospital wards and down the short hall to the front desk at the Large Animal Clinic.

Her mother's behavior was still on her mind, but she wasn't as worried as she had been the day before. The entire family had spent Sunday together in a normal, modern day fashion. They had attended church together and spent the afternoon visiting friends of the family. By the end of the day Jennifer decided that she had been making mountains out of mole hills.

Stephanie, another student who worked part-time in the clinic, sighed with relief when Jennifer opened the office door. "Am I glad to see you."

"Busy day?" Jennifer tucked her purse into the gray metal cabinet beside the desk and took a chair behind the glass partition that separated them from the client waiting area.

"Three emergency surgeries on cows, two bad lacerations on a pair of draft horses and a sonogram to check if a llama is pregnant. Nothing too weird. I just need to get going. I've got an anatomy test this afternoon and I really have to study."

"Is there anything I need to know?"

"Dr. Wilkes just brought in a ton of stuff to be filed." Stephanie transferred a large stack of papers to Jennifer's side of the desk.

"Oh, joy." Dr. Wilkes was notorious for his bad penmanship.

Stephanie bit her lower lip. "Do you want me to stay and help?"

"No, I've got it. Go cram to your heart's content."

"You're a doll, Jennifer."

"Yes, I know," Jennifer said, nodding sagely.

Stephanie giggled, then hurried out the door. Jennifer picked up an armful of papers and carried them to the shoulder high black filing cabinets lining the wall behind her. She peered closely at Dr. Wilkes illegible scrawl and tried to decide if the first letter of the client's last name was an A, an O or a misshapen D.

Fifteen files later, her eyes were beginning to cross when the sound of the front door opening made her look up in relief. Anything was better than this.

To her surprise, Edmond Barnes walked in followed by his chauffeur. His driver held a glass bowl overflowing with a bright bouquet of autumn-colored flowers.

She smiled at Avery's grandfather, happy to see he was looking much better. "Mr. Barnes, what are you doing here?"

He took the bouquet from his driver. "I've brought a small gift to repay your kindness the other day, Miss Grant."

"You didn't have to do that." Jennifer looked at the small opening in the glass partition between them, then hurried out of the office door and around to the waiting area.

He extended the flowers to her. "I didn't have to do it, I wanted to do it."

"How on earth did you know that I worked here?"

"You said you were a veterinary student. A few phone calls was all it took to discover that you both attend school and are employed here."

Taken aback, she said, "That's actually a little scary."

His expression showed his surprise followed quickly by genuine distress. "I'm very sorry, Miss Grant. The last thing I want to do is upset you. Please enjoy the flowers and the knowledge that your kindness touched me deeply."

"I will, thank you very much." She couldn't contain her curiosity any longer. Although it was clearly none of her business, she couldn't help wondering if Mr. Barnes and Avery had made any progress in repairing their relationship.

"Have you been able to accomplish what you came here for?" she asked, hoping he and Avery had been able to heal their breach.

"Reconciling with my grandson? I'm sorry to say I have not, but I'm taking your advice. I don't plan to give up on him. I did that once and it was my biggest mistake. I'll be staying in the area for a while, although the service at my current motel leaves a lot to be desired."

"That's an easy fix." Turning around, she retraced her steps into the office. Setting the flowers on the desk, she pulled her purse from the cabinet and withdrew a card for the bed and breakfast next to the café where her mother worked. She slipped it under the glass toward him.

"This place is on the main street of my hometown. It's only a few miles from here on Highway 24. It's called the Dutton Inn, but it's a bed and breakfast. The owners, Mr. and Mrs. Marcus, belong to our church so I can vouch for them. It's quiet, immaculately clean and the beds have real feather mattresses."

Edmond took the card. "That certainly sounds better than where I've been staying."

"I'm sure you'll like it. The town has a historical section that you may enjoy exploring. If you want a really knowledgeable tour guide, my mother, Mary Grant, works at the café next door. She'll be happy to bend your ear about our history."

"I may do that. Thank you once again for your kindness and consideration."

Just then the outside door opened again. Captain Watson and Avery walked in.

Jennifer pressed her lips together and looked down. How long would it take until the sight of Avery's face stopped twisting her heart with yearning?

Calling herself every kind of fool, she pasted a polite smile on her face and greeted them. "Good afternoon, gentlemen. How may I help you?"

Avery stopped in shock at the sight of his grandfather talking to Jennifer. He had assumed, wrongly it seemed, that the old man had gone back to Boston.

Hanging back as Captain Watson approached the desk and asked to speak with Dr. Cutter, Avery tried to figure out why the head of his family's empire was still in Kansas.

What motive could Edmond have for remaining in the area? Something wasn't right.

His grandfather didn't trust the day-to-day running of his company to anyone. In all the years Avery had known him, he could only remember him missing work once. The day of his son and daughter-in-law's funeral. The next day, he had gone back to his office, leaving Avery alone in the sprawling mansion.

Jennifer picked up the phone and spoke to Dr. Cutter, then hung up and said, "You may go in, Captain."

Avery spoke up quickly. "If you don't need me, sir, I'll wait here."

Captain Watson glanced at Avery sharply, but nodded. "I think I can handle it. I shouldn't be long."

When his captain left, Avery gave his full attention to his grandfather. "I don't know how you knew I would be here today, but I don't have anything to say to you."

Edmond gave him a tight smile. "I'm sorry you feel that way. I simply stopped by to thank Miss Grant for her kindness the other day. I had no idea you would be here."

Avery wasn't sure if he should believe him or not.

With a slight bow, Edmond said, "You have my phone number if you decide you wish to speak with me. Until then, I bid you good day."

He walked past Avery and left the clinic followed closely by his burley and stoic driver.

Avery watched his grandfather leave, but he knew it wasn't going to be easy to dismiss the man from his thoughts. Curiosity had the better of him now. What did Edmond have to gain by staying in town?

For a moment, Avery considered the possibility that his grandfather might actually want a reconciliation. The second the idea popped into his head, Avery dismissed it as foolish. And so was the notion that Jennifer had somehow arranged it. His grandfather never allowed sentimentality to influence his decisions.

"He seems like a nice man." Jennifer said, drawing Avery away from his speculations.

"He isn't."

She looked down. "People change sometimes."

"Not very often."

He stepped up to the glass in front of the desk. Jennifer turned away and began filing papers, allowing him to spend a few moments admiring her feminine curves.

Watching her, he began to consider that he may have lost more than he'd gained when he'd broken it off with her. He'd been angry when he learned Jennifer had gone behind his back to contact Edmond.

Avery didn't want anyone to know what a fool he'd made of himself over a scheming woman. Jennifer had made a mistake, but at least *her* intentions had been good. At the time, her tearful apology and explanation had fallen on deaf ears. All he saw was one more woman who'd betrayed his trust.

He didn't trust easily, but he'd trusted Jennifer more than anyone in a long time. That was what hurt the most. His attempts at revenge hadn't eased his pain. They only managed to make him feel worse.

But he felt better now that he was near her.

I miss her. I miss the way she used to smile at me.

Giving himself a mental shake, he looked down. It didn't matter what he missed. Anything they might have shared between them was long gone. His behavior had made sure of that.

"How have you been?" he asked when the silence had stretched on long enough.

"Fine, thank you."

"That's good. How did your meet go last Saturday?"

"Fine, thank you." Her tone didn't vary.

"I guess that means you won again. Lee says you're one of the best riders in the state."

"Lee is too kind."

"He's a fan of yours, for sure. How is it that I didn't know you were so accomplished? You never went to any shows when we were going out."

"We went out during the winter. The shows run from April through November."

"That makes sense. It's the same for our unit's exhibitions. To become such an expert you must have had a good teacher." His show of interest sounded lame even to his own ears.

"I did." She opened another file drawer without looking at him.

"Who taught you?"

She slammed the file drawer closed and turned to face him. "What do you want?"

He spread his hands wide. "I'm just making conversation."

"I don't think so."

"All right, I'm interested in learning the same type of fancy riding that you do. Who taught you?"

"My grandmother was my coach."

He decided to cut to the chase. "Does she give lessons?"

"She passed away two years ago."

"I'm sorry to hear that." So much for his plan to take lessons from the person who had trained her.

"Thank you. I miss her very much. Perhaps that's why I tried to intervene with you and your grandfather. I know how final it is when you lose them and how much you wish you had had more time with them."

"I've had more than enough time with Edmond. Look,

I need to find someone to teach me the basic dressage moves in the next couple of weeks. Money is not an object. I'll double the going price for lessons. Are you interested?"

She tossed the papers she held onto her desk and folded her arms across her middle. "You're joking, right?"

"I'm rarely serious, but today is the exception to the rule."

"Why?"

"What does that matter?"

She tilted her head. "Humor me."

"Have you heard of the American Cavalry Competition?"

"Of course. I've watched it several times."

"It's going to be held at Fort Riley next month and I plan to compete for the Sheridan Cup."

"I remember now. There's a military dressage class, isn't there?"

"It counts for one quarter of the overall score. The saber class is a lock for me and I'm sure I can finish in the top three with a pistol, but Lee tells me I need a dressage coach and I believe him. He's seen some of the other riders in action. So, what do you say?"

"No."

"What? I just offered you twice the going rate for a few measly lessons."

"And I said no. I don't care what you offer to pay me. Money is not an object."

His temper flared at being thwarted. "You're just afraid you won't be able to keep your hands off me."

Her eyes narrowed. "That is so true. I can picture them around your scrawny neck right this minute."

"That's not a very Christian attitude, Jenny," he chided.

Her eyebrows shot up. She opened her mouth and closed it again without saying anything.

He knew a moment's satisfaction at seeing her speechless, but it quickly evaporated when he watched her bite her lower lip. He had kissed those full sweet lips before. He wanted to kiss her again.

She said, "It wasn't a very Christian thing to say, but as you so clearly pointed out to me when we were dating, you are not a Christian. Good luck in finding someone to give you lessons." She picked up her papers and turned her back on him.

The captain came out of Dr. Cutter's office with a smile on his face. "Good news. Dr. Cutter has cleared Dakota to return to full duty. I can't wait to tell the rest of the men. With proper conditioning, he should be fit to ride in the competition."

"That is good news, sir." Avery glanced toward Jennifer.

She still stood with her back to him. Once upon a time her face would have beamed with delight at such news. She, as much as anyone, had worked to save Dakota and return him to a full and active life. He wanted her to be happy. He wanted her to smile.

As the captain left the building, Avery hung back. Before he could lose his nerve, he rapped sharply on the glass. Startled by the sound, she spun around.

He shoved his hands in his pockets. "I just wanted to say that I know I treated you badly and I'm sorry."

Jennifer clutched the papers she was holding tightly to her chest. An apology from Avery was the last thing she expected. If Isabella had hopped in and asked for a carrot in perfect English, Jennifer might have been more stunned, but not by much.

She waited without speaking. Somehow, he was going to turn it into a jest or an insult, she just knew it.

Only he didn't. For a second, she thought she saw sadness cloud his eyes.

He shrugged and gave her a little smile. "Guess I'll see you around."

With that, he turned and walked out, leaving the bell over the door tinkling merrily and the faintest scent of his cologne wafting through the opening in the partition.

Jennifer stared after him in amazement. The man had actually apologized. She wouldn't have believed it if she hadn't heard it with her own ears.

Perhaps he wasn't such a lost cause after all.

Not that she cared anymore. Reaching out she touched the soft petal of a yellow lily in the bouquet his grandfather had left.

"Who am I kidding?" she whispered. "I do care. Oh, so much more than I should."

Chapter 5

Jennifer realized she was still clutching her files and laid them on the counter. The more she thought about it, the odder Avery's comment seemed.

"Wow! He actually apologized to me. I'm going to have to mark this day on my calendar." She repeated his comment with emphasis and wished she had thought of it before he left.

She couldn't allow herself to be taken in by the man again. She had more backbone than that.

But he *had* sounded sincere. She could almost believe that he meant it.

No, it was way out of character for him. Was he trying to butter her up and get her to change her mind about becoming his riding coach?

"Right. Like that will happen."

She had too much sense to get involved with him

again, even if some small part of her still found him attractive. "Once burned is twice shy, as my grandma used to say."

Brian walked into the office with Isabella in her carrier and a cardboard box balanced on top of it. He deposited his burden on the counter. "Who are you talking to?"

She pulled herself together. "No one. Are you leaving now?"

"I am. Thanks for watching Isabella for us."

"Don't mention it. Where are you and Lindsey off to?"

"We're off to Houston. Do you remember Corporal Shane Ross?"

"The tall Texan from the color guard? Sure."

"He and his wife just had a little girl. He's stationed in Germany, but he's here in the States on a short leave. Annie, his wife, will be joining him overseas when she and the baby get cleared to travel. Since Shane will have to go back before then, Lindsey is going to be staying with Annie for the next few weeks."

"Be sure and tell him that I said hello."

"I will. Any questions about Isabella's care?"

She smiled and shook her head. "None."

"If you need me for anything, you can always get me on my cell phone."

"Don't worry about a thing."

"Remember that Isabella likes to chew on pencils when she is bored, so you should make sure she gets plenty of attention."

"My littlest brother is looking forward to playing with her again, so I don't think that will be a problem."

"I put several of her favorite toys in the box with her

food and litter. I'm sure you know not to give her iceberg lettuce, but a romaine is okay."

Jennifer rose and moved to hold open the office door for Brian. "Isabella will be fine."

"Of course she will."

He started to leave, but stopped and turned to her. "Don't forget that she also chews on any paper she can get hold of."

"Oh, good. I'll use that excuse if I can't get my statistic paper done on time. 'I'm sorry, Professor Carlton, Dr. Cutter's rabbit ate my homework.'"

"You wouldn't."

"I'm kidding." She gave him a gentle push out the door.

"Are you sure you don't have any questions?"

"I'm sure. She'll be fine. Will you?"

He relaxed and grinned at her. "I think so. I just hate leaving her."

"No? I never would have guessed."

"Okay, I'm going." He made it as far as the clinic door before he stopped again. "I almost forgot. Dr. Wilkes is covering my calls while I gone. Be nice to him."

Jennifer waved as Brian walked out the door. When he was gone at last, she returned to her chair and sat down to gaze at Isabella. "Oh, joy, more illegible charts to decipher. What did I do to deserve this? No, don't answer that. I've had enough shocks for one day."

Putting Isabella's cage on the office floor, Jennifer returned to the filing waiting for her and tried to avoid thinking about Avery. It was a losing battle. When six o'clock rolled around at last, she happily turned the office over to the senior vet student who had the night watch and locked the clinic doors.

It wasn't until she pulled into her own driveway and saw her littlest brother come dashing out of the house that she was finally able to banish a certain soldier's puzzling behavior from her mind.

Ryan barely waited until the truck came to a stop before he pulled open her door. "Did you bring her? Did you?"

"I did." Jennifer lifted the carrier from the seat beside her and handed it to him.

He peered into the cage. "Hi, Isabella. Remember me?"

Jennifer smiled indulgently. "I'm sure she does."

"I've got a place for you to sleep all fixed up in my room," he cooed to the rabbit. He looked up at Jennifer with a wide beaming grin.

It was the happiest she had seen him in months. She didn't have the heart to tell him that Isabella had to sleep in her cage. That bit of news could wait until bedtime.

Jennifer glanced toward the spot where her mother usually parked. There was no sign of her truck. The horse trailer was gone, too. "Isn't Mom here?"

"Nope." He jumped down with Isabella's cage and started toward the front door.

"Did she call and say she would be late?" Jennifer asked as she stepped out of her vehicle and pulled Isabella's stuff out from behind her seat. Their mother was almost always home before the kids got out of school. It was one of the reasons she worked the early shift at the café.

"Don't know." Ryan disappeared into the house with the rabbit leaving Jennifer to wonder why her mother wasn't back yet. Surely she didn't have another festival planning meeting.

Following her brother inside, Jennifer saw Toby and Lizzie crowding around Ryan as he lifted Isabella out of her carrier. Watching all three of them stroking Brian's pet, Jennifer knew he needn't have worried that she wouldn't get enough attention.

"Lizzie, did Mom call?" Jennifer asked, setting her box on the pink and white Formica kitchen counter.

Shaking her head, Lizzie said, "She didn't call here."

"That's odd." Jennifer could plainly see there weren't any messages on the answering machine on the counter beside her box.

Toby looked up. "What's for supper? I'm starving."

Lizzie rolled her eyes, "You're always hungry."

"Are the chores done?" Jennifer asked quickly, hoping to forestall an argument between the two.

Ryan piped up. "I took the trash out."

The deafening silence from the others told Jennifer what she already suspected. She pointed toward the door. With a last, quick pat for the rabbit, Lizzie and Toby went out to feed and care for the other animals with only minor grumbling.

Jennifer picked up the phone and dialed her mother's cell phone, but it went straight to voicemail. Staff members at Old Towne weren't permitted to carry cell phones during business hours, but Mary always turned hers on once she left work.

After leaving a brief message, Jennifer hung up and set about finding something to make into a quick meal. Thirty minutes later, Jennifer was dishing out helpings of spaghetti when she heard the sound of her mother's truck pulling in. Her relief mingled with a growing sense of annoyance. She could only hope her mother had a good explanation as to why she hadn't called.

Toby and Lizzie were already seated at the table, but Ryan was still on the floor rolling a red plastic ball for Isabella to chase. At the sound of the truck door slamming, he jumped up and raced toward the entryway. "Mom's home."

Jennifer dropped the pan on the table and made a dive for the rabbit. She caught her just as Ryan threw open the door.

Mary rushed in, still wearing her calico work dress. "I'm sorry I'm late. We had a last-minute meeting with Mayor Jenks. You won't believe what he wants us to do now."

Ryan bounced up and down beside her. "Mom, Mom, Mom, Jennifer brought Isabella home with her. It's okay if she sleeps in my bed, isn't it?" he begged.

Mary's eyes widened as she caught sight of the rabbit squirming in Jennifer's grasp and she snatched up the front of her skirt with both hands. "Do not put that beast on the floor. She ruined two of my best petticoats the last time she was here."

"I've got her," Jennifer reassured her mother.

Later, Jennifer could never be sure if it was the sight of so much white lace or the sound of her mother scrunching up her crinoline that set the rabbit off. Whatever it was, the usually docile bunny suddenly leapt out of Jennifer's grasp and dashed beneath Mary's skirt.

Shrieking, Mary spun around, flapping the fabric of her dress as she attempted to escape Isabella's excited leaps.

Jennifer dropped to her knees and tried to catch the culprit, but Isabella darted underneath her mother's petticoats. Lizzie and Tony began howling with laughter.

Ryan yelled, "Don't step on her!" and threw himself under her skirt to save his friend.

Jennifer saw the fall coming but was powerless to prevent it. Her mother went down in a flurry of white lace and crinoline.

Ryan emerged with Isabella in his arms. Lizzie, Toby and Jennifer all rushed to help their mother up. Clearly shaken, Mary tried to rise, but sank back with a loud moan of pain.

Four hours later, Jennifer sat in the hospital emergency waiting area and listened as the doctor detailed her mother's injury.

"Mrs. Grant has a badly sprained wrist and the MRI shows that she has a severely torn ligament in her right knee."

Jennifer's heart sank. "Will she need surgery?"

"We can try keeping it immobilized, but I think chances are slim that it will heal without surgery. Either way, she is going to need a few months of rehabilitation."

"A few months?"

"I wish the news were better."

"Thank you, Doctor. You've been very kind."

"You're quite welcome. I must say, tonight was a first for me."

"How so?"

"I've never been called on to treat a patient in a Victorian ball gown who claims she tripped over a rabbit."

Jennifer managed a wry smile. "It's a Victorian day dress, actually, but I can see how you might not be up on 1850s fashions. If you knew my family, you would know that this is really nothing too strange for us. Can I see her now?"

"Certainly. We've given her something for the pain and we're getting a splint and crutches for her. She can go home tonight, but she needs to see an orthopedic specialist as soon as possible. This is his number."

Jennifer took the information the doctor handed her along with her mother's discharge instructions and then followed him to the small curtained cubical. Her mother lay propped up on a narrow cart.

"Hey, Mom. How are you doing?"

It was obvious that Mary had been crying. "I'm going to miss my Founder's Day ride. I worked so hard for that."

"I'm sorry, Mom. This is all my fault. I honestly intended to keep the rabbit in my room and not let her out when you were home. I just got sidetracked and forgot that Ryan had her out of her cage."

Mary nodded and reached out to pat her daughter's arm. "I know you didn't mean any harm, dear. I just don't know how I'm going to tell the Festival committee. We have all put so much time and effort into re-enacting Henrietta Dutton's ride. I can't let everyone down this way."

Jennifer was a lot more worried about how she was going to pay the hospital bill. They did have a little insurance, but the deductible was five-thousand dollars. Money already earmarked for Jennifer's school fees. If her mother needed surgery it would mean withdrawing from school until next year.

"You didn't let anyone down, Mom. You have a torn ligament in your knee. It's not like you decided to take a trip to the mall, instead."

"You don't understand. Announcements have been sent to newspapers and historical associations all across the country. We have descendants of the Dutton family coming from as far away as New York and Tennessee for this. We simply can't cancel now."

"Maybe someone else from the committee can take your place."

"I don't know who. Certain not Edna Marcus, even if she is a great-great-great-niece of the woman. She couldn't fit into one of Henrietta's gowns if she stayed on bread and water until doomsday. You're going to have to take my place, Jennifer. I don't see any other way."

"Me?" Her voice actually squeaked.

Mary nodded. "You and I are the same size. We won't have to alter the costume. You're a better rider than I am. You won't have any trouble making the charge up Dutton Heights."

Jennifer shook her head. "I don't think so."

"Please. You know how much this means to me."

Jennifer did know. And it was her fault that her mother wouldn't be able to fulfill the dream she had worked so hard to make come true.

"I suppose I could wear the dress for one afternoon and ride up a hill, but I draw the line at wearing a corset."

Mary scowled and tried to sit up, but winced in pain. Holding her bandaged wrist close, she said sternly, "This is a historical re-enactment, Jennifer. We are striving for the utmost accuracy. The costume must be exact."

"And exactly what does that mean?"

"As was the custom of the day, Henrietta was wearing a corset, pantaloon and three petticoats beneath her simple cotton dress when she pulled a saber from her dead husband's hand, threw herself on his war horse and led a band of ordinary farmers in a battle-turning charge straight up Dutton Heights into the very teeth of a pack of murderous raiders."

Jennifer sighed in resignation. Who could argue with that type of fanatical logic? This was a lose-lose situation. "Okay, okay, I'll do it."

"You will? Oh, darling, you have no idea how happy that makes me." Mary sniffed and used the corner of the sheet to blot her eyes.

When she regained her composure, she said, "You'll have to start practicing right away."

"Practice what? I thought I was just going to ride up a hill in a dress."

"Oh, no. You must do exactly what Henrietta did."

"Mom, she rode up a hill."

Mary shook her head. "Haven't you been listening? She picked up her husband's saber and his pistol and rode straight into the enemy camp. She struck down six of the brigands with her saber and shot two more with her husband's pistol before jumping her horse over the wall where their leader cowered and demanded his surrender at the point of her sword."

"She did all that?"

"Eye witnesses attest to the fact. The Lord was truly at her side."

"He must have been. So I have to wave a sword while I ride up this hill?"

"Not wave it. You'll have to cut down six bandits and shoot two more. Of course, they'll simply be mannequins dressed to look like fearsome raiders. They are rigged to fall down when you strike them or shoot them. It isn't as easy as it sounds. I've been practicing for six months and I'm not perfect yet."

"Mom, do you own a saber and a pistol?" Jennifer didn't try to hide her astonishment.

"Of course, dear. I store them at the Dutton house in a trunk for safe keeping. I wouldn't want the boys playing with them. Someone might get hurt."

Mary bit her lip as her brows drew together in a frown. "With less than three weeks until the festival, you're going to need a professional coach to master using a saber and pistol from horseback. I certainly won't be a position to teach you."

"How on earth did you learn?" Jennifer couldn't imagine her mother galloping across the countryside wielding a sword or shooting a gun.

"Gerard taught me."

Jennifer racked her brain, but could only come up with one Gerard. Surely her mother didn't mean the short, bald man who worked at the local supermarket. "Gerard Hoover from the produce section at the grocery store?"

"Yes. He's a cavalry re-enactor with a Civil War unit. I know he would be happy to help but his unit is in South Carolina for a re-enactment and he wouldn't be back until a few days before the festival. He's playing Colonel Dutton for us. You have friends in the mounted color guard at Fort Riley. Perhaps one of them could show you the basics."

Avery's face flashed into Jennifer's mind. She saw his self-assured smile and that gleam in his eyes.

No, there was simply no way she was going to ask him.

Chapter 6

Avery pulled his apartment door open and stared in stunned surprise at the sight of Jennifer Grant on his doorstep, one hand raised to knock again. She took a startled step backward, her hand going to catch the strap of her purse as it slipped from her shoulder.

She was wearing a blue, short-sleeved sweater over a pair of black jeans. Her hair was loose about her face and the afternoon sun highlighted the honey-colored strands.

A thrill of happiness shot through him at the sight of her. He quickly struggled to suppress the emotion. "Well, well, well. What do we have here?"

She raised her hand again, palm out. "Stop. Don't say anything that will make me regret coming here more than I already do."

Folding his arms over his chest, he waited, wondering what had prompted this visit. Could his grandfather have put her up to it? He wouldn't put it past him.

Lowering her hand, she took a deep breath. "Do you still want a riding coach?"

"Maybe."

"If I agree to give you lessons, I need something in return."

"I've already offered to pay you."

"I don't need the money. Well, I do need the money, but I need something else more than I need the money—which I can't believe I just said—but that's why I've come to you."

"I'm almost afraid to ask what you're talking about."

She shifted from one foot to the other. "I need to learn how to use a sword."

He raised an eyebrow. "I'll bite. Why?"

"It's a long story." She brushed past him and walked into his apartment.

As he started to close the door, he noticed the black SUV parked down the block across the street from his complex. It looked like the same one he had seen several times in the past few days, once behind him when he left the base and once again outside the restaurant where he had dinner. Shrugging off the sensation of being watched, Avery closed the door and followed Jennifer.

In his living room, she dropped onto one of the brown leather chairs that faced his matching sofa across a glass-topped oak coffee table.

"Can I get you something to drink?" he offered. "A soda, some tea?"

"Thank you, but I can't stay long. I have class in half an hour so I'll get right to the point. My mother was recently injured in an accident and she won't be able to ride for several months. I'm taking her place in an authentic re-creation of Henrietta Dutton's charge up Dutton Heights for the Founder's Day Festival."

"In Dutton. Sure I know about it. Our unit will be carrying the colors for the opening ceremony."

"Good. Anyway, to take my mother's place I have to be able to strike down six targets with a saber and shoot two more with a pistol while riding at a full gallop. Can you teach me to do that?"

"Sure."

"In two weeks time?" She looked skeptical.

"Maybe. Why ask me?"

She hesitated, then said, "My mother's instructor is unavailable. I called your captain to ask about getting lessons from your unit's saber instructor."

"Which is me."

"Yes, I was informed that you had taken over the position after Corporal Ross left."

"I told you I was the best, but I'm sure Lee would be happy to teach you what he knows."

"Believe me, I thought about asking him, but I wouldn't be able to pay him for his time."

"He'd do it for nothing."

She looked down at her hands clasped together in her lap. "Perhaps, but I wouldn't feel right about accepting his charity."

"But you're okay with accepting charity from me?"

Her gaze locked with his. "You and I are bartering one skill for another. I teach you and you teach me. No charity involved, no strings attached."

He walked into the small kitchen, opened the refrigerator door and pulled out a bottle of water. He took a drink, then tossed the cap into the trash. Leaning back against the counter, he said, "I'll have to think it over."

Jennifer wanted to wipe the smug look off his face but forced herself to stay calm. For some reason, the good Lord had seen fit to test her with this burden. She wouldn't turn away from it, so she swallowed her pride because her mother was depending on her.

Relaxing her fingers, she rubbed her palms on her pants legs. "If you're worried that our past relationship will get in the way, I can assure you it won't."

"How can I be sure? This might just be a ploy to get back into my good graces."

"You don't have good graces. You have an ego the size of an elephant."

"Insulting the man you want to help you isn't a move I would have made."

She clenched her hands into fists. She hated to admit that he was right.

Forcing a smile to her lips, she said, "I have no interest in renewing our personal relationship. We gave it a shot and we turned out to be wrong for each other. If we leave it at that, I don't see why we can't provide each other with a mutually beneficial service. I know you want to win the Sheridan Cup. I want to keep my mother's commitment. We can work together to make this happen or we can fail separately. It's up to you."

"No strings attached?"

"None."

"No religion shoved in my face?"

Her eyes narrowed. "I will not pretend that my faith isn't an important part of my life."

"If I say yes, what's your plan?"

She relaxed. "My plan is to meet at my house in the afternoons for the next two weeks. We have an outdoor arena. Which horse will you be riding?"

"Does it matter?"

"Yes, it does."

"I plan to ride Dakota."

She nodded. "I know Dakota has had formal training. Lindsey told me her brother used to show him before he gave the horse to your unit. Is he in good enough condition for the jumping part of it?"

"I think he is. He's fast and he loves to jump."

She looked hopeful for the first time. "Then you'll do it?"

"As long as you keep your end of the bargain and this stays strictly business, I don't see that I have anything to lose."

"Good. I'll see you tomorrow at four."

"Make it four-thirty. Shall I bring Dakota?"

"No. You should ride my McCloud. Riding a well-trained horse is one way to learn how it should be done, but bring your own saddle."

Jennifer couldn't believe he had agreed to her proposal so easily. While she was relieved, some small part of her couldn't help but wonder why. Another nagging little voice told her keeping things professional might prove difficult.

Avery drove down the road leading to Jennifer's home at the appointed time the next afternoon. As he approached the double wide mobile home, he couldn't help but compare it to the house he had grown up in. The entire trailer would have fit into the garage that had housed his father's sports cars or into the boathouse where his grandfather's sailboats were moored.

He spotted two boys on a tire swing suspended from the branches of a gnarled oak tree inside the fenced yard.

They must be Jennifer's brothers. Even though he and Jennifer had dated for several months, he had successfully avoided meeting most of her family. He'd been introduced to her younger sister when Jennifer brought her to one of the CGMCG performances. The rest of the time, he managed to pick Jennifer up when she got out of class or right after she got off work.

Meeting family implied commitment—something he avoided like the plague. So why had he agreed to come here today?

Avery had been trying to find the answer to that question ever since Jennifer showed up at his apartment. He wasn't used to studying his own motives but he recognized that guilt was playing an unexpected role.

Of course, he would benefit from their arrangement, too. He couldn't forget that winning the Sheridan Cup was his goal. Spending time with Jennifer would simply be icing on the cake.

As he pulled to a stop, Avery noticed the taller boy turning the tire around and around with the smaller, blond boy sitting inside it. Both of them were dressed in worn jeans and long-sleeved western chambray shirts. The little one's shirt had a patch on one elbow and was baggy enough to make Avery suspect it had been a hand-me-down from his brother.

Avery climbed out of his car just as the older boy finished twisting the rope. He gave the tire a hearty shove and stepped back, letting his brother spin through space with wild squeals of laughter filling the air.

It looked like fun. Until Avery had joined the army he had led a life of privilege few people knew, but the cars, boats and the servants working silently in the cavernous house hadn't supplied a lonely boy with a chance to engage in the kind of amusement he witnessed now. The envy he felt startled him.

When the tire finally stopped spinning, the older boy realized they were being watched. He left the swing and glared at Avery over the fence. His younger sibling tried to follow, but ended up staggering back and forth, then abruptly sat on the ground.

The door of the trailer opened and Jennifer came down the steps wearing blue jeans and a pink jean jacket over a white T-shirt. Her pants were tucked into black riding boots. She looked eager to get to work. He could almost imagine she was happy to see him. He closed the car door and leaned against it as he waited for her.

She stopped a few feet away and slipped her hands in the front pockets of her jeans. "Hi."

Her hair was drawn back into a ponytail, but wisps of it danced free at her temples. They tempted him to smooth them down with his hand, to cup the soft skin of her cheek with his palm and draw his thumb across the fullness of her lips.

He folded his arms across his chest to keep from reaching for her and hardened his resolve against the desire.

There was no sense torturing himself. She'd made it clear she wasn't looking to rekindle their relationship. She needed his help and he needed hers. This was business. He had a trophy to win. She was his ticket to the winner's circle.

"So, who gets their lesson first?" Avery asked. It

wasn't hard to sound bored. He'd had plenty of practice. He knew how to keep a tight rein on his emotions.

Some of the eagerness left her eyes, but she made a
quick recovery and lifted her chin. "Since I have two
weeks to get ready and you have three weeks until your
competition, I think it only fair that we start with me. I
have my mother's horse saddled down at the barn. We
can get started now if you're ready."

"No horse just yet." When Jennifer scowled at him,
he smiled. "The first saber lesson takes place on the
ground."

He turned and opened his car door, then pulled out a
wooden broomstick and offered it to her.

She cocked one eyebrow. "What's this?"

"Your saber, madame."

The older boy snickered. The little one, who had
gained his feet and was standing at the fence, tried his
best to stifle his own chuckles with both hands clasped
over his mouth.

Jennifer sent them both a quelling stare. "Avery, these
are my brothers, Ryan and Toby. Pay no attention to
them."

"I'm Ryan," the little one said eagerly. His older
brother didn't say anything, but the expression on his
face made it clear that he already disliked his sister's
tutor.

Jennifer looked at Avery and then down at the stick
he held out to her. "You're kidding, right?"

"Not at all."

"What can I learn with this?"

"How not to cut off your foot or slice your horse's
neck. Let's see what you've got." He tossed the wooden
dowel to her.

She deftly caught it in the middle. With a quick flick of her wrist, she began twirling it like a baton, spinning it from one hand to the next until it was a whirling blur.

After a few seconds, she tossed the stick into the air, spun around once, caught it neatly by one end and tapped the other end on the ground. Then, tucking the rod beneath one arm, she raised her hand with a flourish. Grinning widely, she said, "That's what I've got. What do you have?"

He snatched it from her grasp. "A long two weeks ahead of me."

She wrinkled her nose. "You're not the only one."

He glared at her and she glared back. Finally, he asked, "Do you want to learn this or not? Because I can leave."

The sound of the door opening caused them both to glance toward the trailer. Jennifer's mother hobbled awkwardly out the front door using one crutch. A long black brace encased her right leg and a blue sling held her right arm close to her body. She carried a bundle of yellow cloth draped across one shoulder. A teenage girl with dark curls followed her out of the house.

Jennifer rushed toward them. "Mother, don't you dare try to get down those steps."

"I'm not. Stop fussing." Grimacing with pain, Mrs. Grant propped herself against the wooden porch railing. She pulled the fabric from her shoulder and held it out to Jennifer. "You're going to need this."

"What is it?"

"One of my skirts. It just ties at the waist. You can slip it on over what you're wearing now."

"I don't need this, yet."

"You'll have to accustom yourself to moving in full

skirts and petticoats. It takes practice and you don't have much time. Aren't you going to introduce me to your friend?"

Avery saw Jennifer's hesitation. He stepped forward as she said, "Mom, this is Avery Barnes. Avery, this is my mother, Mary Grant."

"It's nice to meet you at last, Mr. Barnes. Jennifer has spoken of you often."

"Nothing good," Lizzie muttered, folding her arms across her chest.

"I'm sure," he said with a self-conscious smile. He easily read the wariness on the faces of Jennifer's family.

Mary spoke to her youngest daughter. "Lizzie, don't be rude." Looking at Jennifer, she said, "I'm sure you have lots of work to do so we won't keep you."

"You need to be resting that leg," Jennifer scolded, climbing the steps to hold open the door.

"I'm tired of sitting on the sofa."

"I don't care. The doctor won't start therapy until some of the swelling goes down and it won't go down until you stay off your feet. Lizzie, sit on her if you have to to keep her down."

Mary said, "I'll go back to the sofa when you put this skirt on."

"I'll put it on after you're safely on the couch with that leg on a pillow," Jennifer countered.

"She's quite bossy, Mr. Barnes." Mary said, maneuvering herself to head inside.

"I've noticed that about her," he agreed. Oddly, he also liked that about her.

Jennifer vanished into the house with her mother and sister, leaving Avery alone with her brothers. Toby glanced toward the house then back at Avery. He stepped closer to the fence with a fierce scowl on his face. "If you make my sister cry again I'm going to knock your block off."

"Yeah! That goes for me, too." Ryan added, imitating his brother's defensive stance.

Toby spun on his heels and stalked off. Avery watched him leave, then glanced down at Ryan. The youngster looked as if he wanted to follow his older brother, but he stayed at the fence watching Avery with a mixture of uncertainty and fascination.

Avery had the feeling he had been measured and found wanting. "I'm sorry I made Jenny cry."

"She doesn't like being called Jenny."

Unable to resist the urge to find out whatever this kid was willing to share about his sister, Avery took a step closer. "Why doesn't she like to be called Jenny?"

Didn't this make him guilty of the same conduct he'd rebuked Jennifer for? He was trying to gather information she wasn't willing to share with him. Would she be angry if she knew? Yeah, she would.

"Lizzie says it's because it was our dad's pet name for her and it makes Jennifer sad to think about him. I don't remember him because he died when I was a baby. Are you going to teach my sister how to use a gun? Can I shoot it, too?"

"No."

The boy frowned. "Why not?"

"The guns we use are not toys. They can hurt you."

Ryan sighed. "That's what Mom says. Do you want to see our rabbit? She isn't really our rabbit, she's Dr. Cutter's rabbit but we're keeping her for a while—only she has to stay in the barn now because she broke Mom's leg when Mom tried to step on her."

This kid not only looked like a small version of his sister, he talked like her, too. "Sounds like a dangerous character to me."

A mischievous grin appeared on the boy's face. "Mom or the rabbit?"

Avery chuckled. "My theory is that all women are dangerous characters."

"And mean. My sister Lizzie is always picking on me."

"Does Jenny, I mean Jennifer, pick on you?"

"No, but she makes me do chores and stuff. Come see Isabella." The boy walked to the gate in the fence and motioned for Avery to follow him.

Glancing at the house, Avery saw Jennifer come out the door. She now wore a full, floor-length yellow skirt. She hesitated as she caught sight of him watching, but after only a moment, she grasped the front of her outfit and lifted it enough to walk down the steps without tripping.

When she reached his side, she glared at him. "If you know what's good for you, Avery Barnes, you won't say a word. I know I look ridiculous."

He decided to take her advice and keep quiet, even though he didn't think she looked ridiculous at all.

She looked charming and very feminine in her old-fashioned costume. The flair of the yellow print skirt accentuated her small waist. The sway of the material as she walked and the peek of ruffled petticoat lace at her ankles did funny things to his insides.

"If you remember, I'm the one who goes around dressed as a Union trooper."

She brushed at her skirt. "True, but you and your men manage to look romantic in your uniforms."

Her eyes widened when she realized what she had said.

He hid a smile as he turned away. Oh, yes, at this rate, keeping their current arrangement strictly business was looking less likely by the minute.

Chapter 7

Ryan didn't seem to notice the tension in the air between the two adults. The boy jumped up and down with pent-up excitement. "Avery wants to meet Isabella."

Jennifer relaxed when Avery didn't make any snide remarks about her outfit or her comment that he looked romantic. She hadn't meant to imply that she thought of Avery as romantic, but couldn't think how to explain herself without sounding even more foolish.

Happy to have a diversion, she smiled down at her brother. "Avery met Isabella when the Army had Dakota at my hospital. Why don't you run along and play with Toby, or better yet, go keep Mom company?"

"But Avery wants to say hello to her. Don't you?"

Ryan looked so eager to show off his pet that Jennifer didn't have the heart to discourage him further.

To her surprise, Avery said, "Sure, kid, I'd like to see your rabbit."

Jennifer shot him a grateful look.

"Great." Ryan took Avery's hand and began pulling him toward the barn. Once inside, he let go and dropped to his knees in front of a small wooden and wire mesh rabbit hutch.

"Wait a minute," Jennifer cautioned as she shut the barn door and carefully latched it. Inside the old building, dust motes danced in the air where the late afternoon sunshine cut rectangles of light into the dim interior. Fresh straw crackled underfoot and smelled of hot, dry summer days.

Ryan looked up at Avery. "We have to be careful. She might run away and get lost if she gets out, but I don't think she would. She likes it here."

Unlatching the cage door, he lifted the large brown bunny out and held her close.

Dropping to a crouch beside the boy, Avery stroked the rabbit's head. "I see you're still causing more trouble than you're worth."

He glanced up at Jennifer with a gleam in his eyes. "Do you remember how she had us all searching high and low at the clinic that day?"

Jennifer did. It had been the first day Avery had singled her out for attention. "I remember. She got out of her cage and went into Dakota's stall."

"I remember how mad Dr. Cutter was at Sergeant Mandel. He thought she was trying some new stress reduction therapy for her sick horse."

"He accused her of being hare-brained. I had to straighten the two of them out. I thought for a minute I was going to have to send both of them to stand in the corner."

Ryan piped up. "Jennifer does that to me. I don't like it."

"Count yourself lucky," Avery said. "Brian and Lindsey wound up in more trouble than that."

"How much more?" Ryan asked, wide-eyed.

"A whole lot. They ended up getting married."

Looking uncertain, Ryan asked, "Is that bad?"

Avery nodded. "It's a fate worse than death."

"Don't tell him that," Jennifer said, glaring at Avery. Just when she found herself liking him again, he managed to remind her what a jerk he could be.

"I'm just teasing." He ruffled Ryan's hair and rose to his feet.

She spoke to her brother. "Put Isabella back in her pen and go get washed up."

"Aw, do I have to?"

"Yes. Mr. Barnes and I have work to do." She turned quickly, but stepped on her long hem and stumbled. Regaining her balance, she shot Avery a quelling look, gathered her skirting into a wad in front of her and left the barn.

Avery managed to keep the smile off his face until she was out of sight. He looked down at Ryan. The boy had his cheek resting on his furry friend's head.

"You'd better do as your sister says or she'll send us both to the corner."

"Okay." Ryan's reluctance was clear, but he did as he was told. When the bunny was safely secured, he climbed to his feet and started to leave the barn. It was then that Avery saw the mangled bicycle propped against the wall beside the door.

"Looks like someone had a wreck."

"My mom backed over it with her truck. Jennifer is going to get it fixed as soon as she has the money, but she has to pay for her school and bills first. The bike is a low pry—something."

"Priority?"

"I think so. Does that mean it's not very important?"

"Being stuck without wheels is never a low priority for a guy."

"That's what I think, but Jennifer says food on the table, a roof over our heads and feed for the animals come first." He did a fairly good falsetto imitation of his sister's voice and even managed to give that little shake of her shoulders she did when she was trying to be tough.

"Don't you believe that?"

"I guess I do. I know she and Mom worry a lot about bills. I hear them talking sometimes when I can't sleep."

A familiar sick sensation settled in the pit of Avery's stomach. He knew firsthand the lengths some women would go to solve their money problems. As much as he hated giving Edmond credit for anything, the truth was, his grandfather was the one who had opened Avery's eyes to that painful knowledge. "She should marry someone who is rich, then all her problems would be solved," he suggested bitterly.

"Lizzie says that, but Jennifer says she's only going to marry for love like Mom and Dad did."

Intrigued in spite of himself, Avery asked, "When did she say that?"

"Lots of times. I don't think being rich is a good thing."

"Why is that?" Avery asked.

"Because then you can't make your camel go through

the eye of your needle." He shrugged his small shoulders. "Beats me why you'd want to, anyway."

Avery had to agree. Although he doubted Jennifer's little brother was privy to her true thoughts about marriage, it was oddly satisfying to know she at least paid lip service to marrying for love.

Thrusting aside his curiosity about Jennifer, he scrutinized the twisted metal. "It shouldn't take much to straighten the frame and get you a new front wheel."

"Could you fix it?" Ryan looked hopeful.

"Not without the right tools."

"Oh." The boy's disappointment was painfully clear.

"I know a couple of soldiers at the fort who work in the motor pool. They could fix it."

"Really? How much would that cost?"

"I'm not sure, but you and I could work out a deal."

Ryan tilted his head. "Like what?"

"Did you notice the spokes on my car's wheels?"

"They are, like, maximum sweet."

Avery tried not to laugh at the awe in the boy's voice. "I like them, too, but they're hard to keep clean. I'll get your bike fixed if you wash them for me once a week while I'm out here."

Ryan's eyes grew wide. "Sure."

"I don't mean just throw a little water on them. I mean wash them inside and out, dry them and polish them so that they shine."

He nodded vigorously. "I can do that."

Avery smiled. "Then we have a deal. I'll bring the cleaning stuff with me when I come tomorrow. You'd better get going. Your sister and I have work to do."

As Avery left the barn with the boy, he saw Jennifer waiting for him beside his car. Walking up to her, he handed her the broomstick again. From the corner of his eye he saw her sister and brother come out of the house and park themselves on the front steps to watch.

"I still don't see what I'm going to learn with this," Jennifer said, an edge of annoyance in her voice.

"Hold it straight out in front of you."

She extended her arm. "Now what."

"Nothing. Hold it there until I tell you to put it down."

"This is silly."

He glanced at his wristwatch. "We'll see if you still think that after five minutes."

She stood rock solid for two full minutes before the tip of her stick began to wobble. After another minute a grimace appeared on her face, but she suppressed it when she noticed he was watching. Avery leaned against the front fender of his car and checked his watch again. "Two more minutes."

The tip wavered even more. "I don't see how this will help me hit a target."

"Yes, you do."

"Okay, I'll admit this is showing me which muscles I'll need to strengthen."

"Very good. And?"

Her arm dropped to her side. "It shows me that you like to watch me suffer."

He tapped his watch. "You still have a minute left."

She glared at him but raised her arm again. "How often should I do this?"

"At least ten times a day."

"That won't be so bad."

"I'm not done yet. Today, you can practice with the stick alone, but tomorrow I want you to start adding weight to it."

"How much weight?"

"The sabers we use weigh about eight pounds."

She dropped her arm again and stared at him open-mouthed. "You've got to be kidding. You want me to hold eight pounds out in front of myself for five minutes?"

"Among other things, yes. You have thirty seconds left."

With a long suffering sigh, she extended her arm. "What other things?"

"You're going to study the parts of a saber and of a pistol."

"Why? I'm going to do this stunt one time. I can pretty much promise you that once it's over I'm never touching a saber or a gun again."

"You have to become familiar with the tools you're going to be using. They can be very dangerous in the hands of someone who doesn't understand them. I assume you don't want to injure yourself or anyone else."

"Of course not."

"Did you know that cavalry horses were often shot and killed by their own inept riders?"

"Really?" She glanced at him. The expression on her face was a mixture of distress and disbelief.

He nodded. "Really."

"But I'll be using blanks."

"Blanks still require a charge of black powder that can make a nasty burn or even blind your mount. You can put your arm down now."

She dropped the stick and rubbed her shoulder. He asked, "Are you okay?"

"Remind me to have you spend five minutes holding up your horse before you start your riding lessons."

Chuckling, he said, "That will be easier than trying to hold up the instructor."

Her brother's hearty laughter rang out. Avery kept his eyes on Jennifer's expressive face. It took a second for his teasing comment to sink in. When it did, her jaw dropped.

She punched his shoulder. "I can't believe you said that. I do not weigh as much as a horse. You take it back."

"Fat chance." Ducking away from her outrage, he chuckled as he spun around to put the hood of his car between them.

"Get him, Jen," Lizzie called out.

"Look out, she pinches," Ryan yelled.

His sister elbowed him. "Whose side are you on?"

Jennifer advanced on Avery, a mischievous gleam in her eyes. "I said take it back."

"Or what? You'll make me sorry?" he taunted and took a step back.

"Yes." She lunged toward him, but her feet tangled in her long hem and she fell.

He jumped forward and managed to catch her against his chest. The weight of her slight body in his arms triggered an avalanche of emotions.

Protectiveness, tenderness, an overwhelming desire to kiss her took his breath away. So much for keeping his emotions under control. She looked up at him, her eyes wide with shock. Did she feel it, too? Her lips parted ever so slightly. He bent his head to kiss her.

Chapter 8

Jennifer came to her senses an instant before Avery's lips touched hers and turned her face aside. What kind of fool was she to let this man toy with her emotions again? Hadn't she learned her lesson the first time?

Steadying herself, she quickly regained her footing and stepped back. His hands dropped from her arms and he asked, "Are you okay?"

Did his voice sound breathless or was it her imagination? Why did his aftershave have to smell so good? Why did his touch have to send her heart racing? Wasn't she ever going to get over him? It had been such a bad idea to ask him here.

"I'm fine," she stated, holding her head up and forcing old dreams from her mind. "I guess lesson number two should be how to walk in one of these dresses."

"I'm afraid I can't help you with that."

She managed a small smile and hoped it covered how rattled she was. "I'd give a day's wages to see you try."

"Not a chance."

From the front steps, Lizzie yelled, "Mom says to stand up straight and take small steps."

Jennifer took a deep breath and blew it out slowly. "At least no one in the family missed me making a fool of myself."

A twitch at the corner of Avery's mouth told her he was trying not to laugh. "Tomorrow I'll bring a saber and scabbard so you can practice walking with that in addition to your petticoats."

"Goody, goody. I can't wait. Are we done here or do we have more stick work?"

"You're ready to try riding while keeping that broomstick in your right hand."

He stepped around her and opened the car door. "I also brought this for you." He withdrew a red folder and handed it to her. "Your study guide."

She tucked the folder under her arm. "Fine. Now it's your turn. Did you bring your saddle?"

"It's in the trunk."

"Get it and come along." With her chin up, she proceeded with shortened strides to the corral behind the barn where McCloud and Lollypop stood patiently waiting for riders.

She stopped beside her gray gelding and rubbed his cheek. After a few minutes, Avery joined her and hefted his McClellen saddle to the top rail of the fence.

He moved to stand at her elbow. "Your gelding is a good-looking fellow."

She wished Avery wouldn't hover so close. It made it hard to think straight. "Thank you. This is McCloud.

He's going to help me show you the finer points of horsemanship. The black mare is Lollypop, my mother's horse. She'll be carrying me on my charge as she is apparently already gun trained. I really had no idea how much effort my mother had been putting into this affair."

Hearing a commotion overhead, both Jennifer and Avery looked up. Jennifer's siblings were positioning themselves in the open hayloft doorway. Toby sat with his legs dangling out while Lizzie and Ryan stretched out on their stomachs with their chins propped on their hands.

Avery wagged his eyebrows. "Chaperones?"

"Ignore them. I find that works best. Mount up, soldier. Let's see what you've got."

She ducked under the horse's neck, stumbled on her skirt again, but managed to recover without falling on her face.

These clothes were ridiculous. How on earth had women functioned in long skirts for centuries? Glancing over her shoulder, she was relieved to see Avery was busy saddling the horse and hadn't noticed another less than graceful episode. Opening the gate to the corral, she stood beside it as he led McCloud through.

"What now?" he asked.

"Lead him a quarter way into the arena and halt. Make sure he is standing square, then mount. I want to see you walk once around, then move to a trot for one round followed by a canter."

Standing with her hands on her hips, she watched him follow her instructions, mount and set McCloud into motion. Her trained eye followed his progress, cataloging problems and formulating a plan to address them.

As much as she hated to admit it, he looked good on horseback.

Like that was a surprise. He always looked good. His jeans and long-sleeved gray T-shirt didn't hide the fact that he was fit and well muscled. He wore his modern clothing well, but handsome wasn't even the word for the romantic picture he made when he wore his cavalry uniform.

In her mind's eye she saw him with his saber flashing in the sunlight as he and his fellow soldiers brought history alive in their performances. No wonder the legend of the dashing cavalry soldier still lived in the hearts and minds of people everywhere. If only she could get *her* romance with Avery out of her heart and mind.

Biting her lip, she refused to follow where that train of thought was leading. A handsome face and a well-toned body didn't have anything to do with being a truly good man.

After finishing her instructions, he pulled McCloud to a halt in front of her. He patted the horse's neck. "He's a sweet goer. So what did you think? I'm pretty good, right?"

She told the truth. "You're an average rider."

He sat back and scowled. "What?"

"Okay, you're a good rider, but you're trying to overpower your horse. This event is about harmony between a horse and rider. It's about lightness and relaxation."

"It's also about military bearing and confidence."

"Those you don't need to work on. You have pompous and arrogant down to a science."

"And you've got a master's in peevish."

Taken aback, she said, "I beg your pardon?"

"You should." His tone was so smug she didn't know if she could control herself.

She threw out her arm and pointed at the gate. "If you aren't serious about learning this, get off my horse and go back to the fort."

"Play nice, children," Lizzie called down from the loft.

"Yes," Avery chimed in. "Play nice, Jenny. We both have a lot at stake."

Jennifer glanced from her sister back to Avery. He was right. She had made a promise to her mother. The only way she knew to keep it was to put up with Avery's cockiness.

"All right, I'll play nice but I don't have to like it. Take McCloud down the left side of the corral at a trot and then into a ten meter circle in the center. While you're at it, pay attention to him. He's the one who *does* know what he's doing."

Avery nudged the horse closer and leaned down so only Jennifer could hear. "You're really cute when you're mad. Did you know that?"

Avery's remark succeeded in silencing Jennifer for the rest of the session, except for a few pointed riding instructions from her. His comment had been designed to do exactly that, but he hadn't been lying. She was adorable when she was miffed.

It was too dangerous to give in to the temptation to hold her in his arms and kiss her soft lips, but he'd settle for seeing the icy sparks in her bright blue eyes. Besides, if his teasing kept her at a distance, so much the better. He had no intention of getting emotionally tangled up with her again.

After an hour, she declared the lesson at an end. The sun was getting low in the sky, turning the few bands of clouds in the sky a pale pink.

"That's enough for today." Her tone was cool and clearly meant to sound professional.

Dismounting near the fence, Avery gave McCloud a final pat and unhooked the girth. When he pulled the saddle off, Jennifer came forward and took the reins in her hand. "I'll take him now."

"You don't trust me to cool him down?" Avery challenged.

He waited for her snippy comeback, but she surprised him by saying, "Actually, when it comes to caring for horses, I do trust you. I've seen you in action at the clinic and at the stables. You're good with animals. It's just that McCloud is my buddy and I like to take care of him."

Avery basked in the unexpected warmth of her compliment. "Thanks. Aren't you going to practice with your broomstick on Lollypop now?"

"I think I'll wait until after I've changed out of this skirt. I've appeared foolish enough in front of an audience for one day. I'll see you tomorrow."

"Same time?"

"That's what we agreed on. Every day at four-thirty for the next two weeks."

"I'll be here. Don't forget to study the stuff I gave you." He found he didn't want to leave, but he couldn't think of a reason to stay.

As he walked with slow steps back to his car with his saddle over his arm, Ryan raced up to his side. "You're still going to get my bike fixed, aren't you?"

"Sure, kid."

"I'll get it for you." The boy ran back the way they had come.

Avery aimed his keyless remote at the trunk and the lid popped open. Laying his riding gear inside, he turned to see Ryan struggling to carry his wrecked bicycle across the yard. Avery moved quickly to intercept him and relieve the boy of his burden.

"How long do you think it will take to fix it? Do you think it'll be ready by tomorrow?"

Shaking his head, Avery said, "Probably not tomorrow."

"The next day?" Shoving his hands in the front pockets of his jeans, Ryan bit the corner of his lip.

"I doubt it, but I'll put a rush order on it."

"Thanks. Don't worry about my sister."

Avery closed the trunk. "What do you mean?"

"Jennifer gets all mad and huffy sometimes like she did today, but she gets over it quick. Toby says you just have to give her space and look kinda sorry."

"You just have to look sorry, you don't have to be sorry?"

Ryan leaned toward him. "That's what Toby says, but I think she can tell the difference."

"I'll remember that. See you tomorrow, kid." Avery looked toward the barn but Jennifer didn't appear. Realizing how much he wanted to see her again made him turn abruptly and get into his car.

The following afternoon, Jennifer rushed to get supper started before Avery arrived. Lately it seemed as if she were trying to stuff twenty-eight hours of work, classes and chores into a twenty-four hour day, only now she had to add two more hours of instructions each evening to the mix.

From her place in front of the kitchen sink, she heard the front door open. "Ryan, is that you?"

"Yup."

"Did you feed Isabella?"

"Oops, I forgot."

"Please do it now."

"Okay. You stay here. I'll be right back." The sound of the door slamming made her roll her eyes. That boy was always on the run.

"I'm done," Toby announced. Seated at the kitchen table, he closed his social studies book and slid it into his book bag.

"Good, then you can help me study." Jennifer blew a wisp of hair out of her face as she finished chopping carrots into bite-size pieces and started on the potatoes. "Ask me some questions about equine podiatry. I've got a test tomorrow. My textbook is there beside you."

Jennifer added the diced carrots and potatoes to the pan containing the pot roast, then began to slice the onions on the wooden cutting board on the kitchen counter.

Toby opened her book. After a few seconds, he said, "Describe three ways to manage a horse with a toe crack."

Jennifer tried to concentrate, but all she could think about was seeing Avery soon. Her eagerness to see him again made her wonder if she needed her head examined. She forced her mind back to her studies. "Three methods of treatment are acrylic repair...hoof staples... and... I can't remember."

"The use of a metal band with screws." Toby supplied the answer she couldn't pull out of her brain.

The sound of the dyer buzzer reached her. Jennifer stopped slicing and shouted, "Lizzie, can you hang up my lab coats for me before they get wrinkled, please?"

"I'll get the laundry," Mary called from her bedroom.

"Stay in bed, Mother." Jennifer yelled back. "Lizzie, please? I'm in the middle of making supper."

"Okay—I'll get them," Lizzie called back, vague annoyance clear in her tone.

Toby asked, "What are the advantages of using a treatment plate on a punctured hoof?"

Jennifer closed her eyes and tried to focus. It didn't do any good. "Advantages of a treatment plate include less bandage changes…and something else."

"Increased ease of observation." Toby enunciated each word with care.

"Oh, that's right." Looking down, she finished slicing the onion just as her eyes began to water. Adding the white rings to the pan, she seasoned the roast then opened the warm oven and slid the pan in, taking care to keep her mother's long skirt from getting shut in the door. The costumes were a hassle, but her mother was right. The more she wore the period dresses the more natural moving in them became.

She rubbed her nose with the back of one hand. The pungent odor made her realize she smelled like onions. She moved to the kitchen sink, squirted lemon dish soap on her hands and scrubbed.

"How do you make one?" Toby asked.

Jennifer dried her hands on a dish towel, then flipped it over her shoulder. What else needed doing?

"How do you make one?" Toby asked again.

"How do I make what?" she snapped. Sniffing her

fingers, she frowned. Now she smelled like lemon-scented onions.

Her brother shook his head. "I don't think you're gonna do so well on this test, sis."

She threw him an exasperated look. "Ask me something else."

"What are the parts of a saber?" a deep, masculine voice queried from the doorway of the living room.

She spun around to see Avery leaning casually against the door frame.

"What are you doing here?"

"I'm just waiting on you." Avery enjoyed the stunned look on her face. Her cheeks were flushed, and damp tendrils of hair curled at her temples. She had on another frontier style dress. This one was baby blue with tiny red flowers scattered across the fabric and red cord trim. The colors suited her.

Embarrassed at being caught off guard, she said, "I didn't hear you knock."

"I came in with Ryan. He told me to wait here while he fed the rabbit."

"Oh." She bit the corner of her lower lip. She looked rushed and flustered and a lot like a woman with too much on her plate.

Watching her interact with her family unobserved had been enlightening for him. She managed to get her siblings to help her and each other with only a small amount of encouragement and prodding. Her home, which he once would have considered shabby, struck him as a warm and comfortable place. He'd never known anything like it.

"I've hung up the laundry. Do you need help with

anything else?" Lizzie came into the room and stopped short at the sight of Avery.

"Don't let me interrupt your work," he said, smiling at Jennifer.

She snatched the dish towel off her shoulder and clutched it in her hands, then tossed it on the counter top. "I'm done here. Let me tell Mom and make sure she is okay, then we can go outside."

"You didn't answer my question," he said as he stepped aside for her to pass.

"What question was that?"

"What are the parts of a saber?"

"The toe, which is really the point, the grip, the guard and the blade. The scabbard is comprised of the mouth, the upper hook, the lower hook, the body and the scabbard tip protector." She rattled off the list with barely a pause.

Toby snapped the book shut. "That might impress him, but it isn't going to get you through your equine podiatry exam."

Jennifer pulled her textbook from Toby's hands. "I'm not trying to impress anyone. I'll read the chapter again tonight. Would you check and see if Mom needs anything?"

"I'm fine," Mary called from the bedroom. "You kids should go outside and play."

"Yes, Mom," Lizzie and Toby answered together as they exchanged pointed looks.

Jennifer rolled her eyes. Avery tried not to smile. It was obvious that having her siblings lined up and watching her every move wasn't what she wanted. The door burst open and Ryan came running in.

"I'm sure you kids would rather watch TV or play your video games," Jennifer suggested.

"Not me," Ryan announced. "I've got stuff to do for Avery. Right?"

"Right," Avery agreed and the boy raced out the front door again.

Jennifer followed more sedately. On the porch, she gathered a handful of the floor-length skirt she was wearing and descended the steps carefully. She was definitely getting the hang of moving in her mother's period costumes.

Ryan was dragging the garden hose from the side of the house toward Avery's car. "I got the hose."

Jennifer glanced from her brother to Avery. "What does Ryan need the hose for?"

"He's going to wash and polish my spoke wheels for me."

"Why?"

"It's a deal between us guys. The cloth and polish are on the front seat. Make sure you get all the water spots off."

"I will." Ryan aimed the pressure nozzle at the car and let loose a wide arc of spray.

Avery winced. There would be water spots on more than the wheel covers. He foresaw an evening of hand polishing his pride and joy all over again.

Jennifer glared at Avery, her hands fisted on her hips. "Are you taking advantage of my little brother?"

"No, and I'm ashamed you would even ask that. Are you ready for your next lesson?"

"Certainly."

"Good. Kill the water, sport."

"Yes, sir. I'll get a bucket." Ryan shouted and took his hand off the nozzle.

Avery opened the car door and pulled out a scabbard. "Strap this on."

Jennifer took it from his hand and buckled the belt around her waist. "I still don't see why I have to learn to walk with this thing."

"Because the only safe way to carry a saber is in a scabbard. This is for the welfare of the other re-enactors as much as it is for you. Stop arguing for one minute and do as I say."

"I'm not arguing."

"Yes, you are."

"I am not. Is this right?" She shifted the long weapon to her left side.

"A little farther back." He bent and adjusted it for her. "Do you smell onions?"

She clasped her hands behind her back. "No."

The sound of the front door slamming drew his attention and Jennifer took a step away. Ryan came out of the house carrying a pail. Lizzie and Toby came out and sat on the top step to watch the activity. As the boy set to work scrubbing the first wheel, Avery turned back to Jennifer. "Try walking a few paces."

Jennifer took several steps toward the house. The saber banged awkwardly against her leg. She stopped, then took several more steps with the same results. She grasped the hilt to steady it and glanced at Avery, daring him to laugh.

He folded his arms across his chest. "It's a lot harder than it looks, isn't it?"

"How does Kevin Costner make it look so easy?"

"Practice."

She turned and walked a few paces in the other direction. "Can I keep one hand on the hilt to steady it?"

"For now. Spend a few more minutes just walking and then you can work on sitting with it on."

She walked to the barn and back. "The weight makes a person want to swagger. It's empowering."

"Therein lies the true lure of swordplay for centuries past."

"Does it make you feel the same way?"

"I feel more empowered with a machine gun in my hands, but I know what you mean."

She grasped the hilt and pulled the blade free, holding it in front of her. "Wow. It's a lot heavier than a broomstick. Did I get all the parts right?"

"You did."

She tried several times to insert the tip of the blade back into the scabbard, but kept missing. Avery stepped up, placed his hands over hers and guided the sword home. The feel of her small hand beneath his sent his pulse racing. She drew in a quick breath as her eyes met his. His hands lingered a moment longer.

"Avery!" Ryan shouted. "I got this wheel done. Come and see."

Smiling at Jennifer, Avery said softly, "I should go and inspect his work."

"Yes." She sounded breathless. Was he the reason?

"I'll only be a minute," he added as he moved away.

A minute might not be long enough, he decided as his heartbeat settled to a more normal pace once he wasn't touching her.

He pointed out a few spots that Ryan had missed in his cleaning frenzy, then followed Jennifer with his eyes as she paced back and forth across the gravel drive.

She was smart, sassy, easy on the eyes. She was a woman of principles. The kind who put faith and family first. In other words, she was exactly the kind of woman he wanted to avoid. So why did he find himself drawn to her? He didn't have the answer and it bothered him.

Jennifer walked toward the barn and practiced sitting on a bale of straw beside the door. Managing both the long skirt and the saber took a little finesse, but she was happy to be able to concentrate on something other than her reaction to Avery's touch.

When he walked toward her a few minutes later, she leapt to her feet and unbuckled the sword. Holding it toward him, she said. "It's time we started working on your training. I'll go get the horses."

"You need to sit straighter in the saddle. Move your shoulders forward to center your weight over your hips. Relax, you look like a stick up there."

Avery pulled his mount to a halt and glared at Jennifer sitting perched on the corral fence. She had taken off her skirt and was wearing a pair of well-worn jeans.

"You just told me to sit up straight and now you're telling me to relax. Which is it?"

"Both."

"You're not making any sense." Not only were her instructions contradictory, but her presence was proving to be a distraction that was hard to ignore. Very hard.

"Try not to think of this as a military exercise. Try to think of this as having fun," she suggested. "Become an extension of the horse instead of a lump perched on top of him."

Exasperated, he shot back, "I'm pretty sure military

equitation isn't about having fun. It's about having control of the horse."

"The two are not mutually exclusive. Step down and I'll show you what I mean."

Avery dismounted as Jennifer hopped down from the fence and joined him. He flipped up the saddle leather and began shortening the stirrup for her. They had been at this for over an hour and so far all he had accomplished was feeling like an inept novice.

When he finished shortening the second stirrup, he gave her a leg up and stepped back. With an almost imperceptible nudge of her heels, she set McCloud into motion.

Avery's annoyance evaporated as he watched her ride in a wide circle around him. She and the horse moved with almost flawless grace. She made it look so easy.

"Don't try to overwhelm the horse with control," she said. "If you look at your mount as a true partner, you'll both do better. See how relaxed his stride has become?"

"He's used to you."

She reined to a stop beside Avery. "You're making excuses, but you do have a point."

Kicking free of the stirrups, she dropped lightly to the ground and patted McCloud's neck. "Why don't you take him for a ride down the lane?"

"Are we done?"

"Think of it as recess. It will help both of you because it isn't work. McCloud deserves a little fun, too, and for him that's a good gallop."

Avery closed his hand over hers where she held the reins. "I'll go if you'll join me." It was a rash and risky move, but he couldn't help himself. He wanted to spend time alone with her again.

She pulled her fingers free slowly. A blush colored her cheeks. Stepping back a pace, she shoved her hands in the hip pockets of her jeans. "I should get started on my homework. I've got a big test coming up."

He turned his back on her and began lengthening the stirrups again. "I can understand why you might not trust yourself to go riding alone with me."

"What's that supposed to mean?"

"Nothing."

"No, you were implying something."

"Only that it would just be the two of us and your family wouldn't be scrutinizing your every move." He gestured toward the corral fence with his head. Toby, Lizzie and Ryan were seated on the top rail watching them.

"If you are suggesting that I'll find you impossible to resist once I'm away from prying eyes—you're delusional."

"If you're afraid you can't control yourself, the best thing is to admit it."

"I'm not afraid."

"Guess we'll never know for sure, will we? That's a pity since it would be so easy to prove."

Chapter 9

"All right," Jennifer stated. "I'll accompany you on a ride but only because my mother's horse need exercising."

Avery had his back to her but he could easily imagine the way her stubborn little chin would jut out as she accepted his challenge. He controlled his grin with difficulty. "I'll wait here while you saddle up."

"I'll only be a minute."

"I thought you were going to study for your test," Toby said from the sidelines, glaring at Avery.

"I will. You kids can go in and get ready for supper." Jennifer patted Toby's knee as she walked past him and into the barn.

"I'll wait here," Toby replied and crossed his arms.

Avery had to admire the boy's determined guardianship of his sister, even if she didn't need it.

Jennifer came out of the barn with Lollypop a few seconds later. Grabbing a handful of mane, she swung up onto the mare's bare back and rode up to the gate. She pulled the bolt back and let the gate swing open. Looking at Avery, she said, "Are you coming?"

"Lead on."

Kicking Lollypop into a canter, she took off down the drive. McCloud whinnied as his stable mate took off without him. Avery swung into the saddle. He didn't have to urge McCloud to catch up. By the time they reached the end of the lane, the horses were side-by-side.

Stopping at the narrow paved road, Jennifer checked for oncoming traffic, then crossed the highway. The horses' hooves clattered loudly on the blacktop. Once across, Jennifer led the way through a break in the trees that lined the roadway.

Avery ducked beneath the gnarled thorny branches of the Osage orange hedge. Beyond the trees a large field opened up. The corn crop had already been harvested from it leaving long rows of pale stubble and a few occasional brown stalks waving in the wind.

Jennifer urged her mount into an easy lope toward the tree covered hills rising at the far end of the field. McCloud proved eager to stretch his legs. Soon both horses were pounding across the open ground with only the sounds of their hooves hitting the soft dirt and the occasional crackle of trampled stalks disturbing the evening quiet.

Avery found himself torn between watching his riding companion and helping his horse find his way across the field. Jennifer looked so carefree, so happy as she sat astride the black mare flying over the ground. For a brief second, he caught her with her eyes closed as she lifted her face to the wind. All too soon the distance had been covered and the horses slowed.

At the edge of the field, Jennifer pulled to a walk and cast a grin at Avery. "I needed that."

"You could have just told your family that you wanted to get away from the house and have a good gallop," he suggested, pulling his blowing horse alongside hers.

She cast him a quick glance, then bent to pat Lollypop's neck. The blush in her cheeks might have been from the wind, but he couldn't be sure. No matter what the reason, it heightened her beauty.

"Thanks for giving me an excuse to do it," she said, ignoring his command. "Since Toby and Lizzie have decided it's their duty to chaperone us, I've been feeling like the microbe under the microscope."

"My pleasure. Why not just tell your family you need some time to yourself?" he asked, not willing to let the point drop.

She drew her fingers through the mare's long black mane. "I guess it's partly that I don't like to complain."

"And the other part?"

She wrinkled her nose. "I don't like to admit that I can't do it all."

"Why do you think you need to do it all?"

"Mom has more than enough to worry about. She knows that if she needs surgery it will take most of our savings and it will mean I'll have to drop out of school for this semester. I don't know how much longer we can get along without her income as it is."

"Are you serious?" He knew how hard she studied, how much she wanted to finish school and start supporting her family.

Shrugging her dainty shoulders, she said, "It is what it is. I'm trusting that God has a plan for us."

"What if the plan is something you don't like?"

"I'm human. I'll be disappointed. I'll cry. I'll yell. Then I'll make peace with it because that is what I believe. God is in control. I'm not."

"I don't like the idea that I'm not in control of my life."

"Yes, that is one hard part of our faith, but believing that God is in control doesn't mean we live without direction. I have things I want. Things I plan for and work toward. I want my mother to get better, I want to stay in school and I want to make her proud by re-enacting her heroine's part in history without falling on my face."

"You'll do okay with your charge up Strawberry Hill."

"Dutton Heights," she corrected.

"Whatever. You'll do okay." He relaxed and took a deep breath of the clean evening air. This was nice, riding beside her, talking about things that were important to her.

Shaking her head, she said, "I don't know how you can say that when you have yet to let me hold a saber while I'm on horseback."

"You're determined to do well. That's three-fifths of the battle. Why is this whole thing so important to your mother?"

"I wish I knew. Why is winning the Sheridan cup so important to you?"

"It's not."

McCloud shied as a pheasant flew up ahead of them, and Avery spoke quietly to calm to the horse. Once again Jennifer was struck by how patient he was with animals. If only he treated people as well.

Was the arrogant rich snob the real Avery or was he the dedicated soldier and kindhearted man she sometimes caught a glimpse of? What did his relationship with his grandfather have to do with his behavior?

Uncovering the real Avery Barnes was a tempting idea. One she couldn't easily dismiss. Although she had promised herself she could maintain a strictly business attitude toward him, she found that resolve faltering.

The horses seemed content to amble along together, their tails twitching at the occasional buzzing fly. Jennifer glanced at Avery from beneath her lashes as she narrowed her eyes. "I think winning the cup is very important to you. It has something to do with your grandfather, doesn't it?"

"You're getting nosey again, Jenny," he warned.

She didn't care if he was annoyed. Somehow, she knew it was important for him to talk about his grandfather. "So sue me. He seems like a nice old man."

"Don't let the dapper charm fool you. He has a heart of flint."

She accepted the finality of his tone, but rather than dropping the subject, she tried a different approach. "What was it like?"

"What was what like?"

"Growing up with money, privilege, prominent social status?"

"What was it like to grow up underprivileged?" he countered.

She tilted her head as she considered her answer. "It was ordinary. It was great. I never lacked for anything. I knew my parents loved me. I knew my grandparents adored me. I can't think of a better way to grow up. I think my one real worry has always been that I might disappoint them somehow."

"You don't know how lucky you are. I knew my parents hated each other, but they both loved money enough to stay together. I knew my grandfather has always considered me a weakling and a fool."

A sharp stab of sympathy made her breath catch in her throat. "Why would you say that?"

For a long moment, she thought he wasn't going to answer her. When he did, his voice held a hard edge. "I had asthma when I was younger than Ryan. I was in and out of hospitals constantly for the first six years of my life. Fortunately, I outgrew it, but from the time I was born I was a disappointment to the old man who wanted another strong and ruthless heir to run his empire."

"Is that why you try so hard to make people think you don't care?"

"I *don't* care. I'm a carefree fellow. Ask anyone who knows me and they'll tell you the same."

"I saw the way you worked to help rehab Dakota. I've never seen you make light of the Army or of your unit's mission. You do care. You care about your friends."

"I have made some good friends in the Army," he admitted. "Basic training is a great leveler of men. Crawling beneath strands of barbed wire with bullets from a live machine gun zinging overhead can make you appreciate the people around you in a whole new way."

"Do they really make you do that?"

"That and a whole lot more."

"Wasn't it scary?"

"I think that was the point."

She closed her eyes. "The most scared I have ever been was at my father's funeral."

Jennifer wasn't sure why she needed to share her darkest hour with Avery. Perhaps because she sensed he would understand how alone she'd felt that day. "I was afraid I wouldn't be brave enough for him and for my mother. She took it so hard when he died."

"What happened to him?"

"He had a brain tumor. He died less than five weeks after he was diagnosed. Mother just sat in his chair and cried for days. If it hadn't been for my grandmother, I don't know what would have happened to us. She came in and took over until my mother found her way back from her grief. What happened to your parents?"

"Small plane crash. My dad was a pilot. Mom hated to fly with him. She always said he was reckless, but she went with him that day because they were flying out to Nassau and she loved it there."

Both parents at once. How horrible that must have been for him. "How old were you?"

"Sixteen. How old were you?"

"Fourteen."

He met her gaze. "How did you get through it?"

"My faith got me through it. I kept imagining Dad and God having this great, long conversation. When he was alive, whenever there was something my dad didn't understand, he'd say, 'I'm going to ask God about that when I get to heaven.' What got you through your parents' funeral?"

"Anger."

"At who?"

"God. Fate. My grandfather. He took only one day off work for the funeral. After that, he headed back to his empire and left me wondering what was next."

"Not everyone grieves in the same way," she said softly.

"Some people don't grieve at all," he shot back, a dry, bitter twist in his tone.

A fresh breeze kicked up and Jennifer noticed storm clouds gathering in the west. Reluctantly, she turned her horse toward home. "Perhaps your grandfather is here now because he has regrets?" she suggested.

Avery eyed her intently. "Why do you say that?"

She wanted to tell him that his grandfather was ill, that he might not have much time, but she knew it wasn't her place. She swallowed the words. "I don't know. Why do you think he's here?"

"I think he got bored without me to insult back in Boston."

"And if you are wrong about that?"

He fixed his eyes straight ahead. "Trust me, I'm not."

"You might consider the fact that God brought him here for a reason. Forgiveness heals the forgiver as well as the forgiven."

"That sound like some of your church mumbo jumbo. I thought you weren't going to try and push your faith down my throat."

"I never said I wasn't going to give you good advice."

A smile tugged at the corner of his mouth, but he managed to subdue it. "Is this Jennifer's top ten tips to positive living?"

"I can't take credit for the basic idea. God suggested it first."

"Give it up, Jenny. I'm a lost soul. You can't reform me."

"You're right. I can't—but I know that God can."

Chapter 10

Later, as Avery drove back to his apartment, he tried without success to dismiss Jennifer and her family from his mind.

He had known she didn't come from money like he did, but seeing firsthand the simple way they lived had forged a new respect for her. She attended school full-time, worked almost as many hours at the clinic and still managed to help her mother care for the younger children.

He wasn't sure he could do half as much. The odd thing was, in all the time he had known her, he'd never heard her complain. She never acted as though her life were anything but joyful. How did she manage that?

Turning into the parking lot of his complex, he followed the winding drive to the last building. Low gray clouds were moving in quickly and the first few raindrops splattered on his windshield just before he pulled into his allotted space. Getting out, he sprinted toward his front door with his key in hand.

A tall shade tree surrounded by a black circular metal bench graced the center of the small courtyard outside his building. He saw the man sitting there, but paid little attention as he dashed to the portico over his front door. He had his key in the lock when he heard someone call his name.

Looking over his shoulder, he saw the man from the bench rise. Avery recognized his grandfather and his stomach clenched. "What are you doing here?"

"I was hoping to have a few words with you," Edmond said.

"I don't have anything to say to you."

Shoulders hunched against the cool drizzle, Edmond stepped away from the bench. "Then could I use your phone? I dismissed my driver."

Disgusted with the tug of sympathy he felt, Avery asked, "What's the matter with your cell phone?"

"The battery seems to be dead. Charging it appears to be one of the many things my secretary usually does for me that I fail to notice. I believe I shall have to give her a raise."

It had begun raining in earnest by this time. Avery pushed open his door and tipped his head in that direction.

"Thank you." Edmond walked past him and entered, stopping in the small foyer. Pulling a white silk handkerchief from the inner pocket of his suit coat, he wiped his face.

"How long have you been sitting out there?"

Edmond returned the cloth square to his pocket, then

rubbed his hands together for warmth. "Two hours. I took a chance that you would be here after your regular duty hours."

"Must be odd for you to find out you can be mistaken. The phone is on the wall in the kitchen."

"Thank you."

As Edmond made his call, Avery took a few minutes to change into a clean T-shirt and dark blue running pants, and exchange his riding boots for a pair of sneakers. When he walked back into the living area, Edmond was sitting on one of the kitchen chairs.

It surprised Avery how tired and worn Edmond looked. He remembered his grandfather as a powerful and dynamic man, always on the go and impatient of people without his energy. Edmond rubbed his hands together again. "Collin went back to the inn. It will take him about twenty minutes to return. I could wait outside if that would make you more comfortable."

"How did you find me?"

"Let's just say I have resources."

Avery remembered the dark SUV that seemed to be everywhere he was. "You hired a private eye to follow me."

"Yes."

"You're unbelievable."

"You left me with very little choice."

Avery walked past him into the kitchen. Picking up the coffee maker carafe, he turned to the sink and began filling it with water. "Your coat is wet."

Edmond brushed at his sleeves. "A small matter compared to my only grandson's hatred."

Avery stood staring at the water running over the

sides of the container. Time had dulled the pain of his grandfather's betrayal, but not erased it.

"But you haven't forgiven me," Edmond stated.

Turning away from the sink, Avery transferred the water into the machine, glad to be able to focus on something other than the jumble of emotions he was feeling. "Why are you here?"

"There are things you and I need to discuss."

"Have you decided to cut me out of your will all together?" It was easier to be flippant than face the things he really wanted to say.

"Would it matter to you if I did?"

"Probably."

"At least that's an honest answer."

Avery pulled a bag of gourmet coffee from the fridge, opened it, and spooned the grounds into the filter basket. The rich soothing scent of his favorite blend filled the air.

Edmond slipped his coat off and hung it over the back of his chair. For the next few minutes, the only sound in the small room was the sputter and gurgle of the coffee maker. Finally, Edmond said, "You have a nice apartment. I didn't know enlisted men were allowed to live off post."

"With the return of the Big Red One, barrack space is limited. All it took was getting permission from my commanding officer."

"I've met Captain Watson. He seems like a good man."

Avery scowled at him. "When did you talk to the captain?"

"This afternoon before coming here."

"You can't stay out of my affairs, can you?"

"Miranda was a gold digger. She was after your money. What's more, she was an impatient gold digger. She could have had much more than I offered her if she had been willing to wait until you were married, but she wanted the money in a hurry."

"I was made painfully aware of that by your interference."

"I know you think what I did was wrong, but I did it for the right reasons."

"Did you try to buy off my mother before she married Dad?"

Edmond raised his chin. "I didn't, but perhaps I should have. I wanted my son to be happy. He was wildly in love with her—for a while. Like you, he found someone who loved money more than she loved him. She made his life miserable. I wasn't about to watch that happen to you."

"Why did he stay with her if he was that miserable?" Avery remembered the screaming fights, the tears and accusations. They echoed in his head whenever he thought about settling down and spending his life with one person. Miranda had been able to silence the sounds of his childhood and he had loved her for that.

Only her whispered words of love had been as much a lie as his parents sham of a marriage.

"Your father stayed with your mother because of you."

"Great. Now you're trying to lay their unhappy marriage at my feet. As far as you're concerned, I've never done anything right, including being born."

"That isn't true."

His grandfather expected him to be a failure at everything. Well, he knew exactly how to do that. He'd had years of practice. Avery brushed past Edmond and snatched his car keys from the end of the counter. "I used to wonder why you made it your mission in life to belittle and embarrass me and now I know. Thanks for this heart-to-heart, Gramps. Enjoy the coffee. I'm sure you can find your way out."

Avery left the apartment, slamming the door as he headed into the rain.

Jennifer closed her textbook of equine anatomy and glanced at the silent phone for the hundredth time since she'd gotten home. It was Friday evening and she had turned down an extra shift at the clinic to work with Avery, but he was nowhere in sight.

He hadn't shown up at the prearranged time. Nor had he bothered to call. They had agreed to meet at the same time every evening for two weeks. Where was he? Why hadn't he called?

"It won't ring because you scowl at it." Lizzie was curled up in the corner of the sagging blue sofa filing her nails. The usually overflowing mobile home was blessedly quiet since the rest of the brood had gone to play at the home of some friends, and their mother was taking a nap.

Wishing she weren't so transparent, Jennifer tucked a strand of her long blond hair behind her ear and opened her book again. "I don't know what you're talking about."

"You can call *him*."

"I already left a message. He's a grown man. If he can't be bothered to keep his promises, I'm not going to hound him."

"Poor Jennifer. You're head over heels for the guy."

"Even if I were head over heels—which I'm not—

Avery and I had a deal. If he backs out, I'm not going to beg."

"So he dropped you like a hot rock, again."

"This isn't about personal feelings. This is about honoring a commitment." Jennifer slammed her book shut, making Lizzie look up in alarm.

Jennifer drew up her knees and rested her chin on them. "The man is a player. I don't know why I expected better from him this time."

She thought they shared something special together on their ride yesterday. He had opened up in a way he had never done before. She had started caring about him all over again.

No. That wasn't true. She had never stopped caring about him.

Dejected, Jennifer left her place at the dining room table and crossed the room to plop down beside her sister. Lizzie slipped her arm across Jennifer's shoulders and pulled her close. Appreciating the comforting hug, Jennifer allowed herself a moment of self-pity. "Why couldn't he be dependable instead of charming?"

"Want me to call him and give him a piece of my mind?"

Mustering a grin, Jennifer said, "As kind as the offer is, you don't have much mind left to spare. You'd better hold on to what little you have."

"Ha! Ha!" Pulling her arm away from Jennifer's shoulder, Lizzie used it to elbow her sister in the ribs.

"Hey, that hurt."

"Serves you right for moping over a guy."

"Oh, like you weren't moping over Dale Marcus last week."

"Okay, maybe I was, but I learned my lesson and so

should you. As Mom always says, there are plenty of fish in the sea. Now, show a little backbone and forget about him."

Rising from the sofa, Jennifer fisted her hands on her hips. "You're right. I won't give Avery Barnes another thought. If he can't see what a pearl I am then who needs him? Except... I need him to teach me how to handle a sword or I'm going to make a fool of myself in front of a lot of people."

"Maybe Mom can teach you the rest."

"She needs to stay off her leg."

The phone rang suddenly. Before Jennifer could dash over to answer it, Lizzie grabbed her by the arm. "Let the machine pick up. You don't want to sound like you have nothing to do except wait for him to call."

The second and third ring sent hope rising in Jennifer's heart, but she decided her sister was right. The fourth and fifth rings were almost more than she could stand.

The click of the answering machine coming on was followed by their mother's voice instructing the caller to leave a message after the beep. A shaky male voice said, "Yeah, hey, this is Dale Marcus...ah, could Lizzie... like...call me back?"

With a squeal of delight, Lizzie sprang up from the sofa and grabbed the receiver.

Jennifer walked to the table and picked up her book. A small thread of worry began to unspool in her mind. Why hadn't Avery come by? Why hadn't he called?

Lizzie covered the phone with one hand and turned to Jennifer. "Can I go watch Dale and his band practice for a little while? They're playing at the church youth center tonight. Pastor McGregor will be there and so will a couple of my girlfriends, and their parents. Please?"

At least one of them should be able to enjoy the evening. "Sure. I'll drive you into town. It's not like I'm doing anything else."

"Great. You're the best, Jen."

"I know, I know. God blessed you from birth with me as your big sister."

"It's true." She pulled her hand from the phone. "I'll see you in a few minutes, Dale. Thanks for inviting me."

Jennifer gathered her truck keys from the hook on the wall and checked in on her mother. Mary was sitting propped up in bed reading her Bible. Jennifer put the cordless phone on her bedside table. "I'm going to run Lizzie into town. Do you need anything?"

Mary closed her book. "No. I'm fine. I'm going to catch up on a little more reading and then try a nap. One good thing has come out of this fiasco. I'm not using my busy life as an excuse to avoid reading the Good Book. I needed this time with God."

"He does move in mysterious ways."

"Yes. Who would expect Him to use a rabbit to get me back in the habit of prayerful contemplation?"

"He must really like Isabella. He's used her to change a lot of lives. I've got my cell phone and I'll be back in twenty minutes. Are you sure you don't need anything?"

"If you happen to stop at the Get-N-Go, we need some milk and would you bring me a bag of red licorice?"

"Sure. Was it a favorite of Henrietta Dutton?"

"I have no idea, but it's a favorite of mine. Thanks, honey. Be careful."

After they left the house, it took less than ten minutes to reach the church and drop off Lizzie. Turning back out onto the highway, Jennifer drove another half dozen blocks to the convenience store.

Pulling up, she parked at the side of the building and went in. After picking up a package of the candy her mother wanted, she walked back to the coolers at the rear of the store and pulled a gallon of milk from the rack.

Standing in front of the freezer section, she was debating the cost in unwanted pounds verses the comfort a carton of chocolate silk ice cream might provide when the bell over the door jingled announcing another costumer. The sound was followed by a loud giggle. Jennifer glanced over her shoulder and saw Avery enter.

He wasn't alone. A stunning redhead had her hands clasped around his arm. Standing on tiptoe, she planted a kiss on his cheek and giggled again at something he said. Smiling, Avery happened to glance toward the back of the store and his gaze collided with Jennifer's.

She quickly turned back to stare at the freezer door.

He isn't working late. He hasn't wrecked his car. He has a hot date. I can't believe I spent the last two hours worrying about the man.

Calling herself every kind of fool, Jennifer stood with her head bowed for a few long minutes. Finally, she pulled two cartons of ice cream from the freezer and marched toward the counter at the front. Avery had already paid for his purchases and left. She was treated to the sight of him pulling out onto the highway with Ms. Giggles snuggled close to his side.

Chapter 11

Gravel flew out from beneath his tires as Avery stepped on the accelerator and tore out of the parking lot. He was trying to forget the sight of Jennifer standing at the back of the convenience store. He knew she had seen him. The hurt in her eyes left a hollow feeling in the pit of his stomach.

"I love your car." The woman seated beside him rubbed a hand over the rich leather upholstery.

"Thanks. So do I."

Was her name Bitsy or Betsy? He couldn't be sure. She had been part of a group taking a tour of the stables and museum at the fort earlier that afternoon. It had been obvious from the start that she had little interest in the history lessons being presented. When the group moved on, she had stayed behind, admiring his car. His offer to take her for a spin in it had been met with giggles of delight.

"How do you afford a car like this on Army pay?"

He glanced over and caught the speculative gleam in her eyes. "Family money."

"Really?" Her eyes brightened. "It must be nice. Unless, of course, it's your wife's money."

"No, no wife."

"That's even better. Where are we going?"

Where *was* he going? He was racing headlong down the highway without a destination, without a clue. The woman beside him was a stranger. The woman he wanted beside him was back in the Get-N-Go with a gallon of milk in her hands and eyes filled with disappointment.

He hadn't planned on running into Jennifer. Since his confrontation with his grandfather, he'd just felt like running. Away from responsibility—away from his own insecurities. He'd spent years perfecting the art of being less than what his grandfather expected. A pretty stranger, a fast car and reckless behavior had usually been his answer.

Until now. Until Jennifer.

She wasn't running from her responsibilities or her insecurities. She faced her problems head-on. Where did she find the courage?

The answer was simple. All he had to do was look at the way she lived her life. With faith.

He'd let her down, broken his promises. His grandfather didn't get to witness his stupid performance today— Jennifer did.

Forcing the troubling thoughts to the back of his mind, he glanced at the woman beside him. "Where do you want to go?"

She threw her hand in the air. "Someplace fun. Someplace exciting. Surprise me."

Surprise her. Surprise yourself. Do the right thing for once.

He took his foot off the gas and the car's speed dropped as he contemplated his options. The knot in his stomach eased as he realized he had already made up his mind.

He said, "I'm afraid this is as far as I can go."

"What? Oh, don't say that. We're just getting started. Kansas City is only two hours from here. We can see the sights and try out the nightlife."

When his car slowed enough, he made a U-turn and started back toward the post. "Sorry. I've got to get back to my duties."

"What a bummer." She scooted away from him. "I thought we were going to have some fun."

"The U.S. Army is very strict when it comes to a soldier doing his duty."

"I suppose. It was sweet of you to take me for a ride. I've never been in a Jaguar before."

"It's just four wheels and an engine."

"That is *so* not true."

"Where can I drop you off? I think your tour may be finished at the cavalry museum by now."

She gave him the name of a local motel and he pressed the gas once more, suddenly in a hurry to drop her off. And as odd as it seemed, he felt right about doing it. It was the best decision he had made in months.

An hour later, he knocked at the Grants' front door. Toby opened it, scowling at him. "What do you want?"

"Is Jennifer home?"

"Nope."

Avery reined in his disappointment. "Where is she?"

"Studying."

"At the campus library?" He took a step backward, eager to find her and explain. To tell her he was sorry. To make it up to her somehow.

"Nope." Toby's short reply stopped Avery in his tracks.

"Where is she studying?"

"At a friend's."

Avery could tell by the look in the teen's eyes that he wasn't going to get any more information, but he tried anyway. "I know I messed up. Would you please tell me where I can find her?"

"Nope."

Admitting defeat at the hands of a boy half his age wasn't easy, but Avery knew when to give in. "Would you at least tell her that I stopped by?"

"Sure. If I don't forget." Toby closed the door and snapped off the porch light, leaving Avery standing alone in the dark.

The next afternoon, at twenty minutes after four, Avery drove up to Jennifer's home. She was standing on the front porch, sweeping the steps. She glanced up once, then returned to swinging the broom with renewed vigor.

She looked mad.

He stepped out of the car with a pair of sabers in his hand and waited for her to say something, anything. She just kept sweeping.

He deserved her anger, but the silent treatment wasn't what he had expected. Jennifer wasn't normally at a loss for words.

Deciding that if she didn't mention yesterday, neither

would he, he walked up to her and handed her one of the swords he carried. "I thought today we'd go over some hand-to-hand combat moves."

"All right." She set the broom aside and took the scabbard he held out to her.

Pulling the sword from its cover, she turned and walked to a clear space in the yard. "Is this where I get to say 'on guard'?"

She spun around with the blade extended. Only his quick reflexes allowed him to block her weapon with his own, saving him from a nasty bruise on his arm.

"Will you be careful!"

Her eyes widened and she pressed a hand to her mouth. "Oh, I'm so sorry," she said, her voice thick with disdain.

She took a step back, but the glint in her eyes looked anything but apologetic. Holding her free hand aloft, she extended the point toward him while rocking back and forth on the balls of her feet.

"I thrust like this, right?" She lunged toward him but he struck her blade aside.

"Jennifer, this is serious. You could hurt someone."

Her eyes narrowed as if considering her options. "They aren't sharp. I can't actually cut you—or stab you—or slice you into ribbons."

Extending her blade again, she made tiny circling motions in front of his chest.

Grasping the end of her saber, he forced it down. "If this is about yesterday, I can explain."

Jerking her weapon out of his grasp, she retreated a pace and held it up again. "I saw you with the explanation. She had red hair and she was draped over your arm like a wet horse blanket."

"I thought we wouldn't let this get personal."

"Oh, it's personal, but don't think it's about who you were with. You can date every woman on the planet as far as I'm concerned."

"Then why are you so mad?"

"Because I'm serious about taking my mother's place in the festival. I gave my word that I would do it and I *will* do it to the best of my ability and *you* said you would help me."

"So I took a day off."

"You couldn't call and tell me you couldn't make it? No. You let me worry that something had happened to you."

He tipped his head to the side. "You were worried about me?"

"Yes—no. That's not the point. The point is that you are selfish and self-centered and you don't care about anyone."

"That's true."

"Oh, yes it is!" she shot back automatically.

He held up his hands up in surrender. "I'm agreeing with you, Jennifer."

Her eyebrows shot up. "You are?"

He nodded. "I'm selfish. I'm self-centered. I'm the scum of the earth. I agreed to teach you and I failed to live up to my side of the bargain. Blowing you off yesterday was totally inexcusable."

Clearly puzzled, she lowered her blade. "Yes, it was."

"I'm sorry I worried you by not calling."

Her eyes narrowed and she whipped the sword up, pointing it at his midsection. "You sound contrite, but I'm not buying it."

"I am contrite. I won't miss another day. I'll put it in writing if you want me to."

"You should write 'I'm sorry' one hundred times in your notebook. That's what Mrs. Craig makes me do. Are you going to stab him, sis?" Ryan stood by with Isabella clutched in his arms. The rabbit's eyes were wide. Her nose twitched and her whiskers quivered with excitement. She looked eager to join the battle.

Jennifer lowered her sword, embarrassed and ashamed to be caught menacing Avery. She was usually careful not to lose her temper when her younger siblings were within hearing distance. "I'm not going to stab anyone, Ryan."

"Thank goodness," Avery mumbled.

She ignored him and smiled at her brother. "Avery and I are just…"

"Pretending to be fighting," Avery supplied.

She cast him a grateful look, then scowled. She didn't want to be grateful to him for any reason. Turning her attention back to Ryan, she said, "You shouldn't have Isabella out of the barn."

"But she's tired of being inside. She wants to run around," Ryan insisted.

Jennifer walked to Ryan and dropped to her knees. "We don't have a safe place for her to play. You wouldn't want her to get loose and get hurt, would you?"

"No. I guess not."

"Come on, sport," Avery said. "I'll go with you. Once she's back in her hutch I have something to show you."

Ryan's eyes brightened. "What?"

"You'll see. Let's be responsible first and make sure Isabella is safe. Okay?"

"Okey-dokey."

Jennifer didn't snort at Avery's comment, but she felt like it. He certainly wasn't a poster child for responsibility. When the pair disappeared into the barn, she blew out a deep breath.

Avery had shown his true colors once again. Looking at the weapon in her hand, she sliced it through the air in a wide arc. Any infatuation for him that had been lingering was gone now. She had herself and her emotions well in hand.

Sliding the saber back into its scabbard, she congratulated herself on facing him like the mature woman she was. When he and Ryan came out of the barn, Avery had his hand on one of the boy's shoulders and the two of them were grinning at each other.

So what if he looked handsome and relaxed? It didn't matter.

He and Ryan walked to the rear of Avery's car. From inside the trunk, Avery pulled out a bicycle and set it on the ground in front of Ryan. Her brother's shout of joy startled her as he grabbed the handlebars and straddled the frame.

Ryan quickly peddled around the yard as he yelled, "Look, Jennifer, Avery got my bike fixed! Can I go to Nate's house? Please?"

Avery might be able to charm her little brother into thinking he was something special, but it wouldn't work on her.

When had Avery taken Ryan's bike to get it repaired?

Ryan raced toward her and skidded to a stop a few feet away. "It's as good as new. Can I go to Nate's house?"

His friend Nate lived in the next farmhouse a quarter mile down the road.

"When did Avery take your bike, Ryan?"

"The first day he came to see you. I'm paying him for getting it fixed. That's okay, isn't it?"

"How are you paying him?"

"By polishing his car wheels. I'm going to do it every week that he's here. I've been doing a good job. Avery said so."

"I'm sure you have, sweetheart."

"Can I go to Nate's?"

"All right, but be back before six. It starts getting dark earlier now."

"Okay, thanks." He pushed off, peddling furiously along the edge of the drive.

Turning to look at Avery, she saw he wasn't paying any attention to her. He was pulling a burlap padded target from his trunk.

She closed the distance between, annoyed that he had managed to make her like him a little once more. "You didn't have to fix Ryan's bike. I would have taken care of it before long."

"A guy needs his wheels. Besides, it isn't like I slaved over a hot forge to fix it. A couple of guys at the motor pool did it as a favor."

"Be sure and thank them for us."

"I will. Are you ready for today's lesson?"

"I was ready yesterday." Her remark sounded childish and she regretted it instantly.

"Yeah. I already said I was sorry."

"I only have a week left to learn this stuff. If you aren't going to help me then say so and let me find someone else."

"Jennifer, in spite of what you might think, I'm as serious as you are. Captain Watson, the base brass, they want this win. I want to give it to them."

"Okay then." She resolved to let the matter drop, even though she still didn't trust his commitment. "We will meet here every day next week at four-thirty sharp, ready to work."

He nodded. "We'll also need to meet on the field where you're making your ride as soon as possible."

"I guess that's true. Okay."

"Do you have a pistol?"

"Yes, my mother has one at the Dutton mansion. How soon will I need it?"

"A couple of days, depending on how you do with the saber. Will we be able to shoot here?"

"Yes. Unless the neighbors complain."

"We'll use a small charge of powder to start with. It shouldn't bother anyone. You'll need to learn how to handle a gun on foot before you learn how to shoot from horseback."

"That makes sense."

"Good. Today, I've brought a target so you can start practicing saber hits. Is there someplace we can hang this up?"

Jennifer buckled the sword around her waist and shifted it to the proper position. "Inside the barn would be best."

Leading the way, she helped him hoist and tie up the burlap dummy. He was all business the rest of the afternoon. Part of her wanted to find fault with his manner—she wasn't quite ready to forgive him—but he remained professional and courteous as he demonstrated how to make the slashing strokes the saber had been designed for.

Besides, it was hard not to admire someone who could

wield a sword with such ease and manage to look like a swashbuckling hero straight out of a movie at the same time.

He taught her how to hit targets on both her left and her right sides. It was hard and tiring work, but under his guidance, it wasn't long before she was doing a little swashbuckling herself.

While her skill level rose throughout the afternoon, her determination to remain detached and cool to Avery faded. His smiles and encouraging words weren't flirtatious or deriding for a change, but carried what seemed like genuine warmth. If she hadn't seen him with another woman yesterday, she might have thought he had some affection for her.

Giving herself a mental shake, she decided not to go there and struck the burlap dummy with renewed vigor.

When their lesson was finished and Avery left, she waited until his car was out of sight before she let down her guard and examined the feeling crowding into her mind.

She flexed her sore arm. It was no use. Hitting the dummy hadn't helped. She still cared for Avery, and she didn't know how to change those feelings.

Chapter 12

Avery was ten minutes early again the next afternoon. He had traded his sports car for one of the unit's red pickups and matching horse trailers. As he stepped out of the truck, he realized just how eager he was to see Jennifer again.

He didn't bother trying to hide the truth from himself. He was falling for her—hard and fast.

Glancing at the house, he saw Toby waiting on the front porch. The boy stood and walked toward Avery. He stopped a few feet away, crossed his arms over his chest and fixed his gaze on the ground.

"Thanks for getting squirt's bike fixed." If was apparent Toby had a hard time getting the words out.

Avery knew the boy didn't want to be beholden to him for anything. "It was the least I could do. Where is Jennifer?"

"She took Mom to one of her historical society meetings. She'll be back in a few minutes."

Gesturing toward the truck bed, Avery asked, "Can you give me a hand with this stuff?"

"What is it?"

"A couple of dummies my unit uses for practice. Your sister is ready to start working from horseback. I want to set these up in the corral."

"Why does your outfit ride horses anyway? It's lame."

Avery took a moment to answer. "You think the Army should only be about guns and tanks?"

"I watch the news. You and your buddies aren't riding horses into battle against terrorists. How did you get such a cushy assignment, anyway?"

Avery had heard the question from a lot of visitors to the unit. "Soldiers are assigned to the Commanding General's Mounted Color Guard from various units already stationed at Fort Riley. They do ask for volunteers, but I wasn't one of them. I liked the idea of being inside a tank. I'm attached to one of the armored divisions, on loan to the CGMCG for eighteen months."

"So you didn't have a choice?"

"Not really, but once I realized what the mounted guard is all about, I was proud to be chosen."

"So what is it about?"

"It's about tradition and keeping the spirit of the past alive. I'll bet you think of cavalry troops in the old west as crack shots and daring horsemen."

"Sure. They had to be."

"No. The truth is most of them were boys not much older than you are from cities and small towns and farms. Few of them had ever fired a gun, some had never ridden a horse before they enlisted, almost none of them owned a saber or knew how to use one."

"Are you sure about that?"

"Think of today's Army. How many men have driven tanks or fired missiles before they joined up?"

"Not many."

"A well-trained cavalry was the cutting edge of military tactics a hundred and fifty years ago, the same way laser-guided shells are now. Soldiers in my unit are trained using the same manuals that were used in the Civil War. I'm proud to be a part of that tradition. If that inspires another man to join up and serve his country, then I've done my job."

"Now you sound like my mother."

"I draw the line at putting on a corset to recruit anyone."

That coaxed a ghost of a smile from the boy. "After you've done your time in the color guard, will you go back to your old unit?"

"I will. I'll have two more years to serve before my enlistment is up."

"So, you could be sent to a war zone."

"That's possible."

"Would you go?"

"Yes."

"Would you fight?"

It wasn't the first time Avery had thought about the question, but it was the first time the answer came to him so readily. "Yes."

"Wouldn't you be scared?"

"Yes, I would be scared, but I hope I would do my job. I don't think a man can ever truly know if he will be a coward until he faces that moment, but I know that this country, and what we stand for, is worth fighting for."

Toby regarded him without saying anything else. The sound of Jennifer's truck rolling down the driveway made them both look up. Toby reached into the bed of Avery's truck and pulled out part of the target. "Where do you want this?"

"The center of the corral should be fine."

"I doubt she'll be able to hit it."

"If she doesn't, then I'm a poor teacher."

"You're getting better. At least this time you showed up."

Jennifer stopped the truck beside Avery's and paused to gather her composure. All during church that morning she had prayed for the strength to keep her emotions under control. She was determined to be calm and cool.

If only she would keep her rebellious heart from beating faster at the sight of him.

Ryan jumped out almost as soon as the vehicle rolled to a stop and raced to help his new idol lift something out of the back of his pickup. Jennifer didn't know how to curb Ryan's new hero worship. She wasn't even sure she should try. She certainly wasn't having any success stopping the growth of her own emotional attachment to Avery.

Getting out of her vehicle, she nodded toward him. "What's all this?"

"Your targets. We'll have them set up in a few minutes. Would you mind not wearing one of those skirts this evening?"

She laid a finger against her cheek and tapped it as she considered his request. "Let me see. Look like a fool in a long skirt or look normal in jeans? Decisions, decisions."

"You don't look foolish in the dresses. I'm just concerned about safety. If you're unhorsed, I don't want you getting tangled up in all that material."

Her eyebrows shot up. "Unhorsed? You think I might fall off my horse?"

She couldn't help but feel insulted by his suggestion. They both knew she was a much better rider than he was.

A wary expression settled over his features. Slowly, he said, "In the *extremely* unlikely event…that such a… *freak* accident should occur, I'd rather you were wearing pants."

Mollified slightly, she nodded. "In that case, I'll do as you suggest."

"Good." He relaxed and turned toward the corral with a metal pole and stand in his hands.

She followed him and watched as he and Toby set up two targets. Each tall metal pole had a cross arm that extended out about three feet. A stuffed burlap bag with large red and white circles painted on it hung from the arm about five feet off the ground. As they finished, she saddled Lollypop and rode into the arena.

Avery came to stand beside her and handed her a saber. His hand rested briefly on her knee as he stared up at her. "No funny stuff, no showing off, Jennifer. This is serious. The blade isn't sharp but you can hurt your horse or yourself if you aren't careful."

She took the sword and rested it across the pommel of her saddle. "I'll do exactly as you say."

"Good. Walk Lollypop past both targets and hit them with the slicing motion I showed you yesterday. Keep close to the targets. Don't try to reach for them. You'll unbalance yourself and your horse. That's where ninety percent of riders make their mistakes."

"Okay. I've got it. How hard can it be?"

Nudging Lollypop forward, she rode past the dummy and sliced the blade sideways. It struck the target with a satisfying thud, but the weight of the blade carried it downward and it bounced into Lollypop's flank making the mare sidestep.

"Oh, sorry, baby, sorry," Jennifer crooned to the horse.

Adjusting her grip on the hilt of the saber, she raised it over Lollypop's neck and swung at the target on the opposite side. This time she controlled the blade's descent. It took more arm strength than she expected. It also took her concentration off the horse and Lollypop swerved to the left as Jennifer's weight shifted.

"Not bad," Avery called from the other end of the corral. "Circle back and do it twice more then progress to a trot. Shift your weight more forward in the saddle."

She did as he asked and made two more passes at a walk, then advanced to a trot without any difficulty. Proud of herself, she rode back and stopped in front of Avery. "What do you think?"

"You've got a good seat. You still lack some upper body strength, but you can work on that."

Hoping for a little more praise, she resisted making a snappy comeback. "I want to try it at a gallop."

"I think you should stick to the trot for a little longer."

"No, I can do it from a gallop."

"Okay, if you think you're ready." He stepped back.

When Jennifer kicked Lollypop, the little mare responded by zipping toward the first dummy. Leaning forward, Jennifer extended her arm. She didn't have time to slash downward and ended up stabbing the burlap as she shot past. The blade stayed imbedded in the dummy and yanked out of her hand.

Pulling her horse to a stop, Jennifer whirled around to glare at Avery. If he laughed!

He had one arm crossed over his chest and his other hand covering his jaw. He turned his back to her and took several steps away before turning back. Ryan and Toby, watching from outside the fence, both doubled up with mirth.

Trotting Lollypop back to the target, Jennifer grasped the sword and pulled it free.

Avery waved his hand in a circle. "Try it again."

She heard the amusement brimming in his tone. "If you laugh, so help me…"

He threw both hands up in surrender. "Not laughing. No laughing here."

Ryan fell to the ground in a fit of giggles and Toby sputtered a few times, but recovered himself when she glared at him.

"It's not as easy as it looks," she told them.

"I believe you," Toby managed to say before another guffaw escaped him.

"You work on it a few more times," Avery said, "I'm going to saddle Dakota."

Ignoring her brothers, she focused on galloping past one target and timing her strikes. By the fifth pass, she felt she had the hang of it. Setting Lollypop into a sixth run, Jennifer tried striking both targets. She missed the second one completely and managed to whack her own knee in the process.

She threw the saber to the ground in a fit of temper and rubbed her leg.

Avery rode up beside her. "That will leave a bruise."

She closed her eyes. "This is the most idiotic thing I've ever tried to do. I'm going to look like a moron in front of the entire town and all the visitors and dignitaries, not to mention the famous Dutton descendants. Why did I ever agree to do this?"

"Because you love your mother."

She glared at him from beneath lowered lashes. "Not as much as I did an hour ago."

He chuckled. "You'll get the hang of it. You're not as bad as some of the recruits I've trained lately."

She straightened in the saddle. "Really?"

"No. You're the worst I've ever seen."

Mouth agape, she sputtered, "I am not. Am I?"

"Will you relax? Don't think of this as a military exercise. Think of it as fun."

Ryan had crawled between the fence rails and ran to pick up her sword. He brought it to her and held it up. "You're doing great, sis. You didn't fall off once."

"Thanks, Ryan. Do you want to ride Lollypop while Avery puts Dakota through his paces? I'm done."

She stepped down and hoisted her brother into the saddle in her place, then turned and held the saber out, hilt first, toward Avery. "Why don't you show us how it's done."

Taking the weapon, he held the blade straight in front of his face in a salute. "Yes, ma'am."

Wheeling Dakota, he charged down the corral and effortlessly slashed both targets hard enough to send them spinning. Pulling his mount to a sliding stop, he spun his horse and charged again, striking both dummies before coming to a sliding stop beside Jennifer.

She looked up at Ryan. His eyes were as round as silver dollars. He said, "That was awesome, dude."

Grinning, Jennifer patted her brother's knee. "That's how I'll look when I'm doing great."

"I'm gonna do that someday." He kicked Lollypop into motion and rode around past the targets stabbing them with an imaginary sword.

Jennifer turned to Avery. "I went online and downloaded the required moves that the judges will be looking for in your military horsemanship."

"Great. Were do we start?"

"According to the guidelines, you'll enter dismounted, walk to a predetermined starting point and halt. Then you'll mount and salute. They'll be looking for correct leading and leading on a straight line, correct mounting and they'll also be looking at your horse's calmness."

"A jittery trooper makes a jittery mount?"

"Something like that."

He dismounted and walked beside her to the corral gate. He wasn't particularly tall, but she felt dainty beside him. The small brass spurs on his boots jingled faintly with each step he took. She caught a whiff of his aftershave. He smelled like expensive leather, warm spices and soft woods. A quiver settled in the pit of her stomach and left her smiling softly. There was so much she liked about him. If only she could put her trust in him. If only *he* could learn to put his trust in God.

When they reached the fence, he paused and looked down at her. "Tell me what I'm doing wrong and I'll do better."

She blinked twice. "What?"

"With my horsemanship."

"Oh, right." She wanted to smack her own forehead. Of course he hadn't been talking about their relationship. They didn't have a relationship so how could he be thinking along those lines? Certainly, they had shared a few dates in the past and he had even kissed her then—recalling those brief moments of happiness warmed her to her toes—but since then he'd made it clear that a relationship with her was the *last* thing he wanted..

He tipped his head to the side. "Are you all right?"

Trying for indifference, she replied, "Yes. Why do you ask?"

He leaned closer. "Your face is flushed."

She pressed her hands to her traitorous cheeks. "It is? How odd. It must be all this exercise."

"Shall I start?"

Extending her arm, she motioned for him to proceed. "Yes, go on." *Before I kiss you.*

Chapter 13

For one horrible second Jennifer thought she had spoken aloud, but Avery walked away with Dakota without a backward look.

"Thank you, dear Lord, for small favors," she whispered.

The last thing she wanted was for Avery to discover just how much she cared for him.

This was business. She needed to keep it professional. He needed her help to win the Sheridan Cup. He wasn't interested in rekindling old fires. Was he?

Of course not, and neither was she.

Once she had her mind back on the task at hand, she was able to settle into her coaching mode.

"Ask him to lengthen his stride," she called out, wanting to see Dakota move forward with longer steps.

Immediately Avery tensed. Knowing a horse could

sense mental or physical tension, she wasn't surprised when Dakota's trot became choppy instead of smoother.

"Stop a minute," she called out and walked up to them. She laid a hand on Dakota's neck and stroked him as she looked up at Avery.

Avery let out a frustrated breath. "Tell me what I did wrong."

"You forgot to smile."

"Don't try to be kind. I could feel it wasn't right."

"That's because you know Dakota so well."

"He and I have spent a lot of hours together since Lindsey left the unit. What were we doing wrong?"

"You were thinking too hard."

He relaxed and gave her a half smile. "This is supposed to fun, right?"

"Yup. Who cares what score you get? Riding a horse is *fun.* Can you remember that?"

"I think so."

"Good. Try it again with a smile. Just a little one."

Avery took her suggestions and relaxed as he put Dakota through his paces. The improvement was impressive. While he'd had some trouble communicating with McCloud, he and Dakota were obviously on the same wavelength. Before long, they were operating as a responsive and intuitive team.

Jennifer relaxed, too, and began to enjoy watching them work together.

It was almost dark by the time Jennifer called a halt to the lessons for the evening. Avery couldn't help the pang of disappointment that followed her words. He didn't want the session to end. He didn't want to go home to his empty apartment.

"What do you say to a quick gallop?" he suggested as she held open the gate for him.

"I can't." He heard the longing in her voice, but saw the resolve settle over her face.

"I need to pick up my mother and Lizzie, and then I really need to crack the books. I have a paper due tomorrow."

"Okay." Dismounting, he loosened the girth on Dakota's saddle. He wanted to tease and cajole her into going with him, but he didn't press the issue. Being sensitive to what she needed was harder than he thought. He was used to only thinking about himself.

"I'll take a rain check," she offered as they began walking toward his truck and trailer.

"I'll hold you to that."

Not tonight, but soon, when she wasn't pressed for time or swamped with responsibilities. Once her re-enactment and his competition were over, they might be able to spend a leisurely afternoon together on a trail ride. He knew of a bridle path that meandered along the shore of a local lake. His heart lightened at the thought of spending time there alone with her.

"What's your plan for tomorrow?" she asked.

"Pistols."

She arched her brows. "Really? Am I ready for that?"

"I think so."

Suddenly, Dakota whinnied loudly and began to pull at the reins.

"Easy, boy." Avery patted the big bay's neck to calm him, but Dakota whinnied again. Avery and Jennifer exchanged puzzled looks as the horse stood with his head high and his gaze fastened on the barn door.

Jennifer began to laugh. "He smells Isabella."

Shaking his head in disbelief, Avery allowed the horse to pull him to the barn door. Dakota stretched his head and neck in as far as he could over the lower half of the door and whinnied softly this time.

Jennifer motioned to Ryan. "Get Isabella out of her cage, honey. Dakota wants to see her."

Avery made Dakota back up enough to allow Ryan to slip inside and open the rabbit's hutch. Before he could lift Isabella out, she hopped down and darted to the door. She hopped up and down madly, until Dakota lowered his nose to hers.

As the odd couple nuzzled each other, Avery glanced down at Jennifer standing beside him. "You're right. She is what he wanted."

"It must be love," she noted softly, and glanced up at him.

Their eyes met and held. Her pupils darkened, some deep emotion stirring in their depths. He wanted to reach out and cup her cheek with his hand, but he held back, suddenly afraid that he might destroy what he saw.

"I think they're just good friends," Ryan remarked as he knelt beside Isabella and stroked Dakota's forehead.

Toby, standing a few feet away, said dryly, "Of course they're just friends. They couldn't be anything else."

Jennifer looked away. A blush stained her cheeks bright pink. "I should get going. I don't want to keep Mom and Lizzie waiting."

Reaching out, Avery caught her hand before she turned away. "Why don't you let me pick them up? That way you can get a head start on the studying you have to do."

She shook her head. "Thanks for the offer but it isn't necessary. I can manage."

He leaned closer. "Still won't admit that you can't do it all?"

Rolling her eyes, she said, "I knew I was going to regret telling you that."

"Give me the keys to your truck," he coaxed. "I'll leave Dakota to visit with his bunny friend for a while longer and go pick up your mother and sister."

She bit her lip. He could see her wavering.

Quickly, he added, "Unlike you, I don't have anything else to do tonight."

She seemed to notice that he was still holding her hand. She withdrew it slowly. "I could use the extra time for some online research."

"Great. Where are your keys?" He hated letting go of her, but tried not to show it.

"They're in the truck. Are you sure you don't mind?"

"Friends help out friends. Right? And no, I don't mind at all." He turned to Ryan. "Grab hold of Hippy Hoppy."

When Ryan had Isabella securely in his arms, Avery opened the barn door and led Dakota inside. Pulling the saddle and bridle off, he carried them back outside and closed the door. Dakota lowered his nose to the straw, turned around twice and then lay down. Ryan put Isabella down and she immediately hopped over to her friend.

Avery looked at Jennifer. "What are you still doing out here? Go study."

She grinned. "Thank you. I may actually get my paper done before midnight."

"Not if you stand here talking."

"I'll call Mom and let her know you are on your way." Saluting, she turned and hurried to the house, pausing to look back and wave before she went in.

Happy that he could lighten a small part of the burdens she shouldered, he laid his saddle in the back of his truck and crossed to her vehicle. The keys were in the ignition. Getting in, he started the engine. Before he put it in gear, he noticed a small silver cross dangling from the rearview mirror. Reaching up, he cupped the smooth metal and smiled.

Jennifer took her faith with her wherever she went and she wasn't afraid to display it for everyone to see.

A sharp rap on the window drew his attention. Toby motioned for him to roll down the window. The boy was having a hard time keeping a grin off his face. "It was nice of you to give my sister a break, but don't you think you should ask where my mother is?"

Avery laughed at himself. "I'm sure that would have occurred to me in a minute or two."

"She and the nut cluster are meeting at the Dutton Inn. You can't miss it. There's a big sign out front that says Historical Bed and Breakfast. How lame is that? Like breakfast is a historical meal."

Thankful for Toby's help, Avery rolled up the window and drove off.

On the way into town, his mind kept wandering back to the expression he had seen in Jennifer's eyes.

"It must be love," he repeated to himself, half afraid to say the words out loud.

Had Jennifer been talking about something other than the rabbit's affections? Was it possible she had been talking about her own feelings?

He hadn't given her a reason to care for him. In fact, he had gone out of his way to do just the opposite up until the day before yesterday.

Still, she hadn't kicked him off her property. She

might claim it was because of the commitment she'd made but something told him there was more to it. Perhaps he hadn't damaged their relationship beyond repair. If she gave him enough time, could he prove he was worthy of her affections?

A faint hope began to grow in his heart. He glanced at the cross on the mirror. "If I was a praying man, I'd be asking for Your help."

He smiled as he realized Jennifer would tell him that that was a prayer. And she would be right.

As Toby had promised, the bed and breakfast was clearly marked on the outskirts of town. By the number of people milling around on the wide green lawn, Avery surmised the meeting had just let out. He saw Mary Grant, leaning on her crutches, in animated conversation with several townspeople. Lizzie was sitting on a bench nearby.

A few of the crowd had already headed to their cars lining both sides of the street, and Avery was able to get a parking spot close to the front walk. Lizzie caught sight of him and waved, then headed toward him.

Avery got out and walked around to the passenger's side and opened the door. Lizzie walked past him and climbed in. "Am I glad to see you. This was so borrrring!"

"You're just upset because Dale wasn't here." Mary's voice brimmed with humor. "I know you 'volunteered' to stay with me because you were hoping to see him. You can't fool your mother."

Avery hid a grin as Lizzie rolled her eyes. When he glanced toward Mary, he got a major shock. It wasn't a local man assisting her. His grandfather was walking with her toward the vehicle.

"Be careful of this sidewalk, Mrs. Grant, it's very uneven," Edmond cautioned, keeping a close eye on her halting steps.

"I'm fine, sir, but thank you for your concern."

"Please, you must call me Edmond." He smiled when she cast a shy look in his direction.

"If you will call me Mary."

"I'd be delighted to do so." Edmond looked up and stopped in his tracks when he caught sight of Avery.

Struggling to hide his anger, Avery fumed silently. The old man might look surprised to see him, but Avery didn't buy it. Edmond always had a plan. That he would use Jennifer's family in his attempt to worm his way back into Avery's good graces was a new low—even for Edmond.

Avery inclined his head slightly. "Grandfather. I didn't know you were a history buff."

Edmond recovered quickly. "Neither did I, but Mrs. Grant is showing me the error of my ways."

Mary blushed like a schoolgirl as she handed Avery her crutches and slid in beside Lizzie. "Your poor grandfather was sitting in the parlor reading and I'm afraid we swooped in and surrounded him. We simply take over the inn when we get together."

"That's true," Lizzie muttered.

"I enjoyed myself, Mary," Edmond assured her. "I look forward to watching your granddaughter in the re-enactment of Henrietta Dutton's ride next week. It sounds thrilling."

Avery scowled at him. "You're staying to watch Jennifer's ride? I'm surprised you can be away from the firm for so long."

Mary beamed at Avery as she took her crutches from

him. "Edmond isn't staying just for our festival. He's decided to stay until after the cavalry competition. I can't believe you didn't tell him that you're competing."

Chapter 14

"I don't see why you're so upset he found out you're competing for the Sheridan Cup. It's not like it was top secret information." Jennifer closed one eye and sighted down the barrel of pistol toward a balloon tied to a corral fence post. The two of them were alone. All of her siblings had been banned from the area on direct orders from their mother.

"I shouldn't have said anything to you." Avery regretted mentioning his feelings on the subject almost as soon as the words were out of his mouth.

"No. I'm glad you did. I know you and your grandfather haven't gotten along in the past, but maybe he has changed."

She fired. The balloon continued to wave in the wind. She looked down at her smoking firearm. "Arc you sure this is loaded?"

"Aim a little higher and keep at least one eye open this time. He never came to so much as a soccer practice when I was growing up. Now he's spending a month in Dutton, Kansas, so he can be here to watch me ride. I don't get it. I'd like to know the real reason he's hanging around."

"I had one eye open," she insisted.

"Then you're in trouble. Are you sure you have to actually hit something on your wild ride?"

She blew out a breath and aimed again. "According to my mother I have to gun down two bad guys."

The gun barked and jumped in her hand but her target continued to bob on its string. "Oh, come on! This thing isn't working. If you want to know why your grandfather is here, you should ask him."

Avery took the gun from her and fired one-handed, shattering the balloon. "I don't want to talk to him. I know he's looking for some way to humiliate me."

Her mouth dropped open and she stuck her hands on her hips. "The first two were blanks, weren't they?"

"They're all blanks. There are no bullets. I keep telling you it's the hot powder that pops the targets."

She took the gun back from him and walked down the fence to a second red balloon. "Why are you so sure your grandfather has an ulterior motive in staying here?"

"His track record for one thing."

She had raised the gun with both hands and was sighting down the wobbling barrel, but she lowered it and waited until Avery met her gaze. "What did he do that you can't forgive?"

He jerked his head toward the target. "Shoot."

"If I hit this one you'll tell me?"

"No."

Her eyes narrowed. "Yes, you will."

"Fine. Hit it and I'll share."

Turning sideways, she brought the gun up in a smooth motion with one hand and fired. The target exploded. Her eyes widened. "I did it!"

"Lucky accident."

"It doesn't matter. Share." She folded her arms and stood waiting like Ma Barker clutching a smoking revolver.

"I changed my mind."

"If you tell me why you're so angry at your grandfather, I'll tell you about the time I took off all my clothes and ran through the grocery store."

That was a picture he would have a hard time getting out of his mind. "Okay. You first."

She shook her head. "No. Me after."

He debated the wisdom of sharing his story, but found he wanted to tell her. He wanted to share more with her than he had ever thought possible to share with any woman. He wanted her compassion, her laughter, her worry and her tears. He wanted to be included in her life.

The starting point was this. He took her gun and began to reload it, afraid to watch her face. "After my parents died I got in with a really fast and stupid crowd. I did a lot of things that I'm not proud of now, but then I met a woman named Miranda. She was so pretty and different. She came from a very poor family but that didn't matter to me. She worshiped the ground I walked on, or so I thought."

Jennifer took a step closer. "What happened?" she asked softly.

"I asked her to marry me. We planned a big wedding. I invited all my so-called friends. The marriage of Edmond Barnes's only heir was big news. Only her family pedigree wasn't good enough for my grandfather. He went to her and offered her a lot of money to break it off."

"Did she?"

He stuck the revolver in the holster on his hip. "Yes. A week before the wedding, she and her family moved to another city and into a very fancy home."

"That's terrible. How could she do that?"

"I imagine my grandfather made it plain that he controlled the money and if she had any hopes of getting her family out of the ghetto, his was a one time offer."

Reaching out, Jennifer laid a hand on his arm. Her touch comforted him. "That was a terrible thing for them to do, but you need to forgive them."

"You're saying I should just forget that they made my life miserable? That's not possible."

"You're right. Forgetting such a betrayal isn't possible, but *forgiving* such a betrayal is. Once you find it in your heart to forgive Miranda and your grandfather, you take away the power their act has to hurt you."

Shaking his head, he managed a wry smile. "No. It seems my grandfather isn't the only one with too much pride."

A pensive look clouded her eyes. She took a few steps away to brace her hands on the fence. He watched her with concern. Something was troubling her.

"Ready to tell me about your *au naturel* shopping trip?"

She smiled at him over her shoulder. "I was twelve months old. I apparently escaped from my mother's clutches by crawling under the produce table where I shed my diaper and my top and took off like the gleeful toddler I was. My father chased me down and caught me before I had time to shock the checkout line. He really enjoyed telling that story."

Avery chuckled. "I can imagine he would."

"You wouldn't think twice about embarrassing your own daughter with that story in front of her junior high prom date, would you?" she demanded.

It was easy to imagine a small blond toddler with Jennifer's bright blue eyes and dimpled cheeks getting into trouble right and left. For the first time he considered what stories he might share with children of his own.

"I wish I could have met your father."

She sighed wistfully. "I wish you could have, too. You would have enjoyed his sense of humor. I know death isn't the end, but there are so many things I would have liked to tell him."

Turning away from the fence, she faced Avery. "That's why I'm going to tell you something now that I said I wouldn't."

She shifted nervously from one foot to the other.

"I'm listening," Avery said, worried by her intensity.

"Your grandfather is ill. He's already had one heart attack and a triple bypass surgery."

"How do you know that?" Avery demanded. Was this some kind of trick his grandfather had gotten Jennifer to pull on him?

Quickly, she said, "The first day I met him, after you had left him in the stable, I found him slumped over and in need of a nitroglycerin tablet. He was having chest pain. I thought he was having a heart attack. I wanted to get you or call 9-1-1, but he wouldn't let me."

"He was faking it." His grandfather was made of granite. He'd never been sick a day in his life.

Shaking her head, she said, "You can't fake those kinds of symptoms. He was flushed and sweating. If his pills hadn't helped right away I would have called for an ambulance. He told me he wants to reconcile with you—but I don't think he knows how to start."

Avery took a few steps away. To clear his head. To wrap his mind around what she was saying. "I don't believe it."

"I'm sorry." The sympathy in her voice told him she believed it was true.

He waited, wanting to feel gladness or at least satisfaction that Edmond was facing something he couldn't buy off or bribe his way out of—only those weren't the emotions that came. Instead, sorrow crept in and then pity. For all his money, Edmond was alone now, without family or true friends to stand beside him.

"I used to want to be like him. I *am* like him," Avery admitted slowly.

Coming to his side, Jennifer took his hand and held it between hers. Her warmth drove the chill from his mind. "You don't have to repeat his mistakes. You can be your own man."

Looking down into her eyes, Avery had a glimpse of what the future could be like if she were always beside him. She was an anchor to everyone around her. But why would she have him? He didn't share her faith or her values. She deserved so much more from the man who loved her.

And he did love her.

He loved her bright eyes and the way she threw herself into solving the problems life handed her—even if they weren't her problems. He reached up and brushed a lock of hair back from her face. "Is that another one of Jennifer's top ten tips to positive living?"

Her smile was as soft as the evening breeze. "It's number five."

"Someday maybe you can give me the whole list."

"What would you do with it? Tattoo it on your forehead?"

He flicked her nose with the tip of his finger. "I'd tattoo it on yours. That way I wouldn't have to look in the mirror each time I needed a reminder."

"What makes you think I'll be around when you need a reminder?"

"Good point."

Did that mean she wasn't interested in seeing him once their training sessions were done? He wanted to ask, but he wasn't sure he wanted to hear her answer. Not yet, anyway.

"What are you going to do about your grandfather?"

"Nothing."

Jennifer bit her lip, appalled that her breach of confidence didn't make any difference to Avery. She dropped his hand. "How can you say that?"

"It was easy. I opened my mouth and the words came out." He drew the reloaded gun and held it out to her.

Taking it, she started to turn away, but he reached out and gripped her arm. "I know you want to help, but my family isn't like yours. There isn't any respect or love for one another lurking under the surface. I'm sorry he's sick, but it doesn't change a lifetime of making me feel like I'm his biggest disappointment since learning Santa doesn't exist."

"I'm sorry you were made to feel that way. I just thought you should know he was ill." Blinking back tears of disillusionment, she looked down. All this time she thought Avery's indifference toward people was an act. Perhaps it wasn't. She wanted him to be so much more.

"You can't fix everyone, Jenny."

"I know." She pulled free of his hand and walked toward the next target. Raising the gun, she blasted the balloon to pieces.

"Jenny?"

"What?" She glanced toward him. His smile was incredibly sad. "Don't stop trying."

Heartened, she smiled back. "I don't intend to."

Later that evening, after he had finished instructing Jennifer in the finer points of shooting from horseback and returned Dakota to the stables, Avery found himself once again parked in front of the bed and breakfast in Dutton. Getting out of his car, he stood staring at the building and wondering what he was going to say to his grandfather.

The front door opened and the man he was thinking about came out. Tonight Edmond had a cane in his hand and he leaned on it heavily as he started down the sidewalk. When he caught sight of Avery, he paused.

Avery stayed where he was and after a few seconds Edmond walked toward him. "It's such a nice night, I thought I would take a little stroll before I went to bed. Would you care to join me?"

Not knowing what else to do, Avery agreed. "I guess."

The two men fell into step together, Avery shortening his stride to match the older man's. An awkward silence stretched between them.

The small town was quiet, with only an occasional car going past. The sounds of cicadas and crickets filled the air as they walked beneath the maples and oaks lining the street. Lights shone from the windows of the two-story Victorian homes on both sides of the avenue and occasional voices reached them. A dog in the neighbor's yard began barking, setting off a canine chorus chain reaction down the block.

"This place seems like something out of Currier and Ives," Edmond said at last. "It's obvious the people here take a lot of pride in their town."

"It's okay for Hicksville."

"You young people don't have an appreciation for things of the past century. You're always in a hurry. You want instant everything. Instant oatmeal, instant messaging, instant gratification. Good things take time."

He hadn't come to discuss the vices or the virtues of modern times. Avery said, "Jennifer told me you've been sick."

"I thought as much when I saw you tonight. I must admit I'm surprised that she didn't share that information sooner. According to her mother, she has a very tender heart."

"I hope you aren't planning to use them to get to me."

Edmond stopped and turned to face Avery. "Why are you here?"

"I've been asking myself that same question."

"If you've come to gloat, I don't blame you. I treated you badly." Edmond clenched his fingers and raised his fist. "I thought hardness would make you hard and that would somehow protect you in this cutthroat world."

"From cutthroats like you?"

Edmond's hand fell to his side. "Yes."

"What do you want from me?" Avery asked calmly, keeping his anger and pity out of his voice.

A lopsided smile lifted the corner of Edmond's mouth. "All I want is for you to accompany me on the rest of my stroll this evening. Is that too much to ask?"

He didn't wait for Avery to reply, but began walking.

Avery almost turned around and left. When he realized his hands were clenched into fists at his sides, he relaxed them. If he left now, he'd lose any chance of getting to the bottom of Edmond's plans.

Catching up with his grandfather, he walked beside him in silence until they reached the end of the block. Edmond turned left and continued on.

"My doctor has instructed me to walk for forty minutes twice a day. It's amazing how much you see when you take the time to just walk."

"How sick are you?" Avery asked.

Edmond glanced at him. "According to my cardiologist I may have a few more years. Five if I take care of myself."

"I'm sorry," Avery said quietly.

"Don't be. I'm already eighty years old. Five more would be quite a gift."

"Who is running the firm while you're here?"

"I'd rather not talk about work, if you don't mind."

"That's a switch." Avery almost laughed out loud.

"Yes. My work was my addiction. It cost me my family, my friends, more than you know."

The regret in his grandfather's tone sounded genuine, but Avery wasn't ready to believe it. "You reaped plenty of rewards from your labor."

Edmond stopped and stared at the ground. Quietly, he said, "Yes, I gathered a large amount of wealth. The root of all evil. I thank God I've been given a chance to change and to know Him."

Giving his head a slight shake, he started forward again. "Mrs. Grant told me that you've been helping her daughter learn swordsmanship. Are you really?"

Changing the subject wasn't what Avery wanted, but he went along with it. "Yes. Jennifer is taking part in the town's re-enactment of some woman's charge into the face of certain death."

"The renowned Henrietta Dutton?"

"You've heard of her?"

Edmond chuckled. "Not until I came here. The owners of the bed and breakfast have quite an extensive knowledge of the woman. Apparently Mrs. Marcus is a direct descendent."

"Did you tell her one of our ancestors participated in the Boston Tea Party?"

"I thought about it, but decided my breakfast toast might end up burnt if I one-upped her genealogy. Mrs. Marcus is quite touchy on the subject. On the other hand, Miss Grant seems like a very nice young woman. From something she said I gather you have known each other for a while."

"Jennifer is great. She's—genuine."

"Do I detect an interest on your part?"

"I'd rather leave her out of this conversation."

"Of course. I didn't mean to pry."

They continued walking in silence until they turned the corner toward the inn.

Edmond cleared his throat. "I see we're almost back where we started from."

"I guess we are." Nothing had been solved between them. Avery still didn't know what to make of Edmond's presence. Was it possible his grandfather had come to make peace between them? Mulling over the possibility,

Avery didn't discard the notion as he would have a week ago. Something about Edmond was different.

At the sidewalk leading to the front of the bed and breakfast, Edmond stopped and faced Avery. "Thank you for your company tonight."

"You haven't told me why you're hanging around this one-horse town."

"I'm hoping to discover something."

"About me?"

"About myself. Goodnight, Avery. Perhaps I'll see you at the festival."

Watching his grandfather walk away and enter the house, Avery struggled with a multitude of conflicting emotions. He had spent years detesting the man and trying his best to make his grandfather detest him in return. Yet deep underneath his anger and resentment had always been a childish longing to be loved and respected by the old man.

Avery wasn't sure he wanted to give up his anger. It gave him purpose. But that purpose had led him to behave in ways he wasn't proud of, in ways Jennifer could never approve of.

If he changed—if he wanted to become the kind of man she could respect and care for—he would have to start here. He would have to find it in his heart to forgive. And to ask forgiveness in return.

He knew with sudden clarity that it would be the hardest task he had ever faced.

Chapter 15

Jennifer was reading her homework while mixing the ingredients for a casserole the next day when she heard Avery drive in. She bit her lip as she struggled to keep her battered emotions under control. She had spent a long night in soul searching and personal inventory and she still didn't know how she was going to handle her growing affection for him.

The smart thing would be to stop seeing him all together, but she had promised to coach him until the cavalry competition was over. It was still a week away. Seven days of looking into Avery's dark eyes, of seeing the roguish smile that sent her heart skipping, of wanting to be held in his arms.

"Help me, Lord," she whispered. "I know what is right. I know he's not the kind of man I need in my life, but I can't change how I feel. Show me what You want me to do."

"Are you talking to yourself, Jennifer?" Mary inquired as she crossed the living room on her crutches.

Jennifer felt a blush heat her face. "Actually, I was talking to God."

"He's the best listener in the universe, of course, but I'm available, too. Is it anything I can do to help?"

"No, I'm okay. Thanks." The last thing her mother needed was to start worrying about Jennifer's love life.

Jennifer slipped the green-and-white glass pan into the oven, set the timer, then checked out the kitchen window. She saw Toby and Ryan helping Avery unload Dakota. The three of them seemed caught up in earnest conversation. Lollypop was already saddled and waiting for her inside the corral. There was no reason to hurry outside, except that she wanted to be with him.

Jennifer felt a hand on her shoulder and she turned to her mother. Mary's eyes were brimming with understanding and love.

"I'm not unfamiliar with troubles of the heart, dear," Mary said quietly. "Are you sure you don't want to talk about it?"

Sighing, Jennifer battled the sting of tears. "I like him so much and I know how wrong that is."

"Why is it wrong to care about someone?"

"Because *he's* all wrong. He doesn't share our faith, he doesn't have principles or honor. He thinks money is the answer to everything. He isn't a bit like Daddy."

"You're being rather harsh, aren't you?"

"The truth is harsh in his case."

"Jennifer, if there wasn't something—special—about

that young man, we wouldn't be having this conversation. What is it that you see in him?"

"I don't know what I see in him, except…"

"Except what?"

"Sometimes, I think I see how much pain he is in."

"So you feel sympathy?"

Shaking her head vigorously, Jennifer was quick to deny that accusation. "No, quite the opposite. I want to shake him and tell him to wake up and take a look around. There is so much good in the world and he's making himself unhappy by his choices."

"And you are making yourself unhappy…because?"

"I didn't choose to be unhappy. I didn't choose to fall for a guy that would let me down—twice—or as many times as I let him."

"I'm going to tell you something you already know. A woman who clings to a man in hopes of changing him is destined for a life of heartache."

"I do know that."

"Good. Now I'm going to tell you something you don't know. Before I met your father, he had been to church less than a dozen times in his life. He was my father's nightmare. Good looking, charming and as wild as the hills."

"Dad?" Jennifer wasn't sure she believed what she was hearing. Her father had been a rock of faith and love.

"Yes. He was a sorry case."

"So what changed him?"

"Wanting my love more than anything and knowing that he had it in himself to attain it."

"I don't understand."

"I made it plain to your father that I cared about him, but that I deserved the kind of husband God wanted me to have. I wouldn't settle for anything less. Your father knew that to marry me he was going to have to become that man."

"And that brought him to God?"

"Not right away, but it got his attention."

"Avery thinks religion is a joke."

"Not everyone finds God in a flash of revelation as it happened to the Apostle Paul. People who quietly seek faith through study and through prayer, those people find Him, too. Your father started going to church because I said he should. In time, and by God's grace, he found salvation."

"I hardly think Avery will start attending church because I ask him. In fact, I'm pretty sure he'll say no thanks."

"Then let him say it and show him that what you value can't be cast aside. Follow your own heart. If he isn't the man you think he can be, then God will show you that. Have faith in yourself and in him."

"Thanks, Mom. Are you going to come out and watch me practice?" Her mother had given her a lot to consider.

Mary shook her head. Some of the light left her eyes. "No. I don't think so."

"I've got skills. Even Avery says I'm doing better than he expected."

"I'm sure you are, but I think I'm going to rest for a while."

Jennifer remembered with a sinking heart that her mother had wanted to be the one to make the historic ride. "Of course. Is your leg hurting?"

"No more than usual. I'm just a little tired. They worked me over pretty good in therapy today."

"I'm so glad Mr. Marcus is able to drive you to your

appointment. I've been worrying how I was going to get you there and get back to class on time."

"Yes, it was sweet of Pastor McGregor to ask for volunteers to help us, but Mr. Marcus couldn't make it this morning."

Jennifer cocked her head to the side. "Then who took you?"

"Mr. Barnes was kind enough to take me. Actually, it was his driver who took us. I felt quite special being dropped off by a chauffeur at the clinic."

"I imagine."

"Avery's grandfather is quite taken with you."

"With me?" Jennifer wasn't sure if she was more surprised by the comment or by the fact that her mother had spent the morning in Mr. Barnes's company.

"Yes. He seems to feel that you're a good influence on Avery."

Jennifer hesitated, not sure how much Avery would appreciate her sharing his family troubles. Still, it seemed best to let her mother know how things stood. "Avery and his grandfather are estranged."

"Yes, it's very sad, but Mr. Barnes is hopeful that they can heal the breech. Especially since Avery has taken the next step."

"The next step?"

"Yes, he went to visit his grandfather last night. I think family feuds are the saddest kind, don't you? If someone doesn't have the love and support of those who should be the closest to them, it must leave them feeling rudderless."

"I can't believe Mr. Barnes discussed his family problems with you. I mean, you're practically strangers."

"He doesn't seem like a stranger, he seems like someone I've known a long time. Anyway, I had the feeling he wanted me to understand that Avery wasn't entirely to blame for his…unwise lifestyle choices."

Avery had made poor choices, but Jennifer couldn't help being proud of the choice he had made yesterday. It proved he was willing to change if he had gone to see his grandfather. The hope she had been trying so hard to weed out of her heart blossomed like an early spring crocus.

"Mother, do you like Avery?"

"Dear, the real question is do you like him?"

"A lot. I like him very much."

"And does he like you?"

Jennifer tipped her head to the side as she considered her mother's question. "I believe he does."

"Then don't be afraid. Nurture that affection and trust God to see where it leads."

Standing inside the corral where he had already set up the balloons and burlap bags, Avery was engaged in trying to cheer up Ryan when Jennifer came around the corner of the barn. The sad youngster who knew Isabella was going back to her owner in the morning was forgotten as Avery took in the wide smile on Jennifer's face and the sparkle in her eyes.

For once she looked happy to see him. Not just happy, she looked positively delighted.

She was wearing another prairie skirt. This one was gray with pink bows around the hem. Without breaking stride, she came right up to him, rose on tiptoe and planted a kiss on his cheek.

Not quite sure what to make of her behavior, he asked cautiously, "What was that for?"

"Just because."

"Yuck!" Ryan scrunched up his nose. "Don't do that mushy stuff."

"Pay no attention to the kid," Avery counter quickly. "Do all the mushy stuff you want."

She giggled. "I think we'd better get to work." Smiling at him, she said, "Now fall down dead."

"I'm weak in the knees, but not that weak," he assured her.

Batting his chest, she said, "You're Colonel Dutton. Fall down dead so I can pick up your sword and gun and ride into history. Come on, I've only got three days left to get this right."

Grinning, he stepped back and pressed both hands to his chest. "I'm hit."

He staggered a few feet to the left and spun around once. "They've killed me, Henrietta."

He staggered a few steps to the right. "Don't let my dream die with me."

Ryan began laughing uncontrollably.

Dropping to his knees, Avery drew his sword and held it aloft. "Fight on," he croaked and fell face down in the dirt.

Jennifer chuckled as she pulled his sidearm out of his holster, then tried to pull his saber from his hand. He held on tight.

"Let go," she muttered, pulling harder.

"You have to pry it from my cold dead hand," he whispered.

She rapped his knuckles with something hard.

"Ouch." He lifted his head to see her holding the butt of the gun like a hammer over his fingers. He let loose.

Pistol in her right hand, saber in her left, she headed

for Lollypop. The little black mare was watching the whole performance with wide-eyed interest.

Avery propped his chin on his hands. "Lines!"

Jennifer stopped. "Something, something, can't kill a dream."

Grabbing the horse's reins, she swung into the saddle and charged down the fence line. She missed the first target she fired at, but managed to hit the second one.

Avery jumped to his feet to watch. Dropping the pistol, Jennifer switched the saber to her right hand, narrowly missing Lollypop's ears in the maneuver. The rest of her charge proved she had been practicing as she hit all but one burlap bag.

The course brought her around the corral and back to Avery, where she drew Lollypop to a stop and pointed the saber at him.

"Surrender or die."

Looking into her incredibly blue eyes, he knew she had captured his heart. He held up his hands. "I surrender. I'm yours if you'll have me."

Lowering the tip of her sword, she nudged her horse close to him. He saw uncertainty settle over her delicate features. "Do you mean that?"

Sensing her seriousness, he said, "I do, Jennifer. I never felt this way about anyone. Will you give me another chance?"

She tipped her head to the side. "Yes, Corporal Barnes, I believe I will."

He breathed a sigh of relief. He had no idea what had made her change her mind today, but he was going to take advantage of it. "You won't be sorry, sweetheart. I promise you that."

She stepped down from the horse and smiled shyly.

"I'm going to hold you to that. You and I are going to have some long talks. There are things you need to know and understand before we go any further with this relationship. Things I won't compromise on."

"Such as?"

"My faith and what that means for the two of us."

"All right. I promise I'll listen with an open mind."

"That's all I can ask."

"You are one special girl." Capturing both her hands, Avery smiled down at her, feeling happier than he could ever remember.

Chapter 16

The morning of the Founders' Day Festival dawned bright and clear. Jennifer peeked out her bedroom window at a few minutes after six in the morning and groaned. Apparently a torrential flood or early blizzard wasn't going to get her off the hook. She would have to make her charge up Dutton Heights.

Turning off her alarm a minute before it was set to start blaring music, she wondered if Henrietta Dutton was spinning in her grave.

The dress rehearsal the day before had been a disaster. Not only had Jennifer missed all but one of her targets, but Lollypop had repeatedly refused the final jump at the top of the hill leaving the actor playing the brigand leader unable to surrender to anyone.

Edna Marcus had broken down in tears and declared

she wouldn't be a party to making a mockery of her great, great, great aunt's bravery.

When Jennifer walked into the kitchen, she saw the rest of her family already gathered around the table. The silence was deafening.

Plopping down in her chair, Jennifer began buttering a slice of toast. "You don't have to stop talking about me just because I'm here. I can take it."

Ryan, a smear of strawberry jam on his cheek, leaned toward her. "Lizzie said you messed up big time."

"Tattle tale," Lizzie growled, kicking him under the table.

"Well, she's right," Jennifer agreed. "I'm sorry, Mom. I'll try to do better today."

"You'll do fine," Mary reassured her, but Jennifer could tell she was worried. Her mother had been watching from the sidelines and Jennifer felt the weight of her disappointment.

"I did great the day before when Avery and I went over the course."

She had been so proud of her skills that she had actually been looking forward to demonstrating them in front of the crowds that would be there today. Now it looked as if her accuracy had been a fluke.

At least Avery hadn't been there to witness her paltry effort yesterday. His duties at the fort had kept him away from the dress rehearsal, but he had promised to be at the festival today. She would need a hug from him before and after she made a fool of herself.

Toby patted her shoulder. "You'll do fine, sis. Shake it off."

Ryan jumped to his feet and flapped his hands wildly. "Yeah, shake it off like this."

"Finish your breakfast, Ryan." His mother's stern tone sent him meekly back to his chair. The rest of the meal passed in silence. Jennifer choked down her toast, but it didn't settle her butterflies.

It was nearly nine o'clock when they arrived at the grassy area cordoned off for the numerous horse trailers and campers belonging to the re-enactors. Many of them had been camped at the site since the middle of the week.

She moved quickly to help her mother out of the truck. Mary, dressed in her favorite blue plaid gown, scowled at the crutches Lizzie handed her.

"I wish I didn't need them. They spoil the look of this dress."

Jennifer said, "I don't care. If you don't use them, then I am taking you home."

"She will, too," Lizzie added, slipping out after her mother. Having opted for a modern look, she was wearing green twill pants with a matching white-and-green striped shirt beneath a tan jacket.

"Can we go to the concessions stand?" Toby asked as he climbed out from the rear seat.

"Yeah. I'm hungry, too," Ryan added, trying unsuccessfully to look like a starving waif.

"You can't be hungry already. You only finished breakfast an hour ago," Jennifer pointed out.

"We are," Ryan insisted.

Mary glanced toward one of the white tents set up nearby. "All right, but be back here in ten minutes. We don't want to miss the performance."

"Thanks, Mom," the boys echoed each other, then raced away.

"Lizzie, go keep an eye on them," Mary said.

"Do I have to?"

"Yes." Her mother's tone didn't allow for argument. Lizzie rolled her eyes, but did as she was told.

"I'd like to miss the performance," Jennifer muttered.

Mary shook her head sadly. "And waste all the time you've put into learning how to shoot and wield a sword? When are you ever going to use those skills again if not today?"

"Never. Next year it will be you making this ride." Walking to the rear of the horse trailer, Jennifer opened the door and backed out Lollypop. The mare was already saddled and ready to make her famous run.

Glancing toward the nearby hilltop, Mary sighed. "I hope it's part of God's plan for me, but some things are more important. If I can't ride again, then I can't."

Patting Lollypop's neck, Jennifer glanced at her mother's sad face. Sudden worry struck her. "Mom, you told me the doctor said your knee is getting better."

Mary straightened and managed a smile that didn't quite reach her eyes. "Yes, but I do wish I could be out there today. Since I can't, I'm really glad that it's you."

"You've never told me why this thing is so important to you. If I'm going to go out and make a fool of myself, I think I should know why."

Mary looked down. "My zeal must seem silly to you."

Jennifer studied her mother's face. "A little, but I'd like to know why it means so much to you."

Looking up, Mary met her daughter's gaze. "When your father died, I thought the world ended. You remember how I was. I knew I should be taking care of you children, but I couldn't find the strength. I was in a deep, dark well and I didn't have the courage to climb out. I'm so ashamed of how weak I was, how weak my faith was then."

"Mom, you weren't weak. You were grieving. There is a difference."

"Perhaps, but Henrietta Dutton, a woman who was the same age I was, who had children, who saw her husband shot down in front of her eyes, didn't give in to grief. Unlike me, she did something incredibly brave. She acted the way I wish I had been able to act when your father died."

Tears glistened in Mary's eyes. "I wish I had been as brave for you."

Throwing her arms around her mother, Jennifer hugged her fiercely. "You are every bit as brave as Henrietta was. It just took you a little longer to find that strength, but I see it every day, and I am so proud of you."

Mary returned the hug, then, leaning back on her crutches, she reached up to pat Jennifer's face. "Thank you, sweetie. Now go out there and show the world what kind of strength lurked in the heart of a woman history has overlooked. There were a lot more women like her and their stories deserve to be told."

Jennifer wiped at the tears on her cheeks. "You make me wish I had practiced harder."

"You'll do fine," a deep, familiar masculine voice stated firmly. "You had a good teacher."

Jennifer looked up to see Avery watching her. Mounted on Dakota and dressed in his cavalry uniform, Avery managed to look more handsome than ever. The reassuring smile on his face gave her lagging courage a much-needed boost. "Let's hope I was a good pupil."

All around them, men and women in period costumes, some on horseback or in horse-drawn wagons, were taking their places on the green. Several roped off areas held back the growing crowds who had come to watch. The mayor stepped up to the microphone on a raised platform.

Mary made shooing motions with one hand. "You two should get to your places."

Avery touched his hat in a brief salute. "Yes, ma'am. Will you be all right here alone?"

"Actually, your grandfather will be keeping the children and me company. I see him heading this way." She raised her hand to wave.

Glancing at Avery, Jennifer saw he looked as surprised as she was.

Turning in the saddle, Avery regarded his grandfather's approach with a stoic face. Jennifer couldn't read his expression. She didn't know what he was thinking, but at least there was no sign of the anger that had marked their previous meetings when she was present.

Edmond, looking dapper in a dark blue blazer with a red tie, stopped beside the group. He nodded toward his grandson. "Avery, I'm looking forward to seeing your unit in action. I've heard great things about it."

"Thank you, sir. We'll try not to disappoint."

Relieved that the two were at least speaking to each other, Jennifer breathed a prayer of thanks. "I appreciate your staying with my mother, sir."

"It's my pleasure. I'm sure the pageant will be that much more enjoyable for me due to her keen knowledge of the events themselves."

Mary actually blushed. "Edmond was able to reserve seats for us in the viewing stand with the mayor and the rest of the town council. We'd best be going, too."

Smiling at Mr. Barnes with gratitude, Jennifer

glanced up at Avery. He leaned toward her and said softly, "Go knock 'em dead, Jenny."

"I will."

She mounted her horse and galloped across the short distance to a buggy waiting several dozen yards away. A group of men on horseback dressed as farmers from the 1850s were already gathered beside it. Jennifer tied Lollypop to the rear of the wagon and allowed Gerard Hoover, the grocer turned Colonel for the day, to assist her up to the black leather seat.

Avery watched Jennifer ride away with a heady mixture of pride and love surging through him. He wanted her to succeed as much as he had wanted anything in a long time.

Please, God, if You bother listening to someone like me, I'd like to ask a favor. Let her do well today.

Feeling a bit self-conscious about his attempt at prayer, he turned Dakota and rode back to where his unit was forming up. Maneuvering into position beside his fellow soldiers, he accepted the unit's banner from Lee. Beside him, Sergeant Stone held the U.S. flag.

The mayor of Dutton tapped the microphone and began to speak. "Welcome, ladies and gentlemen, to our Founders' Day Festival and the first recreation of the brave and selfless acts of a husband and wife who helped found our fair city.

"In the days before the great Civil War, our state, referred to by many as Bloody Kansas, had become a war zone. Colonel Arthur Dutton was a firm believer that slavery was a sin. He was instrumental in aiding many escaped slaves and he was determined to see that Kansas entered the Union as a free state. He and four other brave men died here when Bushwhackers attacked this cabin where an escaped slave and his family were in hiding."

Avery found himself listening with interest to the mayor's tale. He realized for the first time that the land he stood on had been stained with the blood of men who valued freedom more than life. Freedom not for themselves, but for others. The knowledge was humbling. He glanced at the men beside him and saw the same look of reverence on their faces.

"Even as Colonel Dutton fell," the mayor continued, "his wife took up his sword and rallied his remaining men by charging into the teeth of the enemy. We are here to bear witness to that bravery."

The mayor paused for breath and Sergeant Stone said quietly, "Prepare to move out."

Avery tightened his grip on the staff of the company's banner. He was here as a representative of all the men and women who served their country in the Army. He was here to honor them.

"To begin our celebration," the mayor said with a flourish, "the Dutton High School band will perform the national anthem as Fort Riley's own Commanding General's Mounted Color Guard brings in our flag."

The band began to play. As the stirring notes reached out across the hillside, Avery's unit moved forward at a solemn walk. In two rows of four abreast, they made a circuit before the crowds. The restless wind tugged at the Stars and Stripes, causing the flag to ripple and flutter. Even the matching bay horses, heads held low, seemed to sense the somber mood.

By the end of the song, the unit had made a complete circle and stopped in front of the mayor's platform. The second row of riders moved up, forming a single row.

"Present Arms," Sergeant Stone barked. The rasp of sabers leaving their scabbards filled the air and sunlight glinted off the blades as the men raised their swords to touch the brims of their hats, then sliced them down to rest beside their boots.

On a second command, Avery nudged Dakota into motion and the line split into columns of twos. Catching the eye of the rider across from him, Avery kicked Dakota into a gallop. The columns separated and turned outward forming a circle, then raced back toward each other, passing in between one another at a run. The crowd erupted into applause.

Jennifer watched the display of military horsemanship with the same awe that moved the crowd of festival goers to thunderous applause. Tears of pride pricked the backs of her eyes. But all too quickly the unit's ride was done and she had to turn her attention from Avery to her upcoming part. Gerard slapped the team into motion and the buggy jerked forward.

At the cabin, Jennifer allowed her pretend husband to assist her in alighting, then made her way to knock on the cabin door. Inside, she waited breathlessly for her cue. It didn't take long. Suddenly the quiet hillside erupted with the sounds of gunfire.

With her heart in her throat and a prayer on her lips that God wouldn't let her make a complete fool out of herself, Jennifer gathered her skirts and ran out of the log cabin to her fallen husband's side.

She dropped to her knees and pulled Mr. Hoover's bald head into her lap. The sounds of gunfire echoed all around her and puffs of blue smoke drifted through the air. She could see Avery standing in the crowd at the roped off area a few yards away.

"Good luck," Gerard whispered from the side of his mouth, his eyes tightly closed in pretend death.

"Thanks," she whispered back as she gently laid his head on the ground. Snatching the saber from his hand, she rose to her feet, held it overhead and froze.

Oh, what is my line? Think.

"Bullets can't…" he prompted softly.

"Bullets can't stop his dream," she yelled, grateful to the make-believe corpse at her feet.

"Take the gun," he growled softly.

She had almost forgotten that part. Stooping, she snatched up the pistol and stuffed it in the waistband of her skirt. Turning, she raced toward Lollypop, still tied to the wagon. Jerking the reins free, she stuck her foot in the stirrup and everything else became automatic.

Crouching low over the mare's neck, Jennifer pulled out her gun and fired off a round at the first bandit's silhouette. To her immense relief, it fell backward as planned. She heard the rallying cry of the men behind her, but didn't allow it to break her concentration. The next marauder fell, too. Dropping the pistol, she raised the saber and urged Lollypop up the hillside. All of the manikins dressed as Bushwhackers fell over when her blade struck them. At the very top of the hill, Lollypop leaped lightly over a small split rail fence and Jennifer brandished her sword toward the last Bushwhacker hiding there.

"Surrender or die!" she shouted.

He threw down his weapon and raised his hands. Seconds later, the rest of Colonel Dutton's men swarmed over the fence and subdued him.

Twisting around in the saddle, Jennifer searched for Avery in the crowd below. She wanted to share her triumph with him more than with anyone. He had made this possible. She scanned the faces but didn't see him. What she did see was a girl in a green striped top and green pants break out of the crowd and begin running up the hill. She recognized Lizzie and her heart stood still at the look of panic on her sister's face.

Wheeling Lollypop, Jennifer kicked the mare into motion and raced down the hill. She reached her sister in a matter of seconds. Slipping from the saddle, she grasped Lizzie by the shoulders. "Liz, what's wrong?"

"It's Mom. She's fainted."

"Fainted? Did someone call 9-1-1? Where is she?"

"On the reviewing stand. There's a doctor with her. Mr. Barnes sent me to get you."

Jennifer hiked up her skirts and began running toward a cluster of people grouped at one end of the platform. She was relieved to see Avery was one of them. Quickly climbing the steps, she rushed to where Mary Grant was still lying on the wooden floor.

Jennifer recognized the man helping her mother as the young doctor from the hospital emergency room. Dropping to her knees beside her mother, she tried to control the fear in her voice. "Mom, are you all right?"

"I'm fine," Mary insisted as she attempted to sit upright. "I simply stood too quickly."

The doctor scowled at his patient. "You need to get out of that corset. It's restricting your breathing. They went out of style for a reason."

Jennifer, struggling to catch her own breath, agreed with his assertion. "He's right."

"Yes, I know." Mary reached out and cupped Jennifer's cheek. "You were magnificent, dear. I'm so proud of you."

"I'm glad you were conscious to see it. Can you get up?"

Avery and the doctor lifted her into a nearby chair. Mary winced and grabbed her leg.

"Did you hurt your knee, Mrs. Grant?" the doctor asked.

"I may have twisted it a little," she admitted with a pain-filled grimace.

"You know it's not going to get better until you have surgery," he said, shaking his head.

Mary glanced at Jennifer, then bit her lip and looked away.

Jennifer's gaze moved from her mother's face to the doctor. "But I thought you said she didn't need surgery."

He didn't say anything, but Jennifer could see that he wanted to. She stared at her mother. "Mom, why would you tell us you were getting better if you weren't?"

"I'm doing fine."

Jennifer sat back on her heels and pressed a hand to her forehead. "You think we can't afford it. You're not having surgery so I can stay in school."

"Your future is more important than my living with a little limp."

Jennifer rose to her feet and faced the doctor. "Exactly what is her prognosis?"

"I'm sorry. I can't discuss it without the patient's permission."

Rounding on her mother, Jennifer propped her hands on her hips and glared at her. "Then you tell me what he said."

Edmond stepped up and laid a hand on Mary's shoulder. "I'm not bound by any vows of confidentiality. He told her that unless she has surgery soon, it was unlikely that she'll ever ride again."

"Edmond, I wish you hadn't. I was upset when I shared that with you." Mary looked ready to cry.

"I'm sorry, my dear, but your daughter deserves to know."

Jennifer sank onto the chair next to her mother and took her hand. "Mom, you love riding as much as I do. I couldn't let you give that up just to stay in school another semester."

"No, you can't quit. I know how it is. Once you leave school you'll never go back. That's what happened to me and I've always regretted it. No. I won't discuss it further. Let's go home. I don't want your wonderful performance today marred by my silliness. Avery, hand me my crutches, please."

He did, but when she tried to rise, her legs buckled and she sat back with a groan. The doctor knelt in front of her and carefully lifted her full skirt to expose her injured knee. He palpated it gently, but his touch brought tears to her eyes.

"The patella is definitely out of place now," the doctor said. "I'm sorry, Mrs. Grant, but I think the decision has been made for you. You're going to need surgery as soon as possible."

"And don't even think about refusing!" Jennifer added. Mary nodded meekly.

Rising to her feet, Jennifer looked into Avery's sympathetic eyes and almost cried herself.

She drew a deep breath. "Avery, do you think you could get some of the men to help carry my mother to my truck if I pull up next to the steps?"

"Sure, and don't worry about Lollypop, or the boys. I'll see that everyone gets home."

"Thank you." Jennifer had actually forgotten about the little mare who was standing quietly exactly where Jennifer had dropped the reins. Her brothers were standing at the edge of the platform with wide, worried eyes.

Avery pulled her close in a quick hug. "It's going to be all right."

"I know."

It would be all right if this was God's plan for them. Next year she would pick up her studies where she left off and her mother would be fully recovered and able to make her ride up Dutton Heights.

Next year. If it was God's plan for them.

Chapter 17

Avery was at the fort's large corral late Monday afternoon when he saw Jennifer's truck pull up beside the fence. He wanted to race over and take her in his arms, but he managed to control the impulse with difficulty. Walking sedately to where she stood was hard, but once she was within reach, he couldn't help himself. She looked so tired and lonely. He wrapped his arms around her and she melted into his embrace.

He kissed the top of her head. "How's it going?"

"Okay, I guess. Do you have a few minutes?"

Looking over his shoulder, he saw Sergeant Stone nod once. Avery nodded his thanks in return, then said, "Sure. What do you need?"

"I just wanted to see you." Her simple statement touched something deep inside him and made his love for her grow.

Drawing back, he cupped her face in his hands. "Here I am."

She gave him a tired smile. "I feel better already."

He wanted to kiss her but he was aware of the men in his unit watching them. "How's your mother?"

"Good. The surgery went well yesterday."

"I'm sorry I couldn't be there. We were in Tulsa for a rodeo. I couldn't get leave on such short notice."

He took her hand and they began to walk toward the shady banks of a creek just beyond the fences.

She sent him a sidelong glance. "You're a soldier. I understand that you have duties you can't just drop. Besides, we weren't alone. Your grandfather has been in to visit every day."

"Really?" He wasn't sure what to make of that information.

"Have you had another chance to talk to him?"

"Not since the festival, but I'd rather hear about you than about him. Did you notify the school that you're dropping your classes?"

"Not yet. I don't know why I'm dragging my feet."

"Jennifer, I can help with the money."

Stopping, she quickly turned to face him and placed a hand on his lips. "I know you can, but I couldn't accept it. You know that."

Grasping her wrist gently, he moved her hand from his mouth and placed it over his heart. "Did anyone ever tell you that you're as stubborn as a little donkey?"

"No, but someone once mentioned I had big ears and a long nose…how did that go?"

"A nose you poked into everyone else's business. I guess I should apologize for that remark."

"That's a fine idea."

"If you apologize for telling that cute second-year vet student that I was ungodly."

Holding up one finger, she wagged it in front of his face. "I never told her that, and she wasn't that cute."

"Jennifer, tell the truth."

Turning away, she started walking again, pulling him along by the hand she still held. "Okay, she was very cute."

"And?"

"I told her you thought religion was a joke and to steer clear of you. She told the other girls."

"Now that I'm going to church, would you tell her I'm available and acceptable?"

"No!" He adored the look of mock shock on her face. "You're not available," she stated firmly.

Cocking her head to the side, she stared intently into his eyes. "Did you go to church on Sunday?"

"Lee and I went to services at the base chapel."

"You did? What did you think of it?"

Remembering the solemness and the sense of peace filling the cool interior of the old stone chapel, he struggled to put his feeling into words. "It was strange to see so many men in uniform bowing their heads in prayer. I mean, these are America's warriors."

"And yet they seek a power greater than themselves."

They stopped beneath the towering branches of a cottonwood tree resplendent with bright yellow fall foliage. He studied her face turned so trustingly toward his. "It made me think about you and the way you face life with such confidence."

She blushed and looked down. "You make me out to be better than I am."

"No. I don't think so."

He caught sight of his sergeant motioning for him to return. Quickly, he said, "The American Cavalry Association always holds a reception and ball the night before the contest begins. Would you come with me as my date? I know it's short notice."

Her face brightened, but then she quickly frowned. "Do I have to wear a period ball gown? Because, I'd rather not."

He chuckled. "Modern dress is acceptable. Will you come? I wanted to ask you at the festival, but things got a little out of hand."

"Yes, they did, and I'd be delighted to go with you if my mother is doing okay. Thursday evening, right?"

"Right. Our unit is performing in Wichita that afternoon, so I might be a little late picking you up."

"What time does it start?"

"Nine o'clock in Wellford Hall."

"Why don't I meet you there?" she suggested.

"You don't mind?"

"Of course not. I'm perfectly capable of driving myself, and that way if I get mad at you for ogling other women, I can just leave."

"I'll never look at another woman except you," he said sincerely.

"Oh, I like the sound of that."

He brushed his knuckles along her cheek. "I wish I could spend more time with you, but I have to get back to work."

"I understand. Can I stay and watch? Friends of my mother are sitting with her and the kids so I have a little time to myself."

"Sure. There are always a few people in the stands when we're here. I'd love to have you stick around."

Hand in hand, they walked back the way they had come. Jennifer said, "You know, I'm still your riding coach for a few more days. I'm going to be taking notes."

He laughed. "I'll be on my best behavior."

"Let me be the judge of that."

Still chuckling, he left her at the gate and remounted. The sergeant soon had them form up and begin practicing the drills they would be doing in the military horsemanship part of the cavalry competition. When Avery finished his turn, he caught Jennifer's eye. She gave him a thumbs up sign and he smiled.

Watching Lee go next, Avery noticed his friend's horse wasn't advancing freely and had trouble making the required gait changes smoothly. Avery nudged Dakota over to where Sergeant Stone sat on his horse. He said, "Lee is having a little trouble with Jasper."

Sergeant Stone glanced at Avery. "He's not as smooth as Dakota, that's for sure. Your riding has really improved. That should give you another leg up in the competition."

"I hope so."

The sergeant leaned forward in his saddle. "Most of us are pretty good troopers, but a lot of us, myself included, are counting on you to win the overall. Now, that doesn't mean I won't try my best to beat you."

After a moment of hesitation, Avery said, "I've had the benefit of a really good riding coach. She's here today. What would you say if I asked her to give everyone a few pointers?"

"I'd say that would lower your chances of winning the Sheridan Cup."

Avery smiled. "Not by much. I'm still the best."

"Then tell your coach we'd be happy to accept some

pointers. There's also a prize for best unit performance and I'd like to win that one."

"I'll do my best to make it happen, Sarge."

Riding to the fence in front of where Jennifer sat on the edge of the bleachers, Avery said, "Jenny, how would you feel about giving the guys some tips?"

A wide smile lit up her face. "Are you kidding? I've been biting my fingers to keep from shouting corrections."

"I thought as much. Come on, the Army can use a woman like you."

The night of the Cavalry Ball, Avery phoned to tell her he would be a few minutes late when Jennifer was already on her way into Wellford Hall. Tucking her cell phone back in her purse, she continued up the steps of the building. She truly didn't mind. Spending the evening in his company once he arrived would be reward enough for her patience. Her relationship with Avery seemed to be the one thing going right in her life.

Her mother's surgery had gone well, but she would need more rehabilitation. Jennifer tried not to think about the mounting cost.

Without her mother's income, even the monthly bills would be hard to cover once Jennifer's savings were gone. She had asked for more hours at the clinic today, but Dr. Cutter wasn't able to promise them. There wasn't a full-time position available and poor students like herself were always eager for the part-time hours.

One thing was certain. Jennifer couldn't share any of her worries with her mother. The last thing she needed was her mother refusing needed treatment or drugs because she felt she was being a burden on her children.

"A penny for your thoughts."

Shaken out of her black cloud by the statement, Jennifer turned to look over her shoulder. "They aren't worth that much, Mr. Barnes."

Edmond, resplendent in a tuxedo, smiled at her. "I think they're worth much more than that. Is my grandson here?"

"He's running a little late. I am surprised to see you here."

"I wanted to show my support. By the way, you look lovely, my dear."

"Thank you. It's last year's dress and I was worried I'd be out of date, but it seems I'm not the only one without a new gown." She glanced around at the numerous women in Victorian and Regency ball gowns. The men were all dressed in formal military attire from various periods in history with only a sprinkling of modern uniforms and an occasional tux.

Jennifer pressed a hand to her waist. "Avery said modern dress was acceptable, but he didn't tell me I'd be in the minority."

She looked down at her dress and hoped Avery would like it. A vibrant red, the gown had a front neckline that was modestly high, but the back had a daring low cut. The full skirt swirled about her legs when she moved but it was her red high heels that made her feel like a movie star.

"Beauty is never out of place," Edmond said with a slight bow. "Allow me to keep you company until my grandson tears you away."

"That's very kind of you, sir." She accepted his arm.

"Have you signed up for the competition? I understand the deadline has been extended until midnight tonight."

"Me? Why would I sign up?"

"For the prize money, of course. The purse is now ten thousand dollars for first place, with two thousand for second and a thousand for third place."

"You must be joking."

"I assure you I'm quite serious. You really should enter. I know you have the skills. I witnessed your daring ride on Saturday, and you handle a saber like a pro."

The possibility of paying her mother's medical bills and staying in school suddenly loomed in front of her like a very plump orange carrot. Then Avery's image took its place. She shook her head. "Avery is determined to win."

"The boy certainly doesn't need the money. Besides, I think the two of you might enjoy seeing who is the more skilled. It will make for an exciting match. Come, the registration table is set up in the back corner of the room."

She tilted her head toward him. "Are you the one who donated so much money?"

"I believe the Cavalry Association's benefactor stipulated that he or she remain anonymous."

"But I can guess."

"You may speculate all you wish." He patted the hand that rested on his arm. "My dear, you have brought about wonderful changes in my grandson. Because of you, I see him becoming the man I always hoped he would be."

"Avery isn't putty in my hands. He's his own man."

"Perhaps, but you have had a strong influence on him and all for the better. A few thousand dollars won't make a difference to me, but if someone needy should win the Sheridan Cup, then perhaps I will sleep better knowing I have done a good service, too."

"I don't know. Avery is very determined to win."

"Goodness, Miss Grant, you speak as if you two would be the only ones entering the event. I've been told there are over a hundred contestants so far."

Mr. Barnes was right. She wouldn't be the only one competing. If she won, it would be on her own merits, the same as every other rider. The prize money was so tempting. It would solve so many problems.

She made up her mind, ignoring the tiny voice of caution in the back of her mind. "All right, Mr. Barnes. I accept the challenge. Show me where to sign up."

"Right over there." He pointed to the far corner of the room. "If you will excuse me for a few minutes, I see someone I'd like to speak with. I'll rejoin you shortly."

"Of course." Taking a deep breath, Jennifer made her way toward the registration table.

Avery spotted Jennifer across the crowded room and froze in his tracks. She looked absolutely breathtaking.

From the tips of her red high-heeled shoes to the elegant upsweep of her hair, she radiated poise and grace. The shimmering red dress she wore floated around her trim figure like the petals of some exotic orchid as she made her way between groups of people toward him.

But it wasn't her outfit or her hairdo that made him think she was the most beautiful woman in the room. It was the way her eyes lit up when she caught sight of him.

His heart kicked into overdrive when he realized the soft smile on her lips that was meant for him alone. If he lived to be a hundred he would never forget how she looked tonight.

"She's a very attractive woman."

Avery spun around at the sound of his grandfather's voice. "What are you doing here?"

"I've discovered I have a passion for this cavalry business."

Avery allowed a small piece of hope to grow. Could it be that the two of them were going to find some common ground after all this time?

Jennifer reached Avery's side and slipped her arm through his. "Avery, I'm so glad to see you," she gushed.

He leaned to whisper in her ear. "You look gorgeous."

With a sparkle in her eyes, she replied, "You don't look half bad yourself. Formal military dress becomes you, but then I've always liked a man in uniform."

"Then I'll stay in one all my life."

"Are you planning to make the military your career?" Edmond asked.

Avery nodded. "I might."

Jennifer, bubbling with excitement, squeezed his arm. "Avery, you'll never guess what? Your grandfather has donated over ten thousand dollars in prize money to the cavalry competition."

Cocking his head to the side, Avery studied his grandfather's face. "Why would you do that?"

"It seemed like a worthy cause."

A sinking sensation settled in Avery's stomach. "You did it to push up the number of competitors. With money like that at stake, every Tom, Dick and Harry will enter."

"And Henrietta," Jennifer added.

Avery frowned as he stared at her. "You plan to enter?"

"I just did. Are you worried?"

Edmond rocked back on his heels. "I saw her ride last weekend. I think she can beat you."

A chilling cold settled in the center of Avery's chest. What Edmond really meant was that Jennifer could humiliate him. His grandfather had found another way to use his money to drive a wedge between Avery and the woman he loved.

Reaching out, Avery gripped her arm. "Don't do it."

"What?" Her eyes widened with shock.

"Don't do it. Don't take his bait."

"What are you talking about?" She looked back and forth between the two men.

"He wants to make a fool out of me again."

Edmond shook his head. "You're wrong, Avery."

"Jennifer, don't fall for this. He wants to prove that money is more important to you than I am."

She shook her head. "Avery, don't be ridiculous. It's a contest. Anyone can win it. You could still win. In fact, I'm pretty sure you will."

"I'll give you ten thousand dollars not to ride."

Her mouth dropped open. "Why would you even suggest such a thing?"

"If it's money you want, why not take it from me?"

Disbelief, then sadness appeared in her eyes. "Because I'm willing to try and win fair and square. I'm not willing to accept a hand-out. I thought you knew me better than that."

"I don't care about your principles. I thought you knew how important this competition is to me."

"Apparently it's more important than our relationship."

He could see everything falling apart in front of his eyes and he didn't know how to stop it. He didn't dare look at his grandfather. He didn't want to see the triumph on the old man's face.

Tears glistened in her eyes, but she raised her chin. "If you gentlemen will excuse me, I'm going home."

Edmond placed a hand on her arm. "Miss Grant, please don't leave. This is my fault. Avery, tell her you don't want her to leave."

Avery clenched his hands into fists at his sides. *Pretend it doesn't matter. Don't give him the satisfaction of seeing how much this hurts.*

Only it did matter and it did hurt.

Jennifer pulled away from Edmond. "The fault is mine for expecting something different the second time around."

With that she hurried away through the crowd and out the doors.

Chapter 18

Jennifer held back most of her tears until she reached home. Once inside her own bedroom, she gave into the pain. Throwing herself down on her bed, she clutched her pillow to her face and let loose the sobs building inside. She was so thankful her mother wasn't present to see what a wreck she had become.

Her mother wasn't home, but her hiccupping sobs, muffled as they were, brought Lizzie to her room.

"Jennifer, what's wrong? Has something happened to Mom?"

Shaking her head and embarrassed that she had worried her little sister, Jennifer managed to eek out a sentence, "Mom's fine—Avery's-a-a—jerk."

"Oh, no. What happened?" Lizzie sat beside her sister on the edge of the bed.

It took several long minutes, but Jennifer was finally

able to control her sobs enough to sound coherent. Sitting up, she told Lizzie what had transpired between her and Avery.

"He actually offered you money to withdraw? What a chicken."

"He's not a chicken." She hiccupped once. "He just wants to win that stupid cup. He thinks it will prove something to his grandfather."

"What are you going to do?"

"Do you think I should withdraw? Not for the money, of course. Why he thinks everything hinges on money is beyond me."

"Duh!" Lizzie said. "Because he's always had it and we haven't."

"I thought he was beginning to see that other things are more important," Jennifer said sadly.

"Well, you can't withdraw. Even if you come in dead last you need to let him know that trying is as important as winning."

"I don't know. I signed up because I was greedy, too. The money would mean so much to this family."

"Yes, it would. Don't think the rest of us kids don't know how hard it's been on you and Mom."

"I'm looking for a job," Toby announced, stepping into the doorway.

"Me, too," Ryan said, worming his way in between his brother and the doorjamb.

Tears stung Jennifer's eyes again as she held out her arms. Toby and Ryan joined her and Lizzie in bed and they all held on to one another.

"I love you all," Jennifer whispered when she could speak past the lump in her throat.

"We love you, too," Ryan assured her. Wiggling out

of his sister's embrace, he sat back. "You're gonna beat the pants off those army guys, aren't you?"

Jennifer ruffled his hair. "Do you think I can?"

"I think you can," Toby stated firmly.

Lizzie smiled. "If Henrietta Dutton could do it in a corset, girl, so can you."

Jennifer pulled them all into a hug again. "With a cheering section like you, I don't know how I can fail."

She managed to keep a smile on her face as she sent them all to bed. When she was alone again she sat on the edge of the bed and pulled her off her shoes with a sigh. She had wanted to look beautiful for Avery tonight.

Wrapping the stilettos in tissue paper, she placed them back in their box and tucked them into the bottom corner of her closet. It would be a long time before she could wear them again without thinking of Avery and the heartbreak of this evening.

Avery stormed into his apartment, replaying every word he had spoken to Jennifer in his head. Throwing off his jacket, he flung himself down on his sofa. He wanted to be mad at her but couldn't get that look of disappointment in her eyes out of his mind.

The hurt went deep in his soul. Deeper even than Miranda's betrayal, because he hadn't loved Miranda the way he loved Jennifer.

He banged his fist into the arm of the couch. If only she loved him back.

Rising, he paced back and forth across the room. He knew she needed the money. It wasn't that he didn't want her to have it. If she loved him, why couldn't she put her scruples aside and accept it from him instead of falling in with his grandfather's backhanded attempt to bribe her?

"God, why did You let me fall in love with her?" he demanded, looking up.

The realization of what he was doing stopped him in his tracks. He was talking to God. Wasn't that what Jennifer said prayer was—just talking to God?

He ran his hands through his hair. *Do angry words count as prayers? Jennifer would know.*

Sitting down in the closest chair, Avery propped his elbows on his knees and dropped his head onto his hands. "I'm such a fool."

Jennifer was *who* she was because of her scruples, because of her beliefs. That was why he loved her.

That was why he had begun to question the life he'd led until now. Because she made him take a long hard look at himself and he didn't like what he saw.

Lord, I've turned away from people who cared about me because I was afraid of being hurt. I see now that I've hurt myself far more than others have hurt me.

Help me to trust, Lord. Help me to make amends. I know I don't deserve another chance with Jennifer, but I love her. I'm begging You. Help me find my way.

A thunderous pounding at his front door startled him. Then he heard his grandfather's voice shout, "Avery William Patrick Barnes, you open this door!"

"Great," Avery muttered. "This is just what I need."

The pounding started again. He rose and went to the door before his neighbors called the cops. He pulled it open to see his grandfather glaring at him. "We are going to speak, young man, and you are not shutting me out anymore."

Shaking his head in resignation, Avery motioned for him to come in.

Edmond looked slightly surprised, but marched in

and spun around to face Avery. "You owe that young woman an apology."

Avery pushed the door shut. "That isn't exactly a newsflash, Grandpa. I've figured that out by myself."

"Oh. Well—good."

"Have a seat." Avery gestured toward the living room.

Edmond drew himself upright. "I prefer to say what I've come to say on my feet. I have never been ashamed of you, Avery. I have always loved you. I ignored you as a child, and that is my loss. I worked to accumulate wealth never knowing that the most important things in my life were slipping away.

"I apologize for the way I treated you, for the things I did and said that hurt you. There. That is all I wanted to say, except to ask that you forgive me."

Avery bit the inside of his lip to hold back the sting behind his eyes. "Would you like to sit down now?"

Edmond nodded and wiped at his eyes as he turned toward the sofa. Sinking into the cushion, he seemed to age before Avery's eyes.

Sighing, Edmond said, "I'm sorry about tonight. Miss Grant and her mother are genuinely caring people. I've come to know Mary well in the past two weeks and I like her a great deal. She is the oddest, most adorable woman I've ever met in my life, but she is very proud."

Avery couldn't keep the shock off his face. He sank into the chair across from his grandfather. "You were trying to help Mary Grant by putting the money up in the hopes that Jennifer could win it?"

Edmond nodded. "It wasn't the best of plans, but it was the only way I could think of that Jennifer might actually accept. Mary is heartbroken that her daughter has to drop out of school because of her."

Avery leaned back and stared at the ceiling. "We've made a mess of our lives, haven't we?"

"Indeed. I've made a fine mess of mine, but you are young and you have a chance to undo the mistakes you've made."

Avery laughed but there was no humor in it. "I broke her heart once because I was scared to death of loving someone. I broke her heart tonight because I want to prove to you that I was worthwhile, that I could excel at something and make you eat your words. Have you ever heard of such a stupid motive for driving away the woman you love? She isn't going to give me another chance."

Avery looked at his grandfather. "I owe you an apology, too. I tried to make your life miserable by my behaviors in the past. Can you forgive me?"

"I think we're both well on the way to forgiveness now."

Avery nodded. "Jennifer once told me that forgiveness heals the forgiver as well as the forgiven."

Edmond smiled. "She sounds like her mother. What are you going to do?"

Avery leaned forward and laced his fingers together. "I'm going to win her back."

"How do you plan to do that?"

"I have no idea."

"I hate to suggest this, but what if you withdrew from the competition?"

"Unfortunately, I have more to consider than my feelings for Jennifer. My commanding officer, the rest of the men in my unit, they're all counting on me to win the Sheridan Cup for Fort Riley. I can't let them down."

Chapter 19

"He's coming," Lizzie hissed in Jennifer's ear the next morning. They were standing with a group of contestants outside the arena entrance waiting for the judges to allow them to walk through the jump course prior to the start of the first event.

The men and a few women around her were all dressed in reproductions of military uniforms ranging from a buckskin clad army scout to a World War I general. Since period clothing was one of the requirements for the competitors, Jennifer had borrowed a Civil War uniform from Gerard Hoover.

Jennifer kept her eyes forward. She wasn't sure she could keep from crying if she looked at Avery. She should have known trying to ignore him wouldn't work, because he walked up and stopped beside her.

"I'm glad to see you, Jennifer," Avery said quietly. "I wanted to wish you the best."

Struggling to hold on to her composure, she replied coolly, "The same to you."

Toby came marching up and stood toe-to-toe with Avery. "I told you if you ever made my sister cry again I'd knock your block off."

"Toby, please don't make a scene." Despite her words, Jennifer wanted to kiss her brave little brother.

"You would be well within your rights to blacken both my eyes," Avery said, surprising Jennifer.

"I could do it, too." Toby raised one fist.

"I wouldn't try to stop you, but I know it would embarrass your sisters."

Some of the anger faded from Toby's face. "Just so we understand each other."

"We do."

Jennifer glanced up to find Avery gazing at her intently. Her heart turned over just as she knew it would. He looked like he hadn't slept at all.

He managed a slight smile. "Jennifer, I humbly apologize for my behavior last night and I hope that you can find it in your heart to forgive me one day."

"That doesn't mean she's going to let you win today," Lizzie piped up.

"Yeah," Ryan added, holding on to Lizzie's hand.

Nodding once, Avery never broke eye contact with Jennifer. "I wouldn't expect anything less from her than her best. I won't give anything but my best in return."

She knew he was talking about so much more than the event they were about to start. She tried to harden her heart against the pull of his intensity, but couldn't.

She looked away. "Words come easily to you. It's hard to judge when you mean them."

"Then I'll let my actions do the speaking from now on."

The arena gates opened and a small, dark-haired woman in jeans and a blue sweatshirt came out with a clipboard. One by one she called off their names and sent them into the course.

Jennifer, happy to escape Avery's overwhelming presence, walked past the low jumps quickly. The course wasn't nearly as complex as the ones she faced at the shows she attended. This would be the easiest part of her day.

If she could keep her mind on what she had to do and not on her aching heart.

Lizzie was waiting with Lollypop outside the gates when Jennifer finished her walk through. Shooting a narrow-eyed glare at Avery's back, Lizzie said, "He has a lot of nerve."

"He apologized. That says something for him." Jennifer mounted and turned her horse toward the gate.

Looking up at her, Lizzie frowned. "Don't tell me you're still soft on the guy."

"I wish I could say I wasn't."

Jennifer managed to keep her wits about her long enough to make a clean run through the jumping component of the day. Avery had a fault-free ride as well, but her time was two seconds faster than his. Fifteen other riders also managed to finish the course without faults including several men from the CGMCG, three riders from Fort Humphrey and two men from the Kansas National Guard unit. Jennifer wound up in third place behind Lee Gillis and the man dressed in buckskins.

Afterward, while they waited for the saber course to be set up, Jennifer joined her brothers and sister in the stands. The bleachers were only half full, which surprised her. She thought more spectators would have come to see such an unusual contest.

Instead of concentrating on the targets being laid out on the field, her eyes strayed constantly to the group of Union troopers seated below her that included Avery.

Had she been rash to rush away last evening instead of talking to him about his accusations? She had been so hurt that he thought she could be bought off. Now, in the light of day, she considered how it must have looked to him.

He had made it clear from the start that winning the Sheridan Cup was very important to him. It must have seemed to him that she didn't care about his feelings, only about the money.

When the announcer called the contestants to the field, she found herself between Avery and Lee in the line up. She smiled at Lee. "You had a great ride this morning."

He patted Jasper's neck. "This fellow is ready to rock and roll today. You did well, too."

The announcer called his name and Lee rode into the course. Jennifer watched as he made another great run, and her heart sank as his time came up on the display board. What was she doing here? These men did this every day. How could she hope to win?

"You should stop holding back, Jenny," Avery said from her other side.

"I wasn't holding back," she insisted. "I beat you, didn't I?"

How like him to try to annoy her when she had been almost ready to forgive him.

"A measly two seconds for a show jumper of your caliber? Either you're holding back or you're scared."

She pressed a hand to her chest. "I am not scared of competing against you."

"Okay, I'm just making sure you have the right attitude for this event."

"There is nothing wrong with my attitude."

The announcer called her name. She drew her saber and kicked Lollypop into motion. The mare responded with a burst of speed and Jennifer felt the satisfying thunk as her blade hit every target she passed while she wove in and out of poles, through a set of gates and over a series of jumps before she came flying across the finish line.

Looking up at her time, she grinned as she realized she had bested Lee by a full second.

She turned to look at Avery as she rode out of the arena. He was grinning from ear to ear. "I knew you could do it," he said, as he rode past her on the way to the starting line.

Ryan and Toby ran up to her. "Wow, you were awesome," Ryan said, his eyes shining with pride.

Jennifer looked over her shoulder to see Avery charging into the first set of hurdles. "It helps if you have the right attitude," she admitted with a little smile.

Although Avery finished first in the saber class, Jennifer managed to hold on to fourth place. In the Mounted Pistol event, she finished tenth. By the end of the day, there was only the Military Horsemanship class to complete.

She and Lollypop moved through the required moves with ease. After she was finished, she watched with interest as the two riders from the National Guard unit finished impressive rounds, as well.

When it was Avery's turn, she noticed he looked almost nervous. As if he sensed her watching him, he looked her way. "Have fun," she mouthed, knowing he was too far away to hear.

A smile broke over his face and he touched the brim of his hat in a salute.

His ride was good. Not as good as hers, but good enough to earn him third place. When the overall scores for the day were announced, Jennifer was happy to see that she was among the top ten riders who would be going after the Sheridan Cup.

As she was loading Lollypop for the trip home, Avery and his group rode past on their way to the stables. He pulled up as the others went on. "You did well, today, Jennifer. You should be proud of yourself."

"I had plenty of encouragement." She nodded toward her family already in the truck.

"They are a great bunch."

"I'm surprised your grandfather wasn't here today," she said, not wanting to leave and yet feeling foolish for wanting to stay.

"He was going to spend today at the hospital with your mother, but he plans to be here tomorrow."

That Edmond was the visitor Mary had assured Jennifer would stay and keep her company today came as a bit of a shock. It must have shown on her face.

"I was wrong about him," Avery said. "He's trying, but he doesn't always go about things in the right way." He tipped his hat. "I look forward to seeing you tomorrow."

As he rode away, Jennifer smiled to herself. She looked forward to seeing him again, too.

At ten o'clock the next morning, Avery found himself in a group of nine men and one woman drawing numbers for their position in the final test of cavalry skills. A single course had been laid out that encompassed jumping, saber and pistol use as men might have faced on a battlefield a hundred years ago.

Jennifer drew number two. He drew number ten. The good thing about that was he would know exactly what he needed to do in order to win when his time came. The bad part was that he would have to wait to ride. He wanted to get it over with.

As the group walked back to where the horses were waiting, he was surprised when Jennifer fell into step at his side. If only he could find a way to keep her there, close beside him.

"Are you nervous?" she asked, pressing a hand to her stomach. The anxious look in her eyes reminded him of the first day he handed her a saber. So much has happened since then that he couldn't believe it had been less than three weeks ago.

"You shouldn't be nervous. You'll do fine," he assured her.

She shot a look toward the stands where her family was sitting. He saw his grandfather seated a few feet away from them. "Will I do well enough to win?" she asked.

"Only God knows the answer to that," he said, quietly, wishing he could make it happen for her. Wishing he could hold her in her arms again.

"That is so true."

By now, they had reached the horses. He held her stirrup as she mounted. Looking up at her, he said, "Don't hold back."

"Do I need another attitude adjustment?" She smiled at him and it warmed his heart and gave him hope.

"No. Have fun, be safe."

"You, too."

Watching her gallop toward the starting area, he knew he would never love another woman the way he loved her.

The first rider up knocked down two rails on the jumps and missed two balloons with his pistol. As he left the field and Jennifer rode on, Avery found himself holding his breath, willing her to do well and praying for her success.

Charging into the course like a true trooper, she had the crowd on its feet cheering for her. Her ride was flawless until the final leg, the pistol range. She missed one balloon, but still managed a good time and he blew out a breath of relief.

When she rode back to his side, he could see the disappointment written on her face.

"Don't look so sad. It was a good run."

"Not good enough."

"You don't know that. Wait and see before you throw in the towel."

One by one, the following riders either failed to hit more targets or finished in longer times. By the time the ninth rider was coming down the stretch, it was clear that Jennifer's score was going to keep her in first place.

Now it was Avery's turn.

He heard his buddies cheering him on and saw Captain Watson giving him a thumbs-up sign. He glanced at his grandfather in the stands and saw Jennifer's family watching intently. The weight of what lay ahead of him seemed almost too much to bear. He knew he could win.

"Don't hold back," Jennifer said, sitting quietly on her horse and staring at him. Her bright blue eyes were shining with deep emotion.

He spurred Dakota toward the starting line. The horse pranced sideways in anticipation of the coming dash. Avery looked over his shoulder to see Jennifer had one hand pressed to her lips and her eyes closed. Focusing his attention back on the course, he drew his saber and charged.

Dakota sailed over the jumps without hesitation, keeping close to the targets and giving Avery every chance to make good hits. Switching to his gun for the last leg, Avery knew his time was good and his run was perfect until Dakota stumbled slightly before the first balloon and Avery's shot went wide. The horse recovered himself and kept going as Avery took out the next three targets until only one remained.

He saw the white balloon coming up on his right, but time seemed to slow down as he swung the barrel of his pistol toward it. His finger tightened on the trigger. He fired as he flew past and time sped up again as he raced toward the finish line and Jennifer's shocked, joyful face.

As he pulled to a halt and dismounted, his buddies all came to slap him on the back and tell him he had done a good job, but he only nodded and headed toward the woman he loved.

Catching hold of Lollypop's reins, he stared up at Jennifer and tried not to show how afraid he was. "I know that I don't deserve another chance with you, but I want one."

She stared at him in disbelief. "You let me win."

"Prove it."

Shaking her head, she frowned at him. "What will your captain say?"

"The Sheridan Cup didn't go to Fort Humphrey so he'll be thrilled. Besides, you're like one of us."

"It's not right," she protested.

He smiled. "It's perfect."

Lee came running up and skidded to a halt beside them. "Did you hear that? They just awarded Dakota best overall horse. Congrats, Jennifer, you were awesome. They'll be giving out the trophies in a few minutes. We've still got a chance to win best overall unit. Come on, Avery, mount up."

"In a minute."

As Lee hurried away, Avery drew a deep breath and looked up at Jennifer. "Darling, I'm in love with you and you're in love with me. Say it."

Jennifer fought back the tears that blurred her vision. She honestly didn't know if they were tears of joy or apprehension. She wanted so much to love him but was she risking more heartache?

"If I say it, you can't break my heart again. I don't think I could stand it."

"I won't. Darling, I'm so sorry for the way I treated you in the past. I want to make it up to you. Tell me how."

"I need a man that I can count on when things get rough."

"I'll be that man."

Oh, how she wanted to believe him. "I need someone who values my faith. If you can't do that—if you can't give God a chance to come into your life—then there isn't any point in our trying to make this work."

"I don't know how to be worthy of a woman as strong as you are. Give me your sword."

"Why?"

"I don't want you armed when I do this."

"Do what?"

"This." He grasped her by the waist, pulled her out of the saddle and into his arms. Which was exactly where she wanted to be. When his lips covered hers, she thought her heart might break as it expanded with happiness.

When he pulled away at last, he touched her cheek softly with the back of his knuckle. "You could do a lot better than a man like me."

"I'll be the judge of that."

"I don't have anything to offer you that really matters."

"What really matters, Avery?"

"Fidelity, honor, commitment, faith."

"You said faith. Does faith truly matter to you? Don't say yes just because you think that's what I want to hear."

A frown put a crease between his brows. "My faith isn't as strong as yours. Praying, trusting Him—it's new to me. I'm taking some baby steps here, but I believe I'm heading in the right direction."

She smiled at him with all the love in her heart. "I believe you are, too."

"I didn't have a clue what faith meant until I saw you putting it into action in your everyday life. I love you so much, Jennifer."

"Oh, Avery, I love you, too."

He shook his head in disbelief. "I can't believe God feels that I'm worthy of you, because I'm not."

She tipped her head to the side. "I can work on that."

His shout of laughter caused some of the people passing by to stop and stare but Jennifer didn't notice them. She was busy being kissed again.

* * * * *

We hope you enjoyed reading

Denim and Diamonds

by *New York Times* bestselling author

DEBBIE MACOMBER

and

A Military Match

by *USA TODAY* bestselling author

PATRICIA DAVIDS.

Both were originally Harlequin series stories!

Love Inspired takes you on an uplifting journey of faith, forgiveness and hope. Fall in love with stories where faith helps guide you through life's challenges, and discover the promise of a new beginning.

LOVE INSPIRED

INSPIRATIONAL ROMANCE

Uplifting stories of faith, forgiveness and hope.

Look for six *new* books every month!

Available wherever books are sold.

Harlequin.com

BACHALO0420B

SPECIAL EXCERPT FROM

HQN

Sarah's long-ago love returns to her Amish community, but is he the man for her, or could her destiny lie elsewhere?

Read on for a sneak preview of
The Promise *by Patricia Davids,*
available June 2020 from HQN Books!

"Isaac is in the barn. Sarah, you should go say hello."

"Are you sure?" Sarah bit her lower lip and began walking toward the barn. Her pulse raced as butterflies filled her stomach. What would Isaac think of her? Would he be happy to see her again? What should she say? She stepped through the open doorway and paused to let her eyes adjust to the darkness. She spotted him a few feet away. He was on one knee tightening a screw in a stall door. His hat was pushed back on his head. She couldn't see his face. He hadn't heard her come in.

Suddenly she was a giddy sixteen-year-old again about to burst out laughing for the sheer joy of it. She quietly tiptoed up behind him and cupped her hands over his eyes. "Guess who?" she whispered in his ear.

"I have no idea."

The voice wasn't right. Strong hands gripped her wrists and pulled her hands away. His hat fell off as he turned his head to stare up at her. She saw a riot of dark brown curls, not straw-blond hair. She didn't know this man.

A scowl drew his brows together. "I still don't know who you are."

She pulled her hands free and stumbled backward as embarrassment robbed her of speech. The man retrieved his hat and rose to his feet. "I assume you were expecting someone else?"

"I'm sorry," she managed to squeak.

The man in front of her settled his hat on his head. He wasn't as tall as Isaac, but he was a head taller than Sarah. He had rugged good looks, dark eyes and a full mouth, which was turned up at one corner as if a grin was about to break free. "I take it you know my brother Isaac."

He was laughing at her.

The dark-haired stranger folded his arms over his chest. "I'm Levi Raber."

Of course, he would be the annoying older brother. So much for making a good first impression on Isaac's family.

Don't miss
The Promise *by Patricia Davids,*
available now wherever
HQN Books and ebooks are sold.

HQNBooks.com

Copyright © 2020 by Patricia MacDonald

PHPDEXP0620TP

LOVE INSPIRED

INSPIRATIONAL ROMANCE

Uplifting stories of faith, forgiveness and hope.

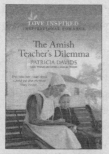

Save $1.00

on the purchase of ANY

Love Inspired book.

Available wherever books are sold, including most bookstores, supermarkets, drugstores and discount stores.

Save $1.00

on the purchase of ANY Love Inspired book.

Coupon valid until June 30, 2020.
Redeemable at participating outlets in the U.S. and Canada only.
Not redeemable at Barnes & Noble stores. Limit one coupon per customer.

52616701

5 65373 00076 2 (8100)0 12456

Canadian Retailers: Harlequin Enterprises ULC will pay the face value of this coupon plus 10.25¢ if submitted by customer for this product only. Any other use constitutes fraud. Coupon is nonassignable. Void if taxed, prohibited or restricted by law. Consumer must pay any government taxes. Void if copied. Inmar Promotional Services ("IPS") customers submit coupons and proof of sales to Harlequin Enterprises ULC, P.O. Box 31000, Scarborough, ON M1R 0E7, Canada. Non-IPS retailer—for reimbursement submit coupons and proof of sales directly to Harlequin Enterprises ULC, Retail Marketing Department, Bay Adelaide Centre, East Tower, 22 Adelaide Street West, 40th Floor, Toronto, Ontario M5H 4E3, Canada.

U.S. Retailers: Harlequin Enterprises ULC will pay the face value of this coupon plus 8¢ if submitted by customer for this product only. Any other use constitutes fraud. Coupon is nonassignable. Void if taxed, prohibited or restricted by law. Consumer must pay any government taxes. Void if copied. For reimbursement submit coupons and proof of sales directly to Harlequin Enterprises ULC 482, NCH Marketing Services, P.O. Box 880001, El Paso, TX 88588-0001, U.S.A. Cash value 1/100 cents.

® and ™ are trademarks owned by Harlequin Enterprises ULC.

© 2020 Harlequin Enterprises ULC

BACCOUP97995

Two fan-favorite stories by beloved storyteller

DEBBIE MACOMBER

Sometimes to find love you have to try again...

Shadow Chasing

The last man Carla Walker's going to count on is a cop—as far as her love life's concerned. Her dad is a police officer, so she's already decided that's not the kind of future she wants. She knows about the long hours, the unpredictable calls, the danger. Carla meets Philip Garrison on vacation, and it's more than a holiday fling. She falls for him. Hard. And then she learns he's a cop...

Yesterday Once More

Three years ago, Julie Houser fled from Wichita, Kansas—and left her husband-to-be practically standing at the altar. Julie couldn't face the vast disparity between her own middle-class background and his family's wealth, not to mention his mother's disapproval. But she never got over Daniel, and now she's back, hoping she can convince him to give marriage another chance.

Coming soon, wherever MIRA Books are sold!

Be sure to connect with us at:

Harlequin.com/Newsletters
Facebook.com/HarlequinBooks
Twitter.com/HarlequinBooks

mira

Harlequin.com

MDM942

Love Harlequin romance?

DISCOVER.

Be the first to find out about promotions,
news and exclusive content!

 Facebook.com/HarlequinBooks

Twitter.com/HarlequinBooks

 Instagram.com/HarlequinBooks

Pinterest.com/HarlequinBooks

ReaderService.com

EXPLORE.

Sign up for the Harlequin e-newsletter and
download a free book from any series at
TryHarlequin.com

CONNECT.

Join our Harlequin community to
share your thoughts and connect
with other romance readers!
Facebook.com/groups/HarlequinConnection

HSOCIAL2020

**_Heartfelt or suspenseful,
inspiring or passionate, Harlequin
has your happily-ever-after._**

With new books published
every month, you are sure to find the
satisfying escape you know you deserve.

SIGN UP FOR THE
HARLEQUIN NEWSLETTER

Be the first to hear about great new
reads and exciting offers!

Harlequin.com/newsletters

HNEWS2020